# DEVIL
## *in the details*

USA TODAY BESTSELLING AUTHOR

# ARIA WYATT

This book is for my author bestie, Kristie Wolf.
Thank you for loving this story and for being you. I'm so happy
to have you in my life!
Love you!

# AUTHOR'S DISCLAIMER

For those who have read my other books—thank you so much—I feel the need to warn you.

I wrote this one at the very beginning of the pandemic, when a lot of crazy shit was happening. I let the words flow, and I didn't hold back. Not even a little. Writing was my escape from the fear and chaos. As you can see, I held on to this story for a while. In fact, I wasn't sure if I'd ever release it. Why? Well, *Devil in the Details* is easily two chili peppers hotter than my previous releases—one might even call it smut—and I worried about alienating my established readers.

While I wanted to stay in my lane (and be consistent with the heat level across all my books), The River had other plans. Very naughty plans.

That said, the emotional connection and character development I strive for in my books is still there. And there's an intriguing plot. (I hope.)

BUT, if the idea of hot sex in a fictional, water-themed kink club bothers you, this isn't the book for you.

Trust me.

Also, I took some liberties with a few New York City details, mainly regarding the parking situation. It's fiction, so don't come at me.

# CONTENT WARNING

*Devil in the Details* contains several topics that may be
upsetting to readers.
Before reading, please review the following list carefully.
Feel free to reach out to me via email with any questions that arise.
Aria@AriaWyatt.com

- Divorce
- Kink club sex (including but not limited to sensory deprivation and spanking)
- Side character with Down syndrome, epilepsy, and cardiac issues
- Heroine with a history of fertility struggles, including a past ectopic pregnancy and a prior first-trimester miscarriage
- Ovarian cysts
- Sexual assault

# DEVIL
## in the details

# *One*

## *Lincoln Kennedy*

The lethal dose of caffeine is ten thousand milligrams. That means the five shots of espresso I ordered won't kill me. Will they help me stay awake? Doubtful. After last night's extracurriculars, I'd need more than a dozen to keep me going.

The strawberry-blonde barista hands me my jet fuel and smiles. "Do you want it dirty?"

My gaze snaps to hers. "I'm sorry, what?"

She holds up a metal carafe. "Your friend's chai. Do you want espresso in that too?"

"Oh." I shake my head to clear the imagined innuendo before I start trying to flirt like a damn fool. "Yes, please."

"Rough night?" She studies my face, her eyes lingering on the dark circles beneath mine.

I glance at her name badge. "You have no idea, Geneva."

"Well, I hope your day is an improvement." She sprinkles some cinnamon on the frothy chai before handing it over with a smile.

"Thanks. Me too," I mutter, snapping the lid onto my to-go cup.

I weave through the café to the table where my best friend awaits and place his beverage in front of him. "I still don't understand why you feel it's necessary for a pre-interview briefing."

Myles leans in. "Because I assured Elinora you were the perfect candidate for the position, and I hate looking like an idiot in front of my boss."

Settling on a stool, I swallow a few sips before answering. The high-octane refreshment is a step above river mud, but I force it down. My focus—and dwindling bank account—depends on it. I rarely order espresso, but I had a late night at the club and need all the help I can get.

"Are you saying you think I'll embarrass you?"

He sighs, rubbing a pale hand over his freckled face. "I know it wouldn't be intentional, Linc."

"For the record, I plan to nail this interview and knock her socks off. You can thank me later for making you look good." I flash him a cocky smirk. "Maybe I'll nail *her* too."

While sex with my boss is a line I'd never cross again, it's fun to goad him because he huffs and puffs more than the big, bad wolf.

Myles snorts. "You have no idea who you're dealing with. Elinora Iverson wouldn't let you within three feet of her. Besides, Iverson Press is an industry anomaly."

"How different can it be from Cooper Press?"

The small, independent publishing house that laid me off last month is on the verge of bankruptcy. My former boss told me he was doing me a favor when he handed me my pink slip. Funny, my idea of a favor involves helping someone—not pulling the rug out from beneath them. I've been an editor for three years, and a skilled one at that, but the New York market is saturated. While I received several offers for positions on the West Coast, relocation isn't an option for me.

Myles pins me with his emerald gaze. "No other woman-owned publishing house has joined the ranks of New York's Big Five this easily. Elinora is a ruthless businesswoman who will stop at nothing to reach the top. If you even *think* about nailing her, she'll trample you and feed you your balls. Then she'll eat you alive."

"You know I love surrounding myself with powerful women."

"You'll change your tune once you meet her," he mutters, sipping his drink.

"I spent a summer in Amsterdam. I think I can handle her."

"Wrong fucking country, Linc. She's from Denmark." He cocks his head to the side. "Did you research the company like I told you to?"

"A little."

"We had two editors leave this month because they couldn't handle the pressure. These are seasoned professionals with decades of experience—not somebody three years out of Emerson College. She only agreed to interview you because I told her you have an impeccable eye for detail, and for whatever reason, she likes me." He knots his hands in his fiery hair. "If you make me look like an asshole, she'll never promote me to the marketing executive position. This is my career on the line."

I grip his wrist. "Myles, relax. I won't let you down."

"I fucking hope not. Iverson Press is big-league shit. It's nothing like what you're used to. We're talking night and day."

"Well, we both know I function better at night."

"How late did you work *last* night?" he probes, his orange brows furrowing.

I glance at my watch. "Let's see, it's eight o'clock now. I got off around five this morning, went home to shower, and here I am."

"You didn't sleep *at all?*"

I point to my cup. "Hence, my vat of liquid alertness."

Myles releases a heavy sigh. "No wonder you look like shit."

"This is a new suit, asshole."

"I'm talking about the circles under your eyes. You've gotta stop this. That environment isn't healthy for you."

I love when he goes all mother hen on me. We've been friends since kindergarten, and he knows me better than I know myself. He's right. My salacious nightlife isn't healthy, but I have no choice—my little sister's life depends on it.

Reagan was born with Down syndrome, epilepsy, and a serious heart condition. For years I've struggled with survivor's guilt over being born healthy. Why was I given that gift when she wasn't? What made me special? Why did she deserve to endure multiple cardiac surgeries and frequent seizures, when the worst health crisis I've dealt with was a sprained wrist in ninth grade?

After our father's stroke three years ago, the family's financial situation hit rock bottom. The measly disability checks he receives from the state don't scratch the surface of Reagan's expenses. Quality assisted living requires money we don't have, so for the past two years, my second job has supplemented our income. Regardless of whether I like it, I'm stuck in this lecherous holding pattern until I've repaid my debts or something changes with Reagan's insurance coverage, which is highly unlikely. According to my calculations, that means I'm on the hook for at least another five years. Not to mention over seventy thousand dollars. Too bad being laid off from my day job wasn't part of the equation. The surplus I'd saved is all but gone now, which is why I picked up a few extra shifts at the club. Myles knows all this, so it would be great if he'd stop riding my ass about it.

I remove my glasses and rub slow circles on my temples to combat the developing headache. While he does have a point about my lack of sleep, it's not like I can add hours to the day. "What choice do I have?"

"Have you thought about what happens if the place gets shut down and people find out you work there? What will your parents think?"

My Irish Catholic parents would lose their shit if they had any idea about my after-dark activities. Father Ignatius DeAngelis, the principal of the Catholic school I attended until the middle of twelfth grade, would roll over in his grave and convince Jesus to hurl lightning bolts at me. Here's how I look at it: I'm already going to hell, so if I do it with good intentions, that should lessen the burn. Right?

"Who will take care of Reagan if she gets evicted from the group home for lack of payment?" I counter, raising a brow at him when he doesn't answer.

Needing a distraction from the sheer panic that possibility triggers inside me, I take a long, slow sip of my espresso and focus on the music drifting from a nearby speaker. Ray LaMontagne croons "Trouble" like a folky omen that twists my stomach into knots. I glance at Myles's blurry face, and for once I'm grateful that I can't see. He's likely sporting his typical holier-than-thou expression, and I'm not in the mood for his shit. I don't need a moral compass—I need a fucking job.

"Just be careful," he murmurs, blotting his mouth with a napkin.

"I *am* careful. Esme doesn't cut corners, and The River is a legal establishment. They won't shut us down."

Esmeralda "Madame Esme" DaVinci, the owner of the kink club where I work nights, is a keen businesswoman. Her exclusive client list features some of New York's most powerful men and women. I'm sure it works in Esme's favor that she, quite literally, has the police chief and district attorney by the balls.

He lowers his voice even more. "Are *all* of your activities legal, Linc?"

*Maybe?*

I shove my glasses back onto my face. "The technicalities are above my pay grade, but Esme is fluent in loopholes and workarounds, so I'm sure we're fine." It also helps that one of her business partners is an attorney.

"That's what I mean. You're taking risks—"

"I'm an in-house escort—not a goddamn prostitute," I whisper-shout, stiffening my spine. "And I never engage in risky behaviors."

"Fucking a stranger doesn't seem risky to you?"

"Not if I take the proper steps to mitigate said risk."

"Yeah, OK."

I jab my finger into his chest. "Look, you have your skill set, and I have mine."

"I wish you'd spend more time focusing on your editor skill set."

"Pretty sure I got laid off, *not* fired." He opens his mouth to respond, but I cut him off. "Not to mention, Cooper Press is going under, so being out of a job was inevitable. I'm doing the best I can, bro." I lower my voice to a true whisper out of respect for the little old lady eating her scone at the next table. "It's not like I sought out The River. The opportunity fell into my lap. It's not about easy pussy, it's about doing whatever's necessary to help my family. Besides, I signed a fucking contract. I'm Esme's until everything's been repaid, and I've met my time obligations. There's no way around it. You know that as well as I do. I'm a damn good editor, an excellent bartender, and an even better fuck. Until I can make it in publishing, this is my reality." Straightening, I meet his gaze. "I'll impress your boss and get you that promotion, my friend. I promise I won't let you down."

"Whatever you do, don't mention her divorce."

"Oh, for fuck's sake." I slap the edge of the table. "I may not be as brilliant as *you*, the legendary Saint Myles Callahan the second, but I'm not an idiot. Why the hell would I ask a stranger about her marital status?"

He squints. "Says the man who fucks strangers for money."

"No, I don't get paid to fuck—I get paid to *be* there. Technically, I'm on payroll as a *bartender*," I explain with air quotes. "And truth be told, the Aqua Suite bar is where I spend most of my time."

"What happens when you aren't mixing drinks?"

"Oh, you know . . . other things. According to Esme, my unofficial title is pleasure concierge, so I guess you could say it's a unique kind of mixing. But either way, I receive monetary compensation for my time. Not what I do with it."

We've never discussed the nitty-gritty details of what I do—thanks to my nondisclosure agreement—but since I listed him as my emergency contact, I've alluded to my job description. That way, it won't be as much of a shock if Esme ever needs to call him. He has no clue what I deal with on a nightly basis. Over the years, I've learned it's better to keep him in the dark. We're both more comfortable this way—content to skirt around the topic like a leather-clad elephant in our friendship.

He rolls his eyes. "Whatever."

"No, it's not 'whatever.' There's a big difference."

"Your *time* entails fucking."

I shake my head. "Not always. My job is to meet the pleasure needs of our female club members, whatever they may be." His scowl tells me his misconceptions are deeply rooted, and I'm feeling chatty this morning, so I elaborate. "Yes, sometimes that involves a bit of kink."

"As in?"

"Use your imagination."

"Are you a Dom or something?"

I laugh. "Not exactly."

"So . . . you're a submissive?"

"No. Submission's not my thing." I purse my lips, trying to think of the best way to explain my River persona, since it's completely at odds with the nerdy version of me the rest of the world sees. "Let's put it this way. Esme has a team of concierges with different talents. I've been known to take control when asked. That said, there are things I will and won't do for a client, but I really can't get into specifics with you." I sip my drink and continue. "The other end of the spectrum is the lonely people who simply want someone to talk to. I've had clients where our playtime was as innocent as dinner and drinks at Oasis."

"What's Oasis?"

"The restaurant affiliated with The River."

"Oh."

"It goes beyond being a rich women's plaything." I rub my jaw, still trying to justify my employment. "Essentially, I provide *companionship* for money, with the occasional martini and cat of nine tails. The kinky fuckery is a perk, not the job itself."

Myles shakes his head. "The devil's in the details, Lincoln."

"Good thing I'm detail-oriented. Maybe I'm the breath of fresh air Iverson Press needs." Rising, I glance at my watch. "Now if you'll excuse me, I've got some Nordic ice to melt."

# Two

## Elinora Iverson

I didn't think it was still possible for my ex-husband's audacity to shock me, but I was wrong. Blood boiling, I clench the phone, unable to believe my ears. "Who the hell do you think you are?"

"Don't be so unreasonable."

"Unreasonable?" I screech, rocketing from my desk chair to pace the office. "I'll tell you who's unreasonable. If you think for one second my lawyers won't rip your little idea to shreds, your head is further up your ass than I remembered."

"Don't swear, Ellie," Charles chides, making my vision go red. "It's not becoming."

"Fuck you." I spit the words with enough venom to give Medusa a run for her money. Right now, I'd pay a small fortune to sprout a headful of snakes and turn that asshole to stone. It's not even ten o'clock, and he's already ruined my day with his outrageous demands. The cheating bastard has the balls to ask for *more* alimony. It shouldn't surprise me though. He's always been the poster child for entitlement.

"When should I expect the deposit?"

"Go to hell." I end the call and toss the phone onto my desk, my stilettos wearing a path into the carpet. Why should I maintain his lifestyle after his third affair nearly destroyed me? Charles is still with the twenty-something supermodel he betrayed me with, and *I'm* required to shell out cash for their fancy vacations? My eyes burn with a mix of rage and sadness. It's not fair he still has the power to hurt me, even after two years. I'm starting to wonder if I'll ever be free of him.

Rounding my desk once more, I blink back tears and sink into my chair with a defeated sigh.

When will karma get off her ass and make things right?

Freya Thorne, my fabulous assistant and close friend, enters my office holding a clipboard and hesitates when she sees me. I blot my eyes with a tissue.

"You OK?"

"Not really."

"Is there anything I can do?"

"Yes, actually. Can you please get me a cupcake from Compass Roasters? I need to eat my feelings." The coffee shop down the street boasts gourmet cupcakes I'd sell my soul for.

Freya grins. "Absolutely. Pick your poison."

"Surprise me."

"Will do." She points to the door. "Myles's friend is here to see you."

"For what reason?"

"You're interviewing him, remember?"

"Shit. That's today?"

"Yes." She gives me a sheepish look. "He's been here since eight thirty, but you were on the phone with Charles, so I didn't want to interrupt."

My lip curls at the mention of my ex's name. "If he calls again, tell him I'm out of the office."

She nods. "So, do you want me to send the guy in? He's been waiting over forty-five minutes."

"He can wait for another five while I use the ladies' room and grab a coffee." Standing, I smooth my skirt and point to Freya's clipboard. "Do you have his résumé?"

"Yeah. I checked all his references for you." She cocks her head to the side. "He's only got three years of experience. You hate newbies—why would you waste your energy?"

I sigh heavily. "Because I have two positions to fill, and I trust Myles's opinion."

She snorts. "There's a shocker. You mean your golden boy's word is gospel?"

"He's not my golden boy." At her arched brow, I add, "Not that I need to justify my reasoning, but Myles is damn good at his job and doesn't give me any shit. If I want something done, he gets it done."

Nodding, she taps her pen on the clipboard. "Well, Clark Kent out there is getting antsy, so maybe you should get started."

"No, he can wait. Around here we operate by *my* schedule. Let him know I'll be with him shortly." I grab my cosmetic bag from my purse. I'm sure my mascara is a disaster, and I'd rather not look like a drugged-up raccoon for the rest of the day. I head for the private restroom attached to my executive suite.

She holds up the résumé. "Don't you want to see this?"

I stop short. "I suppose I can skim it." She hands it over, and I glance at the top. "Lincoln Kennedy? What the hell kind of name is that?"

"Maybe he's American royalty." Freya leans against my desk. "Oh, I should probably give you a heads-up about Clark Kent."

"And that is?" I ask, perplexed by her second Superman reference in five minutes.

"He's smoking hot."

"Good for him." I couldn't care less about my interviewee's appearance. Beautiful men are trouble. I learned that the hard way. "Unless he's Henry Cavill himself, I'm not interested in smoke shows."

# Three

*Lincoln*

This is ridiculous. My eyes have been burning a hole through Elinora Iverson's door for close to an hour. What sense does it make to give someone an appointment if you plan to leave them hanging? My river mud jet fuel is long gone, and I'm fading fast. I need to get this interview over with so I can go the fuck to sleep.

Finally, the door swings open, but it's her cute assistant again. Tall and curvy, with golden curls and hazel eyes, there's something familiar about her, but I can't put my finger on it.

I force a smile. "Do you think it'll be much longer?"

"Ms. Iverson will be with you shortly."

I nod and glance at my watch once more. "You said that thirty-five minutes ago."

She opens her mouth to speak, but someone else's voice comes out.

"In a hurry, Mr. Kennedy?" Elinora Iverson appears at her assistant's side, and I stop breathing.

Years of Catholic school fly out the window as I stare at the porcelain goddess before me. The woman is ethereal. Resplendent. Drop-dead gorgeous. It's a damn good thing I'm seated because my legs would've given out.

It takes every ounce of my energy not to build her a golden pedestal and fall at her feet in worship.

Lustrous platinum blond hair cascades to the middle of her back, shimmering against the navy sheath dress showcasing her willowy frame. Silver stilettos accentuate her legs, making them appear even longer. Her only jewelry is a pair of diamond stud earrings—five times the size of my mother's engagement ring.

Courtesy of my employment at The River, I'm no stranger to provocative imagery. Whether their bodies are hugged in leather or nude, tied up or sprawled out, I've seen more beautiful women than I know what to do with. I learned to control my arousal out of necessity. Years of overstimulation dulled me to normal sexual attraction, which is likely why I don't have an actual love life. I've yet to encounter a woman who can get me out of my head enough to want something more, so I stopped trying.

Right now, staring at the ice queen that is Elinora Iverson, I'm teenage Lincoln again, sitting with my bookbag on my lap in Ms. Fisher's art class. Like the blood in my veins, every thought, rational or otherwise, follows one path. Their destination? My cock.

Elinora's ice-blue gaze narrows on my face. "Hello?"

"No, I . . . uh . . . I'm good," I stutter, as my mind plays the melody for "Let It Go."

"Then you won't mind waiting a little longer."

"Sure, that's fine," I say, even though her glacial tone makes it clear she's not asking for my permission—nor does she care that I've been waiting.

"Freya, show him to my office."

*Freya.* I've heard that name before, but where?

Elinora gestures to me. "Don't touch anything."

Well, fuck. There goes my plan to make a paper clip chain and put sticky notes everywhere. I open my mouth to give a sly retort but stop myself when Myles comes to mind. It doesn't matter how rude or inconsiderate I find Elinora, I refuse to jeopardize his promotion.

I follow Freya into the office, and she directs me to a chair opposite a large ebony desk. "She shouldn't be long."

"Thanks."

Our eyes meet, and hers flare in recognition. Her mouth drops open, but she quickly recovers. "Do you have any questions for me?"

Realization hits me like a battering ram. Her name sounded familiar because she *is* familiar. Her sister, Anya Thorne, is a friend of mine who I met at The River. Courtesy of Anya—and whatever arrangement she has with Esme—Freya is one of the club's newer members.

Which means I'm beyond fucked.

Determined to avoid any awkwardness or make it obvious I recognize her, I clear my throat and ask the first question that comes to mind. "Can she shoot icicles from her fingertips?"

Freya smirks. "Wait until you see what happens when she stomps her feet."

"Do I have any chance of getting this job?"

"I wouldn't count on it, but good luck." She gives me a sweet smile as she leaves.

As soon as she tells Elinora about my employment at The River, which I left off my résumé for obvious reasons, my chances of being offered a position at Iverson Press will hit bottom faster than a lead sinker.

Then again, as a club member, Freya was also required to sign an NDA. I wonder if hers carries the same weight as mine.

I survey the sterile room with its gray walls and sleek furniture. There aren't any pictures adorning the office—hanging, framed, or otherwise. The only décor is a massive oil painting of the Iverson coat of arms. A clock ticks away on her desk, reminding me of a silent classroom during final exams. Except this time, I didn't study.

And I'm naked.

Oh, and I have a boner.

Elinora strides in, carrying a coffee mug, and closes the door behind her. "What brings you to Iverson Press?"

I clear my throat. "Your publishing house is among the most lucrative—"

"I'm not looking for a canned response here, Mr. Kennedy. I want to know why you left your previous place of employment." She sets her steaming beverage on the coaster beside her computer, moving with the certainty of a judge striking their gavel on a sound block. Yet somehow, she manages not to spill a drop.

"Cooper Press is struggling financially—"

"No kidding." She flashes a smug look and settles behind the desk. "I put them there. Anyway, you were saying?"

"I was lowest man on the totem pole, so they laid me off."

This feels like when I told my earth science teacher I wasn't prepared for her midterm. How I couldn't remember the layers of the planet I'd spent my whole fucking life on. Forget the lava core—I froze after mantle.

Elinora points to my résumé. "It says you've been an editor for three years. Elaborate."

"Uh . . ." The woman's a publishing mogul. Surely, she understands my job description? I shift in my seat. "I'm, uh, not sure what you mean."

She rolls her eyes. "What *kind* of editor? Line? Developmental?"

"Oh. Both, but my strength is in line editing."

"Myles praised your attention to detail." She sips her coffee. "Which genres did you work on?"

"Mainly thrillers, mysteries, and crime fiction. I recently finished a sci-fi drama, but I have little experience with sci-fi as a whole."

She gestures to my résumé. "Doesn't look like you have much experience *at all*."

I stiffen my spine, pissed that she's insinuating I don't know what I'm doing. "Yeah, well, that happens when someone's only been out of school three years." The snarky reply is out of my mouth before I can stop it.

Fuck. Now I've really screwed myself over.

Her icy eyes narrow into slits. "I'm aware of the math, Mr. Kennedy. But please," she flicks her hand in my direction, "go ahead and mansplain it to me. I'm sure you've got plenty of experience there."

Why did I subject myself to this level of condescension?

*Reagan.* She's the reason I push forward despite my wounded pride, my exhaustion, and the voice in my head screaming for me to walk out. Reagan is the reason behind everything I do and why I can't afford to fuck up this interview.

"I apologize," I say with a heavy sigh, straightening my glasses. "But Myles gave me the impression you *wanted* to interview me."

She quirks a perfect eyebrow. "For the record, I don't do anything unless I want to."

"Your line of questioning seems a bit aggressive."

"If that's your idea of aggressive, you'll never make it in publishing." She taps her pen on the desk.

I can tell she's ready to dismiss me. Rich women get a certain look on their faces when they're finished with someone. I call it rueful disdain or pity-infused annoyance. Elinora wears a mixture of both. She is moments from sending me on my merry way.

Looks like I'll be trapped in the role of pleasure concierge, kissing wealthy women's asses for the rest of my life. Living in a tiny studio apartment in New York City, while the rest of my family is upstate. Eating microwave dinners more nights than not. Missing out on conventional relationships because I'm too busy fucking the mayor's sister. Abusing my body and mind to make a better life for my sister. I'll do it until the day I die, but it would be nice if just once someone threw me a fucking bone.

Swallowing what's left of my pride, I grip the edge of her desk. "Look, I'm sorry we got off on the wrong foot. I swear I'm not an asshole."

"Could've fooled me."

"Please give me a job. I'll do whatever you want. I'll come in early, stay late. I have no problem being here on weekends." I rake a hand through my hair. "Please, just give me a chance. Even if it's only a temporary position."

"While your résumé is lacking, I suppose your tenacity is acceptable."

"Uh, thanks?" Hope nudges my conscience.

"It was an observation, not a compliment." Derision saturates her tone, matching her snooty face. "That said, Myles Callahan sang your praises, and his opinion is of value to me." Her frigid eyes bore into mine. "Perseverance and word of mouth don't make up for inexperience, but I have positions to fill. I'll give you three months to prove your worth. Against my better judgment, I'm willing to take a chance on you."

"I apprec—"

"But if you fail to meet my expectations, you're done, Mr. Kennedy."

"Thank you, Ms. Iverson. I won't disappoint you." Adjusting my glasses, I lean forward. "Please call me Lincoln."

Elinora raises an eyebrow. "Lincoln Kennedy is a bizarre name."

"My parents are American history buffs with a strange sense of humor. My little sister is named Reagan. They're from Ireland, so it makes it even weirder."

She nods, peering down her nose at me. "You start tomorrow at nine. Freya will show you your cubicle."

"Thank you." I extend my hand to her. "I appreciate the opportunity."

"Welcome to Iverson Press." Clasping my palm with cool, delicate fingers, she thaws slightly, smiling for the first time since we met.

Its effects are devastating. My breath rushes out of me, and goose bumps bloom on my skin. Every nerve ending flares to life, sizzling my insides.

"Thank you so much."

Just when I think I'm off the glacier, she hits me over the head with a block of ice. "I think you'll be a great fit for our romance imprint, Iverson Melt."

"Romance?" I croak, blinking rapidly. "I have no experience editing romance."

"We've already established your lack of experience."

I open and close my mouth a few times. "You want me in *romance*? Sex books?"

Her icy gaze crystallizes the air in my lungs. "If you knew the first thing about publishing, you'd understand romance is a billion-dollar industry."

"I mean, I do, but—"

"Readers crave their happily ever afters, and it's our job to give them what they want. The bottom line is sex sells."

The truth in her statement reaches a level of irony that makes me laugh aloud. Courtesy of The River, I know all about happy endings. I've done every position and acted out every kinky fantasy imaginable. From flowers and fancy dinners with aging debutantes, to tying up politicians' wives, I've been there. Blindfolds, ball gags, hot wax, you name it.

While I have zero experience with the publishing end of the romance spectrum, I know sex better than anyone. You might call me a pleasure guru. Wrangler of female orgasms. Administrator of ecstasy. Superintendent of all things carnal. A bona fide *fucking* professional.

"Is something funny?"

"No, not at all." I force a straight face. "I'm just, uh, surprised you'd task me with love stories."

"If it weren't for Myles, I wouldn't task you with anything."

What's left of my ego cowers behind a rock. "You've mentioned."

She eyes me over the rim of her coffee cup before taking a slow sip. "But, like I said, I have positions that need filling. Iverson Melt is our most profitable imprint, so I can't afford any vacancies there. We've got four manuscripts awaiting line edits and several more headed down the pike." Abandoning her mug, she stands and gestures to the door. "That's my offer, Mr. Kennedy. Take it or leave it."

Rising, I pull my shoulders back and stiffen my spine. "I'll be the best damn romance editor to ever walk through these doors."

"You've got three months to prove it." Elinora crosses her arms over her chest. "I truly hope you surprise me."

"I'll see you tomorrow, Ms. Iverson. And don't worry, I'm full of surprises."

Myles snags me on my way through the office, pulling me into a private conference room. "Well? How'd it go?"

"She spoke highly of you and offered me a position."

I leave out the part about how she stomped all over my self-esteem because I'm ashamed of how deeply her words cut me. For a moment, I could've sworn I was back in high school, reliving the torment of Sister Fitzgibbons, the cruelest nun to ever walk the earth.

Relief floods his face. "Oh, thank fuck. I assume you're replacing Ted, our former mystery and suspense editor?"

"Nope," I say, popping the *p* and reluctantly meeting his gaze. "I'm the new editor for Iverson Melt."

He tries to stifle his laugh, I'll give him that, but Myles's face betrays him. Whether he's angry, embarrassed, or amused, the poor guy is always red. This time's no exception. Flushing from his ears to his neck, his emerald eyes sparkle with mirth. "Wait, she seriously put *you* in romance?"

"Appears that way, doesn't it?"

"Why the hell would she do that when I told her your background was in suspense and thrillers?"

"Maybe she's setting me up to fail?"

"Iverson Melt," he murmurs, shaking his head. "That's intense. Have you ever seen any of their titles?"

"Do I look like a romance reader to you?"

"Bold of you to assume romance readers fit into a specific mold."

"That's not what I meant." Pulling off my glasses, I rub the bridge of my nose. "I don't know shit about love."

"You're right about that one." Myles chuckles. "But you may have an advantage, given your extracurriculars. I'll forward you a few titles in each subgenre to give you an idea of what you're getting into. The most important thing you need to remember is that romance requires a happily ever after—or a happy for now, where it's clear the main characters are together—in the book's conclusion. Bottom line, end of story. Don't let anyone tell you otherwise. You'll figure out the rest. Anyway, I just finished a marketing plan for the release of *Take Me*, an erotic romance that comes out in a few months. Holy fuck, I was seventeen shades of red. This shit's right up your alley."

"Just because I do it, doesn't mean I embrace my lifestyle," I mutter, wiping my lenses on my sleeve. "It's survival, Myles."

"Did she give you a probationary term?"

"Three months."

"Use your expertise wisely and I'm sure you can make your position permanent." He eyes me. "What about pay and benefits?"

"Honestly, I was so happy she offered me a job, I forgot to ask."

"The benefits package starts after someone's been employed for three months, but from what I hear, the pay's competitive."

"Either way, it gets my foot in the door. Maybe I can impress her and make a name for myself." I rub the back of my neck. "Also, you weren't kidding about the whole ice queen thing. She looks exactly like—"

"Right? The resemblance is uncanny. Last week she showed up in a baby blue pantsuit and I swear to God, I almost started singing."

"That's on brand for you." After years in our school choir, I'm shocked he doesn't break into spontaneous song more often. He certainly did back then. "So, what's Freya's story? She seems cool."

Myles nods. "Freya's her right-hand woman. She's cool as fuck, but incredibly loyal to Elinora." He lowers his voice. "I may be wrong, but I suspect something *more* is going on between them, if you know what I mean."

"Interesting. I didn't pick up on that vibe, but I'll take your word for it."

"Richard and I had dinner with them once. He also noticed their closeness."

I curl my lip at the mention of his long-time partner. I'm not a fan and never will be. Twenty years our senior, Richard Pennington acts like he's God's gift to mankind and everyone should fall at his feet—especially Myles. My best friend deserves better than some asshole Brit who thinks his shit doesn't stink. "Sorry, but I take Dick's opinion with a grain of salt."

Myles glares at me. "*Richard* is very attuned to same-sex couplings. He is a sex therapist, for fuck's sake."

"Methinks Dick doesn't know dick."

He snorts. "On the contrary, he *knows* dick. But I really wish you wouldn't call him that."

"I wish he'd treat you better," I counter, crossing my arms over my chest.

Myles sighs heavily. "Lincoln, please. I don't have the energy for this right now."

"It takes a lot of energy for me to watch him take you for granted, so . . ."

"Imagine the energy I expend worrying about some psycho kidnapping you as her sexual pet."

"I'm six foot four, two hundred and forty pounds of solid muscle. I highly doubt any woman could kidnap me without help."

"What if someone drugs you and steals your kidneys? What will you tell your parents if you wake up in a bathtub full of ice somewhere?"

"I *have* woken up in a bathtub." Smirking, I squeeze his shoulder. "I'd probably beg for one of your kidneys."

"You wouldn't have to beg, my friend." Myles shakes his head. "You know I'd give you a kidney if you needed one, but you're not getting my liver. There's far too much wine I need to experience in this lifetime."

"I certainly owe you a bottle for today. Thanks for scoring me an interview, man. I appreciate it."

He nods. "I'm glad it went well. Now, don't fuck up."

"I won't," I say, even though there's plenty of opportunity for me to fail. "Who knows? Maybe one day I'll be able to leave my extracurriculars behind."

# Four

## Elinora

Freya saunters into my office and sits on the edge of the desk, placing a massive pink cupcake in front of me. "I can't believe you gave Clark Kent a job."

While she isn't wrong with her hunky nerd description, the man I interviewed was far from Superman. His arrogance raised my hackles, and I'm still not entirely sure why I gave him a chance.

"I offered him Cindy's position for a three-month trial period."

"Wait, you seriously put him in romance?" she asks, knowing how protective I am of Iverson Melt. "I thought you told me to assign him Cindy's cubicle because Ted hasn't cleaned his out. I didn't realize you intended him as her replacement."

"Ted was caught up, so we don't have a backlog of thrillers waiting to be edited. I put Clark where I need him most."

"How long do you think he'll last?" Freya tosses her golden ringlets over her shoulder. "I give him a week before he quits."

I shrug and rearrange the papers on my desk. "He seemed pretty desperate, so maybe he'll stick it out."

She grins, her hazel eyes flashing. "At least he's nice to look at. And by that, I mean gorgeous."

"I suppose he's a bit of a visual upgrade from Cindy."

Understatement of the year.

Tall and broad, Lincoln Kennedy filled out his charcoal suit like it was hand-tailored for him. His crisp navy dress shirt and silver tie made me question whether he secretly coordinated his outfit with mine. For a moment, I wondered if Myles had tipped him off, but then I remembered I've been in the office since six. I doubt either of them was even awake yet.

The interview went as expected for an interviewee with little experience. My questions clearly rattled Lincoln, which was my intent, but his eye contact never faltered. That's critical for me. If someone can't look me in the eye, I know they're hiding something. Charles was a professional gaze-averter, which should've been a red flag for his infidelity. While I make my living publishing bestselling mysteries, I have no desire to live one. That holds true for every realm of my existence—from Iverson Press to my nonexistent love life.

I skimmed Lincoln's demographics while Freya showed him his cubicle. Age-wise, I've got him by a decade. He's only twenty-five, yet his weary gaze held more depth than I'd expect from a man so young. Hidden behind thick black frames, inky lashes fringed a set of deep blue eyes, but it was the dark circles beneath them that struck me. Lincoln's desperation-laced tenacity reminds me of myself at his age—inexperienced and ill-equipped but driven to succeed at all costs. Maybe he isn't perfect for the romance editor position, but something inside me insisted I give him a chance.

Besides, Freya makes a valid point. With a face carved by the gods, Lincoln is quite the physical specimen, and I could use a better view from my office. Dimples, a sculpted jaw, and a sexy chin cleft add to his Clark Kent appeal. Factor in the glossy black hair he'd swept back from his face, and I'd swear I offered the position to Henry Cavill during his tenure as Superman.

Freya rolls her eyes. "A visual upgrade? You're always so technical."

"Details and technicality make the world go around."

"I think your world needs more plot holes. Maybe a couple kinky twists. Come out with me this weekend."

"You know I don't go out." I unwrap my cupcake and take a bite, nearly moaning when the sweet decadence coats my tongue. "Wow. This is amazing."

"That one's called Strawberry Sex Swing. It's one of my favorites."

My insides flutter with her mention of the carnal contraption I've read about in a few of Iverson Melt's titles. While they more than intrigue me, the chances of me encountering a sex swing in the wild are slim to none. Frustrated by my nonexistent sex life, I switch topics. "Yeah, I'm not really a nightlife kind of girl. The last thing I need is to run into Charles or one of his twenty-seven mistresses."

Freya laughs. "Come to the club with me. I'll introduce you to some of my friends, and we'll get you so drunk you won't remember who you ran into, ex-husbands and mistresses notwithstanding."

"I'm too old for clubbing."

"Elinora, you're thirty-five—not dead. Throw caution to the wind and live a little. What good is building an empire if you never get to enjoy it? There's a spa we can hit up if the dancing scene's not your thing."

"A spa?" I snort. "You go from one extreme to the next. First you want to get me drunk, now we're talking pedicures?"

"Not pedicures, silly. I mean hydrotherapy and massages. If you won't let me relax you with a few drinks, maybe you'll enjoy floating in silence or allow some hot guy to rub your body."

During my marriage, I was too busy "building my empire" to relax. Our sex life suffered, and ultimately, my focus caused my husband to stray. After giving Charles the best fifteen years of my life, I'm reluctant to let another man close enough to touch me.

"No one's rubbed my body in years."

Freya leans in close. "No shit. That's why I'm suggesting it."

"Maybe I'll take you up on that. I could use a good rubdown."

# Five

*Lincoln*

*eople need to get the fuck out of my way.*

Dodging a clump of poncho-wearing tourists on the sidewalk, I hustle past Bryant Park toward Iverson headquarters. I'm never late. Punctuality is something I value almost as much as reliability, so it would be fucking outstanding if I wasn't on the verge of being late for my first day at Iverson Press.

My morning was doomed from the start. First, I missed my alarm and woke an hour later than I planned. Then, I couldn't find my phone. Why? Because I knocked it into my sock drawer while getting dressed. After that, I wasted ten minutes searching for my umbrella, which must have vanished into the ether.

Since I didn't want to show up looking like a drowned rat, I called an Uber. As my luck would have it, a broken water main resulted in ungodly traffic. It was so bad, I jumped out two blocks before my stop and ran the rest of the way. To add insult to injury, my feet are soaked, thanks to a puddle I couldn't see through my foggy lenses.

I push through the front doors of the skyscraper that houses my new job and sprint over to the security desk. "Hi, I'm starting with Iverson Press today. I need elevator access please." I yank my glasses off and dry the lenses on my shirt.

The guy looks over his computer at me. "Name and photo ID?"

"I'm Lincoln Kennedy. You saw me when I interviewed yesterday, remember?" I shove the frames back onto my face.

"I remember." He points to a scanner on his desk. "But I need your ID regardless."

"Fine," I mumble, rummaging in my bag for my wallet, which is buried beneath all my shit. When I finally locate the tattered leather bundle, I withdraw it and pry my ID from its plastic sleeve. I hand it over with a forced smile. "Here you go."

He slides the card through his scanner. "Once Iverson's IT department gives us your personnel info, we can set you up in our system, so you don't have to go through this every time." He hands me back my ID and motions toward the elevators. "Eleventh floor."

"Thanks." I shove everything into my bag, jog over there, and tap the call button. Unnerved by the additional delay, I pace the lobby while I wait, my shoes squishing with every step. Finally, an empty car arrives, and I rush inside. Glancing at my watch, I select the eleventh floor, at the eleventh hour, and sag against a wall.

The damn thing stops on the tenth floor.

"C'mon fucker." Balling my hands into fists, I shift to the side and try to catch my breath.

Except that proves impossible when the doors slide open, and my heart stops.

Elinora stands in the doorway holding a stack of papers, the picture of sleek sophistication with her black power suit and red stilettos. Beneath her unbuttoned jacket, a blood-red camisole accentuates her porcelain skin, and the lacy neckline reveals enough cleavage to make my mouth water. She'd left her hair down, the satiny strands of platinum falling past the lower curve of her breasts. I clench my jaw against the overwhelming urge to press her up against the wall and kiss her neck. My dick goes rogue again, making the situation in my dress pants tighter. I shift my messenger bag in front of me.

Stepping inside, she points to her watch and raises a brow at me. "Cutting it close, Mr. Kennedy."

*Shit.*

With a quick adjustment of my tie, loosening its stranglehold, I clear my throat. "I, uh, there was traffic, so I—"

"I'm not interested in your excuses." She moves to stand beside me.

"I'm sorry." I stare straight ahead, unable to meet the ice-blue gaze that accompanies her frosty tone.

"When we get to our floor, I need to see you in my office."

*Great, she's already firing me.*

I force a swallow and pivot to face her. "What for?" Her eyes narrow, but she doesn't respond, so I backpedal. "I mean, sure. I'll be right in. Is something wrong?" Although I tower over her, I feel like I'm two feet tall, and I can't draw enough air to fill my lungs.

She cocks her head to the side. "Why would something be wrong?"

"It wouldn't. I'm just . . . uh, I was wondering," I stammer, releasing a nervous laugh.

"We never discussed your compensation yesterday," she explains, peering up at me. "I'm assuming you don't plan to work for free?"

"No, definitely not. Time is money." I cringe at my cheesy line.

"Yes, Mr. Kennedy, it is." Elinora purses her full red lips. "Which is why I expect you to be on time. Every day."

"I'm sorry I cut it so close. It won't happen again. When does the building open?"

"Six."

"From now on, I'll arrive by seven." My sorry ass will be here at the crack of dawn, before I even *think* about showing up late.

Her eyes widen, but she gives me a curt nod. "You need to see security for your badge before the end of business today. I'll have IT clear you for early entrance."

We reach our floor, and I step aside so she can exit. "After you, Ms. Iverson."

"Thank you."

I follow her inside the suite like a lost puppy.

Myles waves. "Good morning."

"Good morning, Myles," she says sweetly, handing him the stack of papers. "This is the proposal I need you to work on. Sullivan's agent wants an answer this week, but I need to know if you can market it given the controversial nature of his platform."

Myles nods. "I'll look it over as soon as I finish my meeting with the new distributor we talked about."

"Perfect." She points to her office. "Go have a seat, Mr. Kennedy. I'll be in after I grab your file from human resources."

I rush across the suite to her office and slump into the chair at her desk. I haven't even been employed for twenty-four hours, and I've already had two boners and roped myself into coming in early.

Freya pops her head into the room, her curls piled in a messy bun. "Hey there. You came back for more?"

"Yup." I rub my jaw. "I guess I'm a glutton for a good punishment."

"Me too." She flushes. "I mean, my job isn't to punish—" Squeezing her eyes shut, she shakes her head. "Never mind. I should really be going."

I smile when she finally meets my gaze again. "I'm sure I'll see you around."

"Yeah, I float from here to there." She releases a nervous laugh. "But you already know that, apparently." She gives me a wave and abruptly leaves the room.

I can't figure out why she's so flustered by my knowledge of her River membership when I'm the one whose job is at stake.

After a few minutes, Elinora enters her office with a manila folder. "All right, let's get down to business." She struts to her desk and plops the file in front of me. "How much do you think you're worth?"

*According to Sister Fitzgibbons, absolutely nothing.*

My gaze snaps to hers, and I beat back the shitty high school memories. I open and close my mouth a few times, unable to formulate a response.

"Well?" Impatience laces her tone, but it's the look in her eyes that unnerves me. She's enjoying my discomfort.

And that doesn't sit well with me. I clench my jaw instead of answering.

"Perhaps you didn't hear me, Mr. Kennedy. I asked you how much you think you're worth."

It's a trick question. If my number is too high, she'll mock my arrogance. If I undercut myself, she wins. I'm tired of rich women winning at my expense.

Steeling myself for her rejection, I lean forward. "I made twenty-seven an hour at Cooper Press. I'd appreciate something along those lines."

"Seems vague to me." Elinora cocks her head to the side. "When you said time is money, I figured you had an exact number in mind."

"What I feel I'm worth and what an employer is willing to pay me seldom match up. I need this job, so the ball's in your court."

"Make no mistake, the ball is always in my court." She scans my résumé once more. "I'll pay you thirty dollars an hour. If you make it beyond three months, there will be an associated increase, with the amount to be determined by my level of satisfaction."

"Thank you, Ms. Iverson."

"I expect my employees to earn what I pay them."

I straighten. "I will."

She nods, handing me a slip of paper. "Here's your email login credentials. I'll forward the manuscripts in the order I expect them done. They're all Word documents, so be sure to use track changes so the authors know what you've edited. In addition, I'd like to view the changes for quality control purposes."

Great. Instead of letting me work, she'll be looking over my shoulder. How am I supposed to function with her breathing down my neck?

She raises a brow. "Is there a problem, Mr. Kennedy?"

"No. I'm just accustomed to my employer setting me loose on a project." Not to mention it seems pretty ridiculous that the company's CEO would bother wasting her time on a mere peasant like me.

"Wipe that notion out of your head. Understand that I attach my name to every manuscript that makes it to publication. My standards are extremely high. I expect nothing short of excellence, and until I'm confident in your ability to perform, I'll be closely involved with your projects. Prove yourself, and I'll back off. Are we on the same page now?"

"Yes."

"Good. After you fill out all the necessary paperwork, you can jump right in."

Adjusting my glasses, I rise and sling my bag over my shoulder. "Thank you."

I head for my cubicle to discover a cup of coffee with a note from Myles.

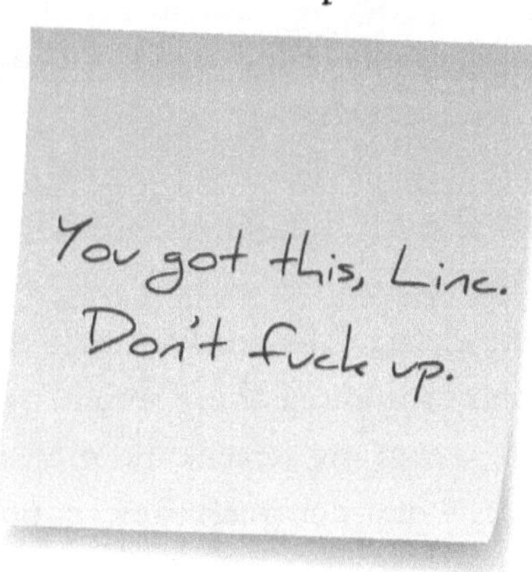

The Callahan brand of encouragement has always amused me. I shoot him a quick text to thank him, then fill out the required forms before diving into my work.

My first project is a steamy contemporary romance set in Ireland. The heroine's a sassy nurse with a guarded heart who finds herself stranded with a cocky Irish actor. I'll probably finish edits on the first few chapters today. My goal this weekend is a romance-reading marathon. Maybe if I immerse myself in this world from the start, I'll have a chance at impressing Elinora.

I work straight through my breaks, which is typical for me. As far as first days go, I really can't complain. My lunch was delicious, my feet are finally dry—thanks to the wad of paper towels I jammed into my shoes—and I'm enjoying the book more than I expected. Plus, the view from my cubicle is breathtaking. Elinora returned from her lunch while I was reading the first sex scene. She sauntered through the suite like a fucking vixen. Powerful, confident, a force to be reckoned with.

Now I have the literary equivalent of blue balls.

Myles appears at my shoulder. "How's your first day going?"

"So far, so good." I point to my computer screen. "This one's a scorcher."

He grins. "So . . . you don't hate it?"

"Surprisingly, no. It's different from what I'm used to, but I'm adjusting."

"How's our favorite She-Devil treating you?"

I snort. "Like a toddler. I get that I'm new, but she insists on babysitting me."

"Speaking of," Myles murmurs, looking over my shoulder. "Hi, Elinora."

"Hello, Myles." She glances at me as she approaches my cubicle. "Are you making progress, Mr. Kennedy?"

"Yes, ma'am."

She cringes. "Stick with Ms. Iverson, please. Ma'am is too old a title for me."

"I'll keep that in mind. How do you want to look at my work? Chapter by chapter, or do you want the entire thing when I'm finished?"

She leans down to peer at my screen, and pieces of her hair brush my shoulder. I nearly moan when her perfume's seductive floral notes drift to my nose. I take a slow, deep breath, drawing in her scent. No joke, the woman smells like heaven. Like a goddess. Images of her naked on a gilded throne tighten my balls. My cock twitches, and I force my thoughts elsewhere. If I'm not careful, I'll weave my fingers into her hair and pull her onto my lap.

I've got a million reasons to resist Elinora Iverson. Not only is she rich, powerful, and gorgeous, but she's way out of my league. More importantly, she's my boss.

And the iciest ice queen who ever iced.

"You've already gotten through your edits on the first sixty pages?" she asks in surprise.

"That's a typical pace for me."

"You realize this needs to be thorough, right?"

I frown. "It's a line edit, is it not?"

"That's what I'm asking you, Mr. Kennedy." When I don't immediately answer, she purses her lips and adds, "I can't have you rushing if it means you miss out on details. If you're going to do it, do it right."

I tense. "For the record, I don't half-ass *anything*—especially not my work." Myles gives me a warning glare, but I ignore him. "I can assure you, not only is it thorough, but it's a significant improvement over what was there."

Elinora raises a brow. "No need to be defensive."

"I'm not being defensive," I snap, clenching my fists in my lap. "I'm stating a fact."

Her mouth curves into a cruel smile. "It seems like you have an issue with my authority."

"No, I have an issue with your insinuation that I'd compromise quality for speed."

Myles grips my shoulder. "Lincoln, chill."

Elinora straightens, her glacial gaze narrowing on mine. "Let me make myself perfectly clear. This is *my* company. I built this empire, therefore I can—and will—insinuate whatever the hell I want. If I'm paying you to do a job, it damn well better meet my standards. You have next to no experience. I have every right to question you and your process, so I'd appreciate if you'd drop your attitude. I'm the queen of this castle. If your ego can't handle my approach, I suggest you find a new kingdom."

I blink a few times before answering. "I'm sorry. I meant no disrespect."

"Could've fooled me." She turns and storms off, her stilettos clicking on the marble floor.

A slamming door rattles my skull, right before Myles smacks the back of my head. "What the fuck is wrong with you?"

"Do you want a list?"

"Are you seriously giving her shit on your first day?" He knots his fingers in his hair. "She's your boss, dude. Grow the fuck up."

"I'm sorry. I didn't mean to overreact, but she struck a nerve."

"Fuck your nerves. You're being an arrogant little dick. If your ego costs me my promotion, I'll kick your ass." Myles storms off in the same direction as Elinora.

"Nice one, Kennedy," I mutter under my breath. "Great first impression."

# Six

## Elinora

That's it. I've finally wasted enough time to make leaving feel like the more productive option. I haven't been able to focus since my run-in with Lincoln after lunch. I release my breath in a huff, picturing the arrogance in his dark blue gaze. Who the hell does he think he is, challenging my authority on his first day? I have every right to question him—I'm the fucking boss. My top priority is to safeguard my company's reputation for quality, and his lack of experience tells me he's *unqualified* to work here.

But when he'd stared up at me as he defended himself, with his haunting eyes and perfectly sculpted face, the cocky bastard weakened my armor. I wanted to tell him to take a hike, but I couldn't bring myself to utter the words. Leave it to me to hire a man whose pride and ego rival my own. Why couldn't he be a simpering, potbellied old guy with a pockmarked face? Why does his thick, glossy hair beg my fingertips to touch it? And why do I have to see so much of my younger self in him?

I log out of my computer and stuff my phone into my purse. After the third call from Charles, I finally took Freya's advice and put the damn thing on silent. It's funny—he calls me more now than when we were married. Not that the reason's a mystery. He wants something from me.

Freya walks into my office carrying her coat and purse. "Are you sure you're OK? You've been stewing all afternoon."

"Charles thinks he deserves more alimony. Maybe if the bastard worked harder, he could support himself." The words drip from my tongue like acid. I have no patience for lazy people who expect others to pick up their slack. It infuriates me that my ex thinks he's entitled to a portion of my success when he did *nothing* to get me here.

"You should block his number."

I shake my head. "He'd call the office or show up here and make a scene." I gesture to my doorway. "Did everyone else already leave for the day?" My employees have a tendency to skip out the second the clock strikes five. I get it, but it's amusing to watch them stand by the elevators like a bunch of idiotic lemmings, when if they gave it a few minutes, there wouldn't be such a delay. I don't have much of a life outside of work, so I'm usually in the office until after six. My elevator ride is always smooth sailing.

Freya smirks. "No, not everyone."

I glance at my watch. "It's six thirty."

"Like your boy Myles told you, Clark Kent is extremely focused and driven," she murmurs, wagging her brows.

I curl my lip. "Clark Kent has an attitude problem."

"So, put him in his place. He'd probably like it."

"Already did," I say with a self-satisfied smile. "There's only room for one queen in this office."

"It's his first day, and you already knocked him down a few pegs?"

"He already pissed me off." I stand and slide my coat on. "Granted, I've been on edge since Charles called, but that's neither here nor there."

Freya perks up. "Speaking of being on edge, have you given any thought to my invitation?"

"What kind of club is it again?"

"It's an elite specialty spa that provides an assortment of relaxation services for its members."

"Wait, you have to be a member to go there?"

She nods. "It's not open to the public. Lucky for you, I'm a member. You can come as my guest."

"You never mentioned being a member of some club. I thought you were kayaking?"

"Kayaking? Where'd you get that from?"

"For the past month or so, you've been talking about going to the river to float."

"The River is the name of the club, Elinora." Freya giggles. "It's, um . . . it's a water-themed luxury spa with a bit of a nightclub scene. There's also an affiliated restaurant called Oasis. They serve amazing food and drinks."

"Oh. That makes way more sense," I say, shaking my head. "I knew hopping into the Hudson down here wasn't a relaxing prospect."

"Did you honestly think I drove upstate multiple times a week to paddle a kayak?"

"Yes." I laugh. "That's exactly what I imagined."

She wraps her arms around me. "Honey, you need to broaden your horizons."

"I don't have time for new horizons."

"There's always time to try something new. Especially if it chills you out. I'm confident The River has a cure for what ails you."

I gesture to myself. "There's no curing this."

"I wouldn't be so sure of that. Come with me tomorrow. It's new members' night, and they're having a mermaid-themed masquerade mingle."

"Seriously? Do I need to dress up as Ariel?"

She snorts. "No, not quite. Think sexy mermaids and mermen. Scantily clad hot guys with hot bodies. Besides, you'd be more like Ursula."

I give her the middle finger. "Ha. Ha. Very funny."

"Maleficent?" Freya grins. "Cruella de Vil?"

"I hate you sometimes."

She kisses my cheek. "Well, I love you. Which is why you're coming with me."

"OK, fine. I'll check it out."

Freya rubs her hands together with glee. "All you need to bring is your bathing suit—I have the perfect mask for you."

"What about a towel?"

"They have towels, robes, and sandals. I'll book us for an overnight room, so we can crash after the mingle."

"You said they do massages? What types?" I rub the back of my neck.

"The spa is all-inclusive, which means you can partake in any activities you wish. As far as massages go, they offer Swedish, hot stone, deep tissue, and sensual."

I raise a brow. "Sensual?"

She nods. "They have waterfalls, hot tubs, whirlpools, mineral pools, and a lazy river. My personal favorite are the private lagoons."

"What happens there?"

"You float. Water lapping at your skin, peaceful music playing—it's glorious. Sometimes, if I've had a rough week, I'll do a sensory deprivation float."

"What the hell is that?"

"There're varying degrees of flotation therapy offered, as well as elective enhancements. Picture this: silence and total darkness, you're drifting in warm water, weightless and free."

I shake my head. "I'm not loving the total darkness part."

"The float is customizable to a member's comfort level, so you can add lagoon lighting. If you don't want it silent, you can add some music or nature sounds. And if you don't enjoy being alone, you can have someone with you," Freya explains. "I'm happy to float with you for your first time."

"Yeah, let's do that. I'd feel more comfortable with you there."

"Perfect. You're gonna love it."

"Don't they worry about people drowning?" I ask, envisioning an adult water park of sorts. With a spa. And a restaurant. Oh, and a nightclub.

"Huh?"

"At the club. I mean, what if someone can't swim? Isn't it dangerous with all that water?"

"No. The salt concentration in the flotation rooms is super high, so your body is too buoyant to sink. You're encouraged to fall asleep in there. It's perfectly safe. There are lifeguards assigned to the mineral pools and lazy river as an added precaution. The owner is a stickler for safety."

"Good to know."

"Oh! I almost forgot. The River even has its own Himalayan salt cave saunas."

"This place sounds like paradise."

She grins. "You have no idea."

We make our way out of my office into the main suite, stopping near Lincoln's cubicle. He's deep in thought, immersed in the manuscript.

"Do I need to order a cot for you?" Freya chirps.

He looks up at her. "No, I'm almost done."

I point to the clock on his desk. "Quitting time was over an hour ago."

He nods. "I set a goal for myself, and I like staying on track."

"That's all well and good, but security didn't clear you for afterhours. It's time to head out."

"All right, let me log off and gather my stuff." He saves his file, emails it to himself, and shuts down his computer. After shoving some items into his messenger bag, he adjusts his glasses and stands, towering over me. "I'll forward the email to you when I'm finished."

"I don't expect you to work from home." I tilt my head to meet his gaze. "Or through your lunch break."

He shrugs. "Like I said, I want to stay on track. You mentioned a backlog, so I'd like to get caught up as soon as possible."

"As long as—"

"I won't sacrifice quality, Ms. Iverson." He rakes a hand through his hair. "And I'm sorry for my behavior this afternoon."

Behind him, Freya smirks and picks at her nails.

I meet his gaze as he adjusts his glasses again. "Can you understand where I'm coming from?"

"Yes."

"Good. We can start fresh tomorrow and finish our week on a positive note."

Freya shimmies her hips. "TGIF."

The ghost of a smirk curves his lips. "That makes tonight Friday eve."

"I like the way you think," she says with a laugh. "Glass half full, right?"

Lincoln rubs his jaw, sighing heavily. "Hell, I'm happy to have a glass to begin with. Half empty, half full—doesn't matter to me. Even one drop is better than nothing."

His comment makes me feel like he's had to fight for his glass, his drop, his place. Like he's climbing a never-ending ladder as life removes rungs before he can grip them. His ladder sways as he clings to it, but he keeps going. The idea bothers me more than it should.

Because I've been there.

# Seven

## Lincoln

*What the fuck is she staring at?*

The three of us ride the elevator in silence, but I can feel Elinora's gaze on me. As much as I try to ignore it, her attention unnerves me. I stare at the lit floor numbers like they're a work of art—or a fucking lighthouse beacon—anything to keep from making eye contact. I can't look at her right now. Not her fancy suit, her red shoes, or her perfect face. None of it. She represents everything I'm not, everything I don't have. Wealth. Sophistication. Power. Today was a shitshow, and now Myles is pissed at me.

Freya breaks the silence. "Got any big plans for Friday eve?"

"Nah, just heading home." I glance at her. "You?"

"I have a yoga class tonight."

"Sounds relaxing." I don't ask Elinora what she's doing because I know she wouldn't tell me. I'm surprised she rides the elevator with peasants like me.

"Where do you live, Lincoln?" Freya asks.

"Near Madison Square Garden."

"I love seeing shows at the Garden." Freya takes another stab at small talk. "So, what do you do for fun?"

I laugh at her loaded question and the mirth in her gaze. "I'm not sure I understand."

"How do you spend your free time? Do you have any hobbies? Special talents? You know, the stuff you do when you aren't working." She elbows me. "Please tell me you have a life."

"I'm *alive*." I meet her gaze. "But I'm always working, Freya. Even when I'm not."

Elinora peers up at me. "You like riddles, don't you?"

I shrug. "Somewhat. I'd classify them with haikus and limericks."

The She-Devil smiles, and it takes my breath away. "Do you have a favorite limerick?"

"As a matter of fact, I do."

The elevator reaches the ground floor, and the doors slide open. We step into the lobby.

"Well?" Elinora narrows her eyes on my face.

"Well, what?"

"What's your favorite limerick?"

*Is she serious?* I fix my glasses, even though they aren't out of place. Myles claims it's my nervous habit. I'm not currently nervous, but I'm not sure how to interpret her sudden interest. "I'll, uh, tell you some other time."

Freya grins. "Oh, c'mon. Tell us now."

*Fuck. Now I've gotta pull something from the archives.* I wrack my brain for the short poems my grandmother told us as kids, but I come up empty.

Elinora shakes her head. "I'm disappointed, Mr. Kennedy. I thought you planned to wow us with your literary prowess."

Her rhyme gives me an idea. "I, um, write my own limericks."

We pass through security and make our way to the bustling sidewalk. From honking cars to sirens, the sounds of New York City fill my ears. I miss the quiet country evenings of my youth. It's always so fucking loud here.

Elinora stops in front of me, propping her hands on her hips. "You can't leave me hanging."

I give her a halfhearted smile. "You'll have to hang until tomorrow because I'm off the clock."

"Minor details," she murmurs, her tone warming with amusement.

"The devil's in the details, Ms. Iverson."

"Put those details to good use, Mr. Kennedy. I want a limerick on my desk tomorrow."

"Is this for extra credit, or something I missed in the company handbook?"

She actually laughs, and the sound makes my cock twitch. "Consider it part of your orientation."

"There once was an editor named Lincoln. His boss soon got him a'thinkin'. She said give me a rhyme. Or I won't pay you a dime. The guy spewed some nonsense without blinkin'." Both women laugh, and I'm not sure whether to be relieved or unnerved, knowing Elinora has a sliver of humanity she refused to show me earlier. I give them a dramatic bow. "Good night, ladies. Until the next rhyme."

"See you tomorrow, Mr. Kennedy."

Her voice skates down my spine as I make my retreat, hustling down the sidewalk to the nearest subway station. While it's only a little over ten blocks to my apartment, and the drizzle has stopped, I don't feel like walking today.

My phone buzzes in my pocket. I peek at the screen to find my sister's name. I'm not in the mood to give her a play-by-play of my workday, but I can't bring myself to ignore the call.

"Hello?"

"Hi, Linky! How was your first day?"

I cringe at her use of my childhood nickname, but don't correct her. Reagan is the only one still allowed to use it. "It was . . . interesting. How was your art group?"

"Fun. I painted you a picture to hang in your fancy new office."

I don't have the heart to tell her it's a tiny gray cubicle. "Thanks, Reag. That was sweet of you."

"Wanna know what it is?"

I smile and step out of the way of a man dragging a rolling suitcase down the sidewalk. "Sure. Unless you want it to be a surprise."

"It's a family portrait from when we used to go fishing. But I made it so Daddy doesn't need his wheelchair."

My chest tightens, remembering how our parents took us camping in the Catskills every summer—before Reagan's epilepsy worsened. And long before our father's stroke. We'd spend hours sitting by the lake and catching fish. I always had to help her reel them in. "I can't wait to see it."

"Can you come visit this weekend?"

"I'm sorry, but I can't. I have to work all weekend, Reag."

"Oh, OK. Bartending?" There's no mistaking the disappointment in her tone.

"Yes." Guilt churns my stomach. I'm sure I'll be doing a lot more than tending bar at tomorrow night's masquerade event, but I'm not about to tell my sister. She thinks I work at an Irish pub near Times Square.

"Maybe next weekend then?"

I squeeze my eyes shut, knowing Esme owns my weekends for the foreseeable future. The best I can manage is a brief Sunday visit upstate. "We'll see. I'll ask my boss."

"How's your new boss? For your editing job, I mean."

A humorless chuckle leaves my lips. "She's a bit frosty."

# Eight

## Elinora

I love mornings. Energized by coffee, breakfast food, and the untapped potential of a fresh start, I push through the revolving door to my office building. I'm not the slightest bit surprised to find a particular colleague already waiting for the elevator.

Garrett Casey owns Hudson Graphics, the design company that shares my floor, and is responsible for the bulk of the book covers for Iverson Press. He's also the only human outside of security to ever enter the building this early. He's a brilliant artist—and businessman—with a work ethic like mine, so I have tremendous respect for him. Not to mention, the man is more gorgeous than he has a right to be. One day, I'll succeed in convincing him to be a book cover model. My Iverson Melt authors would be feral if they ever caught a glimpse of him.

I wave to the security guy behind the desk and make my way over to Garrett. "Good morning."

He smiles. "Howdy. I beat you here today."

I hold up my finger in protest. "That's only because I couldn't find a spot to park."

"Valet's not your thing either?"

"No. I've found it's easier to do everything myself." I'm sure most wealthy executives don't waste their time and energy driving around Manhattan in search of parking, but I'm too neurotic to hire a driver. For one, I'm an extremely nervous passenger. Charles had a lead foot, and we were in two fender-benders. While I only sustained bumps and bruises, the emotional damage went bone deep. It's far less stressful for me to be the one behind the wheel. Beyond that, I've learned I'm the only person I can depend on. I don't need anyone else to transport me where I want to go. I'm an independent woman. Yes, I lose some time in traffic, but it feels safer to always have access to my own vehicle.

Amusement flashes in his eerie gold eyes. "Control freak."

"You know it." The elevator arrives, and we step inside. "Did you hear back from all the authors whose covers need approval?"

"All but one." He rakes a hand through his inky black hair. "I have a feeling McCarthy may be an issue for you. He's not responsive to my emails, and I have to hound him for every little thing."

"I'll reach out to his agent." I press the call button for the eleventh floor.

"Sounds good." The doors slide shut, and we fall into companionable silence for a few moments before he pivots to face me. "Is everything all right with you?"

He's a giant like Lincoln, so I have to peer up at him. "Why do you ask?"

"You seem a little down lately. Like something's bothering you."

"I've had a rough couple of days."

"Your ex being a dick again?"

Garrett is intuitive and easy to talk to. I've been uncharacteristically open with him over the years. It's nice to get a man's perspective sometimes.

I lean against the wall. "Yes. Very much so. He wants more alimony, and it infuriates me." I clench my jaw, refusing to acknowledge the sadness that's clung to me since Charles shattered my heart. "After everything he put me through, he's still trying to make my life hell."

"Want me to kick his ass?" We reach our floor, and the doors slide open. He motions for me to exit before him. "I'll add him to my list."

"As much as I'd love that, I'd hate to see you in jail for assault."

"You're assuming I'd get caught. I'll have you know I'm stealthy as fuck." He nudges me. "But in all seriousness, you know I'm here if you ever need to talk."

"I appreciate that, Garrett." We pause outside the door to my main office suite, and I release a heavy sigh. "I guess I've been a little stressed. I've let a few problematic employees go, and now we're short-staffed. I hired a new guy, but he's barely out of college."

"Lincoln's a good dude. Smart. Hardworking."

I raise my eyebrows. "You know him?"

"Yeah. I met him through my dear friend and AA sponsor, Anya. You know, Freya's sister. Anyway, I run into him all the time at Compass Roasters when I go for coffee. As I'm sure you're aware, he worked for Cooper Press."

"Yes, I know." Guilt tickles my spine. "I'm kinda putting them out of business."

Garrett flashes a wicked grin. "Because you're the Queen of Badassery."

I laugh. "Most people call me an ice queen, so I'll take that as a compliment." While I've accepted my unofficial title, it still hurts knowing people think I'm heartless. I have a heart. It's just a little frostbitten.

"It's definitely meant as a compliment." He glances at his watch. "Anyhoo, I've gotta run. I have a conference call that starts in a few minutes."

"This early?"

"It's a company based out of Dublin. They're five hours ahead of us." He pats my shoulder. "Happy Friday."

"You too."

He smiles and heads toward his suite, pausing to look over his shoulder after a few steps. "Give Linc a chance. He might surprise you."

"I'll try." I wave and enter Iverson headquarters.

*Well, color me surprised.*

It's a quarter to seven, and Lincoln is already at his desk. I didn't actually think he'd show up early to work. None of my employees—not even Freya—arrive before me. People work harder and faster when I'm around, so it impresses me that he took it upon himself to get a head start and dive in, without my presence. Maybe Garrett knows what he's talking about.

Lincoln glances up as I approach his cubicle. "Good morning, Ms. Iverson."

"Good morning." I tap my watch. "You're early."

"I have goals to meet today."

"Did you clock in?"

He shakes his head, his dark hair still damp from his shower. "You didn't authorize overtime, so I'll punch in at nine."

I point to the time clock across the room. "Go clock in. You're my employee—not my servant. I don't expect you to work for free. Also, you're not obligated to come in early or stay late."

"I know," he replies, rising. "But I wanted to."

God, he's tall. I'm five foot eight with heels, and the man towers over me. He's so broad and solid. Muscular, but not bulky. He skipped the suit today, instead opting to wear a teal dress shirt and patterned tie. The greenish hue makes his irises appear a deeper blue—like a lagoon or the depths of the ocean—and I fight the urge to remove his glasses so I can lose myself in his eyes.

I shake my head to focus. "Working extra is not necessary—"

"I want to make this more than a temporary position." His gaze burns into me, laced with a desperate undercurrent that hits me in my stomach. "Understand that I'll do whatever it takes to make that happen."

*Position.* All it takes is that one word to leave his plush lips, and I'm out of my mind with lust, imagining all the ways our bodies could come together. His eyes . . . they warm me in places that haven't felt warmth in years. His stubbled jawline and dimples make my heart race. My mouth waters each time he moves those full, sculpted lips. His deep voice shouldn't send tingles down my spine. My breath shouldn't catch when he smiles, either. I shouldn't want him. I'm a decade older—and oh, yeah—his boss.

Despite all the reasons I shouldn't be attracted to Lincoln Kennedy, we share an undeniable chemistry. It crackles in the air between us like a live wire. Its current pulses through my veins, fluttering in my chest, heating my insides. I know its voltage will destroy me, but my body aches for the shock. For the passion. I need to feel something besides emptiness. It's a position I want Lincoln to fill.

Even though I shouldn't.

"You're off to a strong start," I whisper, quickly retreating to my office. I close the door behind me and plop into my chair. Wrapping my arms around myself, I rub at the sudden chill that simultaneously feels like a hot flash.

What the hell has gotten into me?

# Nine

## Lincoln

I'm not sure what just happened, but I'd know that flushed look any-where. Desire. Could it really be possible that I ruffle Elinora Iverson's feathers? Do I affect her the same way she torments me?

"I'm losing it," I mutter to myself, shaking my head at my stupidity. I remove my glasses and rub my temples. Last night's lack of sleep is playing tricks on my mind.

I told Esme I'd work at The River all weekend if she let me drop my Thursday evening shift. Instead of going to bed early, as I had planned, I did some editing. By some, I mean, I stayed up until three. On the plus side, I'm nearly finished with my first pass-through on this manuscript. I always do at least two full passes to make sure I don't miss anything.

I've been at the office since six thirty. After finally figuring out the ridic-ulously complicated espresso machine in the breakroom, I'm feeling pretty satisfied with myself. Perhaps it's the lingering effects of Elinora's breathy tone, but the confidence seeping into me reminds me of my college days, and that long-lost top-of-the-world feeling I crave. *I've got this.* I know what I need to do and how to do it. Despite my concerns about the romance genre, I'm enjoying it more than I expected. I can and will make this job happen for me.

My cell buzzes with a text from Esme as I walk over to the time clock.

Esme: Don't forget tonight's the Mermaid Masquerade. Make sure you have your sexy merman stuff.

I picture the skin-tight jammers she wants me to wear and groan. Dark teal and patterned to look like scales, the swimwear leaves little to the imagination. I'd much rather parade around in swim trunks than have spandex plastered to my cock. Then again, it could be worse. Last year, she'd concocted an "Aqua Cowboy Adventure Party." My attire that evening was the Speedo equivalent of assless chaps paired with cowboy boots. I looked utterly ridiculous. Curling my lip at the memory, I quickly punch my code into the time clock before responding.

Me: Sounds good.

Esme: It's new members' night. Prepare to give them your best. The goal is to keep them coming . . .

Me: You know I always do.

Esme: That's why you're my favorite.

Me: Correction, I'm everyone's favorite.

Sighing, I stuff my phone back into my pocket and return to my cubicle. Being the favorite is both a blessing and a curse I can't seem to escape. I doubt any of my regulars will be there. New members' night is always packed, so Gwen and Maya usually stay away.

Gwen is a widow in her late fifties who simply enjoys my company. We've done nothing sexual, and I consider her my friend. We have a standing dinner date on the third Thursday of each month. I'm annoyed that I missed her last night because I look forward to our talks. We discuss everything—from the environment to politics to our love lives. She's like the cool aunt I wish I had.

Maya, on the other hand, is a frequent fuck buddy. My friend may be my "client," but she is the one who introduced me to Esme and most of my sexual repertoire. Maya hates chaos, so I doubt she'll show up for tonight's event, which sucks. Like my visits with Gwen, I look forward to my weekly Maya playtime—for different reasons, obviously.

Overall, I enjoy new members' night. It's an opportunity for those who are tentatively adventurous in the bedroom to test the waters. Esme always assigns me the beginners because she claims I'm The River's gateway drug—I get them hooked and keep them coming back for more. My specialty lies in pushing my clients' limits without them realizing it. Some of these women are straight vanilla when we meet. Hell, I was vanilla until I met Esme. Now I'm rocky road—dark, a little nutty, with some scattered soft bits.

My ability to put a woman at ease, while coaxing her beyond her comfort level, still amazes me. I don't consider myself manipulative, but my persuasion game is on point. While I may be a bumbling idiot in real life, I'm the picture of confident, smooth-talking, panty-melting swagger while at The River.

I glance up as Elinora strides into the breakroom with her coffee cup. Lucky for me, I have an unobstructed view from my cubicle. I discreetly watch her, shocked she gets her own coffee. I figured she'd have people for that. Then again, Freya isn't here yet.

Elinora is wearing a cobalt blue sheath dress. The cardigan she had on when she arrived earlier is absent, putting her lush curves on display. On her back, the zipper glints in the light like a beacon. I'd give anything to unzip that dress right now and put my hands on her porcelain skin. Bend her over my desk and grip her hips while I fuck her. Make her moan and scream my name like I'm one of the heroes in the erotic romance novels she publishes. I wonder if she actively reads my newfound genre. What positions she likes in bed. How her lips taste. If she's adventurous or docile. My cock twitches, and I shift in my chair without taking my eyes off her.

Elinora tosses her thick, white-blond hair over her shoulder and pulls the creamer out of the fridge. I want to run my fingers through those silken tresses. Tug the strands and slap her ass while she's tied up. I nearly moan at the visual as my cock stretches the material of my dress pants.

This is bad. Elinora holds my mind and body captive, which is something I haven't felt since I started at The River. I clench my jaw against the visuals dancing through my brain. I can't want her—she's my fucking boss.

"Don't even think about it." Myles's voice from right behind me jolts me back to reality.

Jumping, I nearly knock over my coffee. I snatch my cup to steady it and lean forward to hide my partial erection. "I didn't hear you come in."

"No shit." He appears at my side. "I've been watching you for the past five minutes. You forget that I can read you like a book."

"Your point?"

"Don't. Go. There."

"Not sure what you're talking about."

He grips my shoulders. "I mean it, Linc." He lowers his voice to a whisper. "This isn't Ms. Fisher's art class. You cannot fantasize about your boss. She's forbidden fruit."

So was Ms. Fisher, the sexy teacher who unknowingly tormented me by day and gave me wet dreams on a nightly basis. Sadly, she transferred to a different school when I was a junior.

"Is looking a crime?"

He cocks an orange brow. "I dunno. Is voyeurism what you have in mind when you say looking?"

I roll my eyes. "She's making coffee, for fuck's sake. It's not like I'm watching her shower."

"She's off-limits. Don't watch her. *At all*," he growls, in a tone that reminds me of Father DeAngelis.

I give him a thumbs-up. "Yes, Father Callahan. Or have you risen the ranks to cardinal?"

Myles smirks. "Don't push your luck. I've got all kinds of priestly connections."

"I prefer nuns."

"You're going straight to hell."

"No shit. And according to Sister Fitzgibbons, so are you," I say with an exaggerated eyeroll. She spewed those kinds of threats on a daily basis. Her antiquated beliefs and our school's lack of inclusivity disgusted me.

"Good thing Richard is Buddhist." He scrubs a hand over his face and smirks. "And if you recall, she said I secured my place in hell when I met Henry."

Henry Winthrop was a classmate in the process of entering the priesthood. That is, until Myles "corrupted" him. Now he owns an elite gay club in Albany. He's cool as fuck, and we still keep in touch with him. Even though it's not my scene, I stop by his club to visit from time to time. Henry insists Myles did him a favor when he made him realize he was gay, but courtesy of the toxic clergy at our church's helm, Myles spent years beneath a blanket of guilt. He finally got over it when Henry married Seth, the love of his life.

"You're my favorite blasphemous bastard."

"Likewise." He nods to the breakroom. "Off-limits. Understand?"

"Yep," I mutter.

"What are you doing this weekend?"

"Working."

He curls his lip. "*All* weekend?"

I nod. "I missed Thursday, so I told Esme I'd be there."

"What about your Sunday date with Reagan?"

Every week I try to make the trip upstate to the group home where my sister lives outside New Paltz. I take her out for lunch and some other activity. Sometimes it's a movie or bowling, but lately, we've been going hiking. While a casual stroll around Lake Minnewaska is hardly a hike in my book, it takes a lot out of Reagan. Her heart condition makes her dizzy and out of breath easily, but I try to keep her active. Her fiery spirit is at war with what she's physically able to do. It kills me to see a sixteen-year-old girl trapped in her own body.

I sigh. "Don't worry, I already disappointed her." This was actually the third weekend in a row I've had to cancel.

Myles rests his hand on my shoulder. "How's she doing? I'd love to tag along on your next trip home."

I perk up. "Really? She'd be thrilled." Not to mention, it would help get me back into her good graces after our missed visits.

"Yeah, man. I haven't seen her since we went to your folks' place for Thanksgiving. I miss the little Reag-Bear."

Reagan has had a crush on Myles since she was eight. While I've made it clear he's gay, and in a relationship, my sister still insists she's going to marry him. It's sweet, really. Her face lights up whenever he's around, and he's amazing with her. I'm the family's only non-redhead, so with his red hair and freckles, he looks more like her sibling than I do. And as the youngest of four, I think Myles enjoys having someone look up to *him* for once.

I've always been grateful to my best friend for his kindness. Sadly, some other dudes we grew up with tended to run their mouths. I'll never forget when I overheard Kyle Fink call my sister a retard—to her face. Reagan burst into tears, and the fucker had the audacity to laugh at her. I had the last laugh when I broke his nose and gave him a black eye. Hopefully, that taught him a lesson about being cruel to someone with disabilities.

That shit doesn't fly with me. Kindness is pretty fucking simple, and I have zero tolerance for those who behave otherwise.

"Reagan asks about you all the time." I smile and squeeze his arm. "I'll let her know you're thinking about coming to visit."

He nods. "Did you have enough for her housing this month?"

"Barely, but yeah." I clear my throat. "That's why I've been spending more time at The River."

"Let me know if you're ever in a bind. I'll gladly cover the difference."

"Thank you, man. It means a lot to me."

"I know." He grins and wags his orange brows. "That's what proper ride-or-die blasphemous bastards do for their friends."

I glance at my watch. Five o'clock means quitting time. Normally, I'd stay late, but I have to be at The River by seven, which means I need to get in the right headspace for my extracurriculars. After emailing myself the manuscript I've been working on, I stuff my phone and notes into my messenger bag. Maybe one day I'll splurge on a real briefcase. I rub the stubble on my jaw, knowing it will be a long time before that happens.

*Fuck, I need to shave.*

Esme demands her concierges be clean-shaven to avoid inner thigh scrapes, but that activity is on my no-fly list. Call it a hard limit, if you will.

Yes, I fuck strangers. But, in the unlikely event I find someone who I actually connect with, it would be nice to have something reserved for them. That's why I don't kiss anyone on the lips or give oral at work. To me, kissing is an extremely intimate act. While I have no problem using the tools at my disposal—cock included—I'm more selective with my mouth. That's not to say I don't use my mouth. My skills in the nipple-gasm department are impressive, or so I've been told.

*Speaking of nipples . . .*

My mouth waters, and my cock twitches to life as Elinora floats into view. She approaches my cubicle, and since I'm still seated, her breasts are at eye level. I'd give my soul to peel off her bra with my teeth and put my tongue on her. Kiss and suck every inch of her perfect porcelain skin. Nip and nibble and mark her as *mine*.

Not that it could ever happen.

She motions to my computer. "I don't want you working from home, Mr. Kennedy. Work-life balance is important."

"Do *you* have work-life balance?" The question leaves my lips before I can stop it.

Elinora forces a laugh, her face twisting into a rueful expression. "I'm not sure I even understand the meaning of those words." She meets my gaze. "Which is why I'd like for my employees to have it."

I adjust my glasses with a smile. "Maybe you should lead by example?"

"There are a lot of things I *should* do. Sadly, I don't have the time for most of them. I'm a firm believer that balance improves productivity, even if I don't know how to apply the concept to my life."

I point to her red briefcase. "You can start by leaving work at work."

"I never bring work home. Just my laptop for safekeeping."

"Forgive me if this sounds too forward, Ms. Iverson, but you spend over sixty hours a week here. I get the feeling you make the office your home."

"You're an intuitive man." She smiles and looks me over, making my cock stiffen. "And a bit of a hypocrite."

I raise a brow. "How am I a hypocrite?"

She props her hands on her hips, and I have to clench my fists to keep from tossing her over my knee. "If I recall, you're always working—even when you're not. I believe that's a direct quote."

Shocked she'd remember anything that came out of my mouth, I blink a few times instead of answering.

Arching a perfect brow, she cocks her hip and adds, "Seeing as you're the only employee of mine still working, I'd say that qualifies as hypocrisy."

I lean forward slightly. "Maybe I enjoy working hard?"

"I appreciate hard work."

Hearing the word "hard" leave her lips makes me want to give them something hard in exchange. I don't think I've ever craved a woman this badly. Ever. Not even Ms. Fisher. None of my River playmates even come close to inciting this amount of lust. I can't control the way it's coursing through me, tightening my balls, and making my cock throb. I've had plenty of women, but my new boss surpasses them all.

Oh, the things I'd do to Elinora Iverson if I ever had the opportunity to be alone with her in my private lagoon at The River.

I clench my jaw and force a swallow. "Believe me, I'm no stranger to hard work. In fact, I thrive on it."

She smiles. "Yes, I've noticed this, Mr. Kennedy."

I need her to notice her way onto my cock. Preferably right now.

# Ten

## Elinora

*Fuck. Not these guys again.*

As Lincoln and I exit the building, I stiffen when I spot a trio of men congregating on the sidewalk. They've been there every day this week. I've lived in New York City for years, so I'm used to the catcalls, but something about these guys makes me uneasy.

I stare at the sign for the parking garage down the block and fish in my coat pocket for my ticket. *Shit.* I must've left it on my desk. I'm fairly certain I parked on the third level today. Spot C24. *Wait, maybe that was yesterday.* Note to self: start writing it down. I'm kicking myself for not buying a monthly permit. Or using a car service like normal corporate executives.

The attendant is in his booth, so I doubt the creeps would try anything, but still—it's days like these when I wish I wore sneakers to work.

"Where did you park?" Lincoln asks, following my gaze.

"In the garage."

His eyes narrow on the men. "I'm heading that way. I'll walk you to your car."

"Thanks," I murmur, beyond grateful I didn't have to ask him to escort me.

"Anytime, but you need to walk to my left." He grips my shoulders and guides me toward the inside of the sidewalk, placing his body between me and the creeps.

Tingles race down my spine. His brief touch is warm and firm, yet not overbearing. I'm suddenly at ease. Safe. Protected. Everything I never felt with Charles.

Lincoln's powerful frame towers over me as we stroll past the trio.

One man is brazen enough to let out a low whistle. "Hey, baby." Lincoln shoots him a glare, causing the dirtbag to hold his hands up in surrender. "Just whistling, bro."

Lincoln stops in front of him. "Not at her, you're not. Have some fucking class, *bro*."

Like usual, I straighten my spine and keep walking without acknowledging them. When we round the corner into the parking garage, my breath rushes out of me.

"Does that happen to you a lot?" he asks.

I nod. "I'm used to it, but that group of men is particularly aggressive with the catcalls."

Lincoln presses his lips into a grim line. "Yeah, I noticed." He points to the stairwell. "Which level?"

Gnawing my lip, I meet his gaze. "I don't remember."

Something flashes in his eyes before he runs a hand over his face. "So, you planned to wander up and down dark stairwells alone?"

"I can take care of myself, Mr. Kennedy."

"No one's questioning that." He jerks his thumb over his shoulder. "But they made *me* uneasy, so I'll be escorting you from now on."

I wave him off. "That's unnecessary."

"I'd rather not take the chance, Ms. Iverson." He pauses when we reach the landing on the second level. "Not everyone has good intentions."

"I'm aware," I murmur, suddenly wishing he had bad intentions involving me. I shake my head to clear it. "I'm pretty sure I parked on the third level. Possibly."

We reach the next landing and scan the vehicles. I spot my red Porsche and point. "That's me in the corner."

"Nice car," he says, as we approach the vehicle.

"Thanks. I hate it."

Lincoln cocks his head to the side. "Why? It's a beautiful piece of machiner—"

"My ex-husband bought it for me." I unlock it and yank open the driver's door. "After his first affair."

"As an apology?"

I shrug and toss my purse onto the seat. "Who knows? He had two more, so that negates the implied mea culpa, don't you think?"

His eyes widen. "He had *three* affairs?"

I force a smile. "Those are just the ones I know about. I filed for divorce after I caught him in our bed with his third mistress. You know, three strikes and all that." I shrug. "But he clearly didn't feel my loss since they're still an item."

"I'm sorry he did that to you." He adjusts his glasses and studies my face. "Me too."

He touches my shoulder. "No, really. You deserve so much better."

"Thank you," I whisper.

I'm not sure what prompted me to tell Lincoln about my failed marriage or anything personal, for that matter. I don't share private information with anyone other than my mother, Freya, and Garrett. It's safer that way. People like to cozy up to the ones with money, and I learned a long time ago to stop trusting their false kindness. I won't allow myself to be duped into another financial trap. I'm tired of being used. Despite what Charles has led me to believe, I'm worth more than my bank account.

Yet here I am, still the lonely one who aches for genuine love. Disgusted by my own stupidity, I blink rapidly to dispel the moisture gathering in my eyes.

Lincoln's gaze narrows on my face. "Are you OK?"

"I'm fine." I straighten, grasping on to what remains of my composure. "It's just the wind."

"It's not windy today."

"I don't need a weather update, Mr. Kennedy," I snap, embarrassment clogging my throat. Charles was a professional antagonist. Last thing I need is another man contradicting everything I say and do.

He holds his hands up in surrender and takes a step backward. "Jeez. I was just making an observation. No need to bite my head off."

"Excuse me?"

"Never mind." Sighing, he rubs the back of his neck. "Forget I said that." He meets my gaze with eyes so blue, I'd swear I'm adrift in the Atlantic. "I'm sorry."

"You should be." I can't figure out why I'm so unnerved. Better yet, why I allowed Lincoln to escort me to my car or let him stand up to those creeps for disrespecting me. I can handle myself.

I'm at a loss for why he makes my heart race and weakens my knees. How whenever I'm near him, my palms sweat, and my mouth goes dry. Then, two seconds later, the cadence of his voice makes my mouth water. Most of all, I can't figure out why his apology for my ex-husband's behavior means more to me than anything Charles ever said, but I do know this: Lincoln Kennedy rattles me.

He clears his throat. "I, uh, guess I'll head out. Have a nice weekend, Ms. Iverson."

"You do the same. I'll see you Monday." I sink into the driver's seat and peer up at him. "Thank you for walking with me."

"No problem." He smiles, and my toes curl inside my stilettos. "Don't work too hard. You know, balance and all that."

"We've already established my lack of balance." Guilt nudges my conscience. "And I'm sorry for snapping at you."

"It's fine. It seems like you have a lot on your plate."

"You have no idea."

"Actually, I think I do." Something that feels like compassion colors his tone. I'm not used to anyone giving a damn about my feelings. I'm about to give my rebuttal when he rests his hand on top of my car and adds, "I've learned you can only pile your plate with so much before it gets too heavy and shatters."

Lincoln Kennedy is intelligent, driven, and intuitive. He has tenacity and wisdom beyond his years. At half Charles's age, he has the grit and integrity my ex-husband did not, all wrapped in a sexy-as-hell package. Equal parts nerdy and hunky, Lincoln's the picture of potent, virile male. I'd bet the future of Iverson Press that he's got stamina in bed. Heat floods my core, saturating the panties that were already damp. God knows I haven't encountered stamina—or any sex worth having—in over a decade.

With dark, glossy hair and lush lips, Lincoln is more gorgeous than any man I've seen in real life. Taller and broader too. I can't explain his effect on me, but I need to rein in my libido. Not only is he too young for me, but I've got more baggage than LaGuardia Airport.

And, oh yeah, I'm his boss.

I close my car door, at a loss for what else to say. Lincoln watches me pull out of my parking spot and drive off.

One thing's for damn sure, my weekend would be a hell of a lot more enjoyable with him in my bed.

Freya reaches across our table at Oasis, the swanky restaurant affiliated with The River, and grabs my hand. "I'm so excited you came tonight. You need this."

"Yeah, it's been years since I've had a massage."

"The River Rubdown isn't just any massage, Elle."

"A massage is a massage," I say, spearing a forkful of salad.

"Honey, this is The River. Leave your expectations—and your inhibitions—at the door."

"My inhibitions?" I cock my head to the side. "What do they have to do with anything?"

Freya giggles and wags her brows. "You'll see."

I chew on a piece of cucumber doused with green goddess dressing and eye her suspiciously. "What the hell does that mean?"

"You'll see," she repeats, squeezing my wrist. "But I need you to promise me something."

I set down my fork. "And that is?"

"Promise you'll go with the flow. Dive in and see where the current takes you."

"I'm here, aren't I?"

She chews her lip. "Yes, but I need you to keep an open mind."

"Freya Thorne, what exactly have you gotten me into?"

She points to the far corner of the restaurant. "Look."

I turn in my seat and gasp as what appeared to be a floor-to-ceiling tank of exotic fish, suddenly slides to the right, exposing a cavernous hallway. Blue and teal lights illuminate smooth rock walls, and club music with a heavy bass rhythm reaches my ears. "What's back there?"

"That, my dear, is the entrance to The River."

The music vibrates in my chest as the most beautiful woman I've ever laid eyes on steps into the restaurant. The fish wall closes behind her like a secret portal. Three massive security guards I hadn't noticed before take their places in the shadows along the room's perimeter.

"Who's that?" I ask, nodding toward the woman. "She seems important."

"Madame Esme." Freya's reverent whisper is barely audible. "She owns The River."

"That's an interesting title for a club owner. Is she French?"

Freya doesn't seem to hear me as she waves to the other woman.

Madame Esme scans the room, and her red lips curve into a sultry smile when she spots Freya. She approaches our table. Her body-hugging, teal sequined mini dress shimmers as she glides through the restaurant like a mermaid in a lagoon. Long black waves with streaks of royal blue cascade to the middle of her back. Her olive skin is dewy like she bathes in a fountain of eternal youth.

"Freya, baby," she croons in a lilting voice that drips of sex. "I'm so happy you made it."

"Thank you for allowing me to bring a guest, Madame."

"Anything for you, sugar." Madame Esme leans down and kisses Freya.

On the lips.

With tongue.

My jaw drops open. Freya loves men. And I mean, *loves* them. She's never given any indications she's bisexual, but here she is, passionately kissing a woman. No, make that a sexy mermaid. My nipples prick the inside of my bra, and my lower belly tightens and flutters at the sight. For a fraction of a second, I'm jealous of Freya.

Madame Esme breaks the kiss. "As sweet as always." She straightens and turns to me. "And who might this be?"

"This is my dear friend, Elinora," Freya answers, which is great because I'm still stupefied by what I just witnessed.

"Welcome, Elinora," Esme purrs, taking my hand in her silken palm. Warmth coils inside me with her touch.

*Kiss me.* The thought comes unbidden, and I shake my head to clear it.

"Hi," I murmur, my voice huskier than usual. "Thank you for letting me come." Madame Esme smiles, her honey-colored eyes glittering with amusement, and I cross my legs beneath the table when I realize what I said. "I mean—"

"Elinora, baby, you're in for a treat tonight. Freya booked you our signature service, which is a four-hour block with a concierge."

"Four hours?" My longest massage was ninety minutes, and that cost over two hundred bucks. I sure as hell hope Freya didn't spend her monthly bonus on *me*.

"If you desire more time, I grant extensions upon request."

"I'm sure four hours will be long enough."

"Honey, you haven't seen L yet. Trust me, no amount of time is enough." She closes her eyes for a moment, as if savoring a memory, before returning her attention to me. "Afterward, you're free to partake in any activities you wish."

"You mean the masquerade party?" I ask.

"That's part of it. I'm referring to the other available a-*men*-ities, if you will." At my blank stare, she glances at Freya. "Don't tell me you didn't mention the club."

Freya flushes. "No, not exactly. I told her about the Mermaid Masquerade Mingle, and the spa stuff, but I didn't go into any details about the club amenities."

"Then tonight should be *very* interesting," Madame Esme croons, twirling a lock of my hair. The sensation sends goose bumps over my skin, and I suddenly want her to weave her fingers into my hair and drag her nails along my scalp.

"What amenities?"

Freya grips Madame Esme's other hand and points to me. "She promised to keep an open mind. Right, Elle?"

"I thought I was getting a massage?"

"Oh, don't you worry, Elinora. He'll massage you." Madame Esme runs her fingers through my hair, sending a flare of heat to my core. "The River Rubdown is a full body experience."

"Wait a minute." My gaze darts between them. "Exactly what kind of club is The River?"

# Eleven

## Elinora

I can't believe Freya brought me to a sex club. Then again, knowing my friend for as long as I have, it shouldn't surprise me. We've always been opposites. She gravitates toward all things carnal, while I keep my distance. Full of warmth, passion, and adventure, she's the fire to my ice. I want to be annoyed, disgusted even. I *should* grab my purse and run out the door. Instead, I'm intrigued. Captivated by the taboo concept and the club's beautiful proprietor. Besides, I'm tired of being the ice queen—my tundra could use some fucking flames.

Flanked by Madame Esme and Freya, I force myself to breathe as we walk arm-in-arm along the corridor. We pass a white marble arch, which opens to another, shorter hallway. Someone painted wispy clouds on the pale blue walls and curved ceiling. At the end, a massive spiral staircase seems to vanish into the heavens.

I stop short and point down the hall. "What's at the top of the stairs?"

"The members-only entrance to Vapor, our traditional spa. When I bought this building, it was an abandoned train station. Are you familiar with Grand Central Terminal?"

"Of course."

"The setup is similar, but a little smaller. You know how when you first enter Grand Central at street level, there are upper lobbies where they frequently have exhibits and pop-up shops? I'm talking about *before* you go down the ramp to get to the main concourse with the pretty ceiling."

Envisioning the iconic station I've visited countless times since I moved to New York, I nod. "Yes."

"Well, that's where we have Oasis, our restaurant." She points to several doors further down the corridor we started out on. "Security, client dressing rooms and showers, and everyone's offices are also on the ground floor. Sadly, we don't have a fancy vaulted ceiling like Grand Central because Vapor takes up the building's entire top level. While Oasis and certain parts of Vapor are open to the public, the rest of the club is not."

"I'm assuming there are safeguards in place to ensure the general public doesn't venture into any members-only areas?"

"Absolutely. Our security team is a sophisticated network of manpower and technology. You'll see our guys patrolling all three suites—they're the ones dressed in black with our logo on their shirts. If you ever need anything, don't hesitate to approach them. No one enters this establishment without their knowledge, and we can lock this place down like Fort Knox if need be. You never have to worry about your safety here."

"Good to know." I gesture to the archway at the end of the hall. A huge wrought iron gate blocks the entrance to what looks like a cave. A pair of gold mermaid statues flank the gate, their tridents held high. "What's back there?"

"The entrance to The River's lower realms, Aqua and Glacier. I'll explain more in a bit when I give you the grand tour. This way, I can answer any questions that may arise. But before we get started, I'll fill you in on the basics and take care of the NDA." Madame Esme punches a code into a panel on the wall, then opens the door to a women's dressing room. "Members are assigned their own unique passcodes for the boxes you'll see outside every door. Should you decide to join us, you'll be provided electronic credentials which must be kept secure." She ushers me inside with a brush of my hip, and for the life of me, I can't figure out why I want this woman's hands all over my body.

"I'm going to use the ladies' room," Freya announces, veering off to the left. "Be right back."

Madame Esme gestures to a white leather sofa. "Elinora, have a seat, baby."

I settle, the leather cooling my overheated thighs. "I'm not sure I belong at a club like this."

She slides into the empty place beside me and tilts my chin to face her. For a moment, I think she's going to kiss me. Something deep inside me hopes she does.

Cupping my face, she brushes her thumbs over my lips. "Everyone has a home at The River. It's up to you to find it."

"How do I find it?" My breathy voice makes her smile, and I press my knees together to quell the throbbing ache between my thighs.

"Use the guides. Let them be your compass."

"Guides?"

"My establishment employs men and women whose sole duties are to serve The River's patrons. I call them pleasure concierges. After I get an idea of which amenities a client is comfortable with, I assign them the concierge most equipped to meet their needs. He—or she, if that's the client's preference—serves as their personal guide. However, in your case, Freya gave me a heads-up, so I've already got somebody in mind for you."

"I've never been to a sex club," I blurt.

"This isn't *just* a sex club. It's a pleasure spa. We all have different understandings of pleasure. Some of us seek our comfort near the surface, be it companionship or affection. Maybe you simply want a man to converse with, or someone to hold your hand or rub your back. You'd be surprised by the number of clients who come here simply because they don't want to be alone all the time."

"I'll probably be one of them." I'm shocked by how easily the confession leaves my lips. I've always thought of myself as someone who holds her cards close—especially around strangers. Right now, everything is on full display, and instead of panicking, I'm ready to let someone else play their ace. That has never happened before.

Madame Esme studies me, compassion shining in her eyes. "It's easy to feel disconnected in a world ruled by technology and social media. Dating and relationships aren't what they used to be, and it takes a toll on us. Humans are pack creatures by nature. While some people prefer to lead solitary lives, they often underestimate the power of human touch. How good it feels to be held. Stroked. Kissed . . ." She stares off into the distance for a moment, the wistful look on her face making me wonder if she's describing herself. If so, we have more in common than I thought. Just as quickly, her gaze flicks back to mine, and the sultry edge returns to her voice. "If that sounds like what you're looking for, you can find it at The River. Perhaps your desires run deeper, and you want to make love. We can arrange that too. Maybe you want a thrill, to indulge in something which tantalizes and titillates your senses . . ."

"Like what?" I ask, my insides heating at the images of handcuffs and sex swings dancing in my head.

"Our concierges are skilled in a variety of activities. Many of them follow a BDSM lifestyle and are more than willing to coach interested newcomers. As long as it's one hundred percent consensual for both—or should I say *all*—parties involved, nothing is off-limits at The River. Ménage and group sex are not uncommon here, but there are designated areas for those activities."

Her statement should scare me, but it only turns me on more. I'm starting to wonder if I know myself as well as I previously thought. The Elinora Iverson who walked into Oasis was an ice queen. Seated on this leather couch, openly discussing sex and pleasure, my facade melts into a woman I don't recognize.

"I don't know what I like. I've never done anything like that."

"This is your safe place to test the waters, baby. Keep an open mind, and don't be afraid to express yourself. I encourage you to push beyond your comfort level, but if you have hard limits, voice them so there are no misunderstandings."

"Hard limits?" I squeak.

"Those are the acts you will not allow under any circumstances. Everyone has a threshold."

I know what hard limits are—I publish erotic romance. I've read enough of them to be familiar with the BDSM lifestyle and various kinks. I've never given any thought to my own limits because sex with Charles never pushed them. All he had in his repertoire were predictable, five-minute jackhammering sessions that did absolutely nothing for me. I got used to being the one responsible for my own orgasms, so I've never explored the concept of shared pleasure.

And I certainly never imagined stepping foot inside a sex club.

Madame Esme touches my shoulder. "I'll give you an example. While some women adore nipple clamps, I'm not a fan. A man can do anything else he wants to me, except use clamps. If there's something that's out of the question for you, let him know ahead of time."

No one's going anywhere near my back door, but how does one say that out loud? *Do I wait for him to try, and then refuse?* I grimace at the thought. "What about him?"

"I'm not sure what you're asking."

"Does the man you have in mind for me have any conditions I should be made aware of?"

She nods. "I'm sure he'll make them known, but since you're a first-timer, I'll fill you in. L doesn't kiss women on the lips, nor does he perform oral sex. Those are his hard limits. They are also the only complaints I've ever received about him."

"Complaints?"

"Women who have been with L *always* want more than he's willing to give. You'll understand once you see him. He's got lips to die for, so the ladies get frustrated when he won't kiss theirs." Her gaze drifts from my mouth to my lap for a moment. "Players come here with expectations of good oral. It comes with the sex club territory. So, as I'm sure you can imagine, it's more than a little disappointing when a concierge won't go there. Especially if these women have had partners who had no idea what they were doing, or worse, ones who refused to go down on them."

"Sounds like my ex," I mutter.

"I'm sorry to hear that. Lips are meant to be kissed, and every pussy deserves a skillful tongue. Hence the complaints about L."

My renegade brain conjures an image of her between my thighs, making me flush once more. "They seem like strange activities to have an aversion to," I murmur, forcing my attention to her eyes.

"Everybody's different, baby. I'm sure he has his reasons. Anyway, before we get started, I'll have you sign a nondisclosure agreement. It's a legal document that protects your privacy and that of the club. No one is permitted to discuss what goes on here with any nonmembers. Just like Vegas, what happens in these waters, stays at The River."

"So, no one will smear my reputation?"

Madame Esme purses her lips. "Step one. Lose your negative connotations about sex. Contrary to what you may believe, pleasure is beautiful—not dirty. If you're too worried about tarnishing your image, you won't be in the right headspace. Change your mindset. No one is here to smudge your reputation. Allow The River to flow through you, awaken and indulge the desires you might not even realize you have. All you need to do is float along and see where the current takes you. Let us polish those rough edges. Nothing shines brighter than an orgasm."

"I'm sorry." I backpedal, feeling like an ass for offending her. "It's just . . . I own a corporation, and I don't need my employees knowing about my sex life."

"Understandable, and that is the reason behind the NDA." She hands me a clipboard and pen. "Sign your name on the line."

I scrawl my signature without reading the contract. A big no-no in business transactions. Then again, this isn't a business venture. All I can focus on is the lust coursing through my body. When the hell did I get so thirsty?

"Your first few visits are complimentary. Should you decide to join us, membership dues are paid on a quarterly basis. I can bill you, or we can arrange automatic withdrawals." She brushes the hair back from my face. "After your trial period, it's up to you whether you want to keep your concierge or test the waters yourself. Members are free to interact with whomever they choose."

"I'm nervous," I whisper.

She smiles. "That's why I'm here, baby. Any questions?"

"How do you keep the water clean?" I've always leaned toward the practical side of situations—except for my presence here tonight, obviously—and I have zero desire to contract a weird communicable disease. "I mean, it's got to be tricky for a facility of this scale."

"It is, but we make it a top priority. I'm a firm believer that cleanliness is next to godliness. Rest assured, we don't cut corners when it comes to public health. We follow CDC guidelines for the disinfection of our water and the establishment itself. We chemically treat and triple filter all water. The club is only open nights, so that leaves the entire day for maintenance, cleaning, repairs, what have you. A huge cleaning crew arrives every morning at eight, and they sanitize every possible surface. I'm not exaggerating when I say you could eat off the floor when they're done."

"Good to know."

Freya returns from the restroom and plops onto the couch beside me. "Are you mad at me?"

I shake my head. "Not mad. Just in shock."

"Relax." Madame Esme grips my chin. "You don't have to do anything that makes you uncomfortable." She leans in close and smiles. "We'll start you off slow, so you can dip your toes in." Tilting my chin, she brushes her lips over mine. "Then you can swim deeper." Her tongue darts out, tasting the seam of my lips, which part of their own volition. "And when you're ready, we'll take you under." She sweeps her tongue into my mouth, stroking it against mine in a sensual waltz.

I have never kissed a woman. Ever. I never had the desire to. But I'd allow this woman to do anything she wanted to me. The realization sends a flare of heat to my core. I moan into the kiss and clutch her shoulders.

"Um, this is hot as fuck," Freya murmurs from beside us. "Getting a little lonely out here, ladies."

Madame Esme breaks our kiss, leaving me breathless. "What do you say, Elinora? Are you ready to see where the current takes you?"

"Yes."

She licks her lush lips that taste of honey and chocolate-dipped strawberries. "Excellent. There are a few housekeeping points we need to go over. As I'm sure you've noticed, my establishment is water-themed. Water's versatility makes it my favorite element. As vapor, water is airy like a featherlight caress. You'll find lighter activities—as in, our traditional spa amenities— in the Vapor Suite." She trails her fingertips down my throat. "On the floor below us, we have the Aqua Suite. Think of the main concourse at Grand Central, with its huge open space and train tracks branching out in every direction. Aqua's setup is very similar, except private lagoons, salt saunas, mineral pools, and a lazy river replace the platforms. Does that make sense?"

I nod. "It sounds really elaborate."

"You have no idea, baby. Water, in its fluid state, can trickle like a stream or a brook. It can flow like a winding river, or it can *rush*, surging like rapids or a waterfall. The majority of our concierges play in the Aqua Suite, which is home to our dance floor and The River's main bar. We often host special events in Aqua because it's most conducive for setting up a stage."

"What kind of events?"

"Ones like tonight's masquerade. We also hold auctions, charity benefits, and various demonstrations. Sometimes even the occasional private party."

"I can't imagine having a party at a sex club." Maybe I'll do that for my fortieth birthday in a few years. I'm sure Freya would jump all over that idea.

"Aqua is an oasis of its own. Open your mind to the possibilities." She smiles like she's keeping the world's biggest secret. "And finally, for those whose tastes run a bit kinkier, we have the Glacier."

"What's the Glacier?"

"An elite realm reserved for our most advanced players. Glacier is its own entity within The River. We will not allow you entrance at this time."

My curiosity piques like Belle in *Beauty and the Beast* when he warns her to stay out of his castle's west wing. "What happens there?"

Madame Esme shares a look with Freya, who nods and addresses me, "Things you definitely wouldn't partake in."

"Like?"

Madame Esme meets my gaze. "Glaciers are frozen rivers. Solid and unyielding. Members who follow the BDSM lifestyle are the only persons permitted in Glacier. We want it to be a safe, judgment-free space for them. Some patrons call Glacier a kink club, but I prefer pleasure lounge. Going back to our Grand Central analogy—I'm talking about the bottom floor now, where they have all the food."

"What about the lower tracks? Did this station have those?" I ask, picturing the commuter tracks at Grand Central.

"Yes. Although the setup is a bit different than how we constructed Aqua. Glacier is probably my favorite suite, mainly because I love the architecture. It's essentially an ice palace, minus the cold. So, in addition to the main lounge and several private rooms, Glacier has an underground labyrinth of chambers—we call them ice caves—with each one designed to accommodate a specific kink. There's also a much smaller bar down there."

I can't even begin to imagine the cost and complexity of The River's construction. She must have hired a team of genius architects, engineers, and contractors to make this place a reality. Not to mention the manpower required for regular deep cleaning, daily operation, *and* routine maintenance and repairs.

While I'm beyond intrigued by everything The River has to offer, I'm also a realist. "I'm a Vapor kind of girl."

She rubs circles on my knee with her thumb. "My gut says you can handle Aqua, which is why I'm sending you there."

I gnaw my lip. "I'm not sure—"

"Trust me." Madame Esme brushes her thumb over my mouth to free my lower lip from my teeth. "Like I said, I have someone in mind for you. He's excellent with beginners."

"What if it's too much for me?"

"I'm a woman who enjoys consistency. At The River, we use a standard set of safe words across all suites."

"I thought safe words would be limited to the stuff that goes on in Glacier."

She shakes her head. "Safe words can apply to any sexual situation. When your concierge asks, 'How is the water?' you will choose one of three responses."

"How am I supposed to remember *three* safe words?"

Freya laughs. "Elle, they're self-explanatory. Now shut up and listen."

Madame Esme takes my hands in hers. "As I was saying, your concierge will check in with you periodically. If you are happy with what he's doing, your response should be 'warm.' If you like it, but want him to slow down, you will say, 'cool.' And if at any point, you want him to stop *everything*, all you need to say is 'ice.' Does that make sense?"

I nod. "Warm is like my green light, cool is yellow, and ice is red for stop."

Freya nudges her. "Since she's using a traffic light analogy, we can't leave out the strobe lighting."

Madame Esme laughs. "Good call. If you're having a *really* good time and you want your concierge to ramp up the intensity, say, 'fire.'"

"Fire and ice," I murmur, rubbing my arms to combat the sudden chill. "Hopefully, I can stay at the warmer end of the spectrum."

She slides her hand up my thigh. "Don't you worry, baby. My boy L brings the heat."

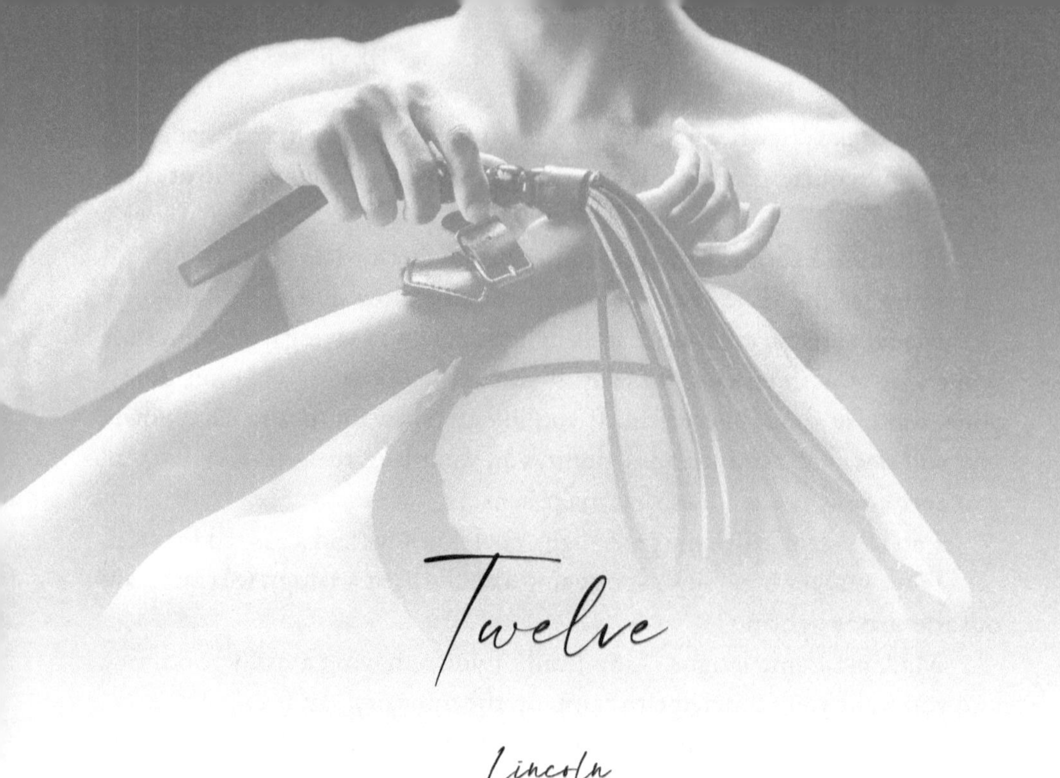

# Twelve

## Lincoln

I've always marveled at The River's impressive security presence, but tonight seems even more locked down than usual. Even Darius King, the club's head of security, is out patrolling the scene.

"What's good, Linc?" He claps my shoulder on his way past the Aqua Suite bar. Unlike the other security guys who roam the club dressed in all black, Esme wants Darius to blend in with the concierges like an undercover cop of sorts. Right now, wearing nothing but skintight navy-blue jammers and a gold mask to match the trident he carries, D is every bit the Mer king. At six foot five, the former Marine is a mountain of muscle. He's also the coolest bastard I've ever met and one of my good friends.

"Same shit, man." I peer at my reflection in the mirrored wall and squeeze a few drops of contact solution into my eyes. I keep a bottle stashed behind the bar because thanks to long hours in front of a computer and late nights at the club, my eyes are always dry. The soothing moisture blurs my vision as I slide my silver masquerade mask back down over my face. "Still can't fucking see."

"Sounds like the sensory dep rooms are perfect for you."

I close the lid and stash the bottle in the cubby beneath the bar. "Sometimes I wonder how I don't trip over my own feet in there."

"That's why you won't catch me in one. I'm not about to bust my ass slipping on wet marble. With my luck, I'd probably hit my head and drown." He points to the growing crowd of patrons. "Gonna be busy tonight. What's your game plan?"

"Dunno yet. Waiting for Esme to enlighten me."

"She's still upstairs prepping a member's newbie friend. My guess says you'll be over in Lagoon Seven with the newbie."

I shrug. "Works for me. You know I love broadening horizons."

He chuckles. "I caught a glimpse of her earlier, and she's smoking hot. You'd better hope I'm right because she's just your type."

"My type?"

"Blonde with curves in all the right places." Darius winks and disappears through the stone archway that leads to the salt cave saunas.

I make my way behind the bar and pour myself a shot of Lagavulin, my favorite single malt whiskey. Yeah, I love blondes with curves, but lately, there's only been one on my mind.

*Elinora.*

I think back to the parking garage earlier, when I wanted to press her up against that red Porsche and fuck her on the hood. How her lips quivered, and her nipples showed through the material of her dress like an invitation. I would've given my soul to hike it up around her waist and bury myself deep inside her. My cock twitches at the conjured visual. I need to chill the fuck out because these thin jammers don't stand a chance at restraining a boner.

Esme crosses the dance floor and saunters up to the bar. "I've got something special for you tonight."

"You say that before every shift."

"I really mean it this time. I just had a taste of her, and she's oh, so sweet."

"Lemme guess . . . she's a newbie?"

"She is." Esme grins and pinches my ass. "You know I reserve the tastiest treats for you, right?"

"Yeah, you take care of me." I smirk. "You know, because I'm your favorite."

She waves a finger at me. "Shh . . . don't tell anybody."

"What am I in for?" I swallow the rest of my whiskey and peer into the empty glass, annoyed with myself for finishing it so quickly. Employees are only allowed to consume one alcoholic beverage per shift, while members can have two. After the week I've had, I could use a whole bottle.

Esme straightens a stack of cocktail napkins. "I'd say she's in her mid-thirties. Drop-dead gorgeous. Currently unattached, she's a recent divorcée in desperate need of a good fuck." She presses her fingertips to her red lips. "She's never been to a sex club or slept with anyone other than her ex-husband."

"Seriously? She's been with *one* dude her entire life?"

"So she claims."

"That makes my job easy."

She tilts her head to the side. "How do you figure?"

"Pretty sure I'll meet her expectations when I've only got one guy as competition."

"I wouldn't be so cocky if I were you. This woman has so much pent-up passion, she's ready to blow. I felt it when I kissed her. I'm telling you, L, she's a river herself. Except somebody put up a fucking dam and blocked her."

"How so?"

"She's gone *years* without pleasure. She's swelling to her breaking point, just waiting for someone to bust through that dam. Her desires run much deeper than she's willing to admit, so don't be fooled by her tentative facade." Esme grips my wrist. "She's *thirsty*, L, real thirsty. And she tastes like warm sugar."

"You know I love sugar. And breaking barriers." I lick my lips in anticipation. "Where is she?"

"Waiting for you in Lagoon Seven." Esme smirks. "And ironically enough, she also goes by L."

I feel the wicked grin curve my lips. "We'll be like the lion and the lamb." I jab my thumb into my chest. "Hint, hint, I'm the lion."

"Yeah, something like that." She points toward the lagoons. "Now get your fine ass in there and cause a flood."

# Thirteen

## Elinora

I can't believe I'm doing this.

Iverson Melt publishes some risqué stories, so I know places like The River exist, but I never imagined I'd be sitting at the edge of a lagoon waiting for some hot stranger to fuck me. I wonder what my pleasure concierge will look like. Will he be patient with me, or will my lack of experience turn him off?

Pushing my white terry robe aside, I ease my feet into the lagoon. Beneath the robe, I've got on a silver string bikini Freya talked me into wearing. The water lapping at my skin is the perfect temperature. I glance at my sparkly silver toenails and smile. I'm glad I took the time to give myself a pedicure this morning. Self-pampering is a rare luxury because, while I could easily afford daily full spa treatments and regular visits to a nail salon, I feel guilty about wasting time on myself.

I take a deep breath and force myself to relax. Something heady, like jasmine or sandalwood, greets my nostrils. The scent mingles with the hint of leather and saltwater.

Private Lagoon Number Seven has a Mediterranean vibe, like the Greek baths in ancient Olympia. The space is dimly lit, save for the iridescent blue glow that emanates from the water and a strand of white lights strewn in a palm tree to my left. The lagoon boasts lofty marble archways and elaborate columns that remind me of the temples in Athens. At the far end of the room, a tranquil waterfall cascades from the ceiling, backlit by teal-colored lights. Tall sea grasses rise from planters adorned with mermaid carvings and sway in the breeze coming from . . . somewhere.

A door opens behind me, and club music floods the room. My heartbeat ratchets up a few notches with the booming bass. The rhythm fades as the door closes.

Every nerve ending flares to life, and goose bumps bloom on my skin. I shift position and adjust my royal blue mask. It obscures the top half of my face, leaving my nose and lips exposed. I draw a shaky breath and peek over my shoulder while fiddling with the end of my braid.

A figure moves through the shadows, placing something on a large, white dais. A towel or blanket, maybe. I know it's a man by the sheer size of him and the way he moves—a primal swagger that makes my inner muscles clench. My breath catches in my throat, and my hands start to tremble.

I shift position to get a better look at him, but it's a little too dark to see more than his outline. "Are you L?" I ask, my voice husky and soft.

"Are *you?*" His reply is more a vibration than anything else.

My nipples harden into peaks, and heat floods my core. My bikini bottoms don't stand a chance. "Yes."

He tosses me a bottle of water. "Drink."

"No, thank you. I'm not thirsty." I set it on the lagoon's edge.

"I said, *drink.*" A dark dominance laces his command, quickening my pulse.

"What if I don't want to?" I defiantly turn my back to him and wiggle my toes in the water. I'm not sure who he thinks he is, making demands just moments after entering the room. I'm used to hearing some basic pleasantries before someone asks something of me.

A low chuckle rumbles from his chest as he prowls closer. "I'm the king of this castle, sugar. You'll do what I tell you, when I tell you, and not a second later."

"Is that so?" I arch my back and toss my braid behind me.

"Damn right, it is."

"Well, I've got news for you, honey. I've got a castle of my own, and I'm used to running the show, so it's gonna take a lot more than words to bend me to your will."

"Turn around," he growls. "*Now.*"

Pulling my legs from the water, I pivot my body to face him and climb to my feet. I prop my hands on my hips. "You know, most people say 'please' when they want something from me."

His silhouette goes as rigid as a statue. In fact, if it weren't for his heaving shoulders, I'd think he *was* a statue. Suddenly, he backs toward the door and leaves without another word.

# Fourteen

## Lincoln

I bolt down a dark corridor to the Aqua Suite bar, nearly knocking Esme off her stool when I finally reach her. "Name," I sputter, gripping her shoulders. "Tell me right now."

She sets down her martini. "Easy, baby. What's the matter?"

I grit my teeth. "What. Is. Her. Name?"

"Your client?"

"Who the fuck else would I be asking about?" I snap, inches from her face.

Esme raises a brow. "Watch your tone, L."

I tighten my hold on her. "Tell me."

"Elinora."

"*Fuck.* I knew it." I release her and spear my hands into my hair. "This can't be fucking happening."

"What the hell's your problem, Lincoln?"

I pace the length of the bar, muttering to myself, clenching and unclenching my fists. It's new members' night. Elinora is a newbie, likely Freya's guest. She came here to get fucked, and I'm about to get fucked out of my job.

Behind the bar, Leo, Gideon, and Rocco are hustling their asses off, making drinks for the throngs of masked patrons. Maybe I can get one of the guys to swap places with me.

"I asked you a question." Esme's tone slices through the air like a whip landing on my shoulders.

I sink onto the stool beside hers. "She's my boss."

"Huh?"

"You heard me. Elinora Iverson is my boss."

"Oh my God. The publisher?"

"Yep, that'd be her." I bury my face in my hands. "You gotta get someone else. I can't fuck my boss. If she finds out it's me, I'll lose my job." My fears snowball into an avalanche that leaves Reagan without care and me spending the rest of eternity as a fuck toy for rich women.

Esme snatches the schedule from behind the bar and skims her finger down the page. "The only concierge who's free right now is Z."

Zarek Petrov. As one of Glacier's resident doms, he has a reputation for the sadomasochism end of the BDSM spectrum—not that there's anything wrong with that on principle—but Zarek is a man who doesn't play by the rules. Only experienced subs can handle what he dishes out, and even then, he's been known to take things too far. In Z's world, respecting safe words is optional. I will never understand why Esme keeps him on the payroll. My blood runs cold at the thought of him with Elinora.

"Absolutely fucking not."

"Excuse me?"

I force an even tone and meet her honeyed gaze. "Anyone but Zarek." I point to my friends behind the bar. "What about them?"

"Gideon leaves in ten minutes, and Leo and Rocco are already spoken for."

"Who's bartending after them?" Most Aqua concierges work half of their shift behind the bar and spend the rest of their time in the lagoons, mineral pools, or the lazy river.

"Rhett and Silas."

"Good. Send one of them in."

She shakes her head. "They're both with clients. Besides, Elinora is here now. We're not about to keep her waiting, are we?"

I dodge her question with one of my own. "What about Cameron?"

"He's off tonight. There isn't anyone else, so I suggest you get your ass back in there before I call Z up to the Aqua Suite. Maybe he's not the right fit for her, but—"

"She's a newbie." I clutch the edge of the bar. "He'd be too rough for her. She can't handle his intensity."

"How do you know what she can handle?" Esme challenges, propping her hands on her hips. "Pretty bold of you to make those assumptions, don't you think?"

There is no way in hell I'll let that fucker near the porcelain goddess I work for. The thought of him marring her flawless skin makes my blood boil.

"You said it yourself—she's only ever been with her ex-husband. She's practically a fucking virgin." I clench my jaw. "You *know* how Z gets. Look at what happened with Maya."

Fire flashes in her gaze. "Those were entirely different circumstances."

"Right, but would you seriously set Elinora up with a Glacier Dom for her first time? That seems reckless."

"First of all, I don't appreciate you insinuating that I don't know what I'm doing." Esme grips my chin, roughly turning my head to face her. "Number two, I don't give a fuck about your opinion of Z. My focus is the bottom line. If she leaves, and we miss out on a membership opportunity, there will be hell to pay. Need I remind you of our arrangement?"

"No," I mutter, feeling sick to my stomach. "But how am I supposed to—"

"I don't care what you do, or how you do it, but you'd better make it happen. Don't forget that *I'm* your boss too. Don't you dare fuck this up." She waves a finger in my face. "I mean it, Lincoln. Be a man and give her what she needs."

# Fifteen

## Elinora

**M**aybe I shouldn't have challenged him. Did my lack of obedience turn him off? Toying with the end of my braid, I pace along the edge of the lagoon and try to reason through the lusty haze in my head. *Maybe I was supposed to—*

The door slides open, and I jump, nearly falling into the shimmering water. A figure enters the room and secures the door before making his way around the perimeter. His height and stature tell me he's the same man as before.

"You're back," I murmur, wrapping my arms around myself. "I thought you'd ditched me." I was moments from grabbing my shit and leaving.

"Sorry. Forgot something."

"Are we all good now?"

"Yeah." He reaches for a switch on the wall and dims the lights—even the ones in the palm tree—to near darkness. I can barely discern the outline of the lagoon. He points to the water. "Get in."

His abrupt retreat had taken some wind from my sails, so instead of fighting him, I slide out of my robe and place it on the dais. Besides, I'm tired of being in control. This is my opportunity to relax and let somebody else call the shots. I tiptoe to the water's edge and ease in until my feet touch the bottom. Water laps at my waist. It's shallower than I expected. There's a splash, but I can't figure out which direction it came from.

I peer into the darkness and wait. "Esme said your name is L. What is that short for?"

"Uh . . ." He coughs. "It's . . . Elliot."

Spinning toward his voice, I blindly reach out. My fingertips brush warm flesh—a shoulder, maybe. *No, that's hair.* His chest.

"Why's it so dark in here? I can't see a damn thing."

"Just feel."

"But I want to see you," I whisper, splaying my hands against his steely pecs before sliding them lower and tracing the ridges of his abdomen. Good Lord, his body is perfection. I'd swear Aphrodite herself carved him from granite. As my fingertips explore the hidden masterpiece in front of me, I decide I don't need to see him. Feeling this man is enough for now.

His huge palms settle on top of my hands, stilling them. He brushes his thumbs over my skin. "Tell me your safe words."

"Fire, warm, cool, and ice."

"You know when to use them?"

"Yes, when you ask me how the water is," I say with a shudder.

"Correct." He lifts my knuckles to his lips and presses a kiss to each one before releasing me. "You all right?"

"Yes, I'm just a little nervous. I, uh, I've never done anything like this before."

"Relax." He clamps his hands on my hips, yanking me up against him. His erection presses into my ribcage as his hot breath tickles my ear. "Just feel, sugar. We've got all night, and I promise I won't push you too far."

"It's been years since anyone's touched me." *And I've never been up close and personal with a man this big.*

He digs his fingertips into my hips and pulls me closer. "How about we make up for lost time?"

"Yes," I whisper, clutching his shoulders.

"Keep your hands there. Don't move them, no matter what I do. Got it?"

"Yes." I can't believe how easy it is for me to obey him. I'm not a docile woman, and you'd be hard-pressed to find a man who describes me as obedient. Yet here I am, following a stranger's orders like I was born to serve him. Maybe there's something in the water, but I feel like I've already been swept away by The River's current. I bite back a moan as his lips find my neck. Tasting, kissing, and sucking my skin. "Oh my God."

He grazes his teeth over my throat, and I knot my fingers in his thick, silky hair, needing him closer.

"Hands."

I jerk them back and find his shoulders once more. "Sorry."

His chuckle is little more than a rumble. "Trouble with directions?"

"I'm usually in charge."

"In here, I'm king. I run the show." He kisses along my jawline, sliding his grip to my waist, his thumbs rubbing circles on my hipbones. "Now, let's try again."

I can't explain it, but his dominance puts me at ease. I want his control, no, I *crave* it. I need him to bend me to his will so I can finally let go of my control. This faceless stranger with his hard body and soft hair, raining kisses on my skin in a dark lagoon, makes me feel . . . *safe*. Protected. Free. I can't put my finger on it, but there's something warm and familiar about him.

He reaches behind me and unties my bikini top. First, the knot at the back of my neck, then the one below my shoulder blades. The halter plops into the lagoon and floats away with the rest of my inhibitions. My breath catches in my throat as he trails wet kisses across my collarbone. I clench my hands on his shoulders.

"How's the water?"

"Warm." I gasp as his mouth moves lower. His lips brush the tops of my breasts, sending a flare of heat between my legs. I clasp the back of his neck and pull his head closer.

He stills. "*Hands*, sugar."

"Shit." I slide my grip to its rightful place. "It's hard to let someone else have control."

He rolls his hips, rubbing his enormous cock against me. "Do I need to tie them behind your back?"

I can't answer him because lust obliterates my ability to speak. Does he need to tie me up? No. Do I suddenly want him to? Fuck yes.

He slides his warm palms up my torso to cup my breasts. Gasping, I press into his touch when his mouth drifts lower and brushes my nipple.

"Oh my God," I whimper, digging my nails into his shoulders.

Wet heat surrounds my nipple. He sucks it between his lips and rubs his tongue over the hardened peak. Flares of pleasure travel the length of my body, igniting me. Burning me alive. I need him to consume me, rage through me, until there's nothing left but smoke. Before I realize what I'm doing, I spear my hands into his hair once more. "*Fire.*"

He snags my waist, tossing me over his shoulder like a rag doll. "Warned you."

My blood rushes to my head as I shriek and claw at his lower back. "What are you doing?"

He makes his way through the water to the staircase at the opposite end of the lagoon. "Earned yourself some restraints."

*Holy shit.*

I wriggle in his hold, flailing and kicking my legs. "Put me down."

"Not a chance." He tightens his arm across my thighs and keeps walking.

"Who do you think you—" His huge palm lands on my ass cheeks with a loud crack. "Ow! Did you just spank me?" I sputter, shocked by how the sting sends a tidal wave of lust through my veins.

"Very observant." He squeezes my ass and snaps the waistband of my bikini bottoms.

"What, are you gonna throw me over your knee and punish me now?"

A dark chuckle leaves his chest as we approach the waterfall. "You gonna stop me?"

No. I will *not* stop him. I'm going to provoke him until he spanks me again. I swat him on the ass and snap *his* waistband, mirroring what he did to me.

He stops short. "This isn't a democracy, sugar. The only give and take is gonna be you," he trails his fingers up the back of my thighs, "taking what I give." He slaps my ass once more. "Got it?"

"Should I call you Sensei? Or would you prefer Captain?"

He nips my side. "How about Your Excellency?"

I snort. "In your dreams, bud."

He steps closer to the waterfall, causing me to shiver in the mist. I arch my back, contorting myself to look around him. In what little light there is, I can make out another door. Behind the waterfall.

"Where are we going?" I squint and crane my neck.

He presses a panel on the wall, and the door slides open. "To teach you some manners."

"Excuse me?"

He slaps my ass. "Stop talking."

We enter a silent room, leaving behind the tranquil rush of the waterfall. My hearing ratchets up a few notches in the total darkness. Our breaths and a pounding drum are the only sounds that remain. After a moment, it occurs to me that the percussion is merely my heartbeat, throbbing inside my skull.

"It's too dark in here." My voice echoes around us. "Is this some sort of dungeon?"

"Shh . . . just feel," he whispers, carrying me deeper into his lair. He pauses next to what I assume is a cabinet, because I hear a drawer scrape open. He rummages inside it and retrieves something before we cross the room.

Since I can't see a fucking thing in the pitch darkness, his familiarity with the room's layout comforts me. His warmth and steady breathing put me even more at ease. None of it makes sense. I'm in a dark room with a stranger who's about to spank me, yet I feel safe.

He stops walking and sets me on my feet in front of him. The backs of my knees make contact with a piece of furniture, and its height and softness tell me it's a bed. "Give me your wrists."

I shiver when his whispered command brushes my ear, but I hold both hands out in front of me. He gently clasps my wrists, securing them with something soft. If I had to guess, I'd say it was a silk scarf. He presses me onto the bed with a nudge of my shoulders.

"Lie down and scoot back." He stretches my arms up over my head and fastens the other end of my restraints to what I assume is a bedpost. The mattress dips beside me, and fabric rustles. I gasp when he skates his palms up my torso over my breasts. Next, he removes my mask, replacing it with a blindfold.

"It's pitch-black in here. Why're you blindfolding me?"

His lips find my ear. "You don't need to see. Listen, taste, and *feel*."

"It would be nice to have a face to go with the sensations."

"I can be anyone you want me to be." His heated whisper sends a flood of desire between my thighs. "Indulge in your fantasies. Make me one of the Hemsworth brothers or Henry Cavill. Or I can be Jason Momoa, and you can call me Aquaman if you want. Trust that I'll give you what you need."

"I do trust you," I whisper, shocked by the truth in my statement.

He traces the shell of my ear with his tongue. "Tell me your safe words."

"Fire, warm, cool, and ice."

"Hard limits?"

It's a good thing he can't see me because I'd bet the heat creeping over my cheeks is in tomato territory on the redness scale. "Uh . . ."

"I need to know this." He punctuates the whispered statement with a nip of my earlobe. "Or we can't go any further."

"No nipple clamps," I say, remembering Esme's declaration from earlier. I have zero experience with the seemingly torturous devices, and I'd like to keep it that way. "And no hardcore S and M stuff."

"Not my style." He feathers his lips over my shoulders. "Anything else?"

*Think, Elinora. Think.*

"No butt plugs," I blurt. "Or anything there, actually."

"Got it. Now I need you to tell me how far you're willing to go tonight."

"All the way."

"Be specific. Tell me what you want."

"I . . . I want . . ." I force a swallow. While I rule the rest of my life with an iron fist and have no trouble making my demands crystal clear at the office, I've never been able to ask for what I want in the bedroom. Mainly because my needs were always shoved to the back burner. "Um . . ."

"Do you want me to touch you?"

"Yes," I whisper.

"Say it louder."

"*Yes.*" My voice reverberates through the room.

"Good girl. That's how I want you tonight. Loud and clear. Understand?"

"Yes." I press my knees together and wait for his touch. "Are you going to make love to me?"

"I don't make love." He licks the column of my throat and brings his lips to my ear once more. "I fuck. Do you want me to fuck you, sugar?"

"Yes," I murmur, suddenly overwhelmed by the enormity of what I'm about to do.

"What was that?" He nips my earlobe.

"*Yes.*" The word leaves my lips on a moan.

"Going forward, the correct response is, 'Yes, sir.'" He palms my breasts. "Now, let's try again. Do you want me to fuck you?"

"Yes, sir."

"That's my good girl." He rewards me with the brush of his thumbs over my nipples.

My back arches up off the bed, my body pressing into his touch, seeking more. "I haven't had sex in almost three years." My confession, however embarrassing, is necessary. Judging by what I felt of him in the water, he's well-endowed. If I'm not careful, I'll be begging him to skip the foreplay my body needs and fuck me this instant. "And I've only had one partner in my life."

He traces the curve of my breasts and whispers, "I won't hurt you."

I know he won't, but I need him to know how completely out of character this is for me. How I've spent the entirety of my life being called an ice queen. A prude. Frigid. How the man who was supposed to love me unconditionally took my loyalty for granted and betrayed me. How I've let no one close to me since. "I'm scared."

He stills. "Of me?"

"No." My reply is unyielding, just like me—Elinora Iverson, publishing mogul. "I'm scared of how badly I need this."

Taking my statement as his call to action, he moves closer. His lips find my throat once more and claim the expanse of skin from my jawline to the tops of my breasts. His lack of stubble tells me he's clean-shaven, and I wish I could touch his face. Cup his jaw while we kiss.

*He doesn't kiss*, my brain reminds me. *I wonder why—*

"How's the water?" His question brings me back to the heat coursing through me.

"Fire."

He groans and grips my waistband, tugging it down. "Was hoping you'd say that."

His fingertips brush over my clit as he removes my bikini bottom. He tosses it aside and kisses my neck, flattening his palm on my lower belly. He inches his way lower and cups me before sliding a finger inside my pussy.

My hips jerk with his touch. "Oh God."

"Let me hear you, sugar." He moves in and out of me, massaging me deep inside. Awakening neglected nerve endings and stoking me hotter.

*"Fire."*

He nips my collarbone and adds a second finger, pumping them into me. His thumb joins the party, rubbing circles on my clit. My thighs fall open, and I clench around his fingers, needing more. Needing him deeper, harder, and faster. I crave a release that's so long overdue, I forget what it feels like. He kisses my neck, shoulders, and jawline. His ragged breaths gusting my skin tell me he's enjoying what he's doing to me.

"How's the water?" he grits out, his voice a deep rumble.

"Fire, sir."

He slides a third finger inside me and increases the pressure on my clit. "Come for me, sugar."

I focus on the sensations building between my legs, loving how his thick, strong fingers fuck me, and his thumb brings me closer and closer to the edge. The room smells like leather and whiskey, and all I can hear is our ragged breathing, my moans, and the wetness coating his fingers as he moves them in and out.

I'd give my soul to taste and touch this faceless stranger. My orgasm hovers in the periphery, needing a final push before I soar. I imagine the celebrities he mentioned, but it's not enough. Their image does nothing to fan the dwindling flames.

So I focus on the one man who I shouldn't fantasize about.

Lincoln Kennedy.

Maybe I'm losing my mind, but I'd give anything to indulge in the fantasy of taking my hunky young employee to bed.

I imagine him with his tall, broad body and gorgeous face. How his deep blue eyes look at me, through me, and within me all at once. I envision myself kissing his full, inviting lips and writhing beneath the heavy weight of his body.

The decadent visual sends me over the edge. "Oh! Yes!" My hips buck wildly as the moans rip from my throat. "Oh, God… *Lincoln.*"

# Sixteen

## Lincoln

$S$he knows it's me.

I freeze, panic gripping my chest. Despite the darkness, the blindfold, and my attempts to deepen my voice, Elinora figured out my identity.

Which means I'm royally fucked.

"Oh my God. I—I'm so sorry. I didn't mean—" she sputters, gasping for breath. "But you—you said to fantasize about someone who—"

*Wait, she was imagining me?*

The guy who begged her for a job like an orphan asking for more porridge? Doesn't she notice how I trip on my words like the poster child for awkwardness whenever I'm around her? Elinora Iverson wants *me*? No, that can't be possible. I shake my head to clear it. Not only do I have my fingers inside my boss's perfect wet pussy, but now I'm losing my motherfucking mind.

*She definitely said my name though.*

Elinora tries again. "He's someone who—"

"Someone who?" My brain, grasping at straws, forces the words from my lips in a cautious whisper.

"You said you'd be anyone I wanted you to be."

"You want him?" I breathe, everything inside me tightening like a coiled spring.

"Yes. I—I've never done anything like this before, so I'm nervous. You told me to come for you, but I couldn't let go until my mind made you *him*. If I'm going to do this, he's who I need you to be." Her words, and the vulnerability in them, steal my breath. My sanity. What's left of my heart.

"Then he's who I'll be," I whisper, as an invisible band squeezes my chest.

Elinora wants me. She wants the real Lincoln, not the pleasure concierge who just made her come. She wants *me* to make her come. I'd give anything to reveal my identity. Pull her close and fulfill all her fantasies while making damn sure she never sought anyone else to do so.

"He's a man who—"

My lips crash down over hers, swallowing her explanation. Wedging her thighs apart, I shift to move on top of her. I cup her jaw with my free hand while the other begins its quest to wring another orgasm from her gorgeous body. Her tight, wet pussy clenches around my fingers, making me groan into the kiss.

My tongue surges into her mouth, tasting and claiming her. I can't remember the last time I kissed a woman on the lips, but it's been *years*. I never kiss my clients. Ever. It goes against all my rules. Self-preservation is critical and—while I may fuck for a living—I reserve my kiss for the rare woman I truly connect with. As pieces of my soul unravel, I realize I'd sell my soul to the fucking devil to keep kissing *this* woman.

Elinora arches her back, thrusting her pussy onto my fingers. I love how her body responds to my touch and how she gasps and moans for me. But more than that, I love the way she said my name.

*She's mine.*

My cock jerks in agreement, begging to join the action, but I need to make sure she's ready. She hasn't had sex in years, and I'm a big guy. The last thing I want to do is hurt her.

I break the kiss. "Make me him again and come. *Now.*"

She cries out, back arching and pussy spasming as she climaxes. "*Lincoln.*"

My name leaves her lips on a moan, and I withdraw my fingers and suck them into my mouth, tasting her sweetness. A growl rumbles in my chest, and I have to force myself not to bury my face between her thighs and lick every fucking inch of her.

"I want—" she begins, gasping.

"Tell me, Elle."

"Please call me Elinora."

"I'll call you whatever you like, as long as you tell me what you want."

"I want you inside me."

I reach up and untie her wrists before snatching the condom I'd tucked in my waistband. I tear open the wrapper and place it in her hand. "Put this on me."

"Are you sure you want to do this?" she whispers.

"Huh?" Is she seriously checking for *my* consent?

"I mean, I just confessed to you that I'm imagining another man. Not to mention, I'm extremely out of practice with anything sexual. Besides, I know this is a job obligation—"

I grab her hand and press it to my cock, dragging it the entire hard length. "Does that feel like an obligation?"

She gasps. "You're huge."

I've heard it hundreds of times but hearing it from Elinora makes me want to roar. Pound my chest. Rear up like a stallion.

"Put the condom on me," I whisper, flexing my hips. "And tell me what you want Lincoln to do to you."

Her grip on my cock tightens. "Everything."

"Tell me."

"I want him to hold me, kiss me, and make love to me."

"What else?" I brush my lips over her ear.

"I want him to fuck me."

The rest of my blood rushes to my cock. "How do you want him to fuck you?" My words are more a vibration than any form of recognizable speech because I'm seconds from fucking her through the mattress. "Tell me."

"I want him to make me feel alive again." Her breath catches. "It's been so long since I've felt . . . anything."

She slides my waistband down, freeing my cock. I take over, shoving the jammers down my thighs and kicking them off. Her soft hands encircle me, and she strokes them up and down.

My eyes roll back into my head. "Condom. Now."

"Yes, sir." As she rolls the condom on, her grip on my cock almost makes me come. "How do you want me?"

"Loud. Screaming m—" *Shit. I almost said my name.* "Screaming his name."

"I mean, what position?" she clarifies.

*All of them.*

"On your back. Legs wide open for me. Hands on my shoulders at all times."

"What happens if I let go?"

"I'll flip you over and spank you."

Elinora's breath rushes out of her. "What if that's what I want?"

"Do you want Lincoln to spank you?"

"Yes," she whispers.

"Then that's what you'll get."

# Seventeen

## Elinora

Need. Pure, raw need. It flows through my body, soaking deep into my soul. I've never felt desire like this, and I've certainly never felt this desirable.

"Can we try other positions?" I ask, eager to dive deeper into the feelings my stranger awakened inside me.

"We'll do every position I can bend you into." He brings his lips to my ear. "By the time tonight's over, I'll make you come on my cock so many times, you won't remember your name."

"Oh my God."

"No. Not God, sugar. There's nothing heavenly about what I'm gonna do to you." He presses my knees apart, positioning himself between them. "Hands on my shoulders."

I reach out and tug the mask covering his face. "Take the mask off."

"How do you ask?"

"Please."

"Please, what?"

"Please, sir," I whisper. "Take it off and kiss me again." His hand brushes mine as he removes it. I stroke my fingertips along his cheeks and jaw like he's the world's most beautiful piece of Braille. "You're perfect."

He exhales roughly, pressing his cheek into my palm. I trace his features, and in this moment, it *is* Lincoln's gorgeous face. I know every curve, every angle, from his thick glossy hair to his jawline and the sexy dimple on his chin. I know his nose, his eyebrows, and those perfect pillowy lips.

"Open your legs wider for me."

My thighs fall open at his command like I was born to serve him. I'm open and vulnerable, yet somehow, I feel comfortable. Safe. *Cherished.* That's right, Elinora Iverson, a woman who trusts no man, trusts this stranger implicitly.

Like I can imagine myself trusting Lincoln.

As the line between reality and fantasy blurs, I want the young editor even more.

Would Lincoln be domineering like my stranger, a man who's willing to bring my darkest fantasies to life? Would *he* take me over his knee and spank me? Tie me up and blindfold me, so I need to rely on touch alone? What would it feel like to be alone with Lincoln, our tongues and limbs tangling while we make love? I'll never know, but in my mind, the flip side of the nerdy, hunky gentleman I employ, is a rogue who drips of sin and sex. The thought sends a flood of arousal to my core. While I can't have Lincoln, I *can* allow my stranger to indulge me in the decadent fantasy of him.

And if that's a sin, tell the devil to take me.

"Hands on my shoulders." His gravelly command makes my heart race.

I slide my fingers along his arms, savoring his bulging muscles. "You feel like a sexy sculpture," I murmur, finally gripping his shoulders as he commanded.

His breath rushes out of him. "And your touch feels like heaven. Now wrap your legs around me, sugar." His hand brushes my lower belly as he reaches between us and lines himself up, the broad head of his cock barely pressing inside me. "How's the water, Elinora?"

# *Eighteen*

## *Lincoln*

I t's the moment of truth. I hold my breath and await Elinora's reply. *Please don't tell me to stop. Please don't tell—*

"Warm, sir."

Harps and trumpets be damned; her breathy whisper is more beautiful than a choir of angels, the Vatican, and the fucking Sistine Chapel.

I press forward, easing my cock inside her. As I fill her, inch by rock-hard inch, she rewards me with a throaty moan.

"The water?" I grit out through a clenched jaw.

"Still warm." She gasps and digs her nails into my shoulders.

"Don't let go of me," I command, drawing my hips back until I'm nearly free of her. I surge forward with a groan. She cries out as her tight, wet pussy takes me to the hilt. "Just like that, sugar. Take me."

"Oh, fuck." She tightens her legs around the back of my thighs. "You're so thick."

Pulling back until I'm nearly free of her body's grip, I seal my lips over hers in a slow, tender dance. While I take my time exploring Elinora's pretty little mouth, her kiss is ravenous—full of hunger and need. I rock my hips, teasing her pussy with just the head of my cock. She bucks beneath me and digs her heels into my thighs. Moaning, she knots her hands in my hair, deepening our kiss.

Esme was right—Elinora is a river, churning with passion, need, and emotion. Swelling past her breaking point, she flows over and through me, pulling me beneath the surface until she's all I know.

Even though my identity is still a mystery, *I'm* the man she wants and needs. And so help me God, I'm gonna bust through her dam, and make *damn* sure my plunge into her waters causes a motherfucking flood.

She cries out as I give her a powerful thrust.

"How's the water?"

She drags her nails down my back and fists my ass cheeks. "Fire."

"Hands," I remind her, rolling my hips. Instead of gripping my shoulders, she pinches my ass. Hard. I deliver a few punishing thrusts before pulling out.

"Why're you stopping?"

I pivot into a seated position and pull her across my lap instead of answering. My palm lands on her plump ass cheeks with a loud crack. A shocked cry leaves her lips, making me hope it wasn't too much, too fast. In the pitch-black, I'm blind to her body's cues, so I can't use the pinking of her skin to gauge her response.

"How's the water?"

"Warm." She squirms against my legs.

Holding Elinora in place with an arm across her shoulder blades, I caress her back, hips, and thighs, my fingertips lingering on her soft bottom. God, *this ass*. I want to stroke, squeeze, and bite it. Clutch her hips while I slam into her from behind. The sultry little vixen wiggles in my lap, so I deliver another swat.

I'm sure I'll look back on this moment with the shock it deserves, but right now, my conscience is nowhere to be found. Reason and caution surrendered to lust. I lose a little more control each minute that passes with my sexy boss naked in my lagoon. Her wanton moans spur me on, unleashing my dominant side.

I pull the elastic from the end of her braid and unravel it, running my fingers through her silken hair. Even damp, it's softer and more fragrant than I could've imagined. I gather the strands into a ponytail at the nape of her neck and gently tug her head back.

"How's the water?"

"Fire."

With one hand knotted in her hair, I slide two fingers into her pussy and stroke them in and out. I desperately want to be inside her, but she's testing the water here, and I don't want to stop the flow.

I yank her head back and add a third finger.

She thrusts her hips to meet my strokes. "Oh, yes." I withdraw my hand, and she writhes in my lap. "Please don't stop—"

I smack her ass once more. Hard.

"*Lincoln . . .*"

My cock jerks, throbbing painfully. Hearing my name rip from her throat is the highlight of my life. Too bad I'm nothing more than a fantasy in her mind. How much further could we take this if it were real? Elinora and Lincoln, two people with a chemistry that crackles in the surrounding air. How much harder could I push her? How much louder would she scream without the smoke and mirrors?

Guilt settles in the pit of my stomach as the reality of what I'm doing comes into focus. It's bad enough my cock earns me an income—now I'm a fraud too. What kind of man knowingly deceives a woman for a fuck?

Moaning, she churns her hips in my lap. My palm collides with her ass cheeks.

"Fire."

Clenching my fingers in her hair, I deliver a few hard spanks, varying the intensity and placement. Her moans grow louder with each one until I can't fucking take it anymore. Flipping Elinora onto her back, I yank her thighs apart and settle between them, rubbing and stroking her pussy.

Her arousal coats her thighs and my fingers. I suck them into my mouth once more, growling low in my throat. "I fucking love the taste of you, Elinora."

She thrusts her hips upward. "I need you."

"I'm right here."

"Hold me and make love to me. Slowly."

My breath catches as her whispered plea cracks my heart wide open. "I've got what you need, sugar."

# Nineteen

## Elinora

**M**y ass is on fire, but that's nothing compared to the desperate ache between my thighs. The place I'd give anything to have the real Lincoln fill. My stranger grips my hips, easing his thick cock inside me, filling and stretching me to my limit. With his ragged breaths gusting my neck, he moves slowly, just like I asked. Since I can't have Lincoln, this warm, strong man is the next best thing. I wrap my arms around him and clutch his back, pulling him closer.

"How's the water?" His gritty tone rasps against my ear.

"Hot."

"Hot's not an option." He rolls his hips. "Try again."

"I want something between warm and fire."

"Tell me," he whispers, kissing my neck. "I want to hear you say it."

"I want . . ." I tighten my legs around him. "Lincoln."

His lips meet mine in a tender kiss. My tongue darts out, twining and stroking against his. He groans and picks up the pace of his thrusts, his cock rubbing places deep inside me. I'm no virgin, but I might as well be because this feels nothing like the sex I've had in my lifetime. It's deeper. Darker. More intense than I could've imagined.

In my mind, Lincoln is the one taking me higher and higher, his thrusts growing more urgent as I near my release. He follows my body's cues, cradling me close, giving me everything I didn't know I needed. Maybe it isn't fair, wrong even, to give life to my fantasy, but at this moment, I don't give a flying fuck.

Closing my eyes, I let go of everything. All the angst, the self-damnation, the fear, and uncertainty. I need this release, this freedom to spread my wings and soar. I'm no angel, but thanks to my Lincoln fantasy, I'm flying among them.

"I'm gonna come." I gasp, clawing his back.

"Let me hear you, sugar. Scream for me."

He grinds his hips in a powerful driving rhythm and crushes his lips to mine once more. The hunger in his kiss sends me hurtling into ecstasy. He swallows my scream as the orgasm slams through me, stealing what's left of my senses. He keeps moving, pumping his hips harder and faster, all while kissing my lips with a reverence that feels like worship. No one has ever kissed me like this. Or made love to me this way. Ever.

"*Lincoln.*" As I lose myself in another climax, I know I can't live without this faceless stranger who ravages and cherishes me in pitch darkness. A man who, when I projected my deepest fantasy onto him, pulled me closer and gave me warmth instead of leaving me in the cold.

"Oh, fuck." He groans, his fingertips tightening on my hips. I feel his cock jerk and pulse before he collapses on top of me. Ragged gasps and reverent whispers of my name leave his lips as he pulls my body close. "Elinora, you're an angel."

Tears spring to my eyes at his declaration. I try to hold them back, but that dam's been broken. My physical climax heralded an emotional release so intense, I feel like I'm drowning.

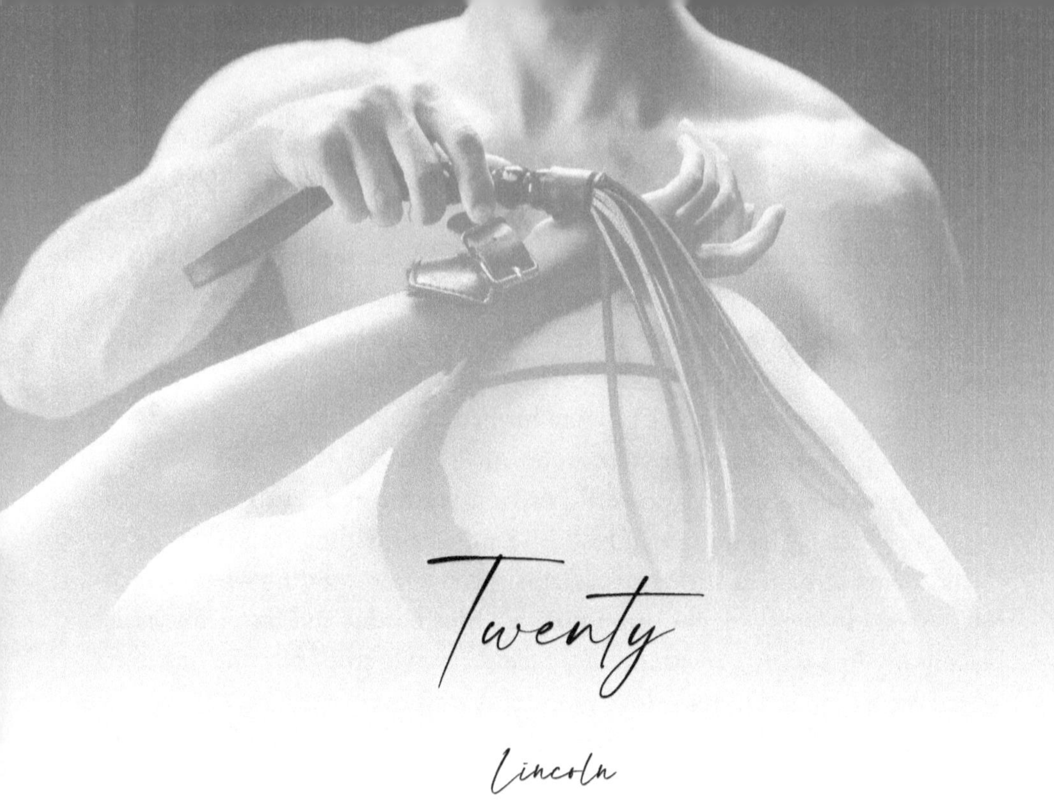

# Twenty

## Lincoln

I f mindfuckery was an Olympic sport, I'd hold a gold medal in every event. In every arena. Since the dawn of the games. I'm beyond fucked physically. And mentally. A sob wracks Elinora's frame, and it's clear I fucked her too.

As guilt knifes my soul, I tighten my arms around her. "Shh . . . don't cry, angel." I run my fingers through her silken hair and pull her even closer. She needs to be held, and I need to hold her.

How could I be so fucking stupid? I should've expected this. Sex without strings doesn't work for everyone—especially not a woman who has only ever slept with one man. I'm no better than her cheating ex-husband. I cheated her too, and that suffocating realization burns me. As her shoulders shake with her river of tears, I hope I drown in them.

"I'm sorry," I whisper.

"You did nothing wrong."

Oh, but I did. My masquerade performance hurt her. I lied to her. I've never felt dirtier than I do right now.

"Why're you crying?" I ask, even though I already know her answer.

"Because it was a lot."

"Too much?"

"No, just a lot." She burrows closer to me, pressing her damp cheeks to my chest. "I'm sorry."

"You have nothing to apologize for."

Her breath hitches. "I projected someone else onto you. It wasn't fair to you or to him."

I squeeze my eyes shut. "We can handle it."

"Yeah, but I can't." A whimper leaves her chest. More tears. Another sob.

I've seen plenty of women become emotional after sex, but never like this. As *my* eyes start to burn, I know I'm in over my head.

"Let's get you cleaned up," I whisper, sliding my masquerade mask back onto my face. "Come float in the lagoon with me."

"I don't think I can walk right now."

"I'll carry you." I say a silent prayer that my legs don't give out after what was, no exaggeration, the best sex of my life. "Your job is to relax."

My orgasm was like nothing I've ever experienced. I'm supposed to give pleasure—not receive it. My time at The River isn't about me, it's about the women I serve. Over the years, I've mastered the art of climaxing without ejaculation. Now, the only client who can force my release is my friend Maya. I trust her enough to let down my guard and lose myself in the sensations. I won't do it with anyone else. Maybe it's because my profession makes me feel dirty. My head, heart, and cock are all on different pages—of entirely different books. But with Elinora tonight, everything converged as one. I lost myself inside her. I don't think I'll ever get that part of me back, nor do I want to. Little does she know, she owns me.

"Your body felt like heaven, Elinora."

Her breath leaves her in a rush. "Heaven's no place for a woman like me."

"I hate to break this to you, but somebody'd better give you a harp, because you just brought me there, angel."

"I'm no angel."

"What makes you say that?"

"I'm a ruthless businesswoman. I've bankrupted many companies. People lost their jobs because of me."

She's not wrong. Even though I was technically laid off—and Cooper Press hasn't gone under yet—it wasn't long ago that I was one of those unfortunate jobless fuckers. Her remorse surprises me though. Maybe she isn't as heartless as everyone claims.

Feeling the urge to comfort her, I say, "That's the price of success."

"Tell that to the unemployed people struggling to pay their bills because I trampled all over their livelihoods. Like I said, I'm no saint."

The self-disgust in her tone mirrors the way I feel about hiding my true identity. She and I fit together like two halves of a puzzle. With our haphazard pieces and inability to see the picture we create, we're perfectly imperfect, and scrambled as fuck.

"Angel or demon, sinner or saint, we've all got a mix of heaven and hell in our blood."

She wipes her eyes. "Yes, well, I'm pretty sure my blood runs hotter than most. I seem to lack that heavenly balance you speak of."

"The devil's in the details, angel." I brush my lips over her ear. "But we don't need to worry about him right now." Needing to place some distance between our activities in the hidden playroom, I scoop her off the bed and carry her back out to the lagoon.

The rush of the waterfall drowns out the voices in my head, and I focus on the woman in my arms. Navigating through the darkness, I make my way around the pool and ease us beneath the water's surface. Facing me, Elinora straddles my hips. She melts into my embrace and rests her head on my shoulder as we settle on an underwater ledge. Warm saltwater laps at our skin. Neither one of us speaks. We don't have to—our bodies do the talking. I cradle her close and gently stroke her back as she clings to me.

I could hold this woman for an eternity, but I'm not that lucky. I'll have to settle for one night.

# Twenty-One

## Lincoln

My Sunday morning coffee tastes bitter, and I can't shake the cloud of guilt that blankets me.

After spending Friday night with Elinora, my Saturday shift at The River was intolerable. How the fuck am I supposed to do my job if I can't close my eyes without thinking of her? Better yet, how can I be a pleasure concierge if my cock refuses to cooperate?

I've never had trouble getting—or keeping—an erection. Ever. Multiple rounds? Bring it. I can hold off my orgasm and suppress ejaculation. When Maya makes me come, I'm quick to recover. Not only is a refractory period unnecessary for my anatomy's repeat performance, it's all but nonexistent. My stamina and blood flow allows me to fuck all night. That's why Esme loves me so much. I'm a sex machine, and if there's one thing I've learned at The River, it's that sex sells. Imagine my embarrassment last night when I couldn't get it up for the pretty redhead who threw herself at me.

If having my cock malfunction wasn't bad enough, a wave of nausea slammed through me, and I nearly puked on her feet. Esme sent me home after that. I called out for tonight's shift, citing nausea. While I'm not currently nauseous, the thought of being inside another woman—Maya included—makes my stomach lurch. I'd rather not humiliate myself again. I need to get my shit together before Thursday. Esme won't buy a week-long stomach bug excuse.

I swallow another gulp of bitter coffee and settle on the couch with my laptop. I've got some editing to do if I want to keep to the schedule I've set for myself. Too bad I don't have a psychological thriller to work on. Nope, I'm balls-deep in an angsty erotic romance. The hero and heroine share an undeniable chemistry, but their sex scenes need some serious attention.

Is any part of my existence *not* ironic?

Like it's been doing fifty-seven times an hour since Friday, my mind drifts back to Elinora. Her warm, soft body and how tightly her pussy gripped me. The way she arched her back and thrust her hips to meet mine. How she raked her nails down my back and screamed my name when she orgasmed. Four times.

I glance at my lap as my cock stands at immediate attention, stretching the fabric of my plaid pajama pants. "Oh, so now you're not broken? Where were you last night?" It twitches at my question as if to say *I did you a favor.* "You've done me enough favors." It twitches again. "You know what? Fuck you too, bro."

My cock still works, but I'm clearly going insane. *That* concrete was mixed when I slept with my boss, poured when I lost control and allowed myself to orgasm, and it hardened to stone when I fell for her afterward.

The way she cried in my arms and melted into me like I was her soul's only source of warmth fucking destroyed me. How she gave me the gift of her body and fell asleep with her head on my shoulder in the lagoon burned me alive. And when she whispered my name in her sleep as I laid her on the dais and covered her with a blanket? That shattered me. And freed a piece of myself I've kept locked away since I first waded into The River's waters.

But I lied to her. I deceived Elinora's mind, body, heart, and soul. God knows there's no freedom in deception. Then again, I am not a free man.

# Twenty-Two

## Elinora

I peer across the table at Freya and sip my mimosa instead of answering her barrage of questions. Sunday brunch at a café near Central Park is our weekly tradition—one of the few things I look forward to.

She leans in. "Well?"

"I'm thinking."

"You do too much of that." She twists a golden curl around her finger.

"I'm starting to think I don't do *enough*."

"You've done nothing but think since yesterday morning. You never came to our room at The River, didn't return my calls last night, and I'm *still* waiting for details." She reaches across the table and squeezes my hand. "Talk to me, Elle."

"It was . . ." I draw a shaky breath and blink back the moisture filling my eyes. *No more tears.* I'm done crying for something I can't have. "Intense."

"Good intense or bad intense?"

I lower my voice even though we're in the café's private back room. "It was the best sex of my life."

Her hazel eyes widen. "Then what the hell's your problem?"

*I want more. I imagined him as my employee.* "It was a fantasy."

Freya runs a hand over her face. "That's the friggin point."

"He was so . . . I mean, I just . . ." I squeeze my eyes shut. "I wish he was real."

"Sweetie, judging by the way you're walking, you didn't *imagine* him inside you. He *is* real." She waggles her eyebrows. "Was he hot?"

"I don't know."

She blinks. "How can you have fantasy sex and not know if the guy's hot?"

"I couldn't see him, Freya. The room was pitch-black, and he blindfolded me. He called it sensory deprivation."

"Holy fuck. I'm surprised you went for that. Did he tie you up?"

"Briefly, but then he untied me. Based on *feel* alone, his body was gorgeous, but he could've had the face of a donkey for all I knew." *Except his face felt gorgeous too.*

"How the hell did you make that work?"

"He told me he'd be anyone I wanted him to be, so I imagined him as someone else." I gulp the rest of my mimosa. "And now I'm feeling the aftershocks of it."

Her gaze narrows on my face. "Oh. My. God."

"What?"

"You envisioned Clark Kent, didn't you?"

*Damn you and your intuition, Freya.* As all my blood rushes to my cheeks, I curse myself for telling her I'm attracted to Lincoln.

A mile-wide grin overtakes her face. "No wonder you're all fucked up."

I roll my eyes. "You're not helping."

"What's the matter? The Lincoln fantasy lived up to your expectations?" She shimmies her hips in a seated salsa dance. "And now you want *more?*"

I hide my face. There's no sense trying to keep things from her—she'll figure it out, eventually. She always does.

Freya pulls my hands away from my face. "Just so you know, we're not leaving this table until I get every detail. And you know damn well I'll follow you home if you try to evade me."

"I hate you sometimes," I mutter with a smirk.

"It's mutual. Now start talking."

Hours—and far more details than I expected to share—later, Freya and I lounge on my couch eating ice cream. The pint of dulce de leche was doomed the second we opened my freezer.

"You know," she begins, licking some caramel off her finger. "Maybe you could go back to the club and see someone different. Esme has plenty of concierges there. She's bound to have someone who can push you further without reminding you of Lincoln."

"What do you mean?"

"I mean, test your limits, and try something new. Maybe play with someone else—with the lights on—and keep Clark out of the equation. It would be a lot harder to picture Lincoln Kennedy when you're staring into the eyes of someone like Darius."

"I thought he was the head of security?"

"He is, but he often lingers after his shift."

"I don't think I could handle him." Darius is drop-dead gorgeous. But he's also the tallest, most muscular man I've ever seen. "He seems intense."

"From what I've heard, he *is* intense." She grins and nudges me. "You might surprise yourself with what you can handle. It doesn't have to be Darius. I play with several guys, depending on my mood."

"Wait, several guys at the *same time?*"

She snorts. "No, I don't think I could handle group sex. Talk about sensory overload. What I mean is, I'm usually with Rocco if he's not bartending. I'm comfortable with him, and we've become good friends. If he's not available, I play with Gideon, who's also a pleasure concierge. Occasionally, I'll play with another club member, instead of one of the men who works there. Like I said, it depends on my mood. Variety is the spice of life, Elle. You should explore your options. You said the spanking turned you on, right?"

I flush. "Yes."

"Well, push yourself further. Clark Kent's a gentleman, and your stranger reminded you of him. I say you skip the gentleman and take a beast for a spin."

"I dunno," I murmur, chewing my lip.

"Like I said, talk to Esme and see who's available. Maybe you'll like it, or maybe you'll hate it. Who knows? But at least this way, you'll have a face to work with. Maybe then you can separate your feelings better."

I take another spoonful of ice cream and ponder her suggestion.

She grins. "Or . . . you and Clark Kent can experiment with your sizzling chemistry." At my raised brow, she adds, "Why don't you let yourself have a fling, and work him out of your system? That's my vote, anyway."

I hold up a hand. "No. That's not an option. I'm his boss. *And* he's a decade younger than me. It would be inappropriate on so many levels. Besides, what would he possibly want with a bitter old divorcée like me? I've got six carousels' worth of baggage." I shake my head. "Oh wait, now I remember. He'd want my money like all the other men out there. That's worth some fucking luggage, isn't it? Well, guess what? I'm done with that shit. There's no way in hell I'd open myself up to another Charles."

"I was going to say he'd want your bitter old vagina, but if you wanna make this about luggage, that's cool too." She wags her brows. "Judging by how big and strong he looks, I'm sure Clark Kent can pack a suitcase *real* full."

Ice cream shoots out my nose. We both cackle like idiots until tears stream down our faces.

"Where did I ever find you, Freya Thorne?"

She snorts. "Should've been a brothel, am I right?"

I elbow her. "Or a sex club."

"So . . . when are you going back for more?"

# Twenty-Three



I stare into my cup. I'm sure it wasn't intentional on the barista's part, but my latte's foam resembles a skull. I hope it's not an omen for today. More than a little creeped out, I snatch a wooden stirrer and swirl it around until there's no discernable design.

*There. That's better.*

"You afraid someone put arsenic in there or something?"

The male voice at my shoulder makes me jump and nearly drop my cup. I whirl to face my friend Garrett Casey. "Dude. Don't sneak up on people this early in the morning."

"I didn't. I said your name twice." Amusement glints in his golden eyes. "Haven't you ever heard of situational awareness?"

It's seven thirty, and Compass Roasters is already bustling. I was so deep in my thoughts I never heard him address me.

"Yeah," I say lamely, snapping a lid onto my cup. "I guess I'm a little distracted."

"You think?" He chuckles and points to my glasses. "Keep it up, and some asshole will mug you for those. Can't do your job if you can't see, am I right?"

"Truth." I'm not exactly worried about someone jumping me for my designer frames, but clearly, Garrett thinks it could happen. I shake my head. "You really take hypervigilance to a whole new level, don't you?"

"Guilty as charged." He shrugs. "But I have my reasons."

"Why? Did someone steal something from you?"

"You have no fucking idea." A shadow darkens his expression for a fleeting moment. Just as quickly, it gives way to a smirk. "So . . . how's the new job?"

"I don't even know where to start."

He gestures to the door. "Walk with me."

When Garrett Casey tells you to do something, you do it. Unless you're an idiot. Since I have at least three functioning brain cells most days—except for when I fucked my boss on Friday—I follow him outside like the good, obedient guy I am.

I keep pace with him as we head toward our office building. "What's up?"

"She's a tough cookie, but she softens once you get to know her."

"She's . . . something."

Garrett sips his coffee. "I saw her at The River on Friday night."

I stop short and pivot to face him. "What were you doing there? Don't you have rehearsals?" He scored the lead in a Broadway production slated to open in November. How he plans to juggle owning a business and his acting gig, I'll never know. Especially since most Broadway shows are scheduled for eight performances a week. Garrett must be Superman in disguise.

"Esme asked my lady to be the event photographer. She's not comfortable going there alone, so I played bodyguard."

"I didn't see you at the bar."

"Because I don't drink. It's never a good idea to put my ass on a barstool."

"Right. Sorry," I mumble, feeling like a tool for forgetting he's a recovering alcoholic.

"No worries. So, yeah, I roamed around the place, doing my typical lurk in the shadows and observe routine." He studies my face, his eerie eyes burning a hole through my skull. "Anyhoo, I *observed* you two going into the same private lagoon . . ."

He already knows, so it doesn't make sense to lie about what happened. Besides, I don't think it's possible for anyone to be dishonest with Garrett. His presence alone feels like truth serum.

I release a heavy sigh as we resume our walk. "Affirmative."

"I saw your masquerade getup. Did she know it was you?"

"Nope, and I'd like to keep it that way."

"How'd you manage that?" He sips his coffee, then steps out of the way of a woman pushing a stroller.

"Lagoon Seven is one of the ones we use for sensory deprivation floats."

He nods in understanding. "Did anything happen?" When I hesitate, he adds, "Not that it's any of my business, obviously, but I consider Elinora a friend." His eyes lock with mine, and the warning in them is crystal clear. "I'm very protective of the people I care about."

"Everything was consensual."

"I'm not doubting that. You're a good dude." He rubs his jaw. "I just don't want to see her get hurt again."

"I'm not trying to hurt her, Garrett."

"Are you aware of her past? I'm referring to the part about her philandering dick of an ex-husband," he asks as we reach our office building.

"Yeah. She mentioned his multiple affairs."

"Did she give you any other details?"

"Not really."

"Her trauma goes deeper than just being cheated on. It's not my place to elaborate, but you need to keep in mind that Elinora values honesty above all things."

"It's not like I set out to lie to her. I didn't have a choice. My situation's pretty complicated. I, uh, had to leave some details out in the name of self-preservation," I mumble, following him into the building.

We swipe our badges and cross the lobby in silence.

Garrett presses the elevator call button before turning to face me. "A lie of omission is still a lie."

Garrett's words have echoed in my mind all morning. Even the mother of all pep talks I gave myself in the restroom earlier didn't prepare me for the cloak of uneasiness his message—and my guilt—draped over my shoulders. After Friday night, nothing could've prepared me to find Elinora in the breakroom, bent over in front of the coffee station, rummaging through boxes of tea. I still can't believe she doesn't have someone else fetch her drinks. As I stare at the luscious ass on display, the guilt dissipates, and my primal instincts roar to life.

*Mine.*

She's wearing a blue dress and black stilettos that make my heart race. Her long platinum locks fall over her shoulders. I clench my fists at the memory of knotting my fingers in her hair while I slapped her plump, gorgeous ass.

I blink a few times and try to breathe. I can't just gawk in the doorway like a dopey Peeping Tom when I came in here to ask her a question. Funny, I can't seem to remember what that question was.

Or my own name.

I clear my throat.

Too loudly because she looks over her shoulder at me. "Good morning, Mr. Kennedy."

"Good morning."

Elinora straightens and opens a tin of tea. "How was your weekend?"

"Busy. Yours?"

Her breath catches. "Memorable."

The rest of my blood rushes to my cock. I can't breathe or think, so I point to the tea bag she selected and try for small talk. "Myles likes it dirty sometimes. How about you?"

She narrows her eyes. "Excuse me?"

*Fuck.*

"Your chai. Espresso. Uh . . . the chai. You have a chai tea bag. It has espresso when it's dirty." I shake my head to clear it. "Myles likes chai in his espresso. I mean, espresso in his chai. Sometimes. Not always, though. Makes him jittery."

Her lips twitch with the hint of a smirk. "Did *you* have espresso this morning?"

"Yes." The barista added three shots to my latte.

"I can tell."

Not only am I stumbling over my words—far worse than usual—but she's making it known she notices my babbling idiocy. Great.

I try again. "I drink too much."

"There're services to help with that. I can get you the information if you'd like. We have alcohol treatment programs offered as part of our benefits package. I know I mentioned the three-month probation, but I'd be willing to start your coverage sooner if you need help."

"Coffee, I mean. Too much caffeine. But I like whiskey too." I rake a hand through my hair and beg my brain to function. "I only drink whiskey on weekends."

"Are you all right?" She peers up at me.

"No. I'm half left."

Elinora bursts out laughing and clutches my arm, stealing what's left of my sanity. "Thank you. I needed a laugh this morning. And to answer your question, I've never had it dirty. But who knows? I might enjoy it."

*Oh, you enjoyed it, sugar.* I blink a few times and open and close my mouth.

"I'm referring to a dirty chai, Mr. Kennedy."

*Right. Tea.* I shake my head. "You should try it sometime—it's delicious." *Like you.*

She nods. "How's the manuscript going?"

Her question jogs my memory. "That's what I was hoping to discuss when you have time."

"I have time right now," she says, squeezing some honey into her mug.

Watching her stir the honey into her chai, I nearly come when I imagine licking it off her nipples. Then she adds a splash of cream and a sprinkle of cinnamon, and I have to clench my jaw to keep from moaning. I've never had this visceral of a response to a woman. Every little thing she does, stokes the lust burning in my blood.

Elinora eyes me expectantly. "Does now work for you?"

I nod, because if I speak, I'm afraid I'll tell her how much I want her.

"Good. Come to my office."

I trail behind her and recite a few Hail Marys on our way down the hall. I haven't been to confession since I was a teen in Catholic school. Something tells me that even if I read the Bible front to back as penance—and say every prayer known to man—it won't be enough to absolve me of my sins. The more Elinora's heavenly ass sways as she walks, the less I care about redemption.

She gestures to a chair in front of her desk. "Sit."

Her authoritative tone reminds me who is in control of the monarchy right now. While I was king on Friday night, bending her to my will while I kissed, spanked, and fucked her, now we're back in her castle. Making her way to the wheeled leather throne, my sexy queen settles and sips her chai.

I ease into the seat she indicated and remove my glasses to wipe a smudge on my shirt. "I hate not being able to see," I mutter, meeting her expectant gaze.

"Have you ever tried contacts?"

*Shit.* "No, uh, I have dry eyes."

"They make drops for that." She reaches for a pen and pad of paper. "What did you want to discuss?"

"I finished *Stranded at the Pub*, which was fabulous, but now I'm working on *Bound Hearts*. Did the previous editor do any kind of developmental edits?"

"As far as I know, yes. Why do you ask?"

"There are some issues." While I flew through the first manuscript—likely because it was set in Ireland, and I fucking love all things Irish—the second project brought my rhythm to a grinding halt. Part of me wonders if she stuck it in my lineup to test me.

"Like what?" She scrawls something on the page.

"The manuscript isn't ready for line edits."

Elinora cocks her head to the side and sets down her pen. "Oh? How come?"

"It's riddled with plot inconsistencies, unnecessary scenes, among other serious issues."

She sips her chai. "Like what?"

"Well, for starters, it feels like the book was haphazardly converted to a dual point of view. Almost like the hero's POV was thrown in there at the last minute. The heroine is outstanding. She's smart, strong, and confident. Her flaws are relatable and well-developed, and her conflict and motivations make sense. From a man's perspective, she's easy to fall for. On the other hand, I can't imagine *any* woman falling for the hero."

"I'm listening."

"He's obnoxious and far too misogynistic. The book explores BDSM, but the author clearly didn't do her research. It misconstrues the principles of dominance and submission in a way that's not only potentially offensive to the BDSM community, but it borders on dangerous. While the hero is supposed to be dominant, he lacks any likable qualities. He's not an alpha, he's a callous dick. His motivations aren't clear, and there's a disconnect between his actions and how they relate to the conflict. His emotional development feels flat compared to the heroine. I understand it's intended as an enemies-to-lovers romance, but aside from sex, there's no love. The happily ever after, if you can even call it that, doesn't feel earned. If the author insists on having a dual point of view narrative, the hero's perspective needs *serious* work."

She graces me with a smile. "You're brutal."

"No, I'm honest," I say, shaking my head. Guilt pools in my stomach as Garrett's words drift through my mind again. I clear my throat and force my brain to follow suit. "I can make the words pretty with my line edits. But in my opinion, for whatever that's worth, if you publish this developmentally flawed as is, you'd be making a colossal mistake. Forgive me for saying this but given what I know of you and your standards, I'm shocked you offered a book deal for this project."

"I didn't." Elinora squeezes her eyes shut. "I stupidly promoted your predecessor to acquiring editor last year. My gut told me she wasn't capable, but the imprint was in such outrageous demand, my romance acquisition team couldn't handle the volume of submissions. Cindy had been with me a long time, so I trusted her to make quality decisions. We've worked with that author in the past, and her platform is well established, so I allowed this deal to fly under my radar. Clearly, that was a mistake."

I nod in understanding. In my experience, many acquiring editors have the authority to make book deals, which is my absolute dream job. Maybe it's my ego or the appeal of the inherent power in the position, but I'd love nothing more than to be a literary gatekeeper. Most publishing houses have some purchasing hierarchy in place, but Iverson Press is an independent corporation which means Elinora can run it however the fuck she wants.

I smile at the gorgeous mogul in front of me. "The good news is that it's not a lost cause. With a rigorous developmental edit, I believe I can fix the issues."

She perks up. "Do you have suggestions for improvement?"

"God yes. I marked the entire thing up with comments, but I didn't want to overstep my bounds and send it back to the agent without first running it by you. I've worked with the agent before, but I haven't developed a rapport with this author, so the last thing I want to do is piss them—or you—off."

Elinora smiles. "I appreciate you coming to me first, and I'd like to read through your comments and suggestions to get a better understanding of the issues here. Depending on the amount of work involved, we may need to push out the publication date. I hate missing deadlines, but I won't allow a poorly written book to reach my readers."

"The book isn't what I'd call poorly written," I begin, feeling a twinge of compassion for the author. "Her writing style is fluid, and she has a strong voice. The story itself could work, if we make extensive revisions to the hero—and the sex scenes."

Elinora raises a brow. "The sex scenes?"

Hearing the words leave her lips makes my cock twitch. "Yes."

"Please elaborate."

"Well, as you'll see, my comments are specific, but like I said earlier, the author didn't research the BDSM lifestyle enough. Also, the action is very repetitive. It feels like they're having the same sex over and over again. I fought the urge to rewrite an entire scene because it was not only offensive, but boring."

"I've never heard of a sex scene referred to as boring."

"You haven't read this one yet. Honestly, if it were possible to reach through the computer and throw a thesaurus at the author, I'd do it."

She chuckles. "Is that so?"

I meet her gaze. "Put it this way, she used the term 'throbbing cock' six times in a single scene." Her face and neck flush, and I realize I should stop talking. Except my brain pushes words out of my mouth against my better judgment. "I mean, there are plenty of alternatives like pulse, twitch, or even jerk." My runaway jaw keeps accelerating, "As someone who has one, I can attest that it does *much* more than throb."

Her mouth drops open, and my verbal freight train comes to a hard stop. *Fuck.*

For a moment, we just stare across the desk at one another. Heat infuses her features, and it doesn't take a genius to figure out why she's squirming in her leather throne. She definitely remembers our night together. Her lips part on rapid, shaky breaths, and I can see the outline of her hardened nipples through her satin dress. I'd bet her panties are damp now, saturated with the sweet arousal I'm dying to lick from her. Too bad she doesn't know it was really me who touched her. Kissed her. Spanked her. Thrust deep inside her. I shift in my seat at the memory, and it doesn't go unnoticed. Her pupils dilate, and her tongue darts out to lick her lips.

"Thank you for the visual, Mr. Kennedy."

"I didn't mean to be inapprop—"

She clears her throat. "I'll read through your comments and approach the agent accordingly, as it would be better received coming from me."

"I'll forward you the manuscript with my edits when I get back to my desk." I rake a hand through my hair. "Listen, I'm not trying to ruffle anyone's feathers, and I'm sorry if I'm overstepping my bounds. I just want to make sure we—uh—*you* publish the best possible book. I'd hate to anger the BDSM community or tarnish Iverson Melt's reputation. Especially when the issues are easily remedied. I'm happy to communicate with the author directly if she requests clarification. Also, we shouldn't need to push out the publication date, as I'm confident I can get the work done before your deadline."

"Never apologize for having my company's best interests at heart." Her gaze burns into me. "That is something I value deeply in an employee. I love the romance genre, which is why I dedicate so much of my resources to Iverson Melt. Unfortunately, my schedule doesn't allow me to give each manuscript the attention I'd like, so it's essential to maintain a quality staff. You surprise me every day, Mr. Kennedy. You've already impressed me with your tenacity, and now you're guarding the company's assets?"

"I'm just doing my job, Ms. Iverson."

"You're doing a damn good job." She rewards me with a toe-curling smile. "If your performance continues on this trajectory, you'll make that position permanent in no time."

Her praise makes me feel like I've won a gold medal. She trusts me and my editorial opinion enough to hear what I have to say, which is more than anyone's ever given me.

Sister Fitzgibbons never wanted my side of the story when Chris Boutros told her I'd vandalized the church. In actuality, I was in the wrong place at the wrong time, but she took the situation at face value. He was the one who spray-painted the chapel and carved dirty words into the pews one drunken Saturday night. But I was expelled for the damage he caused. I can still hear her voice after all these years. *Why should anyone listen to you? You're a disgrace. You'll never amount to anything, Kennedy.* Father DeAngelis was just as bad because he took her word as gospel. *You're an embarrassment to our parish and your family.*

I beat back the ghosts of my past and meet Elinora's gaze. "Thank you for giving me a chance."

"Thank you for covering my ass—I mean, my back."

I stifle a groan, thinking about how well my palm covered her ass on Friday. "The pleasure's all mine, Ms. Iverson."

# Twenty-Four

## Elinora

Lincoln's throat moves on a swallow. Then he smiles, and my inner muscles clench. If he had any idea I screamed *his* name while having sex with a stranger, I'd die.

I knew it would be difficult to face him after conjuring his image Friday night, but I didn't expect it to be *this* difficult. Here I'd thought indulging myself in the fantasy could work him out of my system. Nope. Now I want him even more.

He's wearing a crisp white dress shirt that conforms to the muscles of his shoulders and arms. His marine blue tie matches his eyes. *God, those eyes.* I'd give anything to stare into them while he makes love to me. I slide my hands beneath my thighs to keep from grabbing his silk tie and pulling him across my desk.

Rising, he points over his shoulder. "I'm going to head back to my cubicle now." Then, he smiles again, and I want to fall at his feet.

With his glossy black hair, oceanic eyes, and perfect teeth, my young editor is a masterpiece.

"Mm-hmm." My gaze lingers on his ass as he leaves the room, and I make a mental note to stash some spare panties in my office.

In one encounter, he transformed from endearingly nervous and stumbling to pure confidence. Intelligence and self-assuredness are huge turn-ons for me, but Lincoln discussing his work was the sexiest thing I've ever witnessed. There's no question he knows his shit. He'd already impressed me with the line edits he'd done for *Stranded at the Pub*. Hearing him hash out a book's developmental issues was intellectual foreplay. He claims his strength is in line editing, but I disagree. This man is the total package. Not only is he looking after my company's reputation, but he has my best interests at heart. The fact that, despite his ego and abilities, he came to me first, earns him my professional respect.

I force a few calming breaths and sip my chai. My email chimes, drawing my attention to the computer. Lincoln's name in my inbox makes my heart race.

> Ms. Iverson,
>
> Attached, please find my annotated manuscript for *Bound Hearts*. I've made extensive edits and suggestions for revision. If you need clarification, please let me know.
>
> Again, I apologize for overstepping my bounds, but there was no way I could let these developmental issues slide. Thank you for your willingness to hear me out, and I appreciate any and all feedback you have.
>
> Best,
> Lincoln

I download the attachment while the message behind his words echoes in my head. *Thank you for hearing and trusting me.* I can't imagine anyone *not* listening to this young man. I hardly trust a soul, yet I trust his assessment, and I haven't even read his notations.

I open the document and smile at his first comment, which takes place midway through the third paragraph and references a block of text he'd highlighted.

> I'd consider making this your book's opening line instead. "Don't tell me I left the door unlocked again." has far more impact than, "I parked my car in the employee garage at work." Think about the questions in your readers' minds. Does Sara have a habit of not locking her door? Which door does she mean? Does she live in a dangerous neighborhood? What's making her question herself? These are the things that make your reader

look for answers. Not someone parking in a garage. Public transportation notwithstanding, everyone parks. We all go to work. I want to know what's got her hackles raised about not locking the door. Hook me and pull me in. You've already got the words, just move them around. Also, the vivid description of the parking garage is excellent. I can almost hear the water dripping from the rafters and the jingling of her keys. Great job.

I'm already in love with his editing style, and we're only talking about doors, keys, and parking garages. How the hell am I going to handle the throbbing cocks and sex scenes he referenced?

I've been waiting all day for this.

After stripping out of my work clothes, I adjust my reading light and slide between layers of luxe Egyptian cotton. Goose bumps bloom with the brush of the cool fabric against my bare skin. Then again, I've had goose bumps for hours.

I spent the afternoon reading Lincoln's comments on the *Bound Hearts* manuscript. Moments from masturbating at my desk, I forced myself to close the document before the first sex scene. I rushed to the ladies' room to splash cold water on my face because I was so turned on, I could barely breathe. I'm only ninety pages in, but I know exactly how this story ends. With his ocean-blue eye for detail, a permanent position at Iverson Press is in Lincoln Kennedy's future.

His edits are intricate, yet they don't interfere with the author's voice. He's equal parts blunt and thoughtful with his comments, and every developmental suggestion he's made is fabulous. Since the birth of my company, I've employed dozens of editors. None have compared to this young man.

After he politely walked me to my car, and I once again suppressed the urge to grab his tie and yank him into my back seat, I squirmed the entire ride home. Now, I'm finally in my bedroom, and I can't think of a better way to spend my Monday night than lounging naked in my bed with my laptop and a glass of wine.

I open the document and resume reading. My pulse quickens when I spot a red mark that signifies Lincoln's presence. This particular edit is a sentence rewrite where he'd changed, *"I can feel how soft her cheeks are while we frantically kiss."* to *"I cup her warm, soft cheeks and seize her lips."*

I want someone to kiss me like that. Wait, someone did. My sexy stranger at The River. My eyelids flutter closed, and I lose myself in the memory. *How would it feel to kiss Lincoln?* The immediate flood of heat between my thighs makes me shift, causing the sheet to brush against my clit. I gasp and tug my laptop closer, forcing my attention to his next comment.

Throughout the manuscript, you've referred to Dan as an alpha. As we approach the sex scene, I'm getting some whiplash from his behavior. One moment you have him in caveman mode, and a split second later, he's aloof and disinterested. If Dan is truly an alpha, now is the time to show it. They've been dancing around the act of sex for three chapters. They're holed up in a cabin. The snow isn't letting up anytime soon. Sara's pushing him to his limits by threatening to leave and wander off in the blizzard alone. Alphas don't like their women in danger. Their instinct is to protect and claim. This isn't the occasion for tender lovemaking—it's claiming time.

You made a point of mentioning the handcuffs tucked in his police uniform. Why doesn't he use them? What better way to keep her safe than cuff her to the bed? This is Dan and Sara's first time, so it sets up the reader's expectations for the rest of the book. The way this scene's written, I had no indication Dan was a dominant. You don't introduce BDSM stuff until the second sex scene. By the time we get there, the flogger is unexpected and not in a pleasant way. I literally scrolled back to see if I'd missed something. Nothing here even hints at the lifestyle. If Dan is truly a dominant, that doesn't come and go. He's anxious, frustrated, and desperate to keep Sara safe. He craves her submission on every level. If you're going down the BDSM road, you need to pave the way now.

Think about what we know of Sara. She's feisty as hell but craves strength and direction. She wants Dan to assert his dominance—she's practically begging for it. Sara doesn't want to make love—she wants Dan to fuck her. She comes right out and says it. Give the woman what she needs!

There's a lot you can do to add heat here. Think of the anticipation you can infuse if he cuffs her wrists to the headboard. Maybe he spreads her legs apart before using the belt of her robe to secure them to the bedposts? The vulnerability in her forced submission would make the intimate act more intense. What if he teases her? Uses his tongue to bring her to the brink again and again until she's begging for release? Maybe he spanks her? These are just suggestions—it's totally your call, but somehow, you need to link their first time to the intensity of the future sexual encounters. Don't leave us in left field, use this scene to set the stage. This way, when the flogger and cat-of-nine-tails come knocking, we've got a door to come through.

I set my laptop aside and gulp my wine, but the flush on my skin has nothing to do with alcohol. Lincoln's words have me . . . well, hot. And wet. *Really wet,* I discover, as my fingertips glide through my arousal.

These kinds of acts are in my masked stranger's wheelhouse, not Lincoln's. Everything I know of the nerdy hunk, with his glasses and sexy dimples—and gentlemanly demeanor—is at odds with the image his written words have seared into my head. The man I'm imagining could force a woman into submission with a single word.

What if my new editor *does* have a kinky side? I moan aloud at the thought of Lincoln slapping my ass. What would it be like if *he* cuffed me to a bed, spread my legs wide, and buried his face between my thighs? What if he could make me feel the way L—Elliot—did? I picture Lincoln's face and recall my pleasure concierge's touch while rubbing slow circles on my clit. But it's not enough.

While I only just discovered this fact on Friday, I crave a man's dominance. I need him to claim me, mark me, fuck me. A flare of lust makes me snatch the vibrator from my nightstand. I seldom use it, but the wildfire surging in my blood demands a long, hard orgasm. The kind I can't achieve with my fingers alone.

Lying on my back with my eyes closed, I allow my legs to fall open and slide the toy into my pussy. While my strokes feel amazing, they aren't enough. I press the button on the end and gasp as vibrations pulse through me. I thrust it harder and faster, cranking up the intensity. It's still not enough to satisfy the empty ache that consumes me.

Desperate for my release, I roll to my stomach and pull my knees beneath me. Ass in the air, I pleasure myself with the toy the way I want Lincoln to fuck me—hard and fast—my legs spread wide while he stakes his claim. Moans and gasps spill from my lips, the cries bleeding into the mattress. My inner muscles quiver and finally send me flying. As I climax on a muffled wail, and my knees give out, I know damn well reviewing Lincoln's work will be a bedroom-only endeavor.

# Twenty-Five

## Lincoln

I press my phone closer to my ear. Compass Roasters is packed, and I can't make out what my sister is saying over the noise. "Sorry, Reag. Can you repeat that?"

"Where are you, and why's it so loud?"

"I went out for lunch today and then made a pit stop at that coffee shop I told you about. They're super busy."

"You said your job has a fancy coffeemaker though."

"We do, but sometimes it tastes better when someone else makes it." I had other reasons for stopping here, but I'm not about to share them with her.

"I don't like coffee."

I chuckle. "They have other drinks like cocoa and tea. Also, this place makes the world's best cupcakes."

"Can you bring me one on Sunday?"

It's only Tuesday, but I already know this weekend isn't going to work out. I squeeze my eyes shut. "I'm sorry, Reag, but I don't think I can make the trip up this week."

"Why not?"

"I have a lot of work I need to catch up on."

"You said that last week," she whines.

"I know, and I'm sorry for disappointing you again." I run a hand over my face, adjusting the glasses that are suddenly squeezing my brain. "It's really important that I impress my new boss. She only hired me as temporary, and I want to make sure she changes her mind and keeps me."

She sniffs, and my heart cracks down the center. "Why wouldn't she want to keep you? You're the best."

Not according to Sister Fitzgibbons. Or the cop who arrested me for a crime I didn't commit. Or the school's lawyer who made my parents pay out the ass for damage I didn't do.

I'm about to correct her, but I don't have the heart to tell her not everyone sees me as the hero she believes I am. "Thanks, Reag. I love you."

"Love you too." She sighs. "Maybe since you can't come visit me, Mom and I can come to you? Then you can work while we're there."

"We'll see," I placate her, even though her idea is out of the question. My family has never stepped foot inside my pitifully small studio apartment, so they don't know I sleep on a lumpy twin mattress without a bedframe. They've never seen my barren cabinets or the bathroom that's not much bigger than an airplane lavatory. I'd rather keep them in the dark than let them discover my "big city life" is pretty fucking pathetic. "Listen, I've gotta run. It's my turn to order. Love you."

"Love you too. Bye, Linky."

Forcing a deep breath, I knock on the door to Elinora's office.

"Come in."

I clear my throat. "Hi, Ms. Iverson. You, uh, wanted to see me after lunch?"

"Yes. Have a seat."

I nod and settle across from her. "Is everything all right?"

"Why wouldn't it be?"

I blink, unsure of how to answer. Instead, I place the chai on her desk. "This is for you."

Her eyes widen. "Oh?"

"You said you'd be open to trying it dirty, so I grabbed you. I mean, *it.*

*For* you. I grabbed *it* for *you*. When I got mine." I shake my head to force the language section of my brain to cooperate. "It's a dirty chai."

Elinora's smile makes my cock twitch. "Thank you for the kind gesture, Lincoln."

"You're welcome."

Her eyelids flutter closed as she takes a long, slow sip. "Wow."

"What do you think?"

She meets my gaze. "I think I like it dirty."

"Me too," I murmur, allowing my eyes to linger on her lips as she licks foam from them. "But only when it's hot."

A flush creeps over her cheeks. "Is that so?"

"Yeah, cold espresso's not my thing."

"I also prefer it hot."

*You're goddamn right, you do.* Despite how hard I try to stop them, the corners of my lips twitch into a smirk. Every time I'm alone with her, the air between us crackles. I can't tear my eyes from the heat in her gaze. *She truly wants me.* My smirk widens to a smile.

Elinora arches a brow. "Did I miss the punchline?"

"No, I'm pretty sure—"

Freya marches into the office. "Ugh. I'm sorry, Elle, but the world's biggest asshole is on the phone for you."

Elinora stiffens. "Tell him I'm in a meeting."

"Tried that. He's called six times in a row."

"What does he want?"

"He said he needs to tell you something."

"Take a message," Elinora snaps.

Freya sighs. "Tried that too. He said it's for your ears only."

Elinora squeezes her eyes shut. "Patch him through."

Freya nods and heads back to her desk.

"I'll come back later," I say, rising.

She points to the chair. "Sit. I have no intention of making this a lengthy conversation."

I sit back down like a good, obedient boy and focus on my hands. She's fucking sexy in a position of dominance. I'll submit to her here, but damn . . . I'd love to have her in my castle again.

The phone on her desk rings.

She snatches it. "What do you want, Charles? You'd better have a damn good reason for interrupting a meeting with one of my editors."

I toy with the edge of my sleeve and wonder if the *world's biggest asshole* is her ex-husband or some other douchebag.

"What news?" Elinora's glacial tone makes me glance up at her. She tightens her grip on the phone. "*Excuse me?*" The words leave her lips in a pained whisper. As she listens, a single tear rolls down her cheek. Then another. "Congratulations." She hangs up the phone.

I wait in silence as more tears slide from beneath her lashes. When her shoulders shake with her attempt to breathe, I reach across the desk and touch her hand. "Are you all right, Ms. Iverson?"

With rivers running down her cheeks, eyes that look like melting ice meet mine. "I'm fine." She quickly wipes her tears away like she's pretending I don't see them.

"Is there anything I can do?"

"Can you erase time?"

"No, but if you need someone who will listen, I'm happy to lend my time."

"Do you have an extra fifteen years?" she asks, wiping her cheeks.

*Ah, ex-husband it is.* I glance at my watch. It's a little after two. My rescheduled dinner with my friend and client, Gwen, is at seven. "I've got five hours until I need to be somewhere. I'm all yours until then."

"Thank you, but I'm fine. It's nothing I didn't expect. I shouldn't have allowed him to upset me and interrupt our meeting."

"Tell me." The command slips out before I can stop it. Instead of brushing me off again, her posture softens.

"My ex-husband eloped with his latest mistress." She sniffs and blots her eyes with a tissue. "She's pregnant, and he found it necessary to make that announcement to me." While the slump of her shoulders and averted gaze tells me she's embarrassed, the words spill from her lips as easily as if I demanded she tell me the weather.

"That's low," I mutter. "Did he think you'd care?"

She squeezes her eyes shut and shrugs.

"Look at me." Her gaze snaps to mine, and—God help me—even though she's crying, her submission turns me on. What kind of person does that make me? *An asshole.* I shift in my seat. "Why did he call to tell you that?"

Elinora blinks back tears and sucks in a shallow breath. "He wanted to make sure I knew our fertility issues had nothing to do with his age."

"How old is he?"

"He'll be fifty in September." She wipes her face. "Anyway, our childless state was my fault. I'm the broken one—not him."

"You are *not* broken."

"Yes, well, it solidifies the fact that my body is defective." She sighs. "I didn't mean to get upset, but that was just the gut punch I needed today."

"Nothing about you is defective. Your ex is a fucking dick."

She nods. "He's the world's biggest dick." After a moment, she smirks. "And I definitely mean *is* not has."

I chuckle at her thinly veiled insult. "Well played."

"Sadly, Lincoln, I was the one who was well played."

"It's clear he was a shitty husband, so it stands to reason he'd be an even shittier father. You're better off without him."

"I know." She sniffs and wipes her nose. "But it still really hurts."

"I'm sure it does, and I'm sorry he treated you that way. His actions reflect him. He's the defective one."

"Having a child is all I've ever wanted, but it's been the one gift consistently out of my reach. It's really hard to accept that the vision I had for my life, my future, was a fucking unattainable dream." She blots her eyes again. "And now, the person who was supposed to be my life partner is realizing that dream with someone else."

"I'm so sorry." At this moment, I'd give anything to haul her against my chest and make her pain disappear. Kick her ex-husband's ass and make him apologize for hurting her. Instead, I keep my hands to myself. It's not my place. She's my boss—not my girlfriend.

"It's fine. Thank you for listening." With a deep breath, she tugs on the edge of her jacket and sits up straighter, then clears her throat. "Anyway, the reason I wanted to see you was to let you know I finished reading through your mark-up of *Bound Hearts*."

"That was quick."

"I'm a fast reader." She cocks her head to the side. "I thought during your interview you told me you don't have any experience editing romance?" Now that she's talking about her passion, a faint smile replaces her tears.

"I don't."

She raises a brow. "Are you sure about that?"

"One hundred percent. I'm happy to give you a list of titles I worked on at Cooper Press."

Elinora waves me off. "No, that's unnecessary. I believe you."

I straighten in my seat. "How did I do? Were you pleased with my work? Did I, uh, *it* meet your standards?"

"No."

My stomach drops, and I rub my sweaty palms on my pants. "I can take another—"

"You *exceeded* my standards and then some. I forwarded the manuscript to the agent this morning. She called me after lunch and wanted to know more about my brilliant new editor."

"Really?" I couldn't hold back my grin if I tried. "That's awesome. Thank you so much."

She smiles. "It gets better. The author wants to schedule a call with you for tomorrow."

"Was she all right with my recommendations?"

"According to her agent, she loves them but has some questions for you. What time should I tell her you're available?"

"Anytime works for me." I rake a hand through my hair. "To be honest, I thought you were about to tell me I did a shitty job."

"Far from it. You're a gifted editor, Lincoln."

My grin stretches from ear to ear. "Thank you, Ms. Iverson. You made my day."

"Thank *you* for being part of my team." She holds up her chai and gives me a warm smile. "You made my day too."

# Twenty-Six

## Lincoln

The breakroom is unusually quiet today, but that's fine with me. I need some silence to prepare for my call with the author of *Bound Hearts*. I'm not sure why I'm so nervous—I've worked with dozens of authors. Then again, this is my first romance author. I wonder if she knows I'm a dude. I imagine I'm among the minority there.

Brad Watson, a mystery and suspense editor who works upstairs, enters the room with a can of soda and some chips. He leans against the counter, and I quickly discover he's one of those people who crinkles the fucking bag incessantly. Annoyed that he's disturbing my solitude, I give him the side eye.

"Oh, sorry." He smears his greasy fingers on his dress pants. "How do you like it here?"

"So far, so good."

"Any run-ins with the matriarch?"

"Huh?"

Brad rolls his beady little eyes. "Our boss."

"What about her?" I ask, sipping my water.

"Have you had any problems with her?"

"Nope." I cock my head to the side. "Do *you* have a problem with her?"

He sneers. "I hate that bitch."

"Sorry you feel that way." At this point, I'm done with the conversation and the stupid greasy fuck. Deciding to finish my lunch at my desk, I stand.

"Back to work already?"

"Books don't edit themselves, bro."

"Which genre did she assign you?"

I stiffen my spine. "Romance."

The asshole has the balls to laugh in my face. "That shows how much she knows. Who the fuck replaces Cindy with someone like you?"

"Are you insinuating I don't know my shit?"

"Nah, man. I mean, Iverson's clueless. Her ex-husband cheated on her. I'd say the Ice Queen's views on love are pretty fucked. Then the stupid bitch sticks a dude in romance?"

"First of all, Ms. Iverson's love life is none of your business. As for your opinion of me, I can assure you I'm more than qualified to edit romance." Clenching my fists, I take a step closer to him. "Call her a bitch one more time, and we're gonna have a problem."

He raises a brow. "You're seriously defending her?"

"Yeah, as a matter of fact, I am."

"Listen, man, I've worked here four years. All she does is bitch and nag at people until they quit. She put too much on Cindy's shoulders and now she's gone. Ted from mystery and suspense couldn't handle the pressure either."

"I work well under pressure."

Brad narrows his eyes on me. "Don't think you're immune to her wrath just because you're friends with Myles."

"Myles has nothing to do with my job performance."

"You're new. Trust me, once the honeymoon phase is over, you'll get a taste of her shit. The first time you fuck up, she'll be on your ass. There is no satisfying her."

*I satisfied her just fine.* Since I can't tell him that, I snatch another bottle of water from the fridge.

The stupid fuck keeps talking, "I mean, yeah, she's hot—if frigid's your thing." He chugs his soda. "Personally, the ice queen bit doesn't do it for me. I don't care how nice her tits are, Elinora Iverson is so cold, her pussy could freeze a man's dick right off."

Before I realize what I'm doing, I grab the fucker by the throat and slam him up against the wall, pinning him in place. "Listen and listen well, be-cause I'm only gonna say this once," I snarl, my nose inches from his. "That woman is your boss. This is her castle. If you can't handle the way she runs it, then get the fuck out." I tighten my grip and lift his body off the floor. "If I *ever* hear you disrespect her—or any other woman in this office—like that again, I'll rearrange your face. Got it?"

"Yeah," he grunts.

"I'm not fucking around. You run your mouth again, and you're gonna eat my fist. Are we clear?" When he doesn't respond, I grip his face. "I asked you a question."

"Yes."

"Yes, what?"

"Yes, we're clear."

"Good." I release him and take a step back, then fix my crooked glasses. "Now get the fuck out of here."

Brad staggers forward, gasping and wheezing. I turn and nearly collide with Elinora in the doorway. I don't know how long she was standing there, but her red face and watery eyes tell me she heard everything he said.

"Hello, Mr. Watson. I didn't realize you had such a high opinion of me."

Brad's eyes widen, and all the color drains from his face. "Ms. Iverson, I—"

"Spare me the explanation," she snaps, fire flashing in her gaze. "Your employment with Iverson Press is terminated. Effective immediately."

"What?" Brad knots his fingers in his hair. "You can't fire me."

"It's my business, I can do whatever the hell I want. Grab your things and get out." She points to the door. "Leave in the next five minutes, or I'll have you removed from the premises."

Brad shoots me a death glare before marching from the breakroom. Once he's out of earshot, Elinora sags against the doorframe.

"I'm sorry he said those things about you."

She peers up at me, her tears spilling over for the second time in as many days. "Thank you for defending me."

"Of course."

"No one has ever stuck up for me like that."

"Misogyny doesn't sit well with me, Ms. Iverson. Nor does blatant disrespect. Please don't cry over the bullshit he spewed. He's a dumb fuck."

A weak smile twitches her lips. "The dumbest of fucks."

I touch her shoulder. "Do you want tea or something?"

"No, thank you." She wipes her eyes. "If you want to take his job instead of the position with Iverson Melt, I'm OK with you transitioning to mystery and suspense. I know you mentioned that's your preferred genre."

"I mean, it is, but to be honest, I'm enjoying romance. I'd like to stay where I'm at, if that's all right?"

"Of course. Do you know any quality mystery and suspense editors who need a job?"

The only person from Cooper Press I'd feel comfortable referring is also a romance editor. Tess McPherson is a sweet southern belle who moonlights as a Broadway actress. She'll be performing alongside Garrett in *Prodigy*, the controversial musical theater production opening in November. However, she only works part-time at Cooper, so I'm not sure if her availability would be open enough for Iverson Press. Especially once the show opens.

"No, but I'm happy to take on a few of his manuscripts until you find someone." What I'd *really* like is to beat the shit out of the guy—not do his fucking work—but I don't have time to deal with assault charges. I force a smile even though my heartbeat is racing, and I'm itching for a fight. I don't want her to pick up on those vibes. "Whatever you need from me, just ask and I'll make it happen."

# Twenty-Seven

## Elinora

He can't be serious.

I stare at Lincoln in disbelief. "You're volunteering to take on *more* work?"

"This," he gestures to the room behind us, "is my dream job. I may be a rarity, but I truly love what I do. Besides, if it takes some pressure off you, I'm happy to help. I can easily shoulder a few more manuscripts."

This perfect, beautiful man not only defended me, but now he's trying to make my life easier? It doesn't seem possible.

"Lincoln Kennedy, consider this my offer of permanent employment."

His eyes widen. "I thought there was a three-month probationary period?"

"This," I begin, mimicking his all-encompassing gesture from moments ago, "is my castle. I can fill it with whomever I want, in whatever timeframe I choose. Your work ethic and character speak for themselves. Not to mention the superb quality of your work. I've been doing this a long time, so I know talent when I see it. I'd be a fool not to keep you." I smile and touch his arm. "*And* you've earned yourself a raise."

Lincoln's mouth drops open. He quickly regains control and shakes his head. "While I more than appreciate your gesture, Ms. Iverson, I don't think I deserve a raise."

"Well, *I* think you do." In all my years running this company, I have never had an employee turn down a pay increase. Is he just being humble, or does he truly believe he doesn't deserve it? "And I mean that, Lincoln."

As his expression morphs into one of hope—and pride—I know I made the right decision. In the brief time he's worked for me, this man has lifted me up, defended me, and warmed me. Not to mention, his work ethic is unparalleled. The least I could do was show my appreciation. I flash him a wink. "My castle, remember?"

Lincoln's smile could melt the polar ice caps. "Thank you."

"My pleasure." I touch his arm once more. "Thank you again for sticking up for me."

"Always." His gaze burns into me, breaking what remains of my defenses.

I want to throw my arms around his neck and kiss him, but I nod instead. "Don't be late for your call."

He perks up. "Right. I'll fill you in when I'm finished."

After a good cry in my office over asshole Brad's declaration about my frosty vagina, I head for the ladies' room to clean the mascara from beneath my eyes. I quickly reapply and fix my hair before heading out into the romance suite.

Lincoln is on the phone at his desk. His call with the author of *Bound Hearts* has been going on for nearly two hours. I approach him from behind, silently admiring the confidence in his speech and posture.

He chuckles. "No, that's a common misconception about safe words."

Enticed by the opportunity to hear *his* take on the issue, I linger a few more moments.

"Safe words are an essential means of communication during sex." He sips his water, then pours a little into the plant on his desk—no doubt a gift from Myles—before picking off a dead leaf. He rolls it between his fingers as he speaks. "Not just BDSM stuff, no. They can apply to *any* sex."

Heat floods my lower belly, pooling at my core. The spare panties I tucked in my briefcase will certainly come in handy this afternoon.

"Think about it. Good sex requires open lines of communication. Most partners want the experience to be mutually pleasurable, right?" He drops the leaf into the trashcan beneath his desk. "Well, since people aren't mind readers, we need to check in periodically. With BDSM, this is especially important. When you wrote the second sex scene for Dan and Sara, you made it solely about his pleasure. Not cool. Yes, he's a dominant, but it doesn't work like that. Not only do most dominants want to please their subs, they also get off on *giving* pleasure. It's not some 'take-what-I-give-you-and-I-don't-care-if-you-like-it' arrangement. The balance between dominance and submission is delicate and volatile. If proper techniques and good communication are lacking, the scale can quickly tip into the red zone. During the scene, Dan never once asks Sara how she's doing, which is dangerous."

He gives the author an emphatic nod she can't see. "Yes, literally dangerous. Since Dan has her bound so tightly, he needs to keep her circulation in mind. An hour is not realistic, because lack of blood flow can cause permanent injury. A true dominant cares about their submissive. Their pleasure, safety, *and* emotional wellbeing. While some techniques may be heavier handed than others . . . pun intended." He laughs again, and the deep rumble tickles my spine. "Yeah, I know. I couldn't help myself. Anyway, regarding the pain side of pleasure, a dominant's goal is not to harm the other person. Physically *or* emotionally."

As I listen to Lincoln's conversation, an awareness bubbles in my veins. He's got firsthand experience with the concepts of dominance and submission. Images of him pinning Brad to the wall flash through my mind. The authoritative tone he used yesterday when he forced me to confess the reason behind my tears. The way my body and mind have begun to submit to him without question.

*Lincoln is a dominant.*

The thought zings through my brain—which is currently hardwired to my pussy—and my body's reaction is instantaneous. I'm a mess of tingles as every nerve ending between my legs flares to life.

He and Elliot are not that different after all.

Lincoln runs a hand through his hair, and I clench my fists to keep my fingers from following suit. "Exactly. That's where the safe words come in. Some people only have one. In that case, when a submissive says the agreed upon word, all activity must cease. Other techniques involve the use of multiple words, usually in a scale."

My nipples harden at his confident tone, and I ghost closer.

"Picture a stop light. That's a pretty universal example because even children know that green means go, yellow means slow down, and red means stop. In fact, plenty of couples use those exact words. If that's not Sara's style, maybe she and Dan can agree to words that suit them better." He sips his water and twists into a stretch.

I cover my mouth to stifle a moan at witnessing the bunch and flex of his shoulders. Even hidden beneath a dress shirt, his body is a thing of beauty.

"OK, here's an example using temperature. Let's say a couple is having sex. For the purposes of keeping it relevant to your book, we'll make it a heterosexual couple with the male partner in a position of dominance. Instead of green, maybe they use 'warm.' Yellow can be 'cool,' and she can say 'ice' when she wants him to freeze or stop. Does that make sense? And if things are going *really* well, and she wants him to crank up the intensity . . ." He takes another sip of water.

My inner muscles clench in anticipation of his next words. The auditory foreplay is nearly as arousing as reading his comments in the manuscript.

"If Sara wants *more*, she'll say 'fire.'"

*Oh my God, he's been to The River.*

"Not only does Dan need to pay attention to visual cues, but he can't just wait for Sara to blurt out a safe word. The lines of communication must be open. By that, I mean, he needs to check in with her."

*Like Elliot did with me.*

He nods. "Exactly. Or he can say something like, 'How's the water?'"

My heart skids to a stop. Those exact words, uttered in that same low tone, have haunted me all week. Unable to breathe, I slowly back away and slip into my office.

I sag against the closed door and force my brain to function.

*It's him.* It has to be—it's *his* fucking voice. Lincoln and Elliot are the same person. That's why Elliot blindfolded me and kept his voice at a whisper. That's why he encouraged me to say Lincoln's name. Why I felt so comfortable with him. Why his face felt familiar to my touch.

"I fucked my employee." I wheeze, clutching my chest before sinking into my desk chair and rubbing my temples.

No. It can't be possible. There has to be an explanation. *Think, Elinora. Think.*

Maybe they're brothers—or cousins. Yeah, that's it. Family. This is a crazy coincidence. My decade-younger employee didn't *actually* spank and fuck me last weekend—it was only a fantasy. Since I so desperately wanted it to be Lincoln in that lagoon, I'm hung up on the reverie. My mind is still blurring the boundaries of reality.

I chug some water and try to stop my runaway fantasy train in its tracks, but my brain won't be derailed.

*What if it's really him?*

Desperate for answers, I lurch to my feet and head for Lincoln's cubicle but stop short when I find Myles dangling an open bag of Skittles in front of his face. Lincoln must have just finished his call during my mini freakout. I duck behind a nearby cubicle and discreetly watch them.

"What's this?" Myles demands, propping his other hand on a hip.

"Uh, Skittles . . ."

"I know it's Skittles. I'm talking about what's in the bag."

"My answer's still Skittles." Lincoln grins. "You're only just discovering them? I put the bag there this morning."

"I've been at a meeting." Myles drops the candy onto Lincoln's desk. "I don't want your leftovers."

"My leftovers?"

"Lincoln Elliot Kennedy, if you think I don't know you ate everything but the green ones, you forget that I'm on to your games."

*Elliot? Holy fuck. It's him.* The air inside my lungs crystallizes, and I stagger backward, unable to rip my gaze from the pair of men.

Lincoln pats Myles on the shoulder. "Get your facts straight—I saved you the yellows too."

Myles flicks the side of Lincoln's cheek. "Minor details, Linc."

"It's like I always say . . ." Stretching his arms over his head, Lincoln leans back in his seat and grins. "The devil's in the details."

*Oh.*

*My.*

*God.*

Myles snorts. "You gonna dig through those details to find him, Mr. Bigshot Editor?"

"Nope. Not worried about him right now."

*The devil's in the details, angel. But we don't need to worry about him right now.* My stranger's voice echoes in my head as shock waves reverberate to my soul.

*It's him.*

It was Lincoln all along.

# Twenty-Eight

### Lincoln

The bar in the Aqua Suite is packed for a Wednesday night. Since Rocco is out sick, my buddy Ravi Kalpana jumped in to help mix drinks until Gideon arrives at eight. Ravi is The River's hospitality manager. While he's hilarious and cool as shit, he's not an experienced bartender, so his presence is more of a hindrance than a help.

I decide to switch things up to make my life easier after my third time telling him how to make a cosmopolitan. "Ravi, how about you take care of shots and beer? I'll focus on wine and mixed drinks. That work for you?"

"I'm game. I haven't been in my office to check my messages. Do you know when Gideon's coming?"

I glance at my watch. "Class ended at seven. He should be here any minute."

Gideon Ford is the brains of our bunch. He's currently in the process of getting his MBA. Esme is flexible with his schedule, as she's a firm believer that school comes first—even when it's not convenient.

"Good. I just did the supply order for Oasis, and now I'm starving." Ravi pours some whiskey for himself and quickly knocks it back.

I point to his shot glass. "Liquid dinner?"

"Nah, I'm gonna eat as soon as Gideon gets here to relieve me. Leo is supposed to be here in an hour, so we should be good for the rest of the night. Sorry I'm such a shitty bartender. Good thing I can cook, right?"

What Ravi lacks in bartending skills, he makes up for with his cooking. He loves to feed people. Since we share a passion for the culinary arts, we often trade recipes like a pair of housewives. Last year, when I was sick with the flu, he stopped by every day to drop off his version of chicken soup. Swear to God, it healed me. I'm truly lucky to have him as my friend.

My stomach growls. "Did you bring anything for me?"

"Dude, you should've texted me back earlier. I would've brought more."

"Sorry, I meant to respond, but I was tied up on a call at my other job."

"No worries. Oh, I forgot to tell you." He flashes an enormous grin. "I nailed your grandmother's Irish soda bread recipe the other day."

Ravi is the only man I know who loves Irish cuisine as much as I do.

"Did you get the right butter?" I ask.

"Actually, I couldn't find Irish butter, so I improvised and tried it with ghee. Bro, it was fucking phenomenal."

"What's up, boys?" Gideon calls as he enters the bar area.

"Oh, thank fuck." Ravi claps him on the shoulder. "We're drowning tonight."

"Big daddy's here to save the day." He hands me a clipboard. "Esme told me to have you do the liquor order once shit's under control here."

Since Ravi doesn't spend much time behind the bar, Esme usually tasks me with the booze order because I know what we've used—and are likely to use—each week.

"Sounds good. How was class?"

"Had a test tonight. Pretty sure I aced it."

"You usually do." I have tremendous respect for my friend. The smart motherfucker maintains a 4.0 GPA while juggling two jobs and taking care of his mom.

Gideon grins. "That's because I have a big . . . brain."

Ravi rolls his eyes. "Jesus. Here we go again. Do you ever take a break from talking about your dick?"

"Can't say that I do."

I point to Ravi. "Speaking of breaks, I'm due for mine. Hurry up and go eat. I need you to cover me when you're done. All this food talk has me starving."

Ravi salutes me with a grin. "You got it, Abe."

I shake my head and laugh as he saunters off. The bastard insists on calling me variations of Abraham Lincoln, but I tolerate the nicknames because I love him. I have to admit, it's better than the "Stinky Linky" I heard from the assholes on the school bus when I was a kid. Besides, someone has called me worse.

*Speak of the devil.*

Zarek prowls across the dance floor to the bar. He embodies darkness with his olive skin, spiky black hair, and espresso-colored eyes. The Glacier dominant is a menacing sight at six-three, with a heavily muscled frame wrapped in tattoos.

I swallow a shot of single malt and turn my attention to the margarita a woman just ordered.

Zarek surveys the scene and finds a spot at the end of the bar, perpendicular to where I'm standing. "Everything under control, ladies?"

"Fuck off, Z," Gideon mutters, grabbing more ice from the freezer.

Zarek points to the bottle of tequila I'm holding. "Give me a double."

"I'm not your sub." I slide an empty glass across the bar and plop the bottle in front of him. "Pour your own."

A dark chuckle rumbles in his chest. "Aw, Town Car's hostile tonight."

It had to be Town Car? He couldn't pick a Lincoln Navigator instead? He knows I hate the nickname, but he continues using it because he'd die if he couldn't bust my balls.

I squeeze some lime juice into the margarita glass. "What can I say? You bring out the best in me."

His gaze narrows on something over my shoulder. "Well, hello there. Don't *you* look sweet." He licks his lips, and his expression twists into a lewd smirk. "Keep your tequila, Town Car. I've got better treats to sample."

I spin toward tonight's chosen victim, and my blood turns to ice.

# Twenty-Nine

## Lincoln

**O**h, fuck.

"This is one hell of a plot twist, Mr. Kennedy. Or should I call you Elliot?"

The fury in Elinora's gaze paralyzes me. My heart stops beating, and my lungs refuse to function. She caught me red-handed, with my pants down, and a fucking bull's-eye on my forehead. Now all I need is for someone to throw a noose around my neck and shove my legs out from under me.

*How the fuck did she make the connection?*

"I asked you a question." She grips the bar, drumming her red-painted nails on the granite.

All I can do is stare. No joke, the woman is even more beautiful when she's angry. My gaze follows her shiny platinum hair to where it flows down past the lower curve of her breasts to brush her waist. Her red V-neck shirt accentuates her mouthwatering cleavage, and she's wearing fitted dark jeans. I can't see her ass, but I'd bet my life the denim hugs it perfectly. The casual outfit, while devastatingly sexy, is at odds with the tension she radiates.

"Answer me, damn it."

"Elliot is my middle name."

"No shit. I already figured that out." Her gaze sweeps the length of my body, lingering on my shirtless chest and abs. Esme's love of muscles means our regular uniform is simply dark jeans.

I step forward. "I can explain."

"Oh, really?" Elinora's pupils dilate, and her shoulders move on rapid, shaky breaths. A muscle in her jaw pulses, and for the life of me, I can't decide whether she plans to slap me or kiss me.

"Hello, beautiful."

My scalp prickles at Zarek's voice.

She glances at him. "Hello."

"I haven't seen you here before. What's your name, dollface?"

My vision clouds into a red haze. "Don't answer that."

Elinora narrows her eyes on my face. "Don't tell me when to speak." She turns to face Zarek. "My name is Elinora."

"Welcome to The River, *Elinora*."

"Thank you."

"I'm Zarek." He sets down his tequila. "Why don't you take a walk with me?"

She arches a brow. "A walk?"

He smiles and looks her over, dragging his gaze up and down her body. "I'll give you a private tour."

"She's with *me*."

Elinora flinches at my snarled statement and jerks her head toward me, pinning her widened eyes to my face.

Zarek's offer awakened a part of me I never knew existed. My every bone, muscle, and cell pulse with the primal need to claim Elinora as mine.

Beyond that, I need to protect her.

The ballsy motherfucker slides from his stool and takes a step in her direction. "I think she'll have more fun with me."

The beast inside me snaps.

# Thirty

## Elinora

Lincoln stalks from behind the bar, positioning himself between Zarek and me. I don't need to see his face to know he's seething. His back is a wall of muscle, and his protective stance blocks my view of the other man, which is fine. I didn't come here for him.

He clenches his fists at his sides. "She. Is. With. Me."

"Staking a claim, Town Car?"

"Damn right, I am."

"Looks like Town Car has a soft spot . . ."

A man I haven't seen before comes out from behind the bar to stand beside Lincoln. "Get the fuck outta here, Z. Esme told you to stay downstairs."

As if on cue, Madame Esme rushes across the packed dance floor. "What the hell is going on over here?" Her eyes widen when she spots me. "Elinora, I didn't know you were coming tonight, baby."

"I left a voicemail earlier, asking you to call me, but I found the confirmation I was seeking."

"I'm sorry. I haven't been in my office since lunch." Her eyes dart between me and Lincoln, telling me she knows who I am to him. "Do you have any other questions?"

"Yes, but they aren't for you."

Lincoln stiffens but keeps his attention on Zarek.

Madame Esme approaches the other man. "What are you doing up here? We've talked about this."

"Came to visit Town Car, but I was just leaving."

"Stop looking for new subs in Aqua. You know they can't handle what you're into."

"Doesn't hurt to try." He releases a dark chuckle. "Doesn't hurt *me*, that is."

"Go back to Glacier, Z," Madame Esme commands.

"If you insist." He saunters toward the dance floor, pausing to address me. "Nice meeting you, *Elinora*." His tone makes the hairs on the back of my neck stand on end. "If you get bored with Town Car, you can find me downstairs in cave thirteen."

People part like the Red Sea as he crosses the dance floor. Intrigued by his dark, sinister vibes, I stare after him as he leaves through an iron gate flanked by a pair of enormous gold tridents. Just inside the gate is a frosted glass wall carved to look like ice blocks. Black lighting casts a bluish-purple glow on the wall, and the massive security guards outside the entrance to Glacier make it clear Madame Esme wasn't kidding about the realm's exclusivity.

Behind them, torches flicker like a come-hither from the frozen underworld, and for a moment, I forget why I'm here.

"Let's all take a few deep breaths." Madame Esme's voice brings me back to reality.

Even though Zarek is gone, his absence does nothing to ease the tension rolling off Lincoln in waves. "Breathing doesn't negate the fact that he's a troublemaking dick."

"Enough." She stares up at him, and they share some unspoken message before she looks away and searches the room. "Where's Ravi?"

"I'm coming." A man approaches the bar from the cave-like passageway which leads to the ground floor.

*Are all the men here gorgeous?* Tall and muscled with brown skin and wavy black hair, Ravi is no exception.

His brows pop at the scene. "Whoa. Aren't you guys supposed to be *behind* the bar?"

"Don't ask," Lincoln mutters.

The other bartender glances at his watch. "Back already? Thought you were gonna eat."

"Forgot my phone." Ravi ducks behind the bar, snatches the device, and tucks it into his pocket. He eyes Lincoln. "You know what, why don't you go instead? You seem all hangry and shit."

"Lost my appetite, but I could use a break."

Madame Esme nods. "That's fine, but please do the liquor order before you head home."

"I will," Lincoln says as he grips my elbow. "Let's go."

Despite the confusion swirling in my brain, my body obeys him without question. I hustle to keep up as he tugs me along the corridor which leads to some of the private lagoons.

We pass a gorgeous mermaid statue with naked breasts the size of my head. Carved from gold-veined black granite, she's perched on a rock like a siren, luring sailors to their destruction. There's another mermaid nearby, but she's pearly white, with the slight translucence of quartz. Throughout the Aqua Suite, I've noticed several of these statues in different colors and erotic poses. If I wasn't so mad, I'd admire them for longer.

Lincoln abruptly stops us outside the entrance to Lagoon Seven, and I collide with him. The mere second of contact is enough to ignite me. My traitorous nipples prick the inside of my bra as memories of last Friday flood my mind and panties. Profound lust infuses my fury. It's suddenly hard to breathe.

"I'm not going in there with you," I sputter, attempting to wrench my arm away.

Lincoln tightens his grip. "Beg to differ."

I struggle against his hold. "Who the fuck do you think you are?"

He jams a code into the electronic pin pad on the wall. The door to the lagoon slides open.

My gaze darts to the shimmering blue water. The tranquil rush of the waterfall and rustling grasses drown out the Aqua Suite's club music and my hammering pulse. Jasmine, leather, and saltwater assail my senses and rob me of the ability to inject anger into my words. "I asked you a question."

He yanks me inside and secures the entrance. "Yeah, I heard you."

"How about an answer?"

Lincoln releases me and leans against the door. Gone is the spectacle-wearing, nerdy gentleman from the office who stumbles over his words and blushes. A brutally gorgeous bastard who thinks he can bend me to his will replaces him.

He stares at me in silence, crossing his massive arms over his chest like some brooding asshole who has the right to be pissed. The effects are devastating. To actually see him shirtless, here in the lagoon where he'd spanked and fucked me, untethers what remains of my control. Just like Lincoln and Elliot were two distinct people in my mind, Office Lincoln and River Lincoln seem to be separate entities. His Jekyll and Hyde performance is equal parts confusing and enticing, and even though I'm hurt—and mad as hell—I want him. So help me God, I want them *both*.

Lincoln rubs his jaw. "The better question is, who do *you* think I am?"

# Thirty-One

## Lincoln

Elinora's mouth drops open on a little growl that makes my cock twitch. "Are you fucking kidding me?"

"Do I look like I'm joking?"

She steps closer to me. "No, you look like a man who's about to get slapped."

"I'd like to see you tr—"

Elinora's palm collides with my face. Searing heat spreads from my nose to my ear. My hand flies to my cheek. The warm sting, and the memory of how her plump ass cheeks heated beneath my spanks, hardens my cock.

Her lip curls in a mixture of self-satisfaction and fury. "My handprint looks good on your face."

Pushing off the door, I seize her around the waist. "Keep that up, and mine will look good on your ass." Should I be this cavalier and reckless? Absolutely not. If I were smart, I'd plead my case and beg for forgiveness. Yet somehow, the heat in her gaze incinerates the rational side of my brain, and my apology dies on my lips. Right now, I don't give a flying fuck about my job. The only thing that matters is Elinora, and my gut tells me she's worth the risk. "I'll let that one slide because I know you're angry."

"Angry?" she shrieks, glaring up at me. "No, I'm fucking livid."

I yank her closer. "Tell me all about it, sugar."

"You knew."

"I knew what?" I already know her answer, but I want to make her say it almost as much as I want to make her scream. I need her to know I knew she was fantasizing about me.

She fists my hair and tugs it like I did to hers when I spanked her. "You *knew* it was me last week."

"And what else did I know?"

She grits her teeth and yanks my hair harder. "You knew I made him *you.*"

"Your point?"

Her hand slides to the back of my neck. "You should've stopped us. How could you do that to me?"

I bring my lips to her ear. "You mean everything you asked for?"

"I didn't ask to be deceived."

"Did I force you to do anything you didn't want?"

"You should've told me."

"That wasn't my question." I press the front of my body to hers. "Answer me and do it properly."

"Fuck off."

"Wrong answer." I tug her further into the room, stopping near the water's edge. "Let's try this again. Did I force you to do anything you didn't want?"

"I didn't want to fuck one of my employees!"

"But you wanted to fuck *me.*" I grip her waist. "No one forced you to come here. You showed up in my lagoon ready to get fucked."

She gasps but presses closer to me and flexes her hips. "You should have left."

"I *did* leave."

"Yeah, but instead of coming clean, you came back and fucked me." She catches herself grinding against my hard cock and suddenly stills.

I smirk because, despite her anger, she can't resist me. Good. I want her to crave my body the way I need hers.

"You didn't want clean, and you loved it dirty—"

She slaps my other cheek.

I seize her arms and pin them to her sides. "Keep slapping me, sugar. It'll be my turn later."

"There won't be a later. It shouldn't have happened the first time." She struggles against my hold for a moment. "It's wrong." Her hips rub my cock again, stealing her statement's conviction. Instead of pulling away, she moves closer, pressing her breasts into my chest.

I lick the shell of her ear. "We play by my rules here."

"Your rules don't apply to me, Kennedy. I'm your boss."

"I wasn't your employee that night. And I'm not your employee right now." I nip her earlobe. "Welcome to The River, sugar. You're not the boss here. This is *my* castle. You walk through these doors, *I'm* king." I thrust my hips against her. "We both know you didn't come here to talk."

Elinora draws a shaky breath and meets my gaze. "Fuck you."

"That's not very nice," I murmur, giving her a gentle backward nudge. She shrieks and topples into the lagoon.

# Thirty-Two

## Elinora

Moments later, I resurface from beneath the cool water, coughing and sputtering. I shove my sopping hair back and wipe at the mascara that's no doubt running down my cheeks.

"You bastard!" I screech. "I'm soaking wet!"

Lincoln stands at the lagoon's edge with his fists clenched at his sides, his face in a mask of smug satisfaction. "You were wet before I pushed you in."

My hands fly to my hips. "Who the fuck do you think you are?"

"You keep asking me that, but it seems you're the one who's unclear." He jabs a thumb into his chest. "I know who I am. It's time you figure it out."

I stare up at the brutally gorgeous man whose Atlantic gaze seems to glow. His glasses are gone, which amplifies the breath-stealing effect. Inky tresses fall in pieces over his forehead. He purses those plush lips in a cocky smirk that tells me he's loving the power shift. My eyes roam the expanse of chiseled abdominal muscles before coming to rest at the sizeable bulge in his jeans. My pussy clenches at the memory of him surging inside me. I shudder with the force of the desire throbbing between my legs. It's not fair that he can do this to me—make the lust charging through my veins outrun my fury.

"I hate you."

"Good." Lincoln prowls down the staircase and into the lagoon, closing the distance between us. "Why don't you tell me all about it?" He backs me to the edge. "You know I'm a great listener."

"Fuck you. How dare—"

He seizes my lips. I can't stop the moan that leaves my chest as he kisses me like a starved man, hungrily thrusting his tongue into my mouth. My fingertips dive into his hair, pulling him closer.

His kiss is brutal. Plundering. And I give it back just as hard, nipping at his lips and yanking his hair. He leans his full weight into me and gyrates his hips to make sure I know how hard he is. I drag my nails down his back, making sure *he* knows I'm still angry.

Without breaking contact, he lifts and carries me to the steps. Water sluices off our bodies as he climbs from the lagoon and makes his way to the room behind the waterfall.

No matter what I do, I can't kiss him hard enough, deep enough, to match the frenzy in my body and mind. He flicks on a light and snatches a condom from a dresser drawer before setting me on the edge. A devilish gleam lights his eyes as he tears my shirt down the center.

I gasp as he yanks the material from my shoulders and drops it onto the floor.

He reaches behind me to unhook my bra, tugs it off, and takes a moment to admire my naked breasts. "So fucking beautiful," he murmurs, lowering his mouth to a nipple. He sucks the hardened peak into his mouth.

Then he flicks his tongue.

"Oh, God," I say on a moan.

Lincoln tangles his hand in my hair and roughly pulls my head back. He grazes his teeth over my nipple. "My name is Lincoln. That's the only one I want to hear leaving your lips tonight." He switches breasts, and I wrap my legs around him. After a moment, he kisses my lips again.

I reach for his belt and yank it open while his hands find my waistband. We shove at each other's wet jeans until we're down to our underwear. I bite his lip to get his attention.

His eyes burn into me. "You slapped me twice, and now you're biting?"

Desperate for him to take control, I rake my nails down his back and squeeze his ass instead of answering. I told myself on the ride over that I was only coming here to confront him, but I was full of shit. I wanted more of him. I craved another taste of what he dished out on Friday.

The lust in his eyes turns molten. "Sugar, you're *asking* to get spanked."

I give him a coy smile and dig my nails into his ass cheeks. Hard.

He growls and tosses me over his shoulder, making a beeline for a bizarre piece of furniture in the middle of the room. The black leather bench looks like a tiered kneeler with handles and straps.

I fling my arm toward it. "What the hell is this?"

Lincoln drapes me facedown over the fixture so my knees rest on the padded bottom level. "Spanking bench."

My breath rushes out of me as heat floods my pussy. "What?"

"You heard me." He moves to stand behind me and grips my lace panties. He rips them off and sheds his boxer briefs. I hear him tear open the condom wrapper and roll it onto his cock. He feathers his fingertips over my ass. "Now, I'm gonna spank you . . . *while* I fuck you senseless."

"Oh my God."

His palm lands on my ass with a hard strike. "What did you call me?" He lines his cock up with my drenched entrance.

"Lincoln." I flex my hips back.

"Good girl." He surges forward, filling me to the hilt.

I scream at the sudden penetration and dig my nails into the leather.

"How's the water, Elinora?"

"Fire."

"Hold on tight." Lincoln slams into me, and before I can recover from his thrust, his palm collides with my ass once more.

I cry out and clutch the handles on the side of the bench as he delivers another brutal thrust followed by a spank. "Oh my fucking God, *Lincoln*."

His huge cock fills and stretches me, bordering on pain. But as he moves, stroking and rubbing me deep inside, tendrils of pleasure unfurl.

*Crack.* Another spank.

"Oh!" I press my cheek to the cool leather and flex my hips back to meet his thrusts.

"Fuck," he groans, picking up the pace. "You're so damn tight." He slaps my ass again, then grips my hips. "The water?"

"Warm," I say on a gasp.

He tightens his fingers on my hips as he falls into a pounding rhythm. "You feel so good."

I close my eyes and listen to the sounds filling the room. Another hard spank. My gasps and cries mix with the feral moans and groans leaving his chest. The wet slap of our bodies colliding and the scrape of the furniture moving across the floor heighten the sensations. The heat and sting on my ass, his cock inside me, the leather beneath me. While I still can't see him, this time, I *know* it's Lincoln. And I feel him deeper than ever.

"Lincoln. I want—"

He slows his pace and leans forward, pressing his chest to my back. "Tell me."

Feeling his warmth on my skin confirms my need to have him closer. Deeper. "You."

"I'm here, sugar." He rolls his hips and molds his body to mine while he thrusts. His breaths gust the side of my neck when he grabs my hands and interlaces our fingers. "Spread your legs wider."

I obey his command and feel my orgasm hovering in the periphery. As each slow grinding thrust untethers me, I cling to his hands like they're all that anchors me to the planet. "Oh, *Lincoln.*" I moan his name and clench around his cock.

"Scream for me." He slams into me. Once. Twice.

A wail leaves my lips as his third thrust launches me into orbit. "Yes! Oh, fuck, yes!" He keeps moving, groaning my name while he pistons his hips. I explode a second time, stars bursting behind my eyelids. I dig my nails into his hands and moan his name.

He pounds his cock inside me, drawing out my orgasm, until he finally releases on a bellow. He collapses on top of me, his cock jerking in rhythm with my pussy's pulsing.

With his body curved around me, Lincoln rests his forehead on the leather bench next to my face. "You're an angel, Elinora." His breaths come in harsh bursts against my cheek.

"You said that last time."

"It's still true." He releases one of my hands and runs his fingers through my hair. "You all right?"

"Yes." I swivel my head to meet his gaze. "But I'm still pissed at you."

"How many orgasms would make you un-pissed?"

"I'm serious, Lincoln."

"So am I. Give me a number, and I'll make it happen."

"I mean, we need to talk—not fuck."

# Thirty-Three

## Lincoln

*This is the part where I lose my job.*

"So, let's talk." I grip the base of my cock and slowly pull out, careful to keep the condom in place. I climb to my feet and remove the rubber. Stretching, I toss it in the trash before turning to where Elinora leans against the spanking bench, still panting. Seeing her worn out like this makes me want to pound my chest. Or roar. I stroke her lower back instead. "Are you coming?"

"I don't think I can move yet," she mumbles into the leather.

"I've got you." I lift and carry her to the lagoon. She melts into my arms like I just fucked every ounce of strength out of her.

We settle on the underwater ledge. I position her so she straddles me like last time, and she's too tired to resist. Besides, she's going to fire me anyway, which means I'll likely never see her again. The pain of that thought makes it hard to breathe. I clench my jaw and pull her closer, determined to savor every second of closeness she allows. It's only a matter of time before she regains her strength, slaps me, and leaves.

For a moment, we just stare into each other's eyes while the water laps at our heated skin. My scalp prickles as I try to decipher her unreadable expression. *I was too rough with her.* I brush my hand over her ass cheeks. "Did I hurt you?"

"No."

"Are you sure?"

"I'm fine." She nods and searches my face.

I release a heavy sigh. "You're about to fire me, right?"

"Why the hell would I do that? You're an excellent editor." She grips my shoulders. "I'm pissed at you, but I'm not stupid. I just want to talk."

"I'm listening."

Elinora gnaws her lower lip. "We shouldn't have let that happen again."

"Yeah, but we did."

Her gaze burns into me. "I need to understand why you let it happen the first time."

*Because you're my fantasy.* I tilt my head to the side and shrug. "Like I said, you showed up in my lagoon."

"And you left the moment you figured out it was me."

"I left because I didn't want to disrespect you and lose my job."

"But you came back," she whispers. "Why?"

It doesn't make sense to lie to her. Besides, I need to make damn sure she understands that her safety was the only reason I was willing to jeopardize my career, Myles's promotion, and ultimately, Reagan's housing. I need her to understand that beneath the pleasure concierge facade, I'm an honorable man who cares for her. Even if she'll never truly be mine.

"I asked you a question, Lincoln."

I sigh. "Esme threatened to send Zarek instead."

Elinora stiffens and crosses her arms over her chest. "Oh, so you took one for the team? How noble of you. God forbid the Ice Queen freeze his dick off." The venom in her voice mirrors the pain flashing in her eyes.

"There's no team here. I don't give a flying fuck about Zarek. I was protecting *you.* I don't trust the guy, and there was no way in hell I would've let him near you."

"It should have been my choice—not yours."

"No, you're not understanding me." I bring my forehead to hers. "It wasn't my choice."

"That's great. I *understand* Esme coerced you into having sex with me. What a lucky girl I am."

"Let me make myself abundantly clear. There was no coercion on my end. I wanted you the second I set foot in your office for my interview, and every moment since." Her gaze flares in surprise. "Don't pretend like you didn't know it."

"I didn't know," she protests, looking away.

"Look at me." Her widened gaze snaps to mine at the tone of voice I used. "I don't buy that Ice Queen shit. The woman I know is warm, full of passion and kindness. Fuck anyone who says otherwise. If you think I don't want you, you're dead wrong. I can't even breathe when I'm around you, so imagine how I felt when you showed up in my lagoon ready to submit. Any sense of duty—or doubts about what we were doing—vanished when you slid out of that robe on command." I grip her chin. "And when you put your hands on me and gave me your trust—"

"You said you only fucked. You weren't supposed to hold me and make love to me." She looks away and whispers, "I *trusted* you to be a stranger."

I tip her gaze to mine and brush my thumb over her lips. "But you wanted it to be me." I press my lips to hers in a slow, tender kiss. "You're right. I don't make love, but I made love to you."

"Why?" she asks, breathless.

"Because no part of last week—or tonight—was business as usual for me. Nothing about this situation was normal, but it happened, and I need you to know I acted out of character too."

"How?"

I hold up three fingers. "I can count on one hand the number of women I've kissed in my lifetime. And that includes you." Her eyes widen at my declaration. "We were strangers until you screamed *my* name. Then you were mine. Just like you are right now, Elinora." I lick the column of her throat. "But you sure screamed my name a whole lot louder when you knew it was really me."

"That's not fair," she says, arching into my touch.

"When you come here, you're mine. You know that, right?"

"You can't claim me like I'm some prized cattle." She gasps but doesn't pull away.

"I can." I yank her hips up against my hard cock. "And I will. Not only will you let me, you'll love every second of it. Because I'm not your employee here. And you're not my boss. At The River, we're just a man and a woman who want each other." My hand drifts down between her legs. Even in the water, I can feel her pussy's slick wetness. I slide a finger inside her. "You want me right now, don't you?" I pump my finger in and out of her. "You want my cock inside you again, even though we just finished. Isn't that right, Elinora?"

She moans and shimmies her hips instead of answering.

I reach for the foot of a nearby chaise and yank it toward the lagoon, then snatch one of the condoms I'd left on top of it. If I'm not inside her in the next thirty seconds, I might die. I tear the wrapper open with my teeth and lift us enough to roll it onto my cock. Settling back down, I line myself up with her pussy. "Let's review. Do you know who I am?"

"Yes."

"Say my name." I pull her hips down, pausing when just the head of my cock presses inside. "*Now.*"

"Lincoln."

"Say it louder," I command, rocking my hips slightly to tease her.

"Lincoln!"

"Good girl." I grip her tighter. "Tell me who you came here for tonight."

"You."

"You, what?"

"You, *sir.*" She cries out when she takes me to the hilt.

"Ride me, sugar." Her tight, silky depths steal my sanity as I help her slide up and down my cock. "Just like that."

Elinora clings to my shoulders and buries her face in my neck. "Oh, God, *Lincoln* . . ."

"Look at me," I command, thrusting my hips upward. She meets my gaze. "Keep your eyes on mine. I need to see how pretty the blue is when you come on my cock."

"You have a way with words."

"That's why you can't resist my charms." I kiss her neck. "Here, or at the office."

"Correct. Your attention to detail turns me on." She digs her nails into my shoulders. "Now shut up and fuck me."

After finishing the liquor order, I reenter the lagoon with a robe for Elinora and some food. She's still dozing on the dais, where I laid her after our third go-around this evening. Her naked body against the white leather reminds me of an angel in repose.

Her eyelids flutter open when I touch her shoulder. "Hi."

"Hey." I hand her a glass of water. "Drink."

She presses herself up and chugs the contents. "Thanks."

"I have food for us, and I brought you something to wear." I gesture to her pile of wet clothes and hand over a blue silk robe. "Here you go, angel."

"Thank you." Rising, Elinora slides it on and cinches the belt around her waist. "I thought they only had white ones?"

"We reserve these for elite members, but you look sexy as hell in blue."

"It's my favorite color." She flushes. "I caught you checking me out at the office when I wore my blue dress."

"Which time?" I scratch my head. "I check you out multiple times a day."

"In the breakroom when I was making my tea."

I lick my lips and tug her up against me. "You mean when I went in there to talk to you and found you bent over?"

She laughs. "Yes. Then you started stumbling on your words."

"Another daily occurrence," I point out. "My brain short circuits when I look at you."

"But you seem so self-assured here."

"This is The River, sugar." I flash her a wink. "My castle, remember?"

She peers up at me. "What happens when we're back in mine?"

The question started circling my mind as soon as she made it clear she wasn't firing me. What will happen tomorrow? How will our new normal work? I know *my* role, but I wonder how she'll act around me now that she knows I think her eyes look like forget-me-not blossoms when she comes. How her lips remind me of rosebuds. How she's the most beautiful woman I've ever seen.

"You can do whatever you choose." I cup her face. "But for me, it will be business as usual."

"Oh?"

"By that, I mean, I'll show up on time—or early—and work through my lunch like always. I'll stay late most days, and work from home, even though I'm well aware it's not expected of me. While we're at your office, I'll call you Ms. Iverson and treat you with the utmost respect."

"Like always," she murmurs.

I nod. "I'll continue to give each manuscript my full attention. Bottom line, I'll behave like a professional and help you publish quality books."

Her smile tells me I'm on the right track. *Yeah, this works. We'll keep it professional at work.* I mean, I can't guarantee there won't be a heated glance or two. Or seven. Or once an hour, but I won't do anything inappropriate. Remembering the creeps on the sidewalk, I perk up. "But I *will* continue to walk you to your car afterward—that's non-negotiable. Like I said when you hired me, I'll be the best damn romance editor to walk through those doors. Does that work for you?"

"Yes."

I gesture between us. "If you feel the need to act on our sexual tension, trust me, I'm more than happy to partake, but that ball is in your court. The last thing I want to do is make you uncomfortable—or jeopardize my job—so I need *you* to come to me. This week was an anomaly—I'm usually off on Wednesdays—but I always work here on Thursday, Friday, and Saturday nights."

She raises a brow. "Won't you be busy? Where will I find you?"

"I'm usually behind the Aqua Suite bar."

"But what if you're . . . *with* someone?"

The uncertainty in her tone, and the actual possibility of the scenario she's proposing, are like knives to my chest. How will I fulfill my obligations to Esme? Sure, my bartending hours count, but without *other* extracurriculars, I'll be in a holding pattern. One thing's for damn sure, I refuse to be paid a fucking cent for any time spent with Elinora. She is a privilege I don't deserve, and I'll be damned if I tarnish what we share by classifying her as a client. Nope. Not happening. I'll negotiate those terms with Esme as soon as Elinora heads home.

"I won't be with anyone else. I'll make sure of it," I promise, even though it's not one I'm free to make. Bottom line, Esme owns me. How the fuck am I supposed to be exclusive to Elinora when I'm a pleasure concierge?

Elinora bites her lip. "So that will be our reality? The 'Office Editions' of ourselves behaving like professionals, and on weekends, we'll have the naughty 'River Editions' who are free to indulge?"

I flash her a wicked grin. "Sounds about right. Are you on board with that?"

# Thirty-Four

## Elinora

Does it work for me? Can I maintain two distinct relationships with this man? Charles led two separate lives. Granted, I was only privy to Night and Weekend Charles. Meanwhile, Day Charles fucked other women while I was at the office building my empire. Am I behaving like Charles?

I shake my head. No. I'm nothing like my piece of shit ex-husband. I work hard and give my respect to those who deserve it. In return, I expect the same treatment. I don't play games. What you see is what you get. Unlike Charles, deception is not in my nature.

But what about Lincoln? I hardly know the man, and he already deceived me once. Is Lincoln another Charles?

"What are you thinking?" He brushes the hair back from my face.

"I don't know."

"Yes, you do." He tips my chin up. "Talk to me."

"Let me think about the carnal proposal you've suggested and get back to you."

"Tell me what you're afraid of."

It feels like a win-win arrangement on my end. I get to spend my days working alongside a brilliant editor who outshines those who've been doing it for decades, *and* indulge in mind-blowing sex, three nights a week, with said editor. All this, and I can still reserve Sundays and three weeknights for myself. What do I have to lose?

*Control.* But where has control gotten me, other than deceived, divorced, and lonely as hell? I stare up at the gorgeous young man who makes me feel alive. If I decline his indecent proposal, I lose out on River Lincoln and my freedom to surrender control. My body needs him to call the shots, even if my mind isn't convinced yet. Truth be told, I'm tired of the status quo. I deserve some excitement. Some companionship. Some hot sex.

"What's on your mind?"

"I've never done something like this." I gesture between us. "It's out of character."

"Which part?"

"All of it. Sex clubs, sleeping with my employee, giving up control—"

"Sometimes we need a plot twist to open our eyes to the true conflict."

I raise an eyebrow. "And that is?"

"Maybe your character wants more than what you've been giving her?" He grips my chin. "Maybe her desires run deeper than you're willing to admit? Maybe your needs mirror hers?"

I shrug. "Maybe."

"Tell me what you need from me."

"I can't."

"Why?"

"Because I'm afraid to voice it."

"I need you to explain why a woman who dominates the publishing market would be afraid to speak up in the bedroom."

Maybe because Charles belittled me when I suggested we add some spice to our love life? But Lincoln doesn't need to know all that.

"I don't know."

"I think you do." He traces my jawline. "Did you tell your husband any of your fantasies?"

"No," I lie. He doesn't need to know Charles called me a kinky slut when I voiced my desires. Meanwhile, he was the one getting kinky with multiple sluts.

"Why not?"

"Because I didn't trust him." And I'd been right.

His gaze softens. "Do you trust me?"

"I haven't decided yet."

"How will I know when you do?"

"My trust is not something I give freely, and after my ex, I swore I'd never trust another man." I peer deep into his eyes. "If and when I tell you my deepest fantasies, you will know you've earned my full trust." I clench my fingers on his shoulders. "But don't expect it to come easily."

"I'm a hard worker, Elinora. And it's clear you're not satisfied with the way your story's been written."

I sigh. "No, I'm really not."

He smiles. "Then let me help you make some revisions."

"Lincoln, this draft is so fucked, I'd need to start a fresh one."

"Let's rewrite it." He leans in and brushes his lips over mine.

"Yes," I whisper, desperate for a chance to refresh, revise, and reimagine the rough draft my life has become. "That works for me."

"We'll start right now." He grips both sides of my face. His tongue surges into my mouth and tangles with mine. Moaning, I weave my hands into his hair and lose myself in the kiss. In him. In us. In this new arrangement we've agreed to. One that I hope to God I'm woman enough to handle.

I break the kiss. "Sorry, but there's no way I've got another round in me. I can hardly stand as it is."

He grins. "I'll hold you up?"

I poke him in his chest. "No. We need to eat. Focus on the task at hand."

Lincoln gives me a sheepish smile. "It's hard to do that when I'm around you." He brushes his thumb over my lips. "I need you to stop being so fucking sexy."

"You really think I'm sexy?" I ask, needing some validation.

He snatches my wrist and presses it to the bulge in his jeans. "I'll let you come to your own conclusions."

I grip him through the material and feel the hard, thick length that fucked me senseless tonight. I can't remember the last time I had sex three times in one night. Probably because it never happened. I was lucky if I could get one ten-minute romp from Charles. On the rare occasions when we achieved that, it left me feeling more than a little unsatisfied.

Moisture floods the tender region between my thighs—deliciously sore from Lincoln's thrusting—and for the first time in my life, I'm satisfied.

"You'd better stop rubbing me before I bend you over the dresser for round four."

"Not tonight. I need a couple days to recover." Hopefully, I'll no longer be sore by Friday.

His gaze snaps to mine. "Did I hurt you?"

"That was the most intense sex of my life."

"Bad intense?"

"No, it was amazing." I flush. "I'm just a little sore, which is why you won't be bending me over anything else tonight."

He smirks. "So, tomorrow?"

I shake my head. "Friday."

Lincoln nips my earlobe. "From now until then, every time you walk—or sit—I want you to remember my cock thrusting inside you. Stretching and filling you. Got it?"

My breath rushes out of me at the reminder of his dominance. His mark on my body and mind extends beyond The River, and I *know* I'll feel him when I sit on the throne in my office. It should bother me, him trying to encroach on my kingdom, but the thrill of my submission outweighs the territorial thoughts which try to surface.

"Asked you a question, sugar."

"Yes."

He kisses the side of my neck. "Yes, what?"

"Yes, sir."

"Good girl." He brings his lips to my ear. "Elinora, I plan to make all your fantasies into reality, but I want you to know you're my fantasy too."

I pull up at the curb outside my apartment and hand over my keys to the valet. While I refuse to give up control and hire a driver, I'm happy to let someone else deal with the frustration of finding me a parking spot. Smiling, I tip him and glance across the street to Central Park as he speeds off in my Porsche. The cherry blossoms are in full bloom. They're one of the reasons April *was* my favorite month. Not anymore. What would've been mine and Charles's fourteenth wedding anniversary is next Sunday. The annual reminder now ruins cherry blossom season for me.

Sighing, I glance at my attire, which consists of my jeans and Lincoln's button-down shirt. He wore it at the office yesterday, so it smells like his cologne. I pull it tighter around me and breathe in his scent to dispel memories of Charles.

My Wednesday evening with Lincoln was incredible. After we'd eaten, we curled up on the dais for a nap. It felt so amazing to fall asleep in his arms, wrapped in his warmth and safety. When he walked me to my car this morning with a protective hand at the small of my back, I felt cherished. And when he kissed me so tenderly and whispered my name against my neck, I knew our carnal weekend arrangement would not be enough for me.

I squeeze my eyes shut and remind myself of the reasons Lincoln and I must keep our Office and River editions separate. I'm his boss. Whether or not I'm willing to admit it, I employ him in both settings: at Iverson Press as my editor and as pleasure concierge at The River. Albeit unconventional, what we share is simply a work arrangement. I won't let myself be stupid enough to fall for Lincoln—in either setting—because while we *work together*, we could never work *together*.

*I'm sure he has plenty of other women he services.* The thought turns my stomach sour. He's a pleasure concierge. I'm not special—he fucks for a living. Bottom line, I'm paying for his attention. Just like Charles benefited financially from our marriage.

*Looks like I'm once again the cash cow.*

No. I can't do this. I won't open myself up to that shit again. This time around, I'll protect my heart and wallet. I can't go back to The River with Lincoln. Our Office Edition will have to complete my library because I know in my soul that I'm not capable of juggling both. Besides, I'm a decade-older divorcée who's jaded enough for both of us.

My cell chimes with a text. My heart clenches when I see Lincoln's name.

> Lincoln: Just wanted to make sure you made it home safely.

I respond, letting him know I'm home. As I'm about to tuck the phone back into my purse, it chimes again.

> Lincoln: I enjoyed spending time with you. I'll see you at work later.

I pull his shirt around me and take a deep breath. Reaching out wasn't a job requirement. He checked on me because that's who he is on a fundamental level. Charles never checked on me when I stayed late at the office.

Even that time when I got a flat tire and was three hours overdue, he didn't return my calls. And when I'd walked in, completely frazzled, he informed me he'd already eaten, and if I was still hungry, there were leftovers in the fridge. I remember sitting alone at the kitchen island, gnawing on a slice of cold pizza while the tears rolled down my cheeks.

My phone dings a third time.

> Lincoln: Watson's first manuscript will be in your inbox by Sunday afternoon. I'm ahead of schedule with my own work, so we should be able to meet the publication deadline for both books. Also, in case your character is stuck in her internal thoughts, I meant EVERYTHING I said. Know that. Believe it.

I can't believe the man has a clue where my head is right now. I've known him less than two weeks, but Lincoln is already more attuned to me than the asshole I spent fifteen years with.

I head inside my building, giving the doorman a quick wave as I pass. Exhausted, I take the elevator instead of the stairs and sag against the wall. When I finally enter my home, I settle on a stool and wince. *Every time you walk—or sit—I want you to remember my cock thrusting inside you. Stretching and filling you.* Lincoln's voice flutters through my mind, making my inner muscles clench. Heat and moisture flood the apex of my thighs, as memories of our night grip me.

Who am I kidding? I can't keep my editions separate. I want Lincoln to be part of every book in my lonesome-as-hell library.

# Thirty-Five

## Lincoln

I knock on the door to Esme's luxe office at The River. It's Saturday night. Gideon is off, but Ravi's covering for me behind the bar, which means I'd better make this quick.

"Come in."

Cool blue light and the tranquil rush of a waterfall spill from the room as I step inside and close the door behind me. "Hey, Esme. Can I talk to you for a minute?"

"Sure, baby. I'm just doing payroll." She looks up from her laptop and motions to the white leather chair near her desk. Her electric blue mini dress with its plunging neckline and sequins reflect the room's lighting onto the granite, creating the illusion of moving water. I've always found her strikingly beautiful, and right now, with her smooth, golden skin and red lips, Esmeralda DaVinci is every bit the Mer Queen. "Have a seat."

I settle across from her and rub my jaw. "I have a weird request."

"What's on your mind?"

Studying the river rock mosaic on the wall, I ponder the best way to phrase it. Since she's doing payroll, at least my timing is perfect. I meet her honeyed gaze. "I don't want to be paid for any time spent with Elinora Iverson."

"She hasn't officially become a member, so I've yet to receive money from her. Remember, the first three visits are on the house." She motions to her desk calendar. "If I'm not wrong, she used the last of her complimentary visits yesterday."

"Are you sure?"

"Yes. Her first time here was for the masquerade mingle. Next was when she found you behind the bar on Wednesday, and last night was her third time."

"Did she make arrangements for payment going forward?"

She nods. "There's a credit card on file."

"OK, good. So, back to what I was saying. Once she's officially a member, I don't want any money from *you*, either."

Esme cocks her head to the side. "I'm a little confused by what you're asking."

I sigh and rake a hand through my hair. "When she comes here to see me, I want it to be like we're both members. Meaning, I don't want any compensation for being with her."

She raises a perfectly arched brow. "How's that gonna work? Don't you need to pay for your sister's housing?"

"Yeah, but I'll figure something out."

I've been toying with the idea of picking up a bartending gig elsewhere, but I'm not about to mention that to her.

"How often do you expect her to come?" Esme asks, twirling a lock of her hair.

"Three nights a week." I stiffen my spine. "I also need you to grant me exclusivity."

"That's up to Elinora, baby. She's free to play with whomever she chooses—Zarek included."

I clench my jaw. "He's not touching her."

"Again, that is not your choice." Her eyes burn into me. "What's this about, Lincoln?"

"If Elinora comes here, she's with me and *only* me."

"Do you have feelings for her?"

"Yeah."

"You're crossing a line." Esme shakes her head. "She's your boss."

"Not here, she's not."

"Right." She leans in. "I'm your boss here. Lately it feels like you've forgotten that. I know I give you more freedom than the other guys, but bottom line, you answer to me."

"I'm well aware of the chain of command."

She drums her red nails on the desk. "I have women who pay a lot of money for your time. What happens when one of them requests you?"

"Tell them I'm not available. I don't want to be with anyone else."

"That doesn't work for me, Lincoln. I'm not gonna lose members because you refuse to perform. If you plan to only be with Elinora on the nights she comes here, you'd better pick up three additional shifts to compensate. Otherwise, you're not holding up your end of our agreement."

"Deduct what you would've paid me for the time I spend with Elinora."

She shakes her head and withdraws a manila folder from a desk drawer. "Our contract states monetary and time debts. You're behind on repayment for both." She plops it on the desk in front of me.

I don't need to look at the contract—its terms are burned into my head. I bartered seven years of my life to this woman in exchange for an interest-free hundred grand. I know exactly how much time and money I owe her. Down to the fucking minute and cent. To date, I've worked off two years, four months, six days, nine hours, and six minutes. I've repaid twenty-eight thousand, five hundred and sixty dollars.

"I know. I have five thousand coming to you next week."

"You're The River's very own gateway drug. Your time here is even more valuable to me than getting my money back."

I lean in. "Fine. I'll man the Aqua Suite bar on Mondays, Tuesdays, and Wednesdays. Does that work for you?"

"No. I need you in the lagoon at least two of those nights." She points to a black book on her desk which houses her clients' contact information. "And you *will* play with someone other than Elinora. Your personal life will not impact my business." She jams some numbers into a calculator. "And just so we're clear, even if you paid off the remaining seventy-one grand tomorrow, you would still owe me your time."

I've always liked Esme and respected her cutthroat business tactics. Right now, I fucking hate her. She's not the warm and compassionate madame she leads everyone to believe. She's a calculating kink club owner who has me by the balls. She plasters an alluring smile on her face while she exploits me, squeezing my crown jewels just because she can.

And there's nothing I can do about it.

Rising, I leave her office without another word because if I open my mouth, I'm afraid I'll tell her what I think of her brand of sexual slavery.

I march back to the bar and swallow against the bile rising in my throat. How the fuck is this going to work? I've got my Iverson workload, including the manuscripts I inherited from Watson's dumb ass, and now I've doubled the amount of time I'm required to be at The River. How will I get my work done so I can stay in Elinora's good graces? Somehow, I'll find a way to make it happen, but what about this place?

How can I perform with another woman when I'm falling for Elinora? Better yet, how do I fulfill my obligations to Esme while keeping my word to Elinora? I told her there wouldn't be anyone else. I made a promise I can't keep, and now I'm forced to go behind her back. I'm no better than her piece of shit ex-husband.

Ravi looks up when I reenter the bar area. "You're back. Halle-fucking-lujah." He shoves the drink menu in my face. "Why the fuck does the signature cocktail need to be so complicated?"

"This is The River," I mutter. "Everything's complicated."

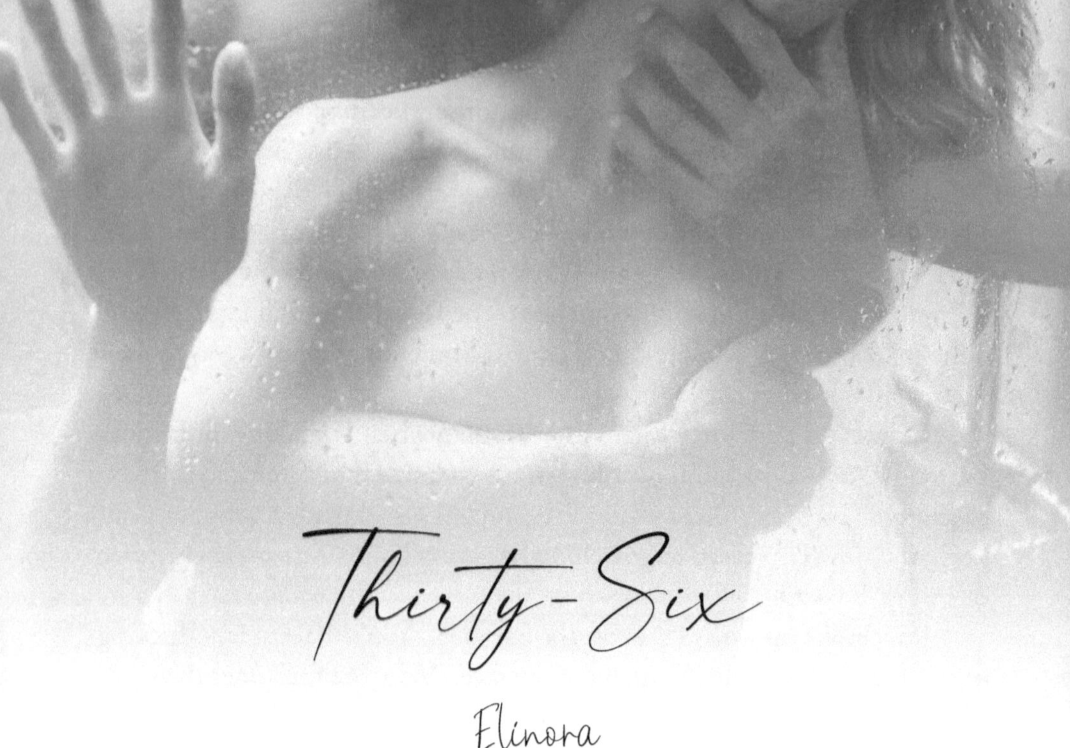

# Thirty-Six

## Elinora

It's Tuesday afternoon, which means I'm a few days into my arrangement with Lincoln. As promised, Office Lincoln has been one hundred percent professional. Polite without a hint of dominance. That should make me happy—this *is* my castle, after all—but every time I look at him, I'm reminded of River Lincoln. I think I need a hybrid version. Or, at the very least, it would be nice to feel like I'm not the only one squirming.

Suddenly warm, I remove my cardigan and drape it over the back of my chair. Lately, it seems like I'm always hot. I'm sure it has something to do with Lincoln. Either way, I need to talk to maintenance about getting my own thermostat up here.

I glance at my watch. He's due back from his lunch soon. The anticipation of his return thrills me to the point where I've gotten nothing accomplished during his absence. Instead, I've been sitting at my desk with my eyes fixed on the romance suite door. I smile to myself at the brilliant layout of Iverson Press's headquarters and my decision to place Lincoln in Iverson Melt.

My company takes up nearly three floors in a ritzy skyscraper near Bryant Park. The floor above me houses the mystery, suspense, thrillers, and crime fiction departments. The floor below comprises sci-fi, fantasy, young adult, and literary fiction. Smack dab in the middle—along with my office and our breakroom—is the romance and women's fiction suite. This was no mistake. Not only is romance my absolute favorite genre, but I need to be in the heart of the action. We share this floor with Hudson Graphics, Garrett's company, so Iverson Press only has about half of the available space. What this suite lacks in square footage, we make up for in profit.

My office overlooks the romance suite. Yesterday, I kept the Venetian blinds closed, discreetly peeking at Lincoln throughout the day. Deep in thought, poring over manuscripts with his glasses and tousled waves, his presence alone turned me on. Today, my blinds are wide open, and his empty cubicle calls out to me like a sex beacon.

Lincoln strides through the main door into the suite as if hearing my thoughts. He's wearing a charcoal suit with a navy dress shirt and silver tie. God, can that man fill out a suit. My lower belly flutters and tightens as he approaches my office and knocks on the door.

"Come in." I force a nonchalant tone.

Lincoln smiles, and I lose my breath. "Good afternoon, Ms. Iverson." He places a brown bag on my desk. "I brought you something."

"Thank you." I peek at the massive cupcake inside the bag. "This looks delicious."

"It's a chai spice cupcake. I thought you might enjoy it. Compass Roasters debuted them yesterday and they're calling them, 'Miles Chai Club.'" He smiles and pats his stomach. "I've already had three. I'm pretty much obsessed."

I peel the wrapper and take a bite, nearly moaning when the decadence coats my tongue. "You have excellent taste."

He sweeps his heated gaze over me, lingering on my breasts for a moment. "Believe me, I know."

A flood of heat dampens my panties. I press my knees together and shift in my chair. Lincoln's eyes track the movement, then snap to mine. Hunger swirls in his gaze. He doesn't say a word, but I hear him loud and clear.

*Every time you walk—or sit—I want you to remember my cock thrusting inside you. Stretching and filling you. Got it?*

"Yes," I murmur in response to his question in my head.

He raises a brow. "Yes, *what*, Ms. Iverson?"

*Yes, sir.* I flush, realizing I'm holding a simultaneous conversation with the River and Office editions of Lincoln. "I intended my response for someone else."

"And who might that be?" The satisfaction on his face hardens my nipples.

"Ask me again on Thursday."

Heat flares in his Atlantic eyes like someone threw gasoline on a bon-fire. He swallows tightly and shifts his stance. His gaze flicks below his belt, then back to mine.

I glance at his crotch. Sure enough, there's a prominent bulge. OK, so maybe he is squirming a little. Good. "Thank you for my delicious cupcake, Lincoln. That was a very sweet gesture."

"You deserve it." He abruptly turns and leaves my office, strutting to his cubicle. Even the way he walks is sexy. Settling, he meets my gaze across the room.

Unable to help myself, I give him my sultriest smile. He slowly shakes his head.

The afternoon dragged on with Lincoln's heated glances from across the suite and the lust they ignited in me. I forced myself to get some work done, but every time I shifted in my seat, I felt him. It's only Tuesday. There's no way I can make it until Thursday, when I feel like I'll combust if I don't have him. This is bad. I'm already failing to keep my editions separate.

I love the way his glasses rest on the bridge of his nose and pieces of hair fall over his forehead. How his eyes light up whenever he looks at me. His sweet gestures, which prove he's thinking of me even when I'm not around. I swear, every bite of that delicious cupcake made me want to kiss him more. Charles never brought me treats for no reason. Hell, he never even remem-bered our anniversary. Meanwhile, Lincoln has shown me more kindness and respect in two weeks than I received from Charles in fifteen years. Even though I shouldn't, I need Lincoln to know how he affects me. What can it hurt if we indulge in a hybrid version of our arrangement to tide us over?

I peek at my watch. It's finally time to go home. Like usual, everyone else filed out at five, leaving behind just Lincoln and me. A shiver of excite-ment courses through me as I reach beneath my desk and slide my panties off, stashing them in a drawer.

I approach his cubicle with a shopping bag full of books, exhilarated by the plan I've formulated. "Ready to go?"

He nods and powers down his computer. Rising, he glances at my bag. "What are those for?"

"Some signed books for a charity raffle we're holding. I figured since I have them in my possession, and haven't read all of them yet, I'd take a peek before I choose a winner."

"Sounds like a good plan." He peeks inside the bag and peruses the titles with a smirk. "Let me guess, they're all romance?"

"Of course. As I'm sure you've noticed, it's my favorite genre."

"I've noticed. Let me carry them." It's a command, not a request.

I hand over the bag. "Thank you."

"My pleasure." He gestures toward the door. "After you."

As we leave the suite, he holds the door open for me like always. We ride the elevator in silence. Lincoln maintains a safe distance away from me, but we may as well be touching. The air between us practically vibrates with sexual tension.

My body heats with every step, and I'm acutely aware of the arousal gathering between my thighs. I've never gone panty-free. Ever. I don't know where this boldness is coming from, but I enjoy this feeling of empowerment as a woman. I glance at the gorgeous man at my side and smile. It's coming from him. He makes me feel this way. Beautiful, respected, and free. Lincoln makes me feel alive.

We make our way to the parking garage and stop at my Porsche. I pop the trunk and motion for him to load the bag of books inside.

Lincoln sets them down and closes the trunk. "Well, I hope you have a nice evening, Ms. Iverson. I'll see you tomorrow."

I grip his tie. "I'm not ready for you to leave yet."

His eyes widen. "I've got work to do tonight."

"It can wait." I trail my fingertips down his chest. "But I can't."

Lincoln rakes a hand through his hair. "I promised you I'd be professional at work."

I smile up at him and gesture to the parking garage. "Does this look like the office to you?"

"Semantics, Ms. Iverson."

I pat the side of the Porsche. "Get in the car."

"I'm bartending this evening," he protests, glancing at his watch. "I don't want to be late."

"This won't take long." Opening the rear door on the driver's side, I tug on his tie once more. "Now get in the goddamn car."

# Thirty-Seven

### Lincoln

I settle on the black leather seat and stare at Elinora in shock. She casts a quick glance over her shoulder and presses me further into the vehicle. I scoot aside as she climbs in, closing the door behind her.

"Someone could see," I warn.

"Don't care." She gently removes my glasses and sets them on the front console for safekeeping, then launches herself at me, landing across my lap in a straddle. Her lips crash with mine in a hungry, desperate kiss. She weaves her fingers into my hair and tugs the strands.

Groaning, I slide my palms to her ass and pull her deeper into my lap. Elinora leads the frenzied kiss, her tongue surging into my mouth, rubbing and stroking with mine. She unbuckles my belt.

I break the kiss and still her hands. "I don't have a condom."

"We're in luck." She snatches her purse and whips one out. "I bought some this morning." She yanks my zipper down and pulls my cock out, rolling the condom on.

I shove her skirt to her hips. "Holy fuck." I breathe, swiping my fingertips over her slick, wet pussy. "You don't have panties."

"I ditched them in my office," she explains between kisses. "Figured they'd get in our way."

There is nothing sexier to me than the fact that she premeditated this. We both moan as she lines herself up and slides down onto me.

"So we're clear, this counts as my castle." Elinora pins my hands at my shoulders and moves, riding me like she'll die if she doesn't fuck me. Her tight wet pussy squeezes my cock in a vise grip, and I'll be lucky if I last a minute.

"You are so fucking sexy," I grit out.

She moans and brings her lips to my neck. Licking and sucking until my eyes roll back into my head.

"Oh my God," I groan.

She nips my neck. "Not God. Just Elinora." She clenches her inner muscles and I feel it to my toes. "That's the only name I want leaving your lips."

My cock throbs at her use of my words. I remember how I felt when I said them, so it turns me on even more to hear it spill from her lips in such a sultry, dominant tone. She tightens her grip on my hands like she's holding the reins to a stallion and changes to a slow, grinding pace. When she rode me in the lagoon on Friday, she admitted she loves how it rubs her clit. But that was different because I ran the show. Right now—with her thighs caging my hips, my hands pinned in place, and her lips on my neck—I'm completely at her mercy. The queen's in the saddle now, and so help me God, submitting to her is the most erotic thing I've ever experienced.

I clench my jaw. "Elinora, you feel like heaven."

She moans and picks up her pace, driving herself onto my cock. Her nails dig into my hands, and she sucks on my neck harder. "I'm gonna come," she says between gasps. "Oh, *Lincoln*." Her pussy spasms as her cries fill the Porsche.

I groan and meet her thrusts.

"Come for me." She moans, riding the wave of her orgasm. "Right now."

Two more thrusts and my cock jerks with my release. Nothing compares to the ecstasy this woman gives me. I have never orgasmed on command. Ever.

I moan her name as my climax rocks me to my soul. "Angel, you're killing me."

Elinora releases my hands and tenderly kisses my lips. I pull her close and kiss her with a reverence that mirrors my desire to worship her. Forever.

She pulls back and smiles, brushing her hand down my cheek. "Thank you for the cupcake."

"If that's what a cupcake can do, I'll build you a fucking bakery."

She laughs. "You're too much. But if you plan to seduce me with treats,

I'll have you know I love chocolate." She touches my neck. "Oops. I gave you a hickey."

"I don't care. You can put them all over me."

Satisfaction flares in her gaze. "Every time you look at it, I want you to remember how tightly my body gripped you when I sucked on your neck."

"Holy fuck." My cock jerks at her words. "Is this payback for what I said to you about sitting?"

She grins and slides my glasses back onto my face. "You're damn right, it is. Now *you* can think about *me* when I'm not around."

"Elinora, all I do is think about you."

# Thirty-Eight

## Lincoln

I t's Wednesday night. I dragged my sorry ass to The River after making out in the car with Elinora again. I bartended on Monday and Tuesday, but tonight I'm in the lagoon.

I swallow against the acid in my throat and head for the bar, needing some whiskey to numb the ache in my chest.

Gideon eyes me. "Why do you look like somebody stomped your puppy?"

Ignoring Esme's one-drink limit for employees, I knock back two shots of Jameson. I'll need the alcohol to survive my shift. "I don't want to be here."

He smirks. "You may change your mind when you see who's on your schedule."

*Unless it's Elinora, there will be no mindset adjustment.* "Oh yeah?"

He holds up a clipboard. "The beautiful Ms. Alvarez."

*Maya.* Before I met Elinora, the mention of my friend's name would more than stir my loins. Tonight? Absolutely nothing.

"Cool."

Gideon grips my arm. "What's going on, man? You've been on edge. Does it have something to do with your boss?"

"Which one?" I snort, pouring a third shot of Irish whiskey.

"Lady E."

I swallow the shot. "Again, which one?"

"Oh, fuck." He chuckles. "That's right. I didn't realize both start with E. That's kinda funny."

"In other circumstances, it would be hilarious. Now? Not so much. I'm fucked, bro."

"Thought you were gonna slit Z's throat when he tried hitting on her that night."

"Yeah." I stare at the wall of glass bottles like they can get me out of this mess. Forget mess, my situation is a five-alarm dumpster fire, and I'm the moron holding the match. Zarek is only the first layer of burning garbage. Supposedly, he's a changed man, but I still don't trust him. Correction, I will *never* trust that asshole. Especially not around Elinora. "He'd better stay the fuck away from her."

"Never seen you like this before." Gideon eyes me while rubbing his jaw. "Normally, you jump at the opportunity to be with Maya."

"My life's normalcy is nonexistent." I lower my voice to a whisper. "I only want to be with one woman. Period. End of story."

"But Esme's got you by the balls?"

"Yep."

"So, what's your game plan?"

I run both hands over my face. "I have no fucking clue."

"Howdy, boys," Maya calls from behind us as she approaches the bar.

I flash Gideon a warning look before spinning around. "Hey. You're not usually here on a Wednesday."

"Heard you were gonna be here, so I figured I'd drop by." She grins and settles on a bar stool, eyeing the bottles of booze. "I'm thirsty."

Gideon smiles. "What can I get you?"

"I'm feeling fruity." She tucks a wayward strand of hair behind her ear and studies the drink menu. "How about Grey Goose and cranberry?"

He grabs a glass. "Light on the cranberry, I assume?"

"You know it."

We have a two-drink limit at The River to ensure members are aware of what—and who—they're doing. Nowadays, Maya only ever orders one, and it's always the same. I'm not sure why she bothers looking at the menu.

"Don't forget her two lime wedges," I add, sipping my whiskey.

She points to my glass. "What are you drinking?"

"Jameson."

"Ah, getting back to your roots?"

Maya always calls me her hot Irishman. She's not wrong about the Irish part—my parents moved to New York from Dublin in their twenties, so I'm full-blooded—but I was born here.

"You can bet the Chilean flag on your ass, Sea Bass."

She and her family emigrated from the South American country when she was ten. With light brown skin, luxe mahogany waves, and a smile that could stop traffic, Maya is as warm as she is radiant. And she does, in fact, have a Chilean flag tattoo on her ass cheek. It's sexy as fuck.

"So, what's new?" I ask.

She shrugs. "Eh, not much. Work's the same. I'm still single. My cat has diabetes."

"Is Pablo OK?" I squeeze her arm, knowing how much she adores her cat.

"Yeah, he'll be fine. I've gotta give him insulin injections though, which sucks." She picks at her nails. "There was something else I was gonna tell you, but I forgot."

"Here you go." Gideon sets her drink in front of her.

"Thanks. Oh yeah, I'm gonna be an aunt."

"Congrats," Gideon says with a broad grin. Whereas most of the guys here grimace at the mention of babies, he adores kids. He's always talking about having a family of his own one day. "I'm referring to the aunt part, obviously."

"Thanks, I guess."

I raise a brow at Maya. "You don't sound thrilled."

"My sister and I don't talk, so my aunt status will be solely based on the title. My mom's excited, so that's cool." She narrows her mocha-colored eyes on my neck and smiles. "*Dios mío.* Kennedy, is that a hickey?"

Leave it to Maya to notice Elinora's mark. Not that I'm surprised—as a paralegal, her attention to detail rivals mine.

Heat floods my face. "Maybe, but I don't kiss and tell."

"Pretty sure you don't kiss at *all*. Now I'm extra intrigued."

Gideon chuckles. "Ask him to fill you in about Elsa."

Maya raises a brow. "Elsa?"

I wave her off. "I'll tell you later."

"Good." She downs her vodka cranberry, rises, and grips my wrist. "Let's go. I'm horny as hell."

I trail behind Maya on our way to the lagoon. Her purple halter dress reveals the extensive scarring on her upper back. My blood boils at the sight because I've seen her naked enough times to know it's only the tip of the iceberg. The marks hidden beneath her clothes are far worse. I shudder to think of what could have happened if I hadn't stumbled upon the scene.

Swallowing tightly, I enter my room code and usher her inside. "I need to talk to you."

"I want you." Maya places her palms on my chest and looks me up and down. "We can talk later."

I squeeze my eyes shut. "I can't do this."

She cups my face. "Tell me what's going on. Did I do something wrong?"

"No, you didn't do anything. This is all me. I, uh, I met someone."

She smiles and takes a step back. "Congratulations. That's awesome."

I sink onto a leather chaise. "She's my boss."

Maya plops beside me. "Wait a minute, you want *Esme?*"

"Fuck no. Maybe I did at one point, but those days are over. I'm talking about my actual boss . . . *Elsa.*" The nickname works, so I stick with it to protect Elinora's privacy. I rub my jaw and sigh. "She's the publisher I work for."

"Does she know?"

"Yes and no."

Maya rolls her eyes. "That's helpful, thanks."

"She knows I want her, but she doesn't know about my contract with Esme, and I'd like to keep it that way." I bury my face in my hands. "I promised her I wouldn't be with anyone else here."

As one of the few people who know about my situation, Maya's been the one who makes it bearable.

"Lincoln, how the hell do you plan to accomplish that? Will Esme let you bartend exclusively?"

"Nope. Already tried that. She got nasty and rubbed our agreement in my face. She said I need to be in the lagoon during at least two of my shifts." I curl my lip. "Then she took it even further, saying I'd need to vary them."

"What do you mean?"

"She plans to fuck with me. Basically, I won't know whether I'm supposed to be behind the bar, or in the lagoon, until I get here. It's her way of ensuring I don't call out sick from my lagoon shifts."

"Damn. She takes manipulative to a whole new level."

"Right?" I knot my hands in my hair. "I don't know what I'm gonna do.

I'm falling for Elsa. Fucking hard. I can't stomach the thought of being with anyone else." I reach over and squeeze her wrist. "Not even you, Sea Bass."

Maya nods. "I get it. You found your one and only."

"Yeah, but I can't be her one and only because she can't be mine. Given her ex-husband's infidelity, me having multiple partners is a hard limit."

She purses her lips. "I may have an idea."

"Does it involve me faking my death or something?"

She giggles. "Not your death, but it involves faking."

I snort. "Are you suggesting we pretend to fuck?"

"That's exactly what I'm suggesting." Maya grabs her purse and withdraws a planner. She's one of those people who prefers paper over the digital kind on her phone. "You tell me the days Esme expects you to be with someone other than your girl, and I'll make damn sure I'm the only woman on your schedule for those nights."

"I won't know for sure since she plans to switch it up, but it will be on assorted Mondays, Tuesdays, and Wednesdays. What will we do, play cards?"

Maya laughs. "I hate card games. We can do whatever we want. Sleep, read, swim, eat—it doesn't matter. Personally, I have a ton of documents I ought to read for my boss's upcoming trial. I'll bring my laptop and get some work done. You can do the same or twiddle your thumbs if you like. If you wind up bartending, I'll hang out at the bar with you."

"Holy fuck, Sea Bass. You're a genius."

She grins. "No shit."

"Since Esme forced me to pick up three additional shifts, I've been freaking out over how I'll get my regular work done. If I bring my laptop here, I'll stay on track with my manuscripts."

"Exactly. Esme is a calculating woman. Why not beat her at her own game? Fulfill your time obligations and let *her* pay you to work on Miss Publisher's manuscripts." She waggles her brows. "I won't tell."

"You're willing to give up three nights a week for me?"

"Lincoln, you're my friend, and I love you. You deserve to be happy. Besides, reading legal jargon is what I'd be doing at home by myself anyway. I'd much rather hang with you."

I wrap Maya in a tight hug. "Sea Bass, I love you."

"Love you more, Lincoln Log." She peers up into my eyes. "After what you did for me, you know you can count on me for anything."

"I appreciate that." I hug her tighter and beat back the images trying to hijack my brain. I can only imagine how the memories torment her. The trauma she endured was horrendous, yet it could have been so much worse.

A few moments of silence pass as we battle the demons in our heads. Determined to always be her life raft, I draw a steadying breath and force myself to focus on the present. And the fact that she's willing to sacrifice her evenings for me. "Wait a minute," I begin, thinking of her voracious appetite for sex. "What about you?"

"What *about* me?"

"You know, your needs."

"I'll live." Maya waves me off. "Celibacy never killed anyone." She gnaws her lip and thinks for a moment. "Right?"

I snort. "Dunno. I haven't been celibate for more than a month since I was seventeen."

"Same."

"But in all seriousness, I know membership here isn't cheap. I feel bad about you spending all that money and not having the chance to partake."

"Esme doesn't charge me."

"Seriously?"

"It's part of our arrangement. Kinda like hush money, I guess."

"Makes sense," I say, even though I'll never understand how she comes anywhere near this place after her ordeal a couple years ago.

She nudges me. "Yeah, so unless you plan to rig a remote-controlled dildo to help a girl out, I suggest you stop worrying about it."

"Do they make remote-controlled ones?"

"Sure do." She flashes a wicked grin. "Anyway, enough about me and my extensive sex toy knowledge. I want every detail about Elsa, including why you let her give you a hickey."

# Thirty-Nine

## Elinora

There's a disruption in the force field. Tingles race down my spine, and my nipples harden. I feel Lincoln's presence even before I lay eyes on him. I glance up from my computer, and sure enough, he's here.

He strides to his desk and furrows his brow at the container of pastries I left for him, on which I affixed a sticky note that reads, "Special treats for my favorite editor."

After he brought me the cupcake the other day, I wanted to return the favor with some homemade Danish pastries. While I'm not much of a cook, I'm a phenomenal baker—especially when it comes to the goodies I learned to make during my early childhood in Denmark.

Lincoln opens the container and smiles. Then he takes a large bite and makes his way to my office while he chews. He pauses in the doorway, shaking his head approvingly.

"You like?" I ask.

"This is the best thing I've ever tasted. I need to know which bakery sells them, so I can buy the place out."

I motion for him to have a seat. "They're an Elinora exclusive."

His eyes widen. "You made them?"

"Yes. I love to bake. It moved me the other day when you thought of me, so I wanted to do something for you." The room is suddenly much warmer, so I fan myself with a stack of papers.

"Thank you," he murmurs, placing a hand on his chest. "That means a lot. Where did you learn this recipe?"

"My mother and I used to make them when we lived in Copenhagen. She owned a bakery, and I was often her assistant. This one is my favorite. It's essentially a chocolate cinnamon roll, but without the cinnamon. We call it a direktørsnegl," I flash a sly grin, "aka boss snail."

He laughs. "I'd say that's an appropriate moniker for this delicacy."

"Well, I was going to make you some wienerbrød, but I thought you'd appreciate the chocolate more."

"Dare I ask what they make *wiener*brød from?"

I laugh and shake my head. "Definitely *not* one of those. When you think of a traditional Danish pastry, the flaky kind with the good stuff in the middle, that is called wienerbrød. It translates to Viennese bread. My mother used to make them with a raspberry filling, which was to die for."

"When did you move to New York?" he asks, taking another bite of his direktørsnegl.

"My father left us when I was six, but my mother wanted to keep the bakery afloat. Unfortunately, she couldn't swing the costs of running a business and raising a child on her own, so she had to sell it. We came to New York when I was ten."

"Does she live in Manhattan?"

"No, Mom moved back to Copenhagen to care for my grandmother when I was twenty-five. I stayed here to run Iverson Press."

"I'm surprised you don't have more of an accent."

"My parents insisted I be bilingual. We had English-speaking neighbors with kids my age, so I gravitated more toward that language. I'm fluent in both, though I rarely speak in my native tongue."

"When was the last time you visited Denmark?"

"Two years ago, after my divorce, I spent three weeks there. Sometimes a woman just needs her mom, you know?" A pang of wistfulness tightens my chest. I should really make an effort to visit more often. "Anyway, I threw myself into baking as a distraction and gained twenty pounds eating pastries. I've lost most of the weight now, and I could probably lose the rest, but that would require fewer pastries—something I'm unwilling to consider."

"You're perfect," he blurts. "I mean, if it makes you happy, I think you should eat as many pastries as you want."

I smile. "Thank you."

"Thank you for making them for me." He meets my gaze. "And for calling me your favorite editor."

I lean in close. "I'll let you in on a little secret. Even if we didn't have our carnal arrangement, you'd still be my favorite editor. Hiring you was one of the best decisions I've made. You're the best I've ever had. And that goes for *both* editions."

Lincoln's breath rushes out of him. He presses his hand to his chest once more and tries to reply, but his words won't come. Finally, he leans forward and holds my gaze. "Thank you." His gravelly tone belies my words' effect on him. "And likewise."

Freya appears in the doorway. "Morning." She eyes Lincoln's direktørs-negl. "Um, is that a boss snail?"

He grins. "It is."

She raises a questioning brow at me. "Funny, no one has ever baked them especially for *me*. Except for on my birthday last year."

"Perhaps if you outshine all the editors I've employed since this company's birth, *and* bring me chai cupcakes, maybe I'll feel compelled to bake you something more often."

Freya chuckles and gestures to him. "Something tells me Clark Kent will inspire a whole new line of baked goods, am I right?"

Lincoln's gaze darts between us. "Clark Kent?"

I give Freya a warning glare, but she ignores me. "Yeah, the boss lady is enamored with a certain hunky new editor who resembles Superman."

While I turn redder than a tomato, Lincoln's grin stretches from ear to ear. "Is that so?"

I meet his gaze. "What makes you think she's talking about you?"

Before he can answer, Freya prances around the room singing Annie Lennox's "Take Me to The River."

Lincoln eyes her. "So much for the NDA, huh, Freya?"

"You're basically a member, so I'm not technically violating the NDA." Freya pats his shoulder. "Besides, secrecy is pointless since she's already been there."

He leans back in his seat and peers up at her, a peculiar expression on his face. "You knew all along, didn't you?"

"Knew what?"

"You knew she'd be with me."

"I have no idea what you're talking about," she says with feigned innocence.

Lincoln leans forward, his eyes locked on her face. "I think you do."

*Wait, what?* My mouth drops open. Freya knew Lincoln worked at The River? Is that why she took me there? *Holy fuck. She set us up.* Esme said Freya gave her a heads-up, which is why she already had somebody in mind for me. That means our first encounter was most definitely prearranged. *That conniving little wench!* I could slap her. And hug and kiss her.

"Freya Thorne, you have some explaining to do." I glance at Lincoln. "As do you, Mr. Kennedy."

Freya waves me off. "Let's focus on the big picture, shall we?"

A wicked smile curves Lincoln's lips. "But the devil's in the details."

I'm still processing everything after a lengthy conversation with Freya, where I learned she and Lincoln recognized each other the day I hired him. While she did, in fact, set me up, Lincoln wasn't part of that ploy. His shock was genuine.

The thing is, I'm not mad. Not even a little. Office Lincoln is the breath of fresh air Iverson Melt needs. River Lincoln, with his heat and passion, is the plot twist *I* need. Workplace hierarchy be damned; I know my thawing heart needs *all* of Lincoln.

Images of him with other women at The River taunt me. Does he show them the same level of care as he's shown me? Does he hold their bodies close in the lagoon, stroke their hair, and whisper their names in reverence after they fuck? He said I'm one of three women he's kissed in his lifetime, but was it just lip service? Could I be as special to him as he is to me, or am I only a fish in his river?

After years of Charles having a side piece, I'm done with sharing my man. Granted, Lincoln isn't officially mine, but I need him to be. I can't stomach the thought of him being with anyone other than me. But who am I to ask that of him?

I'm seated at my desk, skimming a new contract, when Freya pops her head in. "Does the name Stefan ring a bell to you?"

"No. Should it?"

"He said you go way back."

"Which line is he on?"

Freya shakes her head. "He's here. Downstairs in the lobby. Mike from security sent me a pic." She pats the pockets of her dress pants. "Fuck. I left my phone on my desk. Let me go grab it."

"No, it's fine. Just tell me what he looks like," I say, running through the list of publishing contacts in my head.

"Tall. Blond. Blue-eyed." She points to me. "Kinda like a buff, hot, male version of you."

"Stefan Arnold. Holy shit. Send him in."

"Who is he?"

"Stefan owns a publishing company based out of Berlin. We met years ago at a conference. He was interested in me, but I was married to Charles. I wonder what he's doing in New York."

"OK, so we're *sure* he's not a hitman sent by Charles?"

"No, he's definitely not," I assure her with a chuckle. "Actually, you know what?" I rise and smooth my skirt. "I'll go greet him so I can give him the Iverson Press grand tour."

Freya grins. "You never miss a chance to show off your empire, do ya?"

"I try not to. I worked hard for this." I make my way through the suite as she returns to her desk.

"Working hard?" I ask Lincoln as I pass him.

"For you? Always." He flashes me a wink and watches me leave the suite.

I ride the elevator to the ground floor and spot Stefan across the lobby. He's still as handsome as the last time I saw him.

"Stefan Arnold, to what do I owe the pleasure?"

He beams. "I was in New York for business, so I thought I'd stop by." His thick German accent reminds me of one of my college professors.

"Welcome to Iverson Press. My own little corner of the industry."

"From what I hear, it's not a little corner." His pale blue eyes sparkle with admiration as he stretches out his hand. "I'm curious to know how an independently-owned publishing house is giving the Big Five a run for their money."

"I have my ways." I smile and clasp his palm. "How about a tour?"

Stefan's grip is firm. "I'd love one. Perhaps you'd like to join me for lunch afterward?"

"You know what? That sounds wonderful."

We make small talk on the ride upstairs, quickly arriving on the eleventh floor. The doors slide open to reveal Garrett waiting for the elevator, likely for his daily trip to Compass Roasters. He steps aside so we can exit.

"Howdy." He smiles, curiosity lighting his golden eyes.

"Garrett, this is my colleague Stefan Arnold of Arnold Press. He's in the city for business and stopped by to say hello." I glance at Stefan. "Garrett Casey owns Hudson Graphics, the design firm that handles most of our book covers, among millions of other things."

"Nice to meet you, Mr. Casey."

"You as well." Garrett's gaze lingers on Stefan like he's sizing him up. It shouldn't surprise me—my friend has always been protective—but there's something strange about his expression as they shake hands. His eyes flick to mine, and the warmth that was there just moments ago is gone. He gestures to the romance suite's door. "You giving him the grand tour?"

"Absolutely," I say with a laugh.

"Let me know if you need anything today." Garrett searches my face, his eyes burning into mine like twin gold lasers. "I'll be around."

"Great, thank you." I smile, more than a little puzzled by his odd behavior.

"By the way, how's the new guy working out for you?"

My stomach flutters at his mention of Lincoln. "Better than expected."

"Told you." Garrett pats himself on the back and steps onto the elevator, smirking as the doors close between us.

I return my attention to Stefan and motion for him to follow me into the romance suite. I feel Lincoln's gaze the moment we set foot in the room.

"Wow," Stefan murmurs. "This is impressive."

I touch his shoulder. "You haven't seen anything yet. *This* is only the romance suite," I say, making a sweeping gesture with my arm. "Or as I like to say, 'where the magic happens.'"

Stefan raises a brow. "You've dedicated *all* these editors to romance? It seems excessive."

"Not only is romance my favorite genre, but Iverson Melt is by far our most profitable imprint." I force a smile, moderately irked to discover Stefan's one of those people who looks down on the genre. "It's an excess I'm happy to embrace."

Lincoln's gaze tracks our movement as I lead Stefan around the room's perimeter, describing the headquarters' layout and the imprints we publish.

We pass Myles on his way out for lunch. "Myles, I'd like you to meet Mr. Stefan Arnold, CEO of Arnold Press in Berlin." I turn to Stefan. "Myles Callahan is a prized member of my marketing team."

"Thank you, Elinora." He clasps Stefan's hand. "Nice to meet you, Mr. Arnold."

"The pleasure's all mine."

"Enjoy your lunch, Myles. Before you leave for the day, I need to see you in my office."

"I have a meeting this afternoon, but I can come after close of business if that works?"

"That's fine. As long as it's today."

He shifts uneasily, raking a hand through his fiery red hair. "Is everything all right?"

"More than all right. I thought we'd discuss the details of your promotion."

His emerald-colored eyes widen. "What promotion?"

"The one I will tell you about later."

"Oh." His grin stretches from ear to ear. "I'll be there. Thank you." He practically skips out of the office.

Myles busts his ass for me, so his promotion to executive director of marketing is long overdue. Besides, he brought me Lincoln.

I touch Stefan's arm. "There's someone else who I'd like you to meet before we go out. This gentleman is the cream of the crop."

Lincoln's wary gaze locks on to Stefan as we approach his cubicle. The hint of jealousy I detect in the hard set of his jaw and deeply furrowed brow intrigues me. Maybe I have more of an effect on him than I thought.

"This young man is Lincoln Kennedy, the newest addition to the Iverson Press team and Iverson Melt's top editor. Lincoln, allow me to introduce Mr. Stefan Arnold, CEO of Arnold Press."

"You're based in Berlin?" Lincoln asks.

"Yes, that's correct." Stefan smiles and holds out his palm. "You've heard of us?"

"I have." Lincoln nods and shakes his hand. "Nice to meet you."

"Likewise, Mr. Kennedy. You should know you work for a phenomenal businesswoman."

"Oh, most definitely. I'm learning something new each day." Genuine admiration shines in Lincoln's gaze when he turns to me. "If you have a moment later, I'd like to discuss one of the manuscripts."

I open my mouth to speak, but Stefan beats me to it. "Yes, well, that will have to wait. Elinora and I have a lot of catching up to do, so I'm going to steal her away."

Something flares in Lincoln's gaze. "Is that so?"

I bite back a smirk at the possession in his tone and decide to goad him a bit. I need to know how he'd feel if I swam with other fish. Would it bother him? Make him jealous? Or am I the only one who wants more?

"Stefan is an old friend. We're heading out for lunch so we can get reacquainted." I touch Stefan's arm. "I need to grab my purse. Let me show you my office. Have a nice afternoon, Lincoln."

Lincoln clenches his jaw, his gaze burning into me. "See you later."

"Maybe." I shrug and glance at Stefan. "I can't make any guarantees."

# Forty

## Lincoln

My blood boils as I watch Elinora leave with the womanizing bastard from Germany. Courtesy of an old coworker from Cooper Press—who once worked for Arnold—I'm well aware of his seedy business tactics and the way he treats his female employees. He's pushy and self-centered, and from what I've heard, doesn't take well to hearing the word "No." I have half a mind to trail them to make sure he keeps his hands off Elinora.

What the hell did she mean when she said she couldn't make any guarantees? Was I wrong to assume our River rendezvous are set in stone? Is she having doubts about our arrangement? Or worse, is she interested in that dick Stefan Arnold?

I rub the back of my neck and try to focus on the manuscript I'm editing, but Elinora is all I can think about. Her passion for books. The way her eyes light up when she discusses romance. The wistfulness in her tone when she mentioned her mother and Denmark. I can't believe she baked something for me. No woman has ever done that—gone out of her way to show her appreciation.

No one has ever praised the quality of my work like she does. Unlike Esme, she values me, not the money she can make from me. Elinora appreciates my editorial prowess as much as, if not more than, my skills in the sack. That speaks volumes.

I glance at my watch. It's five o'clock, which means Elinora has been gone for four fucking hours. Where the hell is she? Everyone else has already left for the day. Meanwhile, I peck away at my keyboard, determined to finish these fucking edits.

When Garrett stopped by earlier to speak with Elinora, he seemed unnerved when I told him she went out for lunch with Arnold. I questioned him about it, and his reply made me even more uneasy. Evidently, the guy gave him a weird vibe when they met, and it raised his hackles. No one, and I mean *no one*, can read people as well as Garrett. He has a sixth sense that rivals most fortune tellers. The fact that he picked up on something strange, without knowing Arnold's history like I do, tells me I'm not overreacting. Here it is, closing in on dinnertime, and Elinora still isn't back from "lunch."

The door to the suite suddenly opens, jolting me from the worries filling my head. I duck behind a neighboring cubicle as Elinora waltzes inside with Arnold on her tail. Their brisk strides reach her office in no time.

She tosses her purse onto the desk. "It was great catching up with you, Stefan. How long are you in town for?"

"A week. I have business in Los Angeles afterward. What does your weekend look like? Perhaps we can do dinner and a show?"

"Hmm, I'll have to get back to you on that. I may have other plans."

*Goddamn right, you do.*

"I'd suggest canceling them," he murmurs, touching the small of her back.

Elinora stiffens. "Like I said, I'll get back to you."

I slowly rise to my full height. Neither one knows I'm here, and my silent approach is that of a stalking predator, ready to pounce in an instant. The last thing I want to do is interfere with Elinora's potential business dealings, but I can feel her discomfort from across the room.

Arnold grips her waist. "I'm staying at The Platinum in Times Square. Why don't you stop by?"

I clench my jaw tight enough to break my teeth. If that asshole touches her again, I'll break *his* teeth.

Flattening her palms on his chest, she pushes him back. "I think you may have misinterpreted what I meant when I suggested we reconnect. I was referring to a professional connection, you know, as business contacts." She shakes her head. "I'm sorry, Stefan, but I'm not interested in pursuing anything else."

"What if I am?" He clutches her shoulders.

"Unfortunately, you're out of luck. Now take your hands off me."

Instead of doing as she asks, Arnold kisses her.

# Forty-One

## Elinora

Stefan jams his tongue into my mouth, making it hard for me to breathe. I struggle against his hold as panic rises in my chest.

Lincoln appears out of nowhere and grabs Stefan by his throat. He slams him against the wall. "She said she wasn't interested!" His voice reverberates through the empty suite like a thunderclap.

"This is none of your business." Stefan takes a swing.

Lincoln blocks the punch and tackles him, pinning him face down on the floor with his arms behind his back. Pressing his knee between Stefan's shoulder blades, he meets my gaze. "You all right?" I manage a nod, and he turns back to Stefan, who continues to struggle. Lincoln digs his knee deeper. "Tell me, Arnold, do you remember a woman named Ingrid Mueller?"

Stefan immediately goes limp.

"Yeah, I thought so."

"Who is she?" I ask.

"Ingrid is a dear friend of mine who worked for your buddy here." He pulls Stefan's arms back. "Remember her?" When Stefan doesn't reply, Lincoln leans his full weight into him.

"Yes," Stefan gasps. "I remember her."

"Tell Elinora what you did to Ingrid three years ago in an alley behind a Berlin bar."

Stefan mumbles something.

Lincoln wrenches his arms back. "Can't hear you."

"I had sex with her."

"Consensual sex?" Lincoln yanks on his arms.

"No."

My mouth falls open in horror. I was moments from being another Ingrid Mueller.

"It was her fault. She seduced me," Stefan sputters.

"No, she was drunk, and you used your position of authority to take advantage of her. Whether or not a woman's drunk, no means no, mother-fucker." Lincoln nods to me. "Call security."

I snatch the phone from my desk and make the call. Minutes later, Mike and Tim from security rush into the office.

"Here's how this is gonna work," Lincoln lowers his lips to Stefan's ear, "I'll let you walk out of here with them. But if I *ever* catch you near Elinora again, I'll make damn sure your walking days are over. Got it?"

"Yes." Stefan wheezes. "Please get off me."

Lincoln releases him and rises. "All yours, gentlemen."

Mike and Tim take over, haul Stefan to his feet, and escort him from the office.

Lincoln brushes his hands on his pants and watches the other men leave before turning back to me. "Are you sure you're all right?"

"Yes. Thank you."

He jerks his thumb toward the front door. "Were you interested in him?"

"No."

He cocks his head to the side. "You sure?"

I stiffen my spine. "One hundred percent."

"Good. He's a fucking piece of shit. Ingrid still hasn't come to terms with what he did. He's lucky I didn't feed him his dick." He stalks over to me. "You said you were doing lunch. Why were you gone for so long?"

"After we ate, I brought him to a few of the independent bookstores in the area."

He nods. "If you weren't interested in him, why'd you goad me?"

My gaze snaps to his. "Huh?"

"Elinora, if you think I didn't realize you were trying to make me jeal-ous, you're underestimating me." When I don't reply, he raises an eyebrow. "Am I right?"

I huff out a breath and cross my arms over my chest. "And what if I was?"

He steps closer to me. "What if you were, what?"

"Ok, fine. I was trying to make you jealous," I snap, pissed that he's making me confess. "Are you happy now?"

"Tell me why."

I look away. "I don't know."

Lincoln tips my chin to face him. "Yes, you do."

"Because I wanted to see if I was the only one who felt like this."

"Like what?" He backs me toward the desk.

"I'm jealous of the women at The River. I don't want to share you, Lincoln. Not with anyone. And I want more than our office/River arrangement. I want more of you. I shouldn't, but I do." I rub my arms. "I guess I wanted to know if—"

"Listen to me." Lincoln grips the sides of my face. "You are my kryptonite, and I'd sell my soul to be the man you need. I'm all yours, angel." He seizes my lips in a fierce kiss, weaving his hands into my hair.

As our tongues tangle in a frenzied dance, Lincoln lifts me to sit on the edge of the desk. He nudges my knees apart and stands between them. I hook my ankles around the backs of his thighs and tug on his hair, kissing him even harder. Deeper.

My movements dislodge his glasses, which clatter to the desk. "Shit. Sorry."

He doesn't seem to care, even as they fall on the floor when he clears the desk with a swipe of his arm. He hikes my skirt to my waist and groans at the sight of my lace panties.

"These need to go." He peels them off me and flings them onto my chair.

I yank open his belt and zipper, then shove his pants and boxers to his thighs, desperate to feel him inside me. My pussy is soaked and aching for him. My body craves him deeper than I thought possible. He presses me back to lie on the desk without breaking our kiss, then settles on top of me and lines up his cock. Before I can breathe, he sheathes himself inside me with one hard thrust.

I cry out and grip his back, fisting the material of his dress shirt.

"You good?" he asks with a grunt.

"Yes."

He moves with wild, animalistic thrusts like my answer was his call to arms. I'm his land to claim, his kingdom to conquer. What he doesn't realize is that my walls crumbled the first time he made me come, back in our lagoon, with just his fingers. Back when I fell for the fantasy of him. Right now, I've got the real thing. Raw. Unleashed. Knowing his control has snapped empowers me. And makes me fall harder.

Lincoln pushes me higher with each pounding thrust, his cock stroking deeper than I've ever felt him. Our moans mix with the slap of our bodies colliding. My desk lamp crashes to the floor, but he doesn't stop.

I wail his name and shatter into an orgasm, but he doesn't slow his pace, driving his cock inside me like he'll die if we stop fucking.

I dig my nails into his ass cheeks and tighten my legs around him. "Oh, God, Lincoln."

Before I realize it, he takes me over the edge a second time. My entire body spasms and quakes. His thrusts become even more frenzied. He buries his face in my neck, and groans rip from his chest as he passes the point of no return.

"*Elinora.*" His cock jerks and pulses, but he doesn't stop, his hips moving like pistons on a runaway freight train.

I never knew it was possible for a man to keep going after he climaxed. Lincoln is a man and a machine. *He's mine.*

Movement across the room catches my attention.

Myles appears in the doorway. "What the—" His mouth drops open, and his shell-shocked gaze lands on mine.

I shove at Lincoln's shoulders, but his body moves on autopilot. "Ice!" I shriek.

Lincoln lurches upward and rolls off me. Tripping over the pants around his ankles, he lands on the floor behind my desk with a loud thud.

"What's wrong? Did I hurt you?" he sputters, gripping the edge of the desk. He pulls himself to a kneeling position and feels around on the floor for his glasses. "Talk to me, angel." Shoving the spectacles back onto his face, he catches sight of his best friend. "Fuck."

I sit up and frantically fix my skirt and blouse. "Hello, Myles."

"Hi." Myles glares at Lincoln. "What the fuck is wrong with you?"

"What are you doing here?" Lincoln snaps, jumping to his feet.

"I'm supposed to have a meeting with our boss. But you're in here fucking her!" Myles knots both hands in his hair. "Are you out of your goddamn mind?"

Lincoln yanks his pants up. "You can't just barge into her office."

Myles sneers. "Really, man? You couldn't keep your dick in your pants this time? You had to go and fuck her?"

"Stop saying it like that. You make it sound like she's a piece of meat."

"You're acting like she's a piece of meat."

"I would never disrespect her like that," Lincoln snarls, waving a finger at him. "*Ever.* You need to back the fuck up."

Myles points to the desk. "You call *that* respect?"

"Stop!" I hold my hands up. "Both of you. Please, just stop."

The pitch of Myles's voice is an ice pick to my skull, and I can't think after everything I just experienced.

My stomach is suddenly crampy, and it feels like the walls are closing in around me. I need Myles to stop yelling. I don't need Lincoln to defend me. This is my office. I'm responsible for what happens in it. I will explain my actions to Myles, but I can't think clearly with Lincoln around.

"Lincoln, please go home."

His gaze snaps to mine and widens. "But I was just—"

"Go home. I will talk to you tomorrow."

He stalks from the room without another word. Moments later, I hear the door to the suite slam in the distance. Tears well in my eyes.

Myles rushes over to me. "Elinora, I'm so sorry. You told me—"

I hold up a hand. "It's fine, Myles. I'm sorry. Lincoln interrupted some unwelcome advances from Stefan and one thing led to another. I forgot about our meeting."

"I'm incredibly sorry for Lincoln's unprofessional behavior. I had no idea he would—"

"It wasn't our first time." I briefly squeeze my eyes shut. "And it won't be the last."

"Wait, are you saying . . ." Myles scrubs his hand over his face. "I'm confused."

"Me too, Myles." I swipe at a tear. I can't help but wonder why he doesn't know about us. "Lincoln didn't mention our . . . relationship?"

"No."

Freya knows about us, so why wouldn't Lincoln tell his best friend? Now that I think about it, Myles and I have had numerous conversations about Lincoln since he started working here. Never once, has he mentioned a woman in Lincoln's life. While I respect that Lincoln kept details about us private, I guess I hoped he'd talk about me in anonymous terms. Maybe tell his best friend he'd met an interesting woman? Or say he has feelings for someone?

Given Myles's current dumbfounded state, it's clear I'm the only one who's enamored. My heart sinks.

"He really never said anything about us?"

"No." Myles shakes his head slowly. "Swear to God."

"Oh, OK. Wow." Another tear rolls down my cheek. "That surprises me."

He touches my arm. "Probably because he knew I'd give him shit."

I nod and point to the desk. "While I admit the setting was inappropriate, that was one hundred percent consensual."

"I'm not arguing that. Lincoln would never force himself on someone. I'm pissed because he promised me he'd behave like a professional if I got him an interview with you. Now he's making me look like an asshole."

"How do you figure?"

"I warned him not to jeopardize my job. I thought you'd fire me if he made an advance."

"He didn't make an advance, Myles." I wipe more tears. "I did. I came to him. And I'm not firing you, I'm promoting you."

Myles's gaze burns into me. "Elinora, forgive me for saying this, but I don't want a promotion because Lincoln fucked you into it."

"He didn't fuck me into anything. Your promotion is long overdue. I was planning to promote you at the end of the quarter, but I decided it wasn't necessary to wait any longer. Lincoln has nothing to do with how I feel about you or your performance at Iverson Press. I'm promoting you because I want to. You deserve it."

"Thank you."

"Your new position will entail more responsibility, but I'm hoping a twenty percent pay raise will account for the increased workload."

His eyes widen. "*Twenty* percent?"

"I think you know me well enough by now to know I'm more than willing to invest my time and money in those who deserve it. Thank you for all that you do here." I hold up a finger. "There is one caveat. I don't want you to give Lincoln any shit. He makes me feel alive and cherished, which is something I haven't felt in a very long time."

*Make that never.* The thought ricochets off the hollow places inside me, settling in my bones.

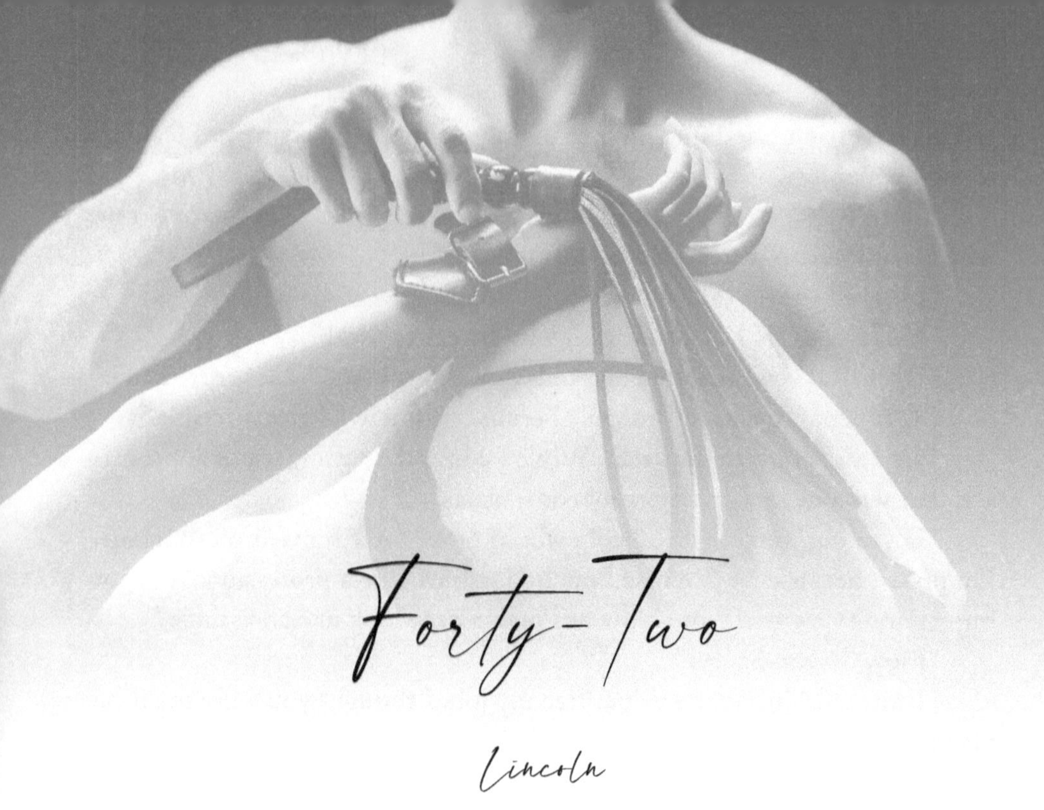

# Forty-Two

## Lincoln

Sister Fitzgibbons was right. I am a disgrace. I promised Elinora to keep things professional at the office. Instead, I fucked her on her desk like an animal. Not only did I fail to keep my word, but I crossed a line. Myles interrupting us was the icing on the fucked-up cake.

My phone rings for the twentieth time today. I glance at the screen. It's Myles again. He's probably itching to ream me a new asshole.

I didn't show up at The River last night. I probably should've called Esme, but my head was too fucked from Elinora's dismissal. Besides, I don't owe Esme my courtesy.

Since I'd never blow off my actual job, I called Freya this morning to tell her I planned to work from home. When she asked if I was all right, I told her I was too sick to come to the office. It's not a total lie—I am sick. Sick to my stomach.

I can't believe Elinora sent me away. She's always appreciated the times I came to her defense in the past. Not this time, apparently.

*You're a disgrace. You'll never amount to anything, Kennedy.* Echoes of my tormenter's voice fill my head. I remember the bitter taste of injustice. Except this time, I *am* in the wrong. I crossed a line and embarrassed Elinora in front of Myles.

What the fuck was I thinking? How can I face her after I disrespected her like that? First, I interrupt her being accosted by Arnold, but then I turn around and fuck her? What kind of man am I?

A text comes through.

> Myles: Answer your fucking phone, Linc.

Nope. Not doing it. I am more than capable of crucifying myself, thank you very much.

Curling my lip, I turn off the phone and snatch my laptop. My letter of resignation won't write itself. I'll hand-deliver the notice to Elinora this afternoon. She deserves more than words on a screen.

She deserves more than what I can give her. So much more. I just hope I'll be man enough to walk away.

# Forty-Three

## Elinora

I'm lucky to have an assistant who doubles as my best friend. In my twenties, I was too focused on building my empire to secure any meaningful friendships, but at least I did something right in hiring Freya.

As if on cue, she enters my office with a cup of tea and sets it on my desk. "It's a chai. I know you love those."

"Thank you." I rub at the chill in my body. I can't seem to get warm today. Maybe I caught something from Lincoln.

"Talk to me."

I take a slow sip before answering. "I can't believe he didn't show up last night."

"He's sick, Elle. It's better he stayed home. He must be down for the count because Myles hasn't been able to reach him today." She brushes the hair back from my face. "Are you all right? Your skin feels really hot."

"I'm freezing."

"I think you have a fever. Clark Kent probably got you sick. Hang on. I think there's a thermometer in the first aid kit." She strides from the office.

Last night, I sat at the Aqua Suite bar and waited for Lincoln. He never showed up. When Esme tried to call him, he didn't answer. I chatted with his friends Gideon and Ravi for about an hour before heading home. Then I cried myself to sleep.

Freya returns with a digital thermometer and slides a fresh probe cover on the tip. "Open up." She places it under my tongue and sits on the edge of the desk to wait for the beep, which happens a few moments later. "Holy shit, Elle. Your temp is a hundred and two."

I shudder and rub my arms. "Come to think of it, I wasn't feeling well yesterday."

Freya drapes her sweater over my shoulders. "What feels off?"

"My stomach is crampy, and I'm a little nauseous."

"Did you eat anything weird?"

"No. Nothing since lunch yesterday. I was too upset to eat."

She points to my calendar. "When is your period due?"

"I have no idea. It's irregular."

"Is there any chance you could be preg—" She stops herself and flushes. Freya knows all about my fucked-up ovaries, my ectopic pregnancy, and my miscarriage. "I'm sorry. I didn't mean to go there. It's just . . ." She squeezes my hand.

"It's all right. No, I'm definitely not pregnant. We always used protection."

*Except for yesterday.*

I was so desperate to feel Lincoln inside me; everything else went by the wayside. Safety, common sense, and my scheduled meeting with Myles all flew out the window when Lincoln kissed me. It didn't occur to me he wasn't wearing a condom until after he left, and I felt the evidence of his release between my thighs. But Freya doesn't need to know about that. The last thing I need right now is a safe sex lecture.

"I think you should go home and get some rest. Grab your stuff. I'll walk you to your car."

I retrieve my purse and shove my laptop into my briefcase. "I'm ready."

Freya takes my arm and leads me from the office. We ride the elevator to the lobby and head outside. The late afternoon sun warms me. I say a silent prayer of thanks when I notice the group of sidewalk creeps is nowhere in sight. We approach the parking garage and climb the two flights of stairs to the level where I parked.

Freya stops short.

"What's the matter?" I ask.

She points to the section of curb near my car where Lincoln sits with his elbows resting on his bent knees and his head in his hands.

"Fancy meeting you here," Freya calls.

His head snaps up. My breath rushes out of me when I see the regret in his gaze.

"Are you lost? Shouldn't you be in bed?" she teases, tugging me toward the car.

Lincoln furrows his brow. "What's going on?"

"I'm not feeling well." I shudder and lean against Freya.

"Looks like you got her sick, Clark Kent."

Lincoln grimaces. "Well, I was hoping we could talk, but if you're sick, I won't keep you."

"I want to talk." I unlock my car and hand over my laptop.

Freya stuffs my bag inside and kisses my cheek. "Call me later. Love you."

"Love you too."

She gives Lincoln a wave and heads back to the office.

He waits until she's out of earshot before climbing to his feet. "Elinora, I'm so sorry."

"For what? What exactly are you sorry for?" My voice gets shriller with each question. "Is that your apology for standing me up last night?"

"What are you talking about?"

"I sat at the bar for over an hour."

His eyes widen. "You went to The River?"

"Of course I did." I blink back the welling tears. "I thought we had plans, but you never came." I rub my temples. "It makes sense, now, obviously."

"Elinora, I—" He rakes a hand through his hair. "Fuck."

"I get that you were sick, but you couldn't bother to let me know you weren't coming? No call, no text, no email? You gave me nothing. I felt like a fool sitting there all alone."

"You dismissed me from your office."

"I didn't dismiss you, Lincoln. I sent you home because your shouting match with Myles was giving me a headache, and I needed to discuss something with him."

"Yeah, but you told me you'd talk to me *tomorrow*, so I assumed last night's date wasn't happening."

"You assumed wrong."

"Fuck." He removes his glasses and rubs his temples, then shoves them back onto his face. "I'm so sorry."

"How are you feeling?"

"I'm not actually sick. I just needed time to write this." He hands me a folded-up piece of paper.

"What the hell is this?"

"My letter of resignation."

"What?" I shake my head. "No. Absolutely not. I won't accept it."

"Elinora, I promised I'd keep our interactions at the office professional." He runs both hands over his face. "Instead, I fucked you on your desk like some animal. Without a condom. I came inside you—"

"I loved every minute."

"You had to use your safe word."

I throw my arms in the air. "Because Myles was standing in the fucking doorway!"

"Exactly my point." He closes the distance between us. "I failed to keep my word, and I disrespected you. That's fucking unacceptable."

"You know what's unacceptable, Lincoln? *This* is unacceptable," I screech, waving the letter in his face before shredding it to pieces. "You did not disrespect me. I told you I wanted more, and you gave it to me. I was the one who forgot about my meeting with Myles."

"Is his job in jeopardy because of me?"

"Of course not. He was long overdue for a promotion, which I gave to him after you left. That's why I sent you home. I couldn't exactly talk business with Myles while you two were screaming at each other."

"Oh."

"*Oh*, is right." I toss the pieces of paper into the air like confetti. "I would never dismiss you, Lincoln. Ever. I need you. You're the most hardworking editor to walk through those doors. Just like you told me you'd be. You breathe life into Iverson Press, so I don't give a flying fuck who walks in on us, you are not leaving."

The relief on his face is palpable. "I'm sorry I didn't call—"

"I'm not done." I stand on my tiptoes and grab his face to shut him up. "You breathe life into me as well. You make me feel alive, which is something I haven't experienced in years. Now that you've shown me what true respect feels like and how it feels to be desired, I don't ever want to lose you. You're *mine*, Lincoln Kennedy. Understood?"

His smile takes my breath away. "Yes."

"Good." I release my grip on his face and sink back down to my normal height. "I'm glad we got that settled."

"You made me fall," he murmurs, touching a strand of my hair.

"Excuse me? You tripped over your own pants. I had nothing to do—"

Lincoln holds a finger to my lips. "And I fell hard."

I push him away from my mouth. "I mean, you're tall, so it's a long way down. Obviously."

He snatches my hand and presses it to the center of his chest. "I mean, *here.*"

Tears prick the corners of my eyes as the meaning behind his words sinks in. "Are you saying—"

"What I'm saying is," he flattens my hand over his beating heart, "I'm falling in love with you."

"Lincoln, I—" Searing pain rips through my lower abdomen. Wrapping my arms across my belly, I sag against the car.

"Angel, what's wrong?"

I squeeze my eyes shut and moan. The agony reminds me of my ectopic pregnancy five years ago. When I was so desperate to carry a child, I ignored my body's warning signs. My fallopian tube ruptured, and my left ovary had to be removed because it was riddled with cysts.

*A cyst!* The cramping, the fever, it all makes sense.

Lincoln grips my shoulders. "Talk to me. What's going on?"

"Rupture," I say on a gasp.

A wave of nausea slams into me. I retch a few times, but my empty stomach yields nothing but acid.

"Rupture? What ruptured?"

I can't answer him. Another round of dry heaves grips me.

He reaches into my purse and snatches my keys. "We're going to the hospital."

I nod and climb into the back seat, where I curl into a ball on my side.

Lincoln jumps into the driver's seat and starts the engine. He peels out of the garage and merges into traffic, slamming on the accelerator.

The warm trickle of blood between my legs tells me I once again ignored my body's warning signs for too long. As Lincoln's sharp turns jostle me, I close my eyes and pray we reach the hospital before I hemorrhage.

# Forty-Four

## Lincoln

The fucking light turns red before the asshole in front of me attempts to turn. "Son of a bitch." I glance in the rearview mirror at Elinora. "We're almost there, angel. A few more minutes, OK?" When she doesn't answer, I twist in my seat. My heart stops at the sight of the blood soaking her pale blue skirt.

The light turns green, and I switch lanes, speeding past the slow fuckers in my way. I reach around the seat and grab her clammy hand. "Talk to me, angel."

"It hurts." She gasps, clutching her abdomen tighter. "Ruptured cyst."

"Your ovaries?"

"Yes. But I only have one."

"One cyst is causing that much bleeding?" My ex-girlfriend once had a ruptured cyst, but she only experienced light spotting and moderate discomfort. Elinora is in agony. I'd move heaven and earth to ease her pain. Up ahead, the signs for New York General Hospital come into view. I step on the gas.

"No, one ovary."

*Jesus Christ, did her whole fucking ovary explode?*

She's not making sense, and it's clearly hurting her to talk, so I stop questioning her. The hospital staff will do enough of that.

The car squeals to a stop outside the emergency room entrance. I throw it into park and jump out, yanking the back door open.

"I'm gonna carry you, angel. Just hold on to me." I scoop Elinora into my arms and sprint inside the hospital.

The woman in triage takes one look at her and buzzes us inside. People rush in our direction. Someone wheels over a gurney and instructs me to set her down.

A nurse swoops in with an oxygen mask and slides it over Elinora's face. "Are you in pain?" When Elinora nods, she adds, "Rate your pain on a scale of one to ten, with ten being the worst."

She holds up all ten of her fingers.

*Sweet Jesus.*

"OK, we'll get you something for that. Any drug allergies?"

"Not that I know of." The mask muffles her strained voice even more.

The nurse reaches around me and raises the gurney's guard rail. "Excuse me."

I move out of her way. "Sorry. I can wait in the lobby if—"

Elinora clamps her hand on my wrist as her glassy eyes meet mine. "Don't leave me."

I raise a questioning brow at the nurse, who nods. I lean down to kiss my woman's forehead and realize she's burning up. "Not going anywhere, angel."

The nurse touches my arm. "You can answer the basic questions for me so she can rest."

"I'll do my best."

"What is her name and date of birth?" She pulls a stylus from her pocket, drawing my attention to her scrubs, which are patterned with cats reading books. While I'm not sure about Elinora's opinion on cats, the colorful stacks of books feel like a good omen. "Hello? You with me?"

"Sorry. Her name is Elinora Iverson. I don't know her birthday." The nurse arches a brow, so I sheepishly add, "She's thirty-five, if that helps."

"July thirteenth," Elinora says with a gasp.

The nurse does some quick math in her head and inputs the date on her tablet. "When did this episode start?"

"Sometime today. She left work early because she wasn't feeling well. She has a fever."

"Was a hundred and two at my office."

"We were talking. One minute she was fine, then suddenly she doubled over. She kinda vomited once, then dry-heaved a few times, but that's it." I follow as the nurse wheels the gurney down the hall, past several occupied rooms.

"When did the bleeding start?"

"In the car on our way here."

"Is there any chance she could be pregnant?"

"Uh . . ." My gaze snaps to Elinora's face. *Holy fuck, is she pregnant?* It's certainly possible, but none of the condoms broke, and yesterday was the only time we skipped one. "Well, um . . ." I clear my throat and try again. "I, uh—"

The nurse stops walking and turns to face me. "Let me rephrase. Is she sexually active?"

"Yes. I'm her . . . partner."

"Now we're getting somewhere." She smiles, and her jade-green eyes meet mine. "When was the last time you had unprotected intercourse?"

While this feels like the Spanish Inquisition, I know it's necessary, so I swallow against my shame. "Yesterday afternoon was the only time we didn't use a condom. It was my fault. I'm an idiot."

"Things happen." She resumes walking and parks the gurney in a nearby room, pulling the curtain closed behind us. "Elinora, when was your last menstrual period?" She grabs her stethoscope and wraps a blood pressure cuff around Elinora's arm.

"April third, maybe? I really don't remember. It's never been regular."

The nurse nods and takes her blood pressure. "Hmm, ninety over forty-five. That's a bit low."

Another nurse peeks her head in. "Lena, what've we got?"

"Rapid onset severe lower abdominal pain. Extensive vaginal bleeding. Fever, nausea, and vomiting. BP is ninety over forty-five. Tell Dr. Evans she needs some pain meds on board STAT, a serum pregnancy test, and a gyno consult."

I squeeze Elinora's hand. "She said something about her ovary rupturing?"

Lena nods. "We'll know more when they do an ultrasound. Our first priority is to get the bleeding under control and reduce her pain." She turns to Elinora. "Trish will be back shortly with some pain medicine. In the meantime, I'll ask you a couple questions. I know it's hard to talk right now, but any information you can give me will help the doctors. Do you have a history of ovarian cysts?"

Elinora claws at her oxygen mask. "My left ovary and fallopian tube were removed five years ago because of an ectopic pregnancy. The tube ruptured, and I became septic. I spent a week in intensive care. Both ovaries were riddled with cysts, but I've never had one rupture."

Lena touches Elinora's shoulder. "It hurts like a bitch. Any other pertinent gynecological history?"

"Fertility issues." Elinora tightens her grip on my hand. "And a miscarriage at eleven weeks." A tear rolls down her cheek. Then another.

My chest tightens. I squeeze her hand and brush my thumb over her knuckles. My mom had two miscarriages before Reagan was born. I remember her crying in bed for weeks at a time. I'd always pick flowers from our garden and bring them to her. She still gets misty-eyed when she talks about the losses. The thought of Elinora feeling that way makes me wish I could grow her a cabbage patch full of babies to love.

Lena wipes Elinora's cheeks. "I'm so sorry to hear that. When did you miscarry?"

"Two years ago. The day I caught my husband having his third affair."

# Forty-Five

## Elinora

Fury flashes in Lincoln's gaze. "He's a dumb fuck. I'd love to punch his face in."

Lena gives him an approving smile. "Your ferocity for her reminds me of my man." She pats my shoulder. "Keep him."

I peer at Lincoln through my tears. "I hope to."

The other nurse reappears with a syringe. "Hi Elinora, my name is Trish. I have something for your pain and something for nausea."

After checking my name and date of birth, she swabs my hip and gives me the injections. "These should kick in pretty fast." She smiles and leaves the room.

I fucking hope so. It feels like evil gnomes are gnawing on my reproductive organs. I glance up at the tall, attractive woman who enters the room in a white coat.

"Hello, Elinora. I'm Dr. Evans. I'd like to do a pelvic exam before I send you for an ultrasound."

I turn my head toward Lincoln. "You don't have to stay for this if it makes you uncomfortable."

At least she's a woman. I remember how awkward I felt with my ectopic when a gorgeous, young male doctor stuffed his hand up my vagina two seconds after he walked into the room.

Lincoln kisses the back of my hand he's still holding. "Not going any-where, angel."

Charles would've run for the hills. Oh wait, he *did* run out of the exam room when I had my ectopic. God forbid he saw some blood. And he was too busy fucking someone else when I miscarried our baby. I got to suffer through that one alone. Then again, was I ever *not* alone when Charles and I were together?

"You will feel some pressure," Dr. Evans explains, sliding her gloved fingers inside me. She presses on my abdomen, making me wince and squeeze my eyes shut.

"Look at me," Lincoln murmurs. My gaze flicks in his direction. He presses his free hand to his chest and holds it over his heart. "I mean it."

I still can't believe he told me he's falling in love with me. My heart did a one-eighty, switching from sheer panic at the thought of him resigning to the state of bliss heralded by his declaration. I focus on his stormy blue eyes and feel something within me settle. Sure, we've only known each other a few weeks—and he's my decade-younger employee—but I can see myself caring for him more deeply than I ever loved Charles.

I touch my chest. "Me too."

Lincoln's smile makes me wish I could throw my arms around his neck and kiss him senseless. He squeezes my hand. "That makes me really happy."

Dr. Evans finishes her exam. "All right, given your extensive bleeding, there's a chance we'll need to operate. I'm ordering IV antibiotics." She addresses Lena. "Please start her on those immediately. I'm also putting in an order for fluids and electrolytes. She seems dehydrated." Dr. Evans pats my shoulder. "Let me check with radiology to see if they're ready for your ultrasound." She motions to Lincoln. "I'm sorry, but you'll have to wait here for that."

He nods and turns to me as she leaves the room. "Do you want me to call Freya and let her know what's going on?"

"Please. Also, please have Myles reschedule our meeting with the owner of Hudson Graphics."

Lena suddenly perks up. "Did you just say Hudson Graphics?"

I nod. "You've heard of them?"

She grins. "I've more than heard of them. Garrett Casey has been my best friend since elementary school."

"No kidding?"

"Yup. He lives on the bottom two floors of my brownstone, so we're neighbors too." Now that she mentions it, Garrett has definitely talked about a female best friend who doubles as his upstairs neighbor. She yanks her phone from her pocket and shows me a picture of them in formal attire. "This was at our friend Jake Bennett's gala back in November. I made Garrett be my date because I enjoy torturing him sometimes."

"Wait. *The* Jake Bennett?" Lincoln asks, his eyes widening. "As in, the multi-platinum singer-songwriter?"

Lena smiles. "The one and only."

"Holy shit. My little sister is *obsessed* with him."

"Your sister has good taste. Jake is a great guy."

"And a phenomenal singer," I add, thinking of his rich baritone voice.

"You should hear the new stuff he's working on." She rubs her hands together with glee. "So, yeah, it's really cool you know Garrett. He's practically my brother at this point."

"Garrett is an excellent friend to have. His skilled team of graphic designers handles all my company's book covers. Small world." I turn back to Lincoln. "Better yet, Lincoln, please get Garrett's contact information from Lena and call to reschedule us for the end of next week."

He pats his pocket. "Don't need to. Garrett's a friend of mine, so I already have his number. I'll give him a call."

"Oh, duh. That's right." I clap my hand to my forehead. "For a moment, I forgot you two know each other. The drugs must be kicking in because my brain is fried. Anyway, thank you for playing secretary."

"Whatever you need, angel."

The steady beeping of the machines by my bed tells me I'm not frolicking in a meadow with the seven dwarves like I woke up thinking. I'm in a hospital. *Wait, why am I in a hospital?*

My brain kicks into gear and fills me in on the events of the past twenty-four hours. Most ruptured cysts cause spotting or light bleeding. I was one of the lucky ones to experience extensive vaginal and internal bleeding, so Dr. Evans deemed it necessary for me to have surgery.

The laparoscopic procedure was non-invasive, thankfully. The surgeon removed what was left of my ruptured cyst and got the bleeding under control without having to take out my ovary. I've got IV antibiotics in my system, along with fluids and pain medicine. All things considered, I feel better.

I lift my head. Lincoln dozes in a chair beside my hospital bed. He left his glasses on my tray table. Long, dark lashes rest against his cheeks. He stayed by my side throughout this whole mess and never once made me feel guilty about it.

Lincoln contacted Freya and even took care of a few business calls for me. His eyes flutter open when he hears the rustle of my blankets.

"Hey," I whisper.

"Hey, angel. How are you feeling?"

"Numb and tired, but OK." I chew my lip. "Thank you for staying with me."

He rises and leans over me, cupping my face. "What did I say about that?"

"That you weren't going anywhere."

"Right." He brings his lips to mine in a slow, soul-melting kiss. We're interrupted a few minutes later, when someone clears their throat in the doorway. Lincoln breaks the kiss and looks over his shoulder. "Hey, Freya."

"Um, excuse me, Clark Kent, but I'm pretty sure she wasn't given the all clear to get hot and heavy." Freya grins and sidles up to my bedside. "How are you feeling, Elle?"

"Better."

She kisses my forehead. "Glad to hear it. I brought bagels for you two."

Lincoln's eyes light up. "Thank you so much. I'm starving."

"Elle, are you allowed to eat yet?"

"I should be fine, but I'll check with the nurse to make sure."

My phone chimes on the tray table, and Lincoln scowls. "Why does your ex-husband keep texting you?"

"Because he's a dick?" Freya offers.

I roll my eyes and reach for the phone. Before I can turn it off, an image appears on the screen. It's a sonogram. The fucking bastard sent me a picture of his developing child with his new slut bride. Bitter tears well in my eyes.

"What's up?" Freya asks, snatching the phone. "Are you fucking kidding me?" She shows the picture to Lincoln.

"Please tell me he isn't rubbing that in your face."

"Oh, he most definitely is."

Lincoln paces the room. "Elinora, I swear to God, I want to kick the shit out of him. Why would he send that to you?"

"He's angry. When Charles gets angry, he acts like a toddler and lashes out. He wants to hurt me."

"What the fuck does he have to be angry about?"

"His sad excuse for a dick?" Freya supplies. "Or his inability to keep it up? I'm sure any of those qualify."

I sigh. "He's angry because he fucked himself over. He didn't think through his plans and now he's losing. Big time."

Lincoln furrows his brow. "I don't get it."

"He eloped with exotic mistress number three. As in, he *remarried*." Thinking of the good news my lawyers shared with me the other day, a slow smile curves my lips. "Which means I'm no longer obligated to pay him alimony. He cut himself off from my money, but he's taking it out on me."

Freya grins. "Karma's a bitch."

Lincoln nods. "The sexiest bitch there ever was."

"I think you should keep paying him," Freya begins. "Two cents a week. Mail him a check and place a big, red lipstick kiss mark on the envelope's seal. Here's your two cents back, you cheap motherfucker."

Lincoln meets my gaze. "I'm with Freya. Give him a taste of his own shit. Sending you that picture was uncalled for. He went out of his way to hurt you, and that doesn't sit well with me."

"Yeah, but then I'm no better than him," I mutter. "Besides, why should I waste money on postage?" My phone rings. "Oh, great. Fucking Charles is calling me now."

Lincoln narrows his eyes on the screen. "Are you going to answer it?"

"No. I have nothing to say to him."

An evil grin transforms his features. "May I answer it?"

"Be my guest." I hand Lincoln the phone. "Tell him to fuck off."

"Hello, Elinora's phone." He smirks. "No, you called *me*, so who are you?" He glances at me. "Charles who? I don't know anyone named Charles."

Freya giggles.

"Her ex-husband?" He tilts his head. "Oh, wait, now I remember. Aren't you that old guy who couldn't satisfy her in bed?" He turns to me. "Sweetheart, what was his name again? The minute man with the soft dick?"

I burst out laughing. "His name is Charles Roth."

"Right. How could I forget about Charlie Softwood?" He laughs. "Hey *speedy*, how about you do yourself a favor and get a job? Maybe then, you can provide for that bundle of joy you keep flaunting. Unless you expect your new wife to pull all the weight too?" Lincoln raises a brow. "Go fuck myself? You mean like *you* fucked yourself out of Elinora's money?" He snorts. "Aw, c'mon, Charlie, what's the matter? Did I strike a nerve?" Lincoln ends the call and hands me my phone with a grin. "He hung up on me."

Freya claps his shoulder. "Clark Kent, you're my fucking hero right now."

Lincoln eyes her. "What can I say? I don't tolerate asshole behavior. Bottom line, don't fuck with the people I love."

*He loves me.*

"You're my hero too." I smile at Lincoln. "Do you feel better?"

"As a matter of fact, I do. You should've heard him sputtering like an old junk car. I doubt he'll call you again. And if he does, hand the phone to me."

"Thank you for standing up for me."

"I will always stand up for you."

# Forty-Six

## Lincoln

We pull up outside Elinora's building, and I signal to the valet guy like I'm an old pro. Meanwhile, I can't imagine having that luxury. Here I am, a dude who lives in a tiny studio apartment and doesn't even own a car. Sometimes, the reminder of Elinora's wealth makes me feel like Julia Roberts's character in *Pretty Woman*. Except I'm not a prostitute.

*Not technically, anyway.*

Pushing the thoughts aside, I glance at Elinora. After emergency surgery and a two-night hospital stay, the doctors finally cleared her for discharge.

It's Sunday afternoon. I gleefully called out sick for my Friday and Saturday shifts at The River. While I feel guilty about canceling my standing date with Reagan again, I can't bring myself to leave Elinora. Besides, I know my sister will forgive me, especially when she sees the surprise I have for her—a CD signed by Jake Bennett. It turns out he lives in Lena's neighborhood. She remembered me saying that my sister is a fan, so she asked him to autograph something for her. I damn near fell over when she brought it in yesterday. Solid proof that it pays to know people sometimes. Reagan is going to flip out. She's one of the few people I know who prefers CDs over streaming her music, and she's amassed quite the collection. Hopefully, this week I can finagle a trip upstate to give it to her.

Seeing Elinora in pain was gut-wrenching. Even now, she claims she's fine, but I've noticed the winces. No matter how hard she tries not to show it, she's most definitely hurting.

"Don't move. I'll come around." I unbuckle my seat belt, jump out of the car, and hand over her valet key. Then I make my way to the passenger side to open her door. "Give me your purse and briefcase."

She surrenders them with a smirk. "My arms work fine, you know."

"I'm sure they do, but I'm still carrying your bags. I'd do it even if they didn't give you lifting restrictions."

"Thank you." She chews her lower lip. "I think I need you to help me out of the car too."

"The surgeon said you'd have trouble getting up and down for a few days, remember?"

"Yes, but I'd hoped she was exaggerating." She grips my arm and allows me to assist her. "I didn't expect to feel so sore."

"Angel, they cut you open and pumped you full of air."

"I know, but *everything* is sore. My throat hurts from the breathing tube."

I thank the valet and guide Elinora to the sidewalk as he speeds away with the Porsche. "I'll make you some tea when we get inside."

"Thank you. You're a godsend, Lincoln." She leans against me as we make our way into the building.

"I dunno about that, but I'm happy to help you in any way I can."

"Hi, Jerry," she calls to the doorman.

He knits his gray caterpillar eyebrows into a frown. "Hello, Ms. Iverson. Are you all right?"

"Yes. I had surgery, but I'm much better now, thank you. This is Lincoln. He is always welcome, so if you see him, please buzz him upstairs." She glances up at me. "I hope you'll be seeing a lot of him?"

"Hello, Jerry." I shake his hand. "You will definitely see me."

"Nice to meet you, Lincoln," he says with a broad smile. "I assume you're skipping the stairs today, Ms. Iverson?"

Elinora grimaces. "God yes. I'll be using the elevator for the time being."

Jerry presses the call button for us. We step inside when it arrives.

"What floor?" I ask.

"Penthouse."

I select the appropriate button on the elevator's digital panel. "It's asking for a code."

"Seven-one-three," Elinora replies. "The top floor is all mine, so the code is for added security."

I raise a brow. "Perhaps you should choose something other than your birthday?"

"I have far too much to remember, Lincoln. By the time I get home most nights, all I want to do is flop onto my bed. I can't stomach the thought of locking myself out of my own apartment because I forgot some random number."

"Fair enough."

We ride to the penthouse floor. The doors slide open into a foyer of sorts with another electronic pin pad.

"Please don't tell me the code is the same for this," I mumble, rubbing my jaw.

"It is."

"Jesus, Elinora. You really need to change that." I enter the code and hear the lock click. I try the knob, but the door won't open.

She smirks and hands me a key. "But you need this too."

"That makes me feel a little better." I unlock the door and hold it open for her.

We step inside, and she flicks a light on. "Welcome to my home, Lincoln."

With crisp, clean lines and a muted color palette, the apartment's sleek elegance strikes me as something out of a magazine. She leads me into her kitchen, and I marvel at the granite countertops, massive island, stainless steel appliances, and more counter space than I'd know what to do with.

"Your kitchen is *amazing*."

"Thank you. I'm surprised you care about a kitchen."

"I love to cook," I explain, eyeing her spice rack and double oven.

"Really?"

"Yes. It's a hobby of mine. Since I live alone, I don't cook as much as I'd like to, mainly because my kitchen's small and I don't have time." I make a sweeping gesture with my arm. "But I could do some serious damage in here."

"While I adore baking, I'm not much of a cook. My poor kitchen hasn't reached a fraction of its potential."

"Woman, I will show you *exactly* what these beautiful appliances are capable of." I set down her bags and slide my hand along the island. "I can't get over all this counter space."

She laughs. "You're adorable."

I turn toward her and brush the hair back from her forehead. "Funny, I feel the same way about you." Cupping her face, I lean down to kiss her. I love the way her lips part for me. How her tongue strokes against mine like a cat rubbing on its owner's legs. A soft, tender claiming of sorts.

She breaks the kiss. "Thank you for being here."

"Always." My gaze lands on a massive floral arrangement. "Who sent you flowers?"

"Let me see." Elinora reads the card. "They're a get-well gift from Myles. Freya must've brought them over."

"He's good like that."

She raises an eyebrow at me. "Please tell me you've spoken to him since Thursday?"

I nod. "Yeah. We talked yesterday."

"Good. It worried me that there'd be residual tension between you."

"The bickering is normal for us. We've been friends since kindergarten, so we're more like brothers. He's a nagging mother hen at times, but I'm used to it. Thanks for not firing him."

"Why the hell would I fire him?"

I shrug. "Myles is a worrier. He made me meet up with him for a briefing before you interviewed me. He obviously knew I'd lose my mind when I saw you, so he gave me a huge lecture about professionalism. As you can see, I ignored him."

Her lips curve into a smile. "You lost your mind when you saw me?"

"You couldn't tell I thought you were the most exquisite woman I'd ever laid eyes on?"

She flushes. "You had quite the effect on me too."

"Plus, you're smart and powerful. Both of which are huge turn-ons for me."

"Most people find me intimidating," she murmurs. "But I turned you on?"

"You did both. My arousal went along with a healthy dose of fear. But now that I've gotten to know you, affection replaces my intimidation."

"So, you don't think I'm a frigid bitch like everyone else?" She shakes her head. "That's what I'm used to hearing."

"I know for a fact you aren't either of those things."

"You're one of the few who thinks that."

"I don't think it, I know it." I reach down and pinch her ass. "If you continue to put yourself down around me, I may have to take you over my knee once you're healed up."

She runs her hands down my chest and flutters her lashes. "If I call myself a super ice queen bitch, will you use the bench again?"

Cue my instant arousal. My breath rushes out of me. "Fuck."

"Is that a yes?"

"What do you think?" I press her hand to my hardening cock. "But you can skip the part where you call yourself names. If you want it dirty, say the word and I'll give it to you." I grip her chin. "But I'm not touching you for two weeks."

"Wait a minute, the doctor said no sex for *one* week," she protests.

"Yeah, but the doctor *also* said the rupture was likely caused by vigorous sex, which, as I recall, happened on your desk less than twenty-four hours prior."

"This wasn't your fault, Lincoln."

Maybe it isn't, but that doesn't erase the guilt that has plagued me since it happened.

"I'm not taking any chances with your health or safety, angel." I stroke her cheek. "The last thing I want to do is hurt you, so I'd feel more comfortable waiting."

"I don't know how I'll last that long. Even though my entire body is sore, I still want you."

"And you'll have me." I grin and trail my fingertips over her breasts. "In two weeks."

She rolls her eyes. "C'mon, let me give you a tour."

Elinora shows me around her luxurious penthouse. We pass by a window in her living room, and I take in the view of Central Park.

"The cherry blossoms are beautiful," I say.

"Aren't they? April was always my favorite month," she replies wistfully.

"Was?"

She grimaces. "Charlie Softwood ruined that too."

I chuckle at her use of my insult. "How did Old Man Softwood ruin April?"

"Because it's—" She tilts her head. "Wait, what's today's date?"

"The twenty-third, why?"

She scowls. "Today would've been our fourteenth wedding anniversary."

"I thought you were together for fifteen years?"

"We were. We started dating when I was seventeen, but we didn't get married until I was twenty-one. The divorce happened shortly before I turned thirty-three. Our marriage lasted twelve years. Truthfully, it should've been half of that."

"From what I know of Softwood, I'd say even less."

"And you'd be right, but I held on to hope. His first and third affairs hurt me the most."

"How come?" I motion for her to sit on the couch and settle beside her.

She sighs. "It blindsided me the first time. This was before I started Iverson Press. We'd been married for two years. I was fresh out of college, full of hope and excitement. I went to a publishing conference in San Francisco hoping to make some business contacts. Anyway, I wasn't feeling well, so I flew home early. I found him in our bed with my best friend."

"That's fucking low."

"Tell me about it. Carolyn was a woman who I'd been friendly with since I moved to America. We were close, and I thought of her as my sister. Since I didn't have any siblings, I grew up feeling alone, so it was nice to have someone who I connected with. Anyway, devastated doesn't begin to describe my state of mind over the betrayal. She was one of those people who I thought I'd get to keep forever, but I cut her out of my life after that."

"But you kept *him?*"

"I was young and stupid, Lincoln. I loved him. I believed his lies that Carolyn had seduced him. Besides, I clearly had some daddy issues."

"How so? You mean with the fifteen-year age difference?"

"That's part of it. My father left us when I was six. My mother swore off men, so a part of me always craved that father figure. I yearned for stability and wisdom, someone who could guide and protect me. When I met Charles, I saw some of that in him. I mean, he was thirty-two and financially stable. He was a software developer with a great job. He seemed wise and strong, capable of making me feel secure. But it was an act. While he's amazing with computers, Charles is lazy. Hard work is a foreign concept for him. He's someone who adores the path of least resistance. His financial security came from the inheritance he received when his grandfather died, most of which he squandered away on frivolous shit. Once my company became successful, I was his bankroll."

"And you tolerated it because you loved him," I murmur, reaching for her hand. We interlace our fingers, and I give her a squeeze.

"Right. I didn't want to be alone like my mother, so I promised myself I'd be true to our vows no matter what."

"When did the second affair happen?"

"About three years after the first. By that time, he managed a solutions company with dealings in antivirus software. She was his assistant," she mutters. "Anyway, instead of being hurt, his infidelity infuriated me. It meant that he'd lied about Carolyn seducing him. He'd established a pattern, so his lapse in judgment was a crock of shit. I threw him out." She shakes her head. "But then I took him back, obviously."

"Why?"

"He said what I wanted to hear. Ever since I was a little girl, playing dolls in the bakery while my mother worked, I've wanted a family of my own. I wanted three children—two boys and a girl. Charles never wanted kids. He promised me he would change his ways. He'd be faithful. He was suddenly open to starting a family. He even laid out the plan for us. When our kids were born, I'd work part-time, so I could have more precious time with them."

"And you believed him?"

"Part of me did. I took him back, and we immediately tried for children. I never expected that I'd have difficulty conceiving. It's funny, I took birth control for years to prevent an unwanted pregnancy—God forbid I upset Charles—meanwhile, I couldn't get pregnant."

"You mentioned two losses though."

"Three. I started fertility treatments when I was twenty-eight. Cycle after cycle, I put my body through the wringer. My life consisted of pills and injections. And good God, the mood swings were horrendous. The first time I got a positive pregnancy test, I sobbed tears of joy. But a week later, I tested negative. The doctor called it a chemical pregnancy. I was crestfallen. We kept trying, but it discouraged me. When I was thirty, I got pregnant a second time, but it was ectopic and ruptured my fallopian tube. I was so desperate to carry a child, I ignored my body's warning signs."

"Jesus Christ, Elinora." I squeeze her hand tighter. "Don't do shit like that."

"I know. Like I said, I was desperate."

"Meanwhile, you were building your empire."

"Right. I never faltered in that quest. Throughout everything, I buried myself in my work. I'd hoped to make Iverson Press successful enough that I'd have the flexibility to work part-time if and when I had a baby. After my father left us destitute, my mother warned me to never depend on a man for financial security. 'Make yourself successful,' she'd preach, while rolling out dough for direktørsnegls. 'Be the boss one day, Elinora.' And my favorite, 'Don't be afraid to climb higher than you think you can reach.'"

I squeeze her knee. "Given what you've done professionally, I'd say that's some sound advice."

"Except my dedication to my career drove my husband to his third affair."

"Wait a minute, he tried to blame his infidelity on *you?*"

"Yes. I worked too much and didn't have time for him. I didn't *want* to have sex with him—it was a means to an end, which in our case involved pregnancy. He was absolutely right. I did work too much. And he certainly lacked my attention. Both inside and out of the bedroom. Sex became a scheduled chore. I finally gave up on fertility treatments. I told him we could stop trying, and I made the effort to spend more time with him. It was the best three months of our marriage. By some miracle, I conceived naturally. I was overjoyed, but given my losses, hesitantly optimistic. The closer it got to the end of my first trimester, the more excited I felt. Freya told me I glowed from within." She shrugs and stares out the window, her eyes brimming with tears. "But then I went home early one day and found him in bed with some slutty model. You'd think he would've learned his lesson and booked a hotel room instead—especially after I caught him with Carolyn—but nope. There they were, going at it like rabbits on my grandmother's fucking quilt. I became so distraught, that when I ran out of our home, I fell down the stairs."

"Holy shit. Did you break any bones?"

"No. But thanks to my injuries, I miscarried our baby. Now *she's* the pregnant wife."

I pull her into my arms, desperate to ease her pain. "Angel, I'm so sorry."

"Thank you. I don't mean to be a downer. I just wanted to make sure you understand where my jealousy stems from."

"Wait, you're jealous of the new wife?"

"No. Sorry, that was a shitty transition. I meant that regarding *you.* I'm jealous of the women at The River. I'm tired of sharing—"

"Listen to me." I grip her chin. "I haven't been with anyone else since our first time together. I can't and I won't. You are the only woman I want." I grab her hand and press it to my chest. "I know it's insanely fast, but I love you."

"I love you too," she whispers. "After everything I went through with Charles, I never expected to hear myself utter those words to another man." She looks away. "But I'm scared."

"I'm scared too. But I need you to know that I am not Charles. I'm nothing like him—I work hard and keep my promises."

"I know you're a hard worker. That's something I love about you. Understand that while I'm fearful, I don't equate you with him."

"I'm not saying you do. I'm just trying to get through to you. I know you're scared, and given your history, you have every right to be. You opening your heart to me is the most beautiful gift I've ever been given. I want you to look me in the eyes right now." She meets my gaze, and I cup her face. "You are my one and only."

# Forty-Seven

## Elinora

I know in my heart Lincoln means what he's saying. His words hold a sincerity that radiates to my soul. His declaration is nothing like Charles's brand of lip service. Yet I can't help but wonder why he clings to his job at The River.

"I believe you. I guess I just don't understand why you still need to work there. I gave you a raise."

"I know, and I appreciate that, but I have tremendous debts to pay. Student loans, credit cards, family stuff, and so on. My father is out on disability after his stroke, so I help my parents however I can."

"Lincoln, if you need money, I'll give it to you."

He grimaces. "Thank you, but outside of what you pay me at Iverson, I will *not* take your money. This debt is my responsibility. I work at The River because it's damn good money, and my goal is to break even in the next few years."

"I'll give you another raise. Then you can quit there sooner." I stare at my lap, hating how desperate I sound.

"Elinora, I need you to understand something about me. While some people have no qualms about being a sex worker, I hate that I have to work at The River. It makes me feel dirty when I think about what I've earned with my body. Survival makes you do crazy shit, I guess." He tilts my chin to meet his gaze once more. "Anyway, those days are over. I'm strictly bartending. Like I said, I haven't been with anyone else, nor do I intend to."

"But if I give you a raise, you can spend less time there," I point out hopefully.

He rakes a hand through his hair. "My pride is the only thing I have left. Aside from my whole heart, I don't have a damn thing to offer you. As a man, that's hard for me to admit. I can't give you financial stability or provide for you. All I can do is love you. I won't let you be my bankroll, Elinora. I don't want your kingdom, your castle, or any of the jewels inside. I only want the queen."

"I'm yours, Lincoln."

"I know, but I need you to trust me."

"I trust you."

"Then please don't make me feel like you think you need to pay to make me yours. I already am. One hundred percent. While I appreciate your offer, I cannot accept it. I don't want your money, I want *you*. My debt is my responsibility to repay."

I stare back at him for a moment before nodding. I never considered that my monetary offer made him feel like less of a man. Charles would've taken my money and run. He'd be content to pay off his debts and bask in the financial security I provided him. Who am I kidding? Charles did take my money, but instead of running, he stuck around to milk more out of me. Too bad the steady cash flow hadn't kept him from stuffing his cock in another woman. Not even when I was pregnant with our child, working to make a life for us.

"I understand. I'm sorry I made you feel that way."

"It's all right. Sometimes I struggle with that whole self-worth thing."

"Lincoln, you are a hundred times the man my ex-husband is. I don't want to hear that you have nothing to offer, because in the few weeks I've known you, you've given me more respect and affection than I received in fifteen years. I'm helplessly in love with you."

"It's mutual, angel."

"I'm not used to this. Our chemistry and passion, the connection we share—you are an anomaly for me. I'm sorry if my history has tarnished my views of love."

Lincoln cups my face. "Let's rewrite your history. In this edition, make *me* your hero instead. Let's start today." He straightens. "You will rest in bed while I go to the grocery store. When I come back, I'll cook the best damn would-be anniversary dinner you can imagine. We'll drink wine and eat chocolates too. I'll give you a massage and kiss you senseless." He wags his brows. "I'll even read you some sexy passages from the manuscript I'm working on."

Heat floods my core. "I'd love that. I must admit, it turned me on when I read your comments in *Bound Hearts*."

His eyes widen. "Really?"

"Yes, really. Let's put it this way, I enjoyed some pleasurable alone time with you in mind."

"That's probably the hottest thing you've ever said to me."

"Pretty sure I told you to fuck me."

Fire flashes in his gaze. "That too. Imagine what will happen when I read to you."

"Oh, I'm imagining," I murmur.

Lincoln kisses me softly. "Let's celebrate this day for what it is—a reminder that divorcing Softwood was the best fucking decision you ever made."

I laugh. "My second-best decision was giving you a chance."

"Exactly." He takes both of my hands and kisses each knuckle. "Let me show you what it means to have my whole heart. We'll erase the bad memories and replace them with fresh ones." He gives me a megawatt smile and winks. "I'm one hell of an editor, angel. I guarantee by the time this day is over, you will never again think of Softwood on April the twenty-third."

# Forty-Eight

## Lincoln

It's a beautiful Monday morning courtesy of the woman dozing beside me. Elinora is out of work for the entire week. She insisted I use her laptop and work from "home" today so I can keep her company. I'm more than happy to oblige. Especially since she's still having difficulty getting around. Besides, I want to make sure she's resting and well-fed. Since I'm obsessive about emailing my work to myself, the current version of the manuscript I'm editing resides in my inbox.

Yesterday was the most romantic day of my life. For Elinora's would-be anniversary dinner, I prepared a feast of filet mignon, roasted vegetables, and portobello risotto. Not going to lie, it was one of my finest culinary creations. Her eyelids fluttered closed when she sank her teeth into the juicy meat. Which turned me on, of course. For dessert, we sipped champagne and fed each other chocolate-dipped strawberries.

Later, we cuddled in bed. Her pain flared a bit in the late evening, but a dose of ibuprofen seemed to help. Since sex was out of the question, it gave us plenty of time to talk. Elinora told me all about what it was like to grow up in Denmark and her first experiences in the United States. We discussed her absent father and how much she misses her mother. She described her days at the bakery in Copenhagen and all the delicious pastries she knows how to make.

I filled her in on the start of my friendship with Myles and our years of shenanigans. We both agreed that his partner, "Dick," is a dick. I described the nuns in Catholic school but left out the part about being expelled six months before I would have graduated. She doesn't need to know I cost my family a fortune just because I stuck my nose someplace it didn't belong. Instead, I told her all about the scenery in Upstate New York and what my parents are like. I purposely left out any details about Reagan.

I'm not ashamed of my sister—or her condition. I'm ashamed of myself and the way I feel. The never-ending, albeit irrational, survivor's guilt associated with my good health.

When I was a child, I wondered if I somehow caused Reagan to be born with Down syndrome. Did my occasional bad behavior affect my parents on some genetic level? Was stress the cause of my mother's two miscarriages? If I'd helped around the house more, would Reagan have been OK?

As an adult, I understand the fallacy of my reasoning. Reagan's precarious health isn't my fault, nor could I have prevented it. But I can make damn sure she gets the care she needs. I'll work seven days a week—and live in a studio apartment for the rest of my life—if it means Reagan can stay at Catskill Manor where the nurses are equipped to handle her seizures and monitor her heart condition. Besides, she adores it there. She lives with a vibrant, engaging group of friends, and the staff treats her like family. Not only has her quality of life improved, but she's flourishing under their care.

I wish I could tell Elinora about my sister and everything she deals with, but that would lead to an explanation of the reasons behind my employment at The River. Then I'd risk violating the terms of my nondisclosure agreement with Esme.

While Gideon, Rocco, Leo, and all the other guys—and ladies—are free to come and go, I'm the only concierge whose employment at The River is contractually bound. Esme doesn't want anyone to know about the interest-free hundred thousand dollars she gave me, mainly because she has no desire to become a loan shark. The confidentiality clause attached to my contract gives her the authority to tack on twenty percent interest if I open my mouth. As it stands, I'm already in violation. Myles and Maya each have a copy of the document. They know the details of my arrangement and understand what's at stake if I fail to uphold my end of the bargain. A gut feeling compelled me to cover my ass in case Esme tried to change the terms. Given her behavior lately, I know I made the right decision. Besides, I trust Myles and Maya with my life, so I know the information is safe in their hands.

Elinora stretches. "Good morning."

I lean over and kiss her. "Good morning, angel."

She points to the computer on my lap. "You're working already?"

"Books don't edit themselves." I smile and touch her cheek. "I promised my boss we'd meet all our publication deadlines. As a man of my word, I intend to make that happen for both mine and Watson's manuscripts."

"Don't be ridiculous. There's no way you can get all that done. Please, just focus on the manuscripts for Iverson Melt. I will reach out to the other agents and let them know we must delay our timeline."

I cock a brow. "You don't think I'm capable of getting it done?"

She shakes her head. "I know you're capable, but your workload has doubled. The last thing I want to do is burn out my favorite editor. Relax with me."

"While I appreciate your concern, I'll remind you I live for this stuff. I work well under pressure and have never missed a deadline." I brush my lips over her ear and relish the goose bumps that bloom on her neck. "Stop distracting me with your beauty."

Elinora snorts and gestures to her pajamas and messy hair. "Radiance at its finest."

"I'd call that a good assessment."

She laughs. "Then you're crazy."

"Also, a good assessment." I run my fingers through her hair. "Are you hungry?"

"A little."

"Do you like omelets?"

She nods. "Especially if there's cheese in them."

"Lucky for you, I picked up some damn good cheddar." I set the laptop aside. "I'll make some breakfast for us."

"Thank you." Elinora attempts to get up and winces.

I walk around to her side of the bed. "Let me help you." I lift her to her feet, and she sags against me.

"I hate feeling so helpless. And gross. I could use a shower, but it hurts to twist and bend."

"Let's eat first." I flash a wolfish grin. "Then I'm more than happy to wash you, sugar."

Once breakfast is done, I lead Elinora into the bathroom. She runs a brush through her hair as I adjust the water. While I prefer hot showers, I don't want to burn her perfect, porcelain skin. Once satisfied with the temperature, I help her undress.

My gaze sweeps the length of her body. I gesture to her healing incisions. "Are you sure they can get wet?"

She nods. "The doctor said two days."

Her surgery was Friday night, so we're in the clear. I motion for her to step inside her fancy doorless shower. She's got a rainfall showerhead with a smaller detachable one connected to a hose. The rose gold granite walls infuse the entire room with an elegance that is totally Elinora.

She steps beneath the stream and sighs in bliss as water cascades over her beautiful body.

"Is the temperature OK?" I ask.

"It's perfect, thank you."

I step out of my boxers and join her under the water, pressing my chest to her back. "Relax and let me take care of you, angel."

She leans against me, and I squeeze some vanilla-scented bodywash onto a cloth. I gently wash her neck and shoulders. As my hands move lower to cleanse her breasts, I lose the battle against my hardening cock.

Elinora chuckles. "Wondered when that would happen."

"Yeah, good thing you couldn't hear my internal monologue."

"Oh? Waxing poetic in your head?"

I laugh. "More like threatening my dick to keep his shit together." She shimmies her hips so her lush ass rubs my cock. A ragged breath leaves my chest. "That's not helping."

She reaches down and takes the cloth from me, hanging it on the hook. She guides my hands to her breasts. "Touch me."

Soft, succulent flesh fills my palms. I brush my thumbs over her nipples, making her moan. Her soapy hand encircles my cock and strokes me from root to tip.

"Fuck, that feels good." I lean against the wall and absorb the sensation of her hand sliding up and down my length.

"Close your eyes and let me take care of you," she murmurs, tightening her grip and increasing the pace.

Her touch feels incredible. Soft delicate fingers stroking and rubbing me. Harder and faster, bringing me closer and closer to release. In my mind, I'm still massaging and rolling her nipples, but in reality, I'm just holding them now, because I can't think enough to do anything else. "Oh, God, you're gonna make me come." She picks up her pace, and I lose it. "Elinora, *fuck*." My cock jerks and spurts, my release washing down the drain.

She turns to face me and flashes a coy smile. "Feel better?"

"Holy fuck. What was that for?"

"I like making you come."

"Oh, it's fucking mutual." I grip her hips. "When you're healed up, I'll be damn sure to return the favor."

She smiles. "I look forward to it."

I perk up. "Actually, I have an idea."

# Forty-Nine

## Elinora

I love when Lincoln gets ideas because they usually involve mind-bending orgasms for me.

His lips curve into a wicked grin. "Turn around and lean against me like you were before."

I take my time obeying him and purposely rub my ass on his cock. He loops an arm around my ribcage and holds me to his chest. Dipping his head, he kisses my shoulders and reaches for the detachable shower head with his free hand.

"Let me take care of *you* now." He angles the stream so it spatters my upper thighs, then inches his way higher until the water sprays my pussy.

I gasp and buck my hips.

"You like that?" He moves his wrist in circles. Gyrating streams of water dance on my clit.

I moan and clutch the arm he's wrapped around me. "Oh my God."

He nips my ear. "Not God, sugar."

"Lincoln." His name leaves my lips on a moan.

"That's right. Now, close your eyes, and open your legs wider for me." He sucks on my neck, his stubble rasping the delicate skin. "Have you ever done this to yourself?"

"No." I gasp, writhing my hips.

"Good. Then I'm your first." He slides the lever on the nozzle to adjust the stream, increasing the pressure to a pulsing flow.

My hips jerk in response.

"How's the water, Elinora?"

"Fire."

He rotates his wrist. The pleasure is incandescent as he takes me higher and higher. It feels like ten ruthless tongues licking and flicking my clit.

"Come for me," he commands, moving the nozzle closer.

The intensity sends me over the edge. "Lincoln. Oh, fuck . . . yes!" I wail my pleasure. My knees give out, but he holds me up.

He nips the side of my neck. "We're not done yet." He slides the lever once more, changing the stream to a steady flow, and focuses on my clit.

I orgasm in a matter of seconds. It's too good. Too much. "Cool," I say on a gasp, hips writhing.

He angles the stream to my feet. "You all right?"

"Yes. Too much."

"Sorry. I didn't mean to get carried away." He turns off the water and snags a towel, wrapping it around me. "But you're so fucking sexy when you moan my name."

"Mm-hmm." I can't speak or think.

He tips my chin up. "You sure you're OK?"

"Yes. That was amazing."

He smiles and kisses me. "Wait until you feel what I can do with my tongue."

I raise a brow. "Thought oral sex was a hard limit for you?"

"Where'd you hear that?"

"From Esme."

He curls his lip. "When it has anything to do with her establishment, it's a hard limit."

"So, your comfort level is location specific?"

"No, I'm saying I've reserved parts of myself—and things I'm willing to do—for the women I love."

I chew my lip. "Women, plural?"

"There has only ever been one." He tips my chin up. "Until you."

"But you said I'm one of *three* women you've kissed?"

He nods. "One of those was a mistake."

"But you've slept with—"

"Countless women." He rakes a hand through his hair. "Listen, I'm not proud of that, but I want you to know I've always been safe about it. I get tested every two months for my peace of mind. The only time I've had sex without a condom was on your desk. I'm sorry for being reckless and disrespecting you like that."

"You didn't disrespect me, Lincoln."

"Yeah, I did. But I need you to understand why you're different for me." He places a hand on his chest. "Aside from my first girlfriend, you're the only one who holds a place here." His gaze burns into me. "And I mean that."

"Other than what I felt for Charles an eternity ago, you are the only man in my heart. I love you, Lincoln. It scares the shit out of me, but I do."

He cups my face. "I know it's fast, but I love you more than I have a right to. You make me feel free."

"You make me feel alive," I murmur, standing on my tiptoes to kiss him.

We dry off, then head back to my bedroom for more lounging. Lincoln slides his glasses back on and opens the laptop.

"What was she like?" I ask, realizing he's never spoken about his romantic history. "Your first girlfriend."

"Jill was sweet and compassionate. We dated throughout high school, and she was my first everything. I loved her, but once it was time for college, it became clear we were on different paths. She moved to California for school and still lives out there."

"You didn't consider going to college together?"

He shakes his head. "My family is in New York."

Wondering what would happen if she showed up on his doorstep, I ask, "Do you two keep in touch?"

"Yeah, we talk here and there. I went to her wedding two years ago. She just had a baby last month."

"It's refreshing to hear about someone having an amicable relationship with their ex," I say, somewhat ruefully.

"While I was heartbroken over our split, Jill didn't hurt me. We were only kids when we got together, and we still had a lot of growing up to do. The last thing I wanted was to hold her back from her dreams. I'm proud of what she's accomplished. She's planning to start her own law firm in San Francisco. She met her husband in law school."

"Good for her. I can respect a female entrepreneur." I wink.

"I have tremendous respect for them."

"What about Esme? Do you respect her?" I'm curious to learn the reason behind the disgust on his face a few minutes ago.

Sure enough, it's back. He sneers so hard his nostrils flare. "There was a time in my life when I respected her. Those days are over."

"Was she the mistake?"

His gaze snaps to mine as he sets the laptop aside. "The biggest mistake of my life."

"Did you sleep with her?"

"Yes." He clenches his jaw. "Before I started working there."

"So, your skills in the sack got you the job?"

"Yep." Lincoln squeezes his eyes shut. "Is there anything else you'd like to know?"

"Why did you start working there, or better yet, why do you continue your employment, if it makes you feel dirty?"

"She gave me an offer I couldn't refuse."

"And that was?"

Lincoln scrubs a hand over his face. "I'd rather not talk about it."

"I'm sorry. I didn't mean to pry."

"It's all right." He squeezes my hand. "Just understand that if things were different, that chapter of my life would never have been written."

# Fifty

## Elinora

It's Saturday morning. After a week of being the sweetest, most attentive partner a woman could ask for, a shirtless Lincoln stands at the stove making pancakes. From my place at the kitchen island, I scope out the flex of his back muscles while he folds fresh strawberries into the batter. While I should focus on catching up on my emails, all I can think about is his perfect ass.

"You know," I begin, tracing a pattern on the granite countertop.

Lincoln looks over his shoulder at me. "Know what?"

"It's been a week . . ."

He chuckles and shakes his head. "I said two, remember?"

I huff out a breath. "Pretty sure you're not a surgeon."

He points the spatula at me. "No, but you weren't exactly lucid when you listened to her instructions." His lips curve into a devilish smile. "I'll read to you after breakfast."

"I don't want you to read to me. I want you to . . ." I flush and look at my feet.

Lincoln turns off the stove and prowls across the kitchen. "Tell me."

My breath rushes out of me, and heat pools between my thighs at the command in his tone. Who knew I'd love having a man tell me what to do?

He brushes his lips over my neck. "I wanna hear every detail."

"I want, uh, I—" I force a swallow. Bold as I am, I still can't voice my fantasies. "I just want you."

"I want you too." My head falls back as he kisses my neck and shoulders. "But I need you to work on making your desires known." He tips my chin up. "You have no trouble at the office."

"That's different. I'm the boss there."

"Setting doesn't matter. In my eyes, you're always queen."

I raise a brow. "Are you saying I'm bossy? Or do you mean you'd follow me into battle?"

"Both." He nips my earlobe. "Your assertiveness is something I love about you. One of the many qualities that made me fall." He kisses my throat. "Now, tell me your fantasies."

"I can't. It's hard for me to say."

"You can tell me you love me, but you're still afraid to talk to me?"

"I'm not afraid to talk to you. It's just . . ."

"I don't have your full trust yet?"

I squeeze my eyes shut. "We'll get there, Lincoln. I just need more time."

He nods, but I can tell he's offended. "I get it. Fifteen years is a lot of damage to undo. Understand that I'll do whatever it takes."

"I know you will." I reach for his hand. "We're almost there. You're doing everything right."

"Maybe I'll give you an assignment? Since we're not having sex for at least another week, it gives you plenty of time to think about other ways to communicate."

"An assignment? Are you suggesting I get some sidewalk chalk and make you a mural or something?"

"No, I'm suggesting you let yourself trust me. I want all of you—mind, body, heart, and soul. I wanna know how I can make you feel secure in what we share. If straight up telling me your darkest desires is too hard for you, find another way. Make a list or something."

The late afternoon sun filters through the blinds in my living room. I'm lounging on the couch with a romance novel while Lincoln uses my laptop.

He stretches and sets the computer aside. "Do you feel like going for a walk?"

I glance up from my book. "That would be wonderful. Give me a minute—I have two pages left in this chapter, and I need to see how the heroine reacts to something."

Lincoln chuckles. "Make sure her reaction aligns with the goals, motivation, and conflict."

"You didn't edit this one, so no guarantees." I skim through the remaining paragraphs and grimace. "Nope."

"I see it's a romantic suspense. Is she one of the 'too stupid to live' types?"

"No, but she's overly blasé about critical shit, which annoys me," I mutter, closing the book. I stand and stretch. "Where do you feel like walking?"

He points to the window. "The cherry blossoms are fading. We should enjoy them while they last."

"Good call."

We make our way outside and cross the street into Central Park. I loop my arm through his, and we stroll along the walkway. The chilly breeze makes me glad I wore a sweater.

Lincoln stops us near a cluster of cherry trees and pulls out his phone. "May I take a picture of you with these in the background?"

I flash him a coy smile. "For what purpose?"

"Alone time."

"Well, in that case." I snatch his phone and switch it to selfie mode. "Let's give you better material." I stand on my tiptoes and kiss him, capturing the image on the screen.

Heat flares in his eyes. "Thank you. I'll print that one out and hang it over my bed."

I snap a few more pictures of us together before handing back his phone. "Please send them to me, so I can do the same."

# Fifty-One

### Lincoln

I love this woman so much it hurts. With her flushed cheeks, she's more beautiful than the infamous Central Park cherry blossoms. We continue our walk, pausing every so often to snap a picture.

Elinora points to an empty bench. "Let's relax for a few minutes. I have something I'd like to discuss with you."

My heart sinks because I know she's going to bring up The River again. Maybe I should just ignore the NDA and tell her about my contract.

We settle on the bench. I rake a hand through my hair. "I know what you're going to say."

She arches a brow. "Do you?"

"Yeah. You're gonna tell me I should quit The River."

"While I'd love if you did, this has nothing to do with your side job." She straightens, her tone all business now. "Not this Monday, but the following one, I'd like for you to attend an event with Freya, Myles, Lynn, and me."

"I'd love to," I blurt, relieved she's not pressing me about Esme, and honored to be grouped with Lynn, a member of Iverson Melt's elite. She's an acquiring editor who specializes in historical and sweet romance. I haven't had many interactions with her, but she seems cool.

Elinora chuckles. "I haven't even given you the details."

I shrug. "Doesn't matter. If it's something I get to do with you, I'm in."

Emotion wells in her eyes. "Following me into battle?"

"Always." Taking her hands in mine, I kiss each of her knuckles. "Why? Do I have to wear a bunny suit or something?"

She laughs. "No, work attire is fine. I want you to come with me to the Romance Writers Conference at The Platinum Hotel in Times Square. It's a two-day event featuring published and aspiring authors from all over the country."

"Sounds great. Of course I'll come. Do you have a booth you need me to man?"

She shakes her head. "No, Freya and Myles will run our booth. The first day, you'll be with me. I have two workshops to teach and a few panel discussions. It will be a good experience for you to see this end of things. Plus, you'll be better suited to answer editorial questions during the panels."

"That sounds awesome. Let me know if there's anything I can do to help you prepare."

Elinora nods. "I'll have you read through my workshop materials to see if everything makes sense. On day two, I'm sending you out on your own." A broad smile crosses her features. "I would like you—my top editor—to take part in the editor pitch sessions. In the past, this conference ran them like speed-dating, which worked well. Assuming they follow suit, authors who wish to pitch their novel can sign up for ten-minute time slots with the editors or agents of their choice. Given the success of Iverson Melt, our editor sessions have always been full. I feel confident about you and Lynn representing the company."

I press my hand to my chest. "That means a lot to me, Elinora. But this is acquiring editor stuff . . ."

"Maybe I want to see if you have what it takes to fulfill that position. I seem to recall you saying something about that being your dream?"

"Oh, it most definitely is. I'm stoked to be part of this."

"Lynn went last year and discovered two amazing new authors. When we get back to the office, she can fill you in on the process. Her strength has always been with quirky historical romance and the sweeter stories." She trails her fingertips down my neck. "And we both know which subgenre you prefer."

My cock twitches. "So, you'd like me to only focus on erotic romance?"

Raindrops start to fall, but she ignores them. "No, I want broad spectrum coverage. If someone pitches you a brilliant concept for a historical, please request a partial submission. Same goes for the wholesome stuff. While I know Lynn won't purposefully turn her nose up at higher heat levels, she's apt to shy away from the super kinky ones." She slides her hand up my thigh as the rain comes down harder. "I know I can count on you to balance things out. Besides, there's nothing shy about you, Mr. Kennedy."

"If you're trying to seduce me, Ms. Iverson," I brush my lips over her ear and whisper, "it's working."

She bites her lower lip. "This is coming from the man who said he wouldn't touch me for two weeks?"

"I'm open to revisions."

# Fifty-Two

## Elinora

The enormous bulge in Lincoln's jeans creates an answering throb between my thighs. My surgery was a week ago, and I feel fine— other than the all-consuming lust thrumming in my veins.

I drop my gaze to his lap. "Let's go take off these wet clothes."

Lincoln brushes the damp hair back from my face. "We can mess around, but my two-week rule still stands."

"But you just said—"

He cuts me off with a passionate kiss. Every time our lips meet, it feels like he's changing me. Rewriting the bitter cold draft of myself into something vibrant and new. Erasing the pain Charles caused and infusing this version with warmth. Respect. Love. All the things my ex-husband never gave me. Each kiss with Lincoln feels like a new beginning. The rain pours down on us, washing away our pasts.

He breaks the kiss and rests his forehead against mine. "You don't know what you do to me, Elinora."

"If it's anything like what I feel, then yes, I most certainly do." I grip his shoulders. "Let's go home. I need you to hold me."

We leave the park bench behind and make our way back to my pent-house, smiling at Jerry the doorman as we pass. Once upstairs, Lincoln seizes my lips again and backs me into my bedroom.

After shedding our saturated clothes, we towel off and slide between the luxe Egyptian cotton sheets. Our lips collide once more. His hands roam my body, cupping my breasts. I deepen the kiss, pulling him closer and wrapping my legs around him. Desperate to feel him inside me, I reach between us and grip his cock.

Lincoln breaks the kiss. "Nice try."

"I need you," I say, flexing my hips against him.

"I'm here, angel." He kisses my neck and shoulders, gradually making his way to my breasts. He sucks and licks my nipples, my ribcage, my belly. And lower. Trailing wet kisses across my hips, he nudges my thighs farther apart and settles with his face between them.

"Lincoln, you don't have to—"

Thunder crashes, making me jump. In unison with a flash of lightning, the swipe of Lincoln's tongue against my pussy renders me speechless. I know he mentioned oral sex is only a hard limit for him at The River, but part of me worries he feels obligated to pleasure me.

"Lincoln." I gasp. "Please don't force yourself—"

"No one's forcing anything." He groans, palming my ass cheeks. "I've been dying to taste you." He pulls me closer and licks up my center as more thunder booms.

I fist the sheets. "Oh, God."

He spears his tongue inside me and growls low in his throat, fingers clenching my ass. "Just like heaven, angel. Open your legs wider and watch me lick you."

I lift my head and meet his gaze. Possessive and burning with desire, his Atlantic blue orbs lock on to mine while his lips and tongue unravel me. Another flash of lightning. He rapidly flicks his tongue on my clit. With his dark lashes fluttering against his cheeks, he groans and sucks my clit between his lips. My toes curl, moans coming freely. Lincoln pleasures me like a man starved for the taste of my body. A storm of hunger more powerful than the one raging outside my window.

"Oh, *Lincoln.*"

"Tell me you're mine."

I knot my fingers in his hair. "I'm yours."

He groans and ramps up the intensity. The pleasure is indescribable. Charles rarely went down on me, and when he did, it was lackluster. I remember the dozens of times I faked an orgasm so we could move on to sex.

As Lincoln draws my climax steadily closer, I realize exactly what I've been missing.

Arching my back, I press my pussy to his mouth. Seeing his handsome face between my thighs, pleasuring and loving me the way only he can, while his hands pull me even closer, is enough to send me over the edge. Lightning strikes and the lights flicker as I come.

"Yes!" My hips thrash in his hold as my release slams through me, stealing my breath.

He doesn't stop, and his marauding tongue makes me climax again, wailing his name this time. It becomes clear he's in a holding pattern, sucking and licking me into oblivion. I need more. I need him inside me.

"Make love to me," I plead, pulling at his shoulders. "Lincoln, *please*."

He lifts his head. "I don't have any cond—"

"I'm infertile, and I trust you." I meet his gaze fiercely. "I need you to make love to me. Right now."

He presses himself up and resettles on top of me. His lips brush my ear. "I don't want to hurt you."

"Go slow." I reach between us and line us up. "I need you."

Lincoln brings his lips to mine, giving me the salty sweet taste of myself. He deepens the kiss and eases his cock inside.

I moan as his thick length fills me, soothing the empty ache the way only he can. "You feel so good."

He clenches his jaw and rolls his hips. "You too, angel." Interlacing our fingers, he presses my hands to the bed at my shoulders.

I tighten my legs around him, close my eyes, and savor each stroke. Lincoln buries his face in my neck and moves slowly, like he'd be content to thrust for days. Weeks. Months. Years. An eternity. That's what I need from him—his time. I need his years, his future. Our future.

"Tell me you'll always be mine."

He lifts his head. "Always."

"Only mine?" I breathe, tears welling in my eyes.

"Only yours." He kisses me and tightens his grip on my hands as if to solidify his vow. "I'm all yours, angel."

"Hold me," I whisper.

He releases my hands and pulls me close, rolling us onto our sides. I loop my upper leg over his hip and clutch his back. Our face-to-face position feels more intimate than any time we've been together. Maybe it's because

I love him now. Or because I know beyond the shadow of a doubt that he's meant to fill the emptiness inside me.

A tear rolls down my cheek at the depth of what I feel for this man. It's a single drop, but it ought to be a downpour.

His gaze focuses on mine. "Am I hurting you?"

"No. I just . . ."

"Just what?"

"I love you." I grip him tighter. "So much, it's hard to breathe."

He cups my face and kisses me slow and deep, pouring his soul into it. "I love you too."

I close my eyes and surrender the final holdout of my heart, body, and soul. I give him everything that's left of me and pray he's strong enough to hold on to it.

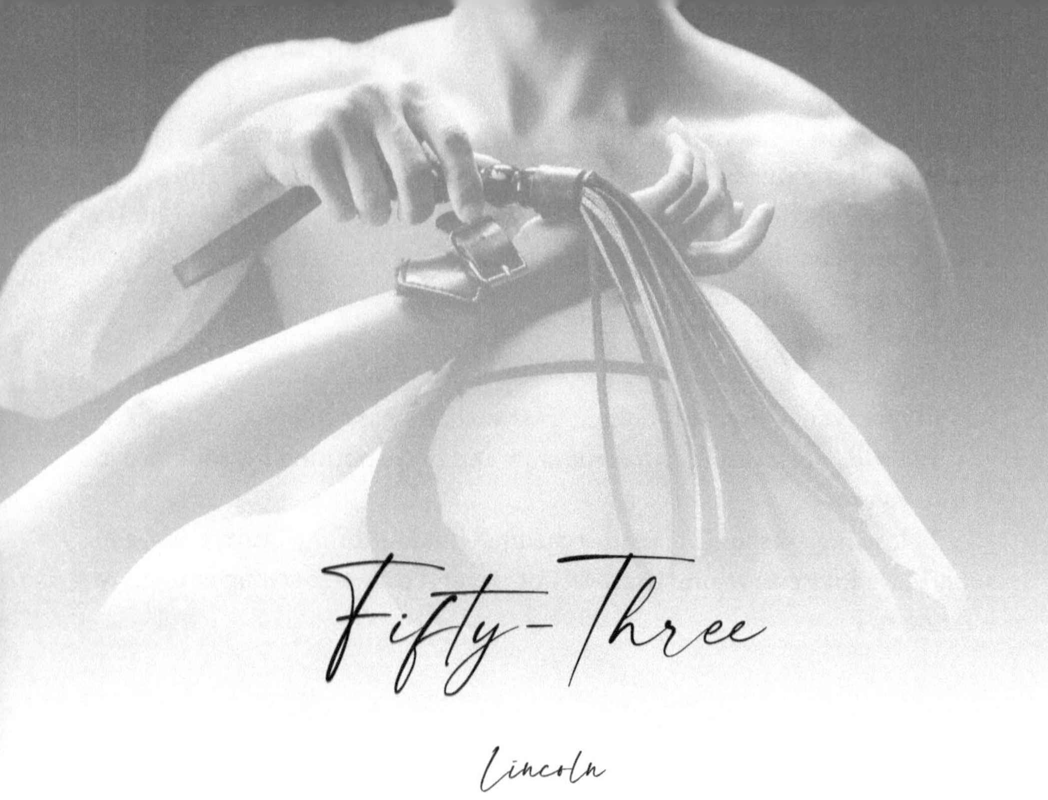

# Fifty-Three

*Lincoln*

It's Sunday morning, and I'm exhausted from last night's bartending shift. Elinora has her weekly brunch with Freya, so despite my fatigue, I seized the opportunity to visit my sister. Catskill Manor is unusually chaotic today. Staff and residents crowd the reception desk, making it difficult for me to sign in. Reagan doesn't know I'm coming, and I can't wait to surprise her. Since I'm impatient, I tuck the signed Jake Bennett CD beneath my shirt, tighten my grip on the paper bag from Compass Roasters, and head for the nurses' station instead. After all, it's not like they don't know me here.

Perplexed to find the nursing desk in Reagan's unit unattended, I head down the hall toward her suite. I reach the doorway, and ice fills my chest when I realize everyone's in her room. My sister is lying on the floor.

"What happened? Is she OK?"

Sue, one of the nurses assigned to Reagan, looks up at me from where she's kneeling beside her. "She's OK. Coming out of a grand mal seizure. She's still extremely groggy."

Cynthia, the nursing supervisor, uses her stethoscope to listen to Reagan's heart. "Everything sounds good."

The other three nurses leave the room and return to whatever it was they were doing before.

"Did she fall? Hit her head?" I squat beside my sister as my stomach twists into knots. I'll never forget how terrifying it was when she had her first seizure.

"No. She felt it coming and told me, so I was able to lower her to the floor before it happened." Sue gently brushes the hair back from Reagan's face and adjusts the folded-up blanket beneath her head. "This one only lasted two minutes, so we didn't need to medicate her." There have been times when her seizure went on for more than five minutes, which is a true medical emergency that requires the administration of antiepileptic drugs. Sue points to a rectal syringe on a nearby chair. "I had everything ready just in case."

"Thank you." The smell of urine tells me Reagan lost bladder control during the episode, which is sadly a common occurrence. A glance at her damp sweatpants confirms my hunch. I know how much it embarrasses her when she wets herself. "Can we please get her out of the wet pants?"

"As soon as she's more alert, we'll get her freshened up." Sue pats my arm. "I know it's upsetting to see, but I promise we have everything under control."

"I know, and I appreciate everything you do. I just hate that she has to deal with this shit."

"Linky?" Reagan's eyes flutter open. "That you?"

"Yeah, Reag. I'm here."

She blinks up at me in confusion. "I didn't know you were coming."

"That's because I wanted to surprise you."

She suddenly scrunches up her face. "Oh no. I peed."

My heart breaks as I gently squeeze her shoulder. "It's OK, honey. We'll take care of it in a few minutes."

"Do you think you're ready to sit up?" Sue asks.

"Yes, but my legs hurt."

"That's from the contractions, sweetie." Cynthia blots the saliva at the corners of Reagan's mouth with a tissue. "I'll get you some muscle cream."

"Why is she still having seizures with all the medication she's on?" I ask.

"In Reagan's case, the breakthroughs often happen in conjunction with hormonal changes. That seems to be the pattern with her," Cynthia explains.

"What do you mean, a pattern?"

Sue lowers her voice. "Let's call it a *monthly* pattern."

*Oh. Now I get it.*

"Don't tell him I have my period," Reagan whines, her cheeks turning pink as she covers her face with her hands.

"It's OK, Reag. I'm your brother. And an adult." Most of the time.

"But you're a boy."

"I have an idea." I slowly climb to my feet. "How about I leave the room for a little while so you can get cleaned up?"

"Wait." She clutches my arm. "Please don't go home yet."

Guilt settles in my stomach. I really need to make my visits more of a priority. I feel like a dick for neglecting her these past few weeks. "I'm not going anywhere."

"Promise?"

"I promise."

"Lincoln, why don't you check out Reagan's artwork in the lobby while you wait?" Sue suggests.

"Good idea." I head for the lobby, pausing to admire my sister's beautiful watercolor paintings. She's always enjoyed art, but I guess I'd forgotten about her innate talent.

"Wanna see mine?" asks a teenage boy in a wheelchair, who I've seen during a few of my visits.

I smile. "Sure. What've you got?"

"This way." I follow as he wheels himself to the opposite side of the room. He points to a landscape painting. "I made that."

"Great job." I recognize the Shawangunk Mountains outside New Paltz, and the Sky Top Tower on the Mohonk Preserve. He even included some of the nearby cornfields. "I like the details."

"Thanks." He eyes me. "You're Reagan's brother?"

"I am."

"She's my friend. You should come visit her more. She cries sometimes when she doesn't get to see you."

"Thank you for letting me know." Rubbing the back of my neck, I release a heavy sigh, hating myself for being a shitty brother. "I never want to make her sad. My job is a little crazy, but I'm going to do better." And that's a fucking promise. "What's your name?"

"Keith."

"Lincoln, you can come back now," Sue calls.

"Be right there." I turn toward Keith. "Thank you for being Reagan's friend."

He nods. "She's the best."

"She really is." I give him a smile and head back down the hall.

Reagan lounges on her bed, wearing yoga pants and a T-shirt. She looks up when I enter the room. The palpable relief on her face tightens my chest. "You're back."

"I told you I would be, didn't I?" I settle on the foot of her bed.

"Yeah, but I was worried."

The never-ending well of guilt spills over, but I force myself to smile and focus on the present. She doesn't need to see me cry. "How are you feeling?"

"Tired, and my head hurts."

"Make sure you rest today. But before that," I crinkle the paper bag in my hands, "I brought you a special treat."

Her eyes light up. "What is it?"

"Pretty sure I promised you a cupcake." I hand her the bag.

She peeks inside with a grin. "That's the biggest cupcake I've ever seen."

"I guarantee it'll also be the tastiest. It's, uh, strawberry." The cupcake's actual name is Strawberry Sex Swing, but I'm not about to share that tidbit with my little sister.

"I love strawberries." She gleefully unwraps it and takes an enormous bite.

"I know you do."

"Wow. It's so good."

"Best cupcakes in New York." I can't help but smile, seeing her happily enjoy the treat. Once she's finished, I hand over the CD. "I'm sure you already have this album, but I picked up a special edition copy for you."

"Ooh, Jake Bennett! I love him so much!" She hugs the CD case to her chest. "I didn't know he had any special editions."

"He technically doesn't. Open it and look inside."

She opens the case, and her eyes widen when they land on the personalized disc. "Oh my God, Linky! Did he really sign it?"

"He sure did."

"How does he know my name?" Squealing, she holds it up for me to see. "Look! He wrote it right there! He even spelled it right."

Reagan,

Thank you so much for listening. I appreciate you!

Jake Bennett

"Oh, you know, he's friends with a friend of my friend, so—"

She throws her arms around my neck. "Thank you."

I wrap her in a tight hug. "You're welcome. The next time he goes on tour, I'll take you to see one of his concerts."

"I'd love that." She pulls back to look at my face. "Do you think maybe we could go backstage so I could meet him?"

"I'm not sure how one coordinates those types of things, Reag." Maybe I'll nonchalantly mention something to Garrett when I see him. It's a big ask, and I'm not sure how Jake Bennett handles fan meetings, if he does them at all. Also, it's really cute that she thinks I have those kinds of connections with celebrities of Bennett's caliber. "My friend says he's a really nice guy, so you never know."

"That would be amazing," she swoons, staring at the enormous poster of Bennett beside her bed. "And *of course*, he's a nice guy. He's Jake Bennett."

I chuckle at her matter-of-fact tone. "You're definitely the authority on all things Jake. Speaking of nice guys, talk to me about Keith."

Her widened gaze darts to mine, and she flushes. "How do you know about him?"

I tap my head. "I'm your big brother. I know everything."

"Uh . . ." She opens and closes her mouth a few times, like the idea of me knowing all her secrets is horrifying.

I nudge her. "Relax. I met him in the lobby."

"Oh." Her breath eases out of her. "Keith is in my art group. He's really kind to me."

"Good. He should be."

"How is your job going?"

"You trying to change the subject?" I tease.

She flushes again. "Maybe."

"I'll let you get away with it since you had a rough morning. My job is going well. My boss offered me a permanent position."

Her eyes light up. "That means you can come see me more like you promised! Right?"

"Yeah." I force a smile. "That's right." Except I've doubled the amount of time I'm supposed to be at The River *and* inherited Brad's work. I'm lucky I have time to shave every morning. But she doesn't need to know all that.

I have no clue how I'll do it, but come hell or high water, I'll keep my promise.

# *Fifty-Four*

## *Lincoln*

My first day back at the office was uneventful. Elinora wasn't there because she had her follow-up appointment in the morning and went home for a nap afterward. While I truly enjoyed spending the week with her, it's nice to get back to my routine. It's challenging to focus on a manuscript with her lying in bed beside me. Especially since I'd love to act out some scenes.

My cock stirs at the memory of our weekend. Sex on Saturday night was the most soul deep connection I've ever felt. I'm grateful for my decision to reserve oral sex for someone I love, and I think I enjoyed it as much as she did. I can't get enough of Elinora's honey-sweet taste, and I love making her come with my mouth. I lost track of how many times it happened. Should I have gone to the store to pick up condoms? Probably. But when our bodies joined, and her tight, wet pussy gripped my bare cock, I knew I could never go back. She's mine. I want no barriers between us.

Too bad I belong to another woman.

It's Monday night. I stretch and peer across the lagoon to the chaise where Maya lounges with her computer. Dressed in black yoga pants and a pink T-shirt, she's deep in thought, twisting one of her mahogany-colored waves around a finger.

"Having fun?" I ask.

"This case is fucking riveting."

"Really?"

She snorts. "No. I may die from boredom, but whatever. It needs to get done." She points to my laptop. "Working hard for Elsa?"

*Looks like the nickname stuck.* Given that Elinora is my boss, I decided it was best to keep her identity quiet. People like to talk, and the last thing I want is for someone to overhear something. I can't jeopardize my career or her reputation by running my mouth.

"Always. She fired one of our suspense and thriller editors for being a misogynistic fuck. I inherited some of his manuscripts."

"Even though it's more on your plate, you love suspense and thrillers, so that's kinda cool."

"I mean, I've always enjoyed the genre, but I like romance more."

Maya flutters her lashes. "Is Lincoln Log in *love*?"

"Yeah."

"I'm so happy for you, Linc."

"Thank you. I appreciate you spending time with me here."

"Like I said, if it helps you and fucks Esme, I'm in." She sets her laptop aside. "Have you given any thought to what happens if she finds us out?"

"Who, Esme?"

"I mean both of them. Obviously, Esme will be pissed."

"I don't give a fuck—it's not like she'll fire me."

"No such luck, right?" She scans the lagoon. "Hey, I can't believe I never thought of this, but are there cameras in here? I'd hate for her to see us chilling and somehow retaliate against you."

"No, there are no cameras in the lagoons. Esme has no way of knowing what we do—or don't do—in here."

"That's good."

"Yeah."

"In these circumstances, it works in our favor, but doesn't that seem kinda dangerous? I mean, obviously not with you and me, but what about others?" She chews her lip. "What if things get out-of-hand?"

"I don't think Esme expects there to be any issues in Aqua, because most clients don't venture into the rooms behind the waterfalls. Very few even know they exist because only pleasure concierges have the access codes."

"I'm assuming they have to be accompanied by a concierge to go in there?"

"Yes. And we're each assigned a specific lagoon." I point to the waterfall. "That room is mine, meaning not only am I the only concierge permitted to use it, but I'm responsible for what goes on in there. It's also my job to ensure the playroom—and everything in it—is properly sanitized after every shift."

"Even though I've been in there with you like a zillion times, I never realized the behind-the-scenes stuff."

"Most people don't. Probably because we aren't supposed to tell anyone. Oops."

She laughs. "Always the rebel."

"You know it." I scratch my chin. "Yeah, so Esme installed cameras—with audio—in all of Glacier's playrooms. The security guys monitor activities and sometimes listen in to make sure everything's consensual and safe words are respected. Those updates were put in place shortly after your . . . incident."

"Good." She shudders, her mind likely taking her back to the trauma. "Do players know they're on camera? There's gotta be legality issues there. What if footage gets leaked?"

"There are safeguards in place. You know Ravi's sister is a silent partner, right?"

"Really?"

"Yup. One of several. Anyway, Indira Kalpana is a tech and communications whiz. She takes care of all our computers and surveillance. She partners with Darius King for security stuff and The River's attorney, Lyra Frost, to ensure everything's copacetic on the legal end."

"Wow. I've always assumed Esme was the sole owner, seeing as she's the face of the establishment."

"Nope. Esme owns the property and seventy percent of the company's assets. The remaining thirty percent belongs to the other shareholders."

Maya widens her eyes. "How come I've never heard about any shareholders?"

"Because the whole thing is very hush-hush." I nudge her. "That's why they're called silent partners. Get this—other than Darius, they're all rich, powerful women. Mostly entrepreneurs."

"That's queen level stuff. Who are they?"

"I only know of a few, and that's strictly because I overheard some things I probably shouldn't have."

"That sounds ominous," she muses, lifting an eyebrow.

"Yeah. I'm not kidding when I tell you they're fucking secretive. Darius calls them the Feminati."

"Wait, so they're like a sex-positive female secret society?"

"Exactly. I shouldn't even know they exist, but like I said, I've heard some things. Probably because they hold their monthly meeting in Lagoon Eleven, which is pretty close to this one."

Her eyes light up. "*That's* why I saw a group of women go in there together one night?"

"Yup. The room behind the waterfall in there is their secret gathering spot."

"Do they all sit back there in sex swings or something?"

"No. That room isn't set up for sex. It's kinda like King Arthur's Round Table, but they have comfy chairs and a fancy private bar. It's pretty fucking swanky. Anyway, you know Aurelia Bishop and Valentina Caruso?"

Her eyes widen to saucers at my mention of some of New York's wealthiest women. "Holy shit."

"Right. There's a lot of fucking money in these waters." I slowly shake my head, wishing I had a drop of their fortune. "Anyway, back to what we were originally talking about. Anyone who ventures into Glacier receives a detailed notice about surveillance and must sign a waiver as part of the clearance process. This is part of the reason why Aqua has become so much more popular."

"And why Esme doesn't want to lose you," she points out.

"Right." I rub my temples. "And why I'm fucked."

Maya rises and walks over, settling on the chaise beside me. "Why are you fucked? Does Elsa want more too?"

"Yeah. She says she loves me, Maya. And she wants me all to herself." I shake my head. "But how can I make those kinds of promises to her when Esme's got me by the balls?"

"Is Elsa OK with you bartending?"

"She doesn't love the idea, but she tolerates it. It's the lagoon stuff that's a deal breaker. I told her that I only work at The River so I can pay off debt."

"Surely she can understand the situation with Reagan?"

I rest my head in my hands. "I didn't tell her about Reagan."

Maya grabs my arm. "Lincoln, why the fuck wouldn't you tell her?"

"Because I didn't want to field a million questions about why I work here." I meet her mocha-colored gaze. "And I don't want her money."

"She offered you money?"

"She said she'd give me money if I needed it," I mutter.

"Uh, I'd say you need it, Linc."

"Yeah, but then I'd feel even more like a fucking loser. Or like she's paying to make me hers exclusively. Then I'm just another broke ho."

"You need to get over that shit. If she loves you, she wants to help you. It's not like she's holding out a few Benjamins and telling you to fuck her."

"But Esme owns me."

"And you could change that if you accept your woman's financial offer."

"Except my contract here applies to my *time* too."

Maya straightens. "I'll talk to my boss and see if he can work something out."

"I can't go to a lawyer. The contract explicitly prohibits me from discussing its terms with anyone. That factor should've been a red flag from the get-go, but I was desperate when I signed it. I'm a dumb fuck for skimming the details," I mutter, massaging the back of my neck. The irony of me, an editor, missing details makes me want to punch my younger self in the dick. If only it were possible to go back in time. "Besides, she'll tack on twenty percent interest if I open my mouth. I'm already having a hard enough time making payments for Reagan's housing and staying current with my rent. There's *nothing* left, Maya."

She grips my shoulders. "Which is why you need to lose your pride and accept some help."

"I've tried getting personal loans, but the bank declined me."

"Fuck the bank. If you're too stubborn to take money from Elsa, I'll lend you money. I can easily borrow against my 401k, and you know damn well I'd do that for you."

I take her hand in mine and squeeze it. "I know you would. And I appreciate that more than you'll ever know, Sea Bass."

"As far as legality issues, Julian has a ton of experience with NDAs and blackmail cases. He's pricey, but I'm sure he'd cut you a deal since you're my friend. Besides, if it gets you out of this situation, it's money well spent." She grips my chin, her gaze burning into mine with a ferocity I've never seen from her. "I *will* get you out of this contract, Lincoln."

I finished cleaning out my inbox before Elinora arrived at the office on Wednesday morning. I'm on schedule to finish all my manuscripts before their deadlines. Seated at my cubicle, I feel her the moment she enters the suite. The hairs on the back of my neck stand on end as she approaches.

"Good morning," she sings, placing a direktørsnegl in front of me.

"Good morning, and thank you. You're a goddess," I murmur, peering into her beautiful eyes. "How are you feeling?"

She smiles. "Better than I've felt in years."

We share a lingering look, and I mouth the words I can't say aloud at the office.

"*Jeg elsker dig.*" At my questioning brow, she adds, "What you said, but in my native tongue."

"I love all of your tongues," I whisper.

"Likewise."

I watch as she sashays to her office and settles behind her desk. We make eye contact, and I discreetly flash her a wink while eating the delicious pastry.

A while later, my cell rings. I snatch it and frown at the 845 area code. It's never a good sign when I receive a call from upstate.

"Hello?"

"Hi, this is Angela from Catskill Manor, may I please speak to Mr. Lincoln Kennedy?"

"This is Lincoln. Is Reagan all right?"

"Yes, she's fine. I'm from accounts receivable."

My scalp prickles. "What's up?"

"This is a courtesy call to remind you we're sending out the renewal packages this week. All forms must be filled out in their entirety and signed by a notary."

"I'll take care of everything as soon as I receive it."

"Another thing, Mr. Kennedy. Unfortunately, because of increased operating costs, all our one-on-one residents face a ten percent increase for this upcoming year's housing."

"Ten percent?" I clench the phone. "That's a bit steep, don't you think?"

"We offer a state-of-the-art facility and highly skilled nursing staff, Mr.

Kennedy. Your sister's care requires a great deal of manpower, and that kind of thing doesn't run cheap."

"I'm well aware of that, Angela," I snap. "I'm referring to the fact that last year it was only a five percent increase. We're talking double here."

"I'll remind you we have a cardiac nurse assigned to Reagan so we can monitor her heart at all times. If the cost is too much, we can scale back—"

"No." I slam my fist on the desk. "*Nothing* is to change. I'll sign your damn papers." I hang up and rest my head in my hands.

Myles approaches with a concerned expression. "Why the hell are you slamming shit and yelling?"

"Ten percent," I croak, fisting my hair. "Ten fucking percent."

He stops beside me. "What are you talking about?"

"Reagan's housing. I have to sign papers for a new lease. They want an additional ten percent to cover the cost of monitoring her heart. Plus, she had another fucking grand mal seizure the other day, and the new antiepileptic meds they want to try aren't covered by her insurance." My eyes sting, but I clench my jaw, refusing to let any tears escape. "I'm barely making it happen as it is."

He rakes a hand through his hair. "We'll figure it out, Linc."

"How the fuck am I gonna come up with more money?"

Myles grips my shoulders. "Tell you what, I'll cover the difference."

I shake my head. "I can't let you do that, man."

"You don't have a choice." He squeezes my shoulders, his emerald-colored eyes burning into me. "I'm not about to let them jeopardize Reagan's health just because they're a bunch of money hungry fucks."

My eyes water beyond the point of my control. "Thank you," I whisper, quickly wiping my cheeks. "So fucking much."

"That's what friends are for, Linc."

"Is everything all right?" Elinora's voice makes me jump and drop my phone on the floor.

I duck beneath my desk to retrieve it and take a few deep breaths to compose myself. Between Maya and Myles, I have some of the best friends a man could ever ask for. I don't deserve their kindness. And I certainly don't deserve Elinora's heart.

I straighten and meet her gaze. I know I should let her in on all the details, but I can't bring myself to say the words. "Yeah, it's all good."

# Fifty-Five

Elinora

Something happened. Myles wouldn't be comforting Lincoln for no reason. His beautiful eyes have tears in them. He's not fine; he's lying. And I want to know why.

"What's going on, Lincoln?"

"Nothing," he mutters, wiping a hand over his face. "Family stuff."

What happened to his family? Are his parents in trouble? He's mentioned a sister, but he never talks about her. I rest my hand on his shoulder. "Is there anything I can do?"

He touches my hand. "No. But thank you."

With my heart sinking at his forced smile, I nod and head back to my office. Why won't he let me in? Better yet, why would he lie to me? If something's upsetting him, I want to help. I wish we weren't at the office—I'd throw my arms around him and kiss his worries away in private. Maybe I'll suggest we go out for lunch.

Myles walks past my doorway, which gives me an idea. I pull out my phone and send him a text asking if Lincoln's all right.

> Myles Callahan: Yes. Linc's a worrier,
> but everything's been worked out.

What the hell does that mean? Why is he worried?

Freya knocks on my door. "Do you wanna grab lunch?"

I chew my lip. "I was going to ask Lincoln . . ."

She shrugs. "Clark Kent can come. Heroes need sustenance too."

"I wanted to talk to him about something." I straighten and meet her gaze. "In private."

She eyes me. "Is everything OK?"

"I don't know."

My lunch idea was a bust because Lincoln wasn't at his cubicle when I went to invite him. In fact, he didn't return until midafternoon. I have no problem with him taking extended lunch breaks, but the three-hour absence isn't like him. Given his behavior this morning—and his refusal to talk to me about it—I'm more than a little concerned.

The workday is over now, so I power down my laptop and stuff it in my briefcase before making my way to his desk. "Ready to go?"

"Yeah." He rises and grabs his stuff, his brow deeply furrowed. "Lost track of time, sorry."

We head out of the suite and stand by the elevators in silence. The ride down is silent too. My heart sinks deeper with each descending floor and lands at my feet by the time we reach the sidewalk.

I parked on the ground level of the garage today, making the trip to my car much shorter than usual. I press the unlock button and toss my stuff inside before turning to face him.

"Did I do something?" I blurt, blinking rapidly to hold back the welling tears.

Lincoln pulls me into a hug. "No, of course not, angel. I had a terrible day, that's all."

"But why?" A tear escapes and rolls down my cheek.

He brushes it away. "I have a lot on my mind. I'm sorry I've been moody." His gaze softens. "Please don't cry."

"Why won't you tell me what's bothering you?"

"Because it isn't your problem to fix." He kisses my forehead. "You've got enough on your plate."

"But you're part of my plate."

He gives me a weak smile. "You wanna eat me now, huh?"

"You know what I mean." I hug him tighter. "Come out for dinner with me."

"I'd love to." He releases a heavy sigh. "But I can't. I have work tonight."

"Call in sick," I suggest, grasping at straws.

"That wouldn't make me a dutiful employee, now would it?"

"No." I sigh heavily enough to blow down a skyscraper. "It would be irresponsible, which is not your character."

"Right." He gives me a quick kiss on the lips, but it's over far too fast.

"Will you think of me when you're there?"

His steady gaze meets mine. "I'm always thinking of you, Elinora."

"Only me?" I whisper, unsure why the raging insecurity is consuming me today. Maybe I'm PMSing, but I feel like I could curl into a ball and weep.

"Only you, angel." He kisses me again, deeply this time. He threads his hands into my hair and pulls me closer.

I moan and lose myself in Lincoln, holding on to him with a desperation that feels raw. Each moment that passes, immersed in his kiss, soothes me. Reassures my heart. Makes me love him more.

He breaks our kiss. "I have to go now. Love you."

"I love you too."

"I'm giving you a homework assignment." He flashes a wicked smile. "It's due tomorrow."

"And what might that be?"

"I want you to come up with a list of at least three things you desire. By that, I mean, stuff you want to try at The River. I want to hear your deepest fantasies."

"You know I can't do that."

"Yes, you can." He brushes his lips over my ear. "And I promise to make them a reality this weekend."

# Fifty-Six

## Lincoln

I spent most of Thursday morning on the phone with the author of *Bound Hearts*. She's nearly done with revisions using the developmental edits I sent. Once everything's in place, I'll do a second pass wearing my line editing hat.

Bartending last night was rough. Gideon's mom is in the hospital, so it was all me. Then again, being busy certainly kept my mind off the Catskill Manor debacle. One thing is for certain, until my financial situation changes, I have no choice but to accept Myles's help.

I chug what's left of my coffee and glance at my watch. It's nearly lunchtime. Elinora has been quiet today—not that I blame her. My lack of an explanation for yesterday's outburst hurt her, and made her question my feelings, which is something I never want to happen. Hopefully, I reassured her enough. If not, I'll make damn sure I do it tonight.

*Wait a minute, she never did her homework assignment.*

I snatch my phone and tap out a text.

> Me: Should I deduct points for lateness?

She retrieves her phone and types a reply before meeting my gaze with a coy smirk.

> Elinora: Maybe I didn't feel like doing your assignment.

> Me: Is that so?

> Elinora: Too challenging.

I flash her a grin.

> Me: I want a list on my desk by three o'clock.

> Elinora: Tell me, Clark Kent, what happens if I don't give you one? Will there be . . . consequences?

> Me: Perhaps. But I GUARANTEE you'll like my reward much better.

> Elinora: I'll keep that in mind. Now stop distracting me with your roguish charm. I have work to do.

My stomach growls.

> Me: Are you hungry? (for food)

> Elinora: I had a sandwich already.

> Me: Damn. I was hoping for a lunch date quickie.

I can see her blush from across the room. My palm twitches at the thought of making her sweet little ass pink too.

> Elinora: Mr. Kennedy, I need you to meet me in the 12th floor conference room in ten minutes.

Cue my instant hard-on. I jump to my feet and haul ass upstairs to wait for her.

Stiffly pacing the conference room, I clench and unclench my fists with anticipation. She enters ten minutes after me, locking the door behind her.

We collide without a word. Lips crashing, tongues thrusting in a feverish kiss. I back her to a wall and hike up her skirt, thrilled to discover she ditched her panties. She loosens my belt and yanks my zipper open, then shoves at my boxers and frees my cock.

I lift her by the thighs. "Wrap your legs around me and hold on tight. This is gonna be hard and fast."

Elinora clings to my shoulders and cries out as I plunge deep inside her.

I fuck her against the wall the way I've wanted to since the moment I laid eyes on her. Hips slamming, the slap of our bodies spurs me on. She digs her nails into my skin and moans as she takes my cock like it was made for her.

"Oh, *Lincoln.*"

"I love fucking you." I nip her earlobe. "Do you like being fucked?"

"Yes," she says on a moan.

"Yes, what?"

"Yes, sir."

I slam my hips forward, making her cry out. "That's it, sugar. Feel how hard and thick I am. How deep your pussy takes me." I know dirty talk drives her wild, and that's exactly how I want her. "You're so hot and wet. Fucking perfect."

"God, Lincoln, you're gonna make me come already." She gasps, tightening her legs around me.

"Let yourself go." I pound my cock inside her, taking her over the edge.

She bites down on my shoulder to stifle a scream. Her pussy spasms and flutters around me, squeezing my cock. I bury my face in her neck and fuck her harder. Deeper. A few more thrusts, and I join her with my release.

Gasping, we cling to one another in silence for a few minutes.

"You all right?" I ask.

"Yes." She straightens my glasses and wipes the sweat from my brow. "More than all right."

I'm still inside her and make no move to pull out. I kiss her instead. Slowly and deliberately. "I love being inside you."

"I love when you fuck me. And make love to me. And when we kiss. I just love *you*, Lincoln. Everything about you."

"It's mutual, angel."

"Also, I need a rain check for tonight. The conference coordinators called and told me one of their speakers backed out. They asked me to fill in, so I need to come up with a presentation."

*Damn.*

"What kind of presentation? Can I help you?" I ask, slowly pulling out.

"It's on marketing strategies. Thankfully, it's one I've done before, so I can use the materials I came up with a few years ago. I need to account for some newer avenues and make sure everything is current. I'll have you read it over when I'm done. I'm sorry I have to skip the lagoon tonight." She kisses me and whispers, "But I'm all yours tomorrow night."

I smooth her skirt and stuff myself back in my pants. "I look forward to it."

"And I fibbed about not doing your assignment . . ."

I raise a brow. "Oh?"

"Yes, but I'm still working up the courage to tell you what I want."

"I hope you know you can tell me anything."

"I do, but I wish you felt the same way toward me." Her gaze focuses on mine. "I can't help but feel like you're shutting me out."

*Tell her.*

I open my mouth to speak, but a blaring fire alarm silences me. The ear-splitting screech is enough to cause an eternal migraine.

I grip her arm. "Let's go."

We make our way to the nearest stairwell and follow the hordes of people down to the ground floor. Outside, the wail of approaching sirens assaults my brain. I spot Garrett and a few people from Iverson Press and nudge Elinora in that direction.

Crowded on the sidewalk, with the throng of evacuated people, is the perfect place to forget about the secrets between us.

# Fifty-Seven

## Lincoln

TGIF. And it's Cinco de Mayo, no less. I sip my coffee and stare at the computer screen, delighted by the author's revisions to *Bound Hearts*. She truly upped her game, which instills me with a sense of pride. I love being an integral part of the publication process, and this job has been an absolute gift.

Elinora is a gift. She's angelic in white today. I can't wait for all the devilish things I plan to do to her tonight. She still hasn't expressed her desires, but that's all right—I have some things in mind.

Speaking of my lady love, she approaches my cubicle with an armload of books and places them on my desk.

"What are these?"

"My completed assignment."

"I'm confused."

"You're a smart man, Lincoln." She touches my arm. "I'm sure you'll figure it out." With that, she turns and walks away, retreating to her office.

I study the stack of six books. They're all erotic romances published by Iverson Melt. Selecting the top one, I open the cover to find a sticky note written in Elinora's handwriting.

I flip to the page and grin when I discover she's highlighted a passage. My pulse quickens. It's a BDSM sex scene featuring a bound woman giving her dominant a blow job. My cock immediately hardens with the implications. I stare across the room through the open door of Elinora's office. The sultry little vixen winks.

I cannot believe one of her fantasies is giving me head. I read through the scene and snatch the second book.

The note inside its cover reads:

Turning the pages, my eyes land on another BDSM scene. My cock throbs, stretching the material of my dress pants. Here, a dom is eating his sub's pussy while a spreader bar holds her legs wide open. *Holy fuck.*

I grab the next book, nearly ripping out a page. It's a sensory deprivation scene with cuffs and a feather. I clench my jaw and lock eyes with Elinora. She trusts me enough to make her desires known, but what I wouldn't give to hear them spill from her lips.

The fourth book's spanking scene makes my palms twitch. My cock grows impossibly harder. Elinora's confession that she loves the bite of pain with her pleasure as much as I love taking her over my knee, makes me one lucky fuck. I can't wait to see the flush bloom on her plump little ass tonight.

Book five. A blindfolded woman stands spread-eagle, awaiting a dom armed with a vibrator and a riding crop. At this point, I'm seconds from jerking off at my desk.

Hands shaking, I clutch the last book. I can't breathe through the fog of lust in my brain. The doggy style sex scene makes me groan. I fucking love holding on to her hips and taking her from behind. Watching my cock slide in and out. Feeling the slap of my hips against soft flesh. Pressing her shoulders into the mattress. Pulling her hair. Spanking her gorgeous ass while I thrust.

I lurch to my feet and prowl to her office.

"May I help you, Mr. Kennedy?" Elinora flutters her lashes and does the little lip bite thing that drives me crazy. Her gaze drifts to my cock.

I stop in front of her desk. "At eight o'clock tonight, I want to find you in that lagoon, wearing nothing but your birthday suit."

A coy smile curves her lips. "I take it you read the passages?"

"Yeah, and I'm gonna make them happen."

"I certainly hope you up the ante." She taps her nails on her desk. "You know, show me who's king of the castle."

"When I'm done, there will be no question of who you belong to. First, I'm gonna watch those pretty rosebud lips take my cock and see how deep you can suck me. Then I'll lap at the river running between your thighs until you can't take it anymore." I clutch the edge of her desk and lean in close. "Don't worry, I'll make that sweet ass pink and fuck you so good you'll feel me inside you for days."

She gasps and squirms in her seat. "Shh . . . someone will hear."

"All five boroughs will hear your screams tonight."

# Fifty-Eight

## Elinora

My entire body trembles with excitement as I stand outside the entrance to Lagoon Seven. It took a tremendous amount of nerve for me to give those books to Lincoln and flirt with him after he read the passages.

I lightly tap the door and gather the rest of my courage as the portal slides open.

A leather-clad Lincoln steps into the light. "Hello, sugar."

"Good evening, handsome." I bite my lip. "The leather is hot." And so are the handcuffs dangling from his waistband. I once suggested to Charles that we try handcuffs. He laughed in my face. The look on Lincoln's face is far from laughter.

"You asked for authenticity, so I'm gonna give it to you." He ushers me inside and twists the lock. With a wicked smile, he rests his hands on my shoulders. "Tonight will be intense. You're going to see a side of me you've never seen, and I'll push you further than I've ever pushed you. I need you to be open with me. If you don't like something, say the word and I'll stop. Understand?"

"Yes."

He tips my chin up. "Yes, what?"

"Yes, sir."

"Good girl." Lincoln kisses my lips briefly, then grips my elbow. "Come with me." He leads me behind the waterfall to the playroom. "I want you naked. Now."

I swiftly undress, leaving my clothes in a pile on the floor. I meet his lust-filled gaze and await his next directive.

He takes a moment to circle me, tracing his hands on my skin. "So beautiful," he murmurs, kissing the side of my neck. I gasp, and my head falls to the side to give him better access. "That's it, sugar. Open yourself to me. I want complete surrender."

"What are you going to do to me?"

"You'll see." He leads me deeper into the room to an apparatus suspended from the ceiling. "Get in."

"Is this a sex swing?" I whisper, my stomach fluttering.

"It is." He helps me slide my arms into the straps, then adjusts the pads beneath my butt and shoulders. "You're gonna be here for a while, so you need to tell me if anything's uncomfortable."

One thing's for damn sure, this is nothing like the swing sets of my youth. I breathe in his clean, heady scent and clutch the stiff nylon, feeling something within me settle. "You sure this is sturdy?"

"Holds up to three-hundred and fifty pounds. Do your back and neck feel like they have enough support?"

"Yes."

Lincoln nods and presses my legs wide open, guiding my feet into the sex swing's stirrups. "You asked for a spreader bar, but this gives the same effect."

I glance down at the arousal glistening on my pussy and feel my nipples tighten. I catch him admiring the excitement between my legs. Goose bumps cover my flushed skin when he licks his lips. No one has ever looked at me this way. Part of me wants to close my legs, but the lust in his gaze stops me from trying. Right now, all splayed open like this, the part of me that wants him to look is slowly taking over. I trust Lincoln—mind, body, heart, and soul—which, after my failed marriage, is something I never imagined I'd give to another man.

"Don't be shy with me, angel." He kisses me, brushing the hair back from my face. "I love having every inch of you on display, like a rare flower blooming just for me." He slides his hands up my thighs. "From these gorgeous stems," his fingertips graze my pussy, "to the soft, pretty petals here."

No one has ever described me with such reverence. In Lincoln's eyes,

I'm a goddess. I have no doubt he'd build a temple to worship me. It feels incredible to be desired instead of used.

Gasping, I press into his touch. "You have a way with words."

His thumb makes slow circles on my clit. "And an incredible attention to detail. Do you have any questions before we get started?" Moisture floods my pussy at the dark promise in his tone. He grips the cable and swivels me around.

"My God, it spins?"

"Yes, and the straps are adjustable for when I flip you over later." Standing behind me, he abruptly tilts the swing back, then leans down and brushes his lips over mine, giving me an upside-down kiss of sorts. He nips my lower lip. "I'm gonna watch you bloom from every angle." Our tongues dance for a moment before he pulls back and adjusts the swing's height.

He presses on my shoulders until my head is near his waist. I stare up at him as he cups my breasts and rolls the nipples between his thumbs and forefingers. Leaning forward, he sucks a nipple into his mouth and grazes his teeth over the sensitive peak. He alternates breasts while his hands roam lower, inching closer to my pussy.

I gasp and arch my back, feeling his hard, leather-covered cock press on the top of my head. Just when I think he's about to touch my clit, he straightens. "You ready to suck me?"

My breath catches in my throat. It's been ages since I've given a blow job, and I've certainly never done it while bound in a sex swing. I hope my skills live up to his expectations. I'd let Charles down in the bedroom in real life when what I'd wanted was the stuff of fiction. Could real life and fiction meet? Is that what Lincoln is? My fantasies come to life?

"Yes."

"Yes, what?" He lowers his zipper and meets my gaze.

"Yes, sir."

Satisfaction flares in his stormy blue depths. He shoves the leather pants down over his hips, freeing his cock, then steps out of them and kicks them aside. "Open those pretty lips for me."

Arching my neck, I follow his command. He grips the base of his cock, guiding the tip to my mouth. My tongue darts out to lick him.

Lincoln groans, gradually easing his hips forward. Satin-covered steel fills my mouth. He slides in further, claiming me.

# Fifty-Nine

## Lincoln

The heat of Elinora's wet mouth surrounds my cock. I don't want to overwhelm her with the position's intensity, but it takes every ounce of strength for me to move slowly.

"Just like that, sugar. See how deep you can take me." I ease forward.

She massages the top of my shaft with her tongue, her teeth grazing the underside. Her neck is elongated into a beautiful arch. I brush my fingers across her throat. Her moan makes my balls tighten.

"Oh, fuck *yes.*"

Elinora releases the straps overhead and arches back further, clamping her hands on my hips. One of them trails down to cup my balls, rolling them in her palm as she sucks my cock deeper.

I groan, slightly rocking my pelvis. "Your tongue feels like heaven."

This may be her fantasy, but damn if it isn't mine too. Her enthusiasm makes me feel like I'm a hundred feet tall. I push further—a little too far because she presses against my thighs.

I immediately pull back. "Sorry."

In response, she swirls her tongue on the head before rapidly flicking it through the slit at the tip.

"Shit," I growl, clutching her breasts. At this point, I'm so turned on it's more like groping. Since that's not the effect I'm going for, I pull out and help her sit back up. "OK, it's your turn now."

"Talk about a head rush." She gasps. "Why'd you stop me?"

"Because you would've made me come in the next twelve seconds, and tonight's about your fantasies." I know it took a tremendous amount of courage for her to reveal her desires, and I want to make sure I live up to her expectations.

"Putting my mouth on you is one of my fantasies."

"And that makes me one lucky fuck." I spin her around to face me and seize her lips in a kiss, knotting my fingers in her hair. "Your tongue felt incredible."

She nips my lower lip. "Next time, I won't let you cut it short."

"We'll see about that." Reaching for the nearby dresser, I snatch a blindfold and hold it up with a devilish grin. "You ready?"

"I think so." Elinora's pupils dilate. Her shoulders rise and fall as her breathing picks up speed when I slide it down over her eyes.

I love watching her body's response to me. Her growing excitement ratchets mine up a few notches. She trusts me to take care of her, and I'm going to make damn sure I do.

I guide her hands to the swing's straps again. "Keep your hands here no matter what I do. Got it?"

"Yes, sir."

Her submission makes my cock even harder. I pick up a feather tickler and riding crop, holding one in each hand. Standing between her legs, I start at her neck, lightly trailing both toys over her skin. "What do you think these are?"

"One's a feather," she says on a gasp. "The other feels like the tip of a belt."

"It's a riding crop." I lightly tap her ass with it. "How's the water, Elinora?"

"Fire, sir."

Next, to throw her off, I switch hands and repeat the featherlight caresses. This time, starting from her ankles. While circling her right kneecap with the tip of the feather, I swat her left calf. She gasps and writhes her hips. I trade hands again and move to her wrists, working my way inward. Even though I've done this scene on other women, nothing about tonight feels routine. I'm not worried about my client getting her money's worth or if she's down for a fuck. Instead of thinking about how much money I owe Esme and when my shift will be over, my focus is solely on Elinora and the perfect body she's offered up to me. The way she moans my name and writhes with pleasure.

I tickle her breasts with the feather and tap her ass with the riding crop again.

"Oh, God, Lincoln . . ."

Trailing the feather down her belly, I sink to my knees between her thighs and place the crop on the floor. I can tell she's waiting for another slap, but I'll save that for later. I brush the feather over her nipples and lower my lips to her pussy. I don't touch her yet, instead allowing my hot breath to gust over her clit.

She flexes her hips. "*Lincoln.*"

I move closer, brushing the tip of my nose in the crease of her thigh, softly kissing now. Then I switch sides and lick from her kneecap to her groin, carefully avoiding her pussy. Her hips churn with her attempts to get closer, but I kiss her other thigh instead.

"I know you're teasing me."

"Maybe." I chuckle. "What're you gonna do about it?"

"Please," she whispers.

"Please, what?"

"Please, sir." She fists my hair.

"Hands, sugar." While I love that she's calling me sir, it's not the answer I'm looking for. Some primal part of my manhood needs to hear Elinora voice her desires. It goes beyond lust and desire for me. I need her to give me her full trust and say what she wants instead of highlighting passages in a book. I wait until she moves her hands to their rightful position before continuing. "I wanna hear you tell me what you want."

"You."

"Tell me what you want me to do," I whisper, mere inches from her body's entrance. She hesitates, and I close my eyes in frustration. The walls are still up. Despite my efforts, I haven't won her over yet.

"I want—"

"Tell me."

She clutches the straps. "I want you to lick me until I scream."

# Sixty

## Elinora

"**Y**our wish is my command." Lincoln's voice is a deep rumble that vibrates my clit. Gripping my hips, he drags his tongue through the moisture that gathers at my center and groans. "Fuck, I love the taste of you."

My toes curl, and I arch my back, pressing my hips closer to him. He sucks my clit between his lips and swirls his tongue. With the blindfold covering my eyes, everything is more intense. Lightning bolts of sensation spear through me, making my thighs tremble.

"Lincoln, that feels amazing," I say between moans, my head falling back.

He spears his tongue inside me the way he'd thrust his cock. Urgent and deep. He alternates swirling licks with rapid flicks of his tongue, teasing every inch of needy flesh between my legs. My moans come freely as he takes me higher and higher. He presses my legs wider apart and slides a finger inside me, focusing his lips and tongue on my clit. With each thrust of his finger, he gives me a hard suck to match the rhythm.

I grip his hair and tug on the strands. He pulls back and presses featherlight kisses to my inner thighs.

"Why are you stopping?" I sputter, thrusting my pussy toward his mouth.

"Where are your hands?" His tone is full of amusement.

"I can't help it." I reluctantly release his silky hair. Before I realize what's happening, something cold encircles both wrists. Handcuffs. My heart rate and breathing kick up a notch. "That's not fair."

His low chuckle makes my pussy ache. "You asked for these, remember?"

He's right—I did. And he's bringing every part of my delicious fantasies to life. "Yes."

"How's the water, Elinora?"

"Fire."

He lifts my arms overhead, and I hear another click as he fastens my wrists to something—probably the swing's built-in bar. He tips me back, pressing against my thighs. A low hum tells me he's holding a vibrator. As he trails the buzzing tip across my breasts, he puts his mouth on me once more.

I moan loudly at the contact and flex my hips. With my arms restrained and my legs held in place by the swing, I'm completely open to him. Vulnerable as hell, yet safe. *I trust him.* But beyond that, I love him. Truly and deeply.

Lincoln's tongue embarks on a merciless crusade, bringing me to the edge in moments. He increases the intensity, dragging the vibrator between my legs to tease the entrance to my pussy. He doesn't enter me, just holds it there while sucking my clit.

I fall apart. Every nerve and every cell explode into a screaming orgasm.

He doesn't stop licking me. He trails the tip of the vibrator toward my rear, but instead of tensing, I absorb the pulsing vibrations that radiate from my pussy to the crack of my ass. He's pressing my boundaries but not crossing them.

There's a part of me deep inside that wants him to push me further.

"How's the water?"

"Warm."

Lincoln spears his tongue inside me for a few strokes, then returns to my clit, quickly bringing me back to fire. I come immediately. Every inch of me pulses and spasms with my release.

"Lincoln, I want—" I buck my hips wildly. "Fuck me."

He turns off the vibrator and unlocks the cuffs, freeing my wrists. Helping me to sit up, he removes the blindfold and kisses me slowly and deeply. "Are you good to stay in the swing, or do you want to move to the bed?"

"Swing."

"Good." He releases my feet from the swing's restraints and picks something up off the floor. "Now, turn over so you're facedown, and stick your feet back into the stirrups. I want those legs wide open for me."

I do as I'm told and suddenly realize there's a mirror across the room. I take in the sight of Lincoln standing behind me, armed with the riding crop, powerful and brutally gorgeous. His huge cock juts proudly.

"How's the water?"

"Fire."

*Crack.* The crop lands on one of my ass cheeks. The stinging warmth spreads across my skin. I cry out and clutch the swing.

Lincoln strikes the other cheek. Hard. "The water?" His voice comes out on a low growl that tells me how much this is turning him on.

*"Fire."*

He meets my gaze in the mirror. "Hold on tight, sugar."

# Sixty-One

## Lincoln

This may be the only time I'm grateful for my employment at The River, and Elinora isn't the only uninhibited one tonight.

Again and again, I slap her plump little ass with my palm. "You like that?"

"Yes!" Her throaty moans tighten my balls. "Lincoln! Oh, fuck!"

I strike the other cheek with the riding crop. Alternating between my hand and the toy, I make sure to gauge her reaction. The last thing I want to do is push her too far or hurt her. My palm collides with a loud crack.

Naked and spread wide open for me, it's not just Elinora's body on display. It's her heart and soul, too.

*She trusts me.*

A wave of emotion crashes into me, stinging my eyes. She believes in me, both here and at the office, so I owe it to her to come clean about my dealings with Esme. And I will. But not now. Tonight is about Elinora's fantasy—not my problems. But one thing's for damn sure, I'll make this right. I'll give her my honesty. I'll devote every part of myself to our relationship, even if I must take Maya up on her offer of financial help to gain my freedom.

Elinora wails my name. I can't wait another second to be inside her.

"I'm gonna fuck you now," I growl, savoring my hand's warm sting. I toss the riding crop on the floor and line up my cock with her pussy. "Tell me how you want it."

"Hard. Don't hold back."

I slam into her. "Like this?"

"Yes!" She claws at the floor. "Lose control with me."

I've already lost control. Elinora owns me—heart and soul. It's high time I give her the rest of me.

I clutch her hips and fall into a pounding rhythm as her cries mix with the groans leaving my chest. Looking down to where we join, I watch my thick length slide into her warm, wet depths. She takes me so deep, I don't know where I stop and she starts. Each thrust takes me higher, bringing me closer to the heaven I seek inside her. Nothing compares to Elinora and what I feel for her. I want to be the man she deserves, and I'll do whatever it takes to get there.

Even if it costs me everything.

My strokes take her over the edge, and she wails my name as her pussy spasms around me. I fuck her even harder, losing any semblance of restraint. I'm no longer a man. Pure, animalistic lust fuels me.

Something I don't recognize inside me claws its way to the surface. Possession. I want my mark on every fucking inch of her body.

This woman unhinges me.

I knot one hand in her hair and yank her head back. "You're mine, Elinora."

She whimpers something and clenches around me, desperately trying to dig her nails into the floor.

"How's the water?"

"*Fire,*" she wails, arching her back. Sweat glistens on her skin. Her hair is tangled in my fist. Even though I'm pounding into her, she's still flexing her hips back, pulling me deeper.

If she wants more, I'll give it to her.

Gliding my thumb between her thighs, I gather her juices and spread them back. I'm not sure how much she'll allow, but I'm dying to find out. She gasps when I massage slow circles on her ass.

I hesitate for a moment, but instead of pulling away, she tightens her thighs around me. "You like that?"

"Yes."

I take it even further, slowly easing a finger inside. Stroking and rubbing.

Exploring. The exhilaration of pushing her limits is nothing compared to watching her surrender control.

I go a little deeper. "Tell me to stop, and I will."

She flexes her hips back. "Don't stop. Oh, God, *please* don't stop."

Satisfaction bubbles in my veins as I slow my thrusts to match the rhythm of my hand. I love how her pussy squeezes my cock. How she leans into the forbidden touch instead of pushing me away. Most of all, I love that she trusts me enough to tell me what she wants.

Her movements get wilder and more erratic. Then she bears down on my cock and explodes into another orgasm. "Oh! Lincoln! Yes!"

"Fuck, baby. That's it." I slam into her a few more times until I can't hold back any longer. Groaning, I come long and hard, giving her everything I've got. My cock is still jerking when I collapse forward and bury my face at the back of her neck.

We stay this way for a few minutes, me draped over her like a blanket, both gasping and shuddering with the aftershocks of the most intense sex we've ever had. I couldn't move if I wanted to.

"I love you, angel." I kiss her shoulders. "So fucking much." Panic fills my chest and seeps into my veins when she doesn't respond.

*Her ovary.*

Pulling out, I gather Elinora in my arms, disentangling her from the swing. It's only two weeks out from her ruptured cyst surgery. How the fuck could I forget and lose control like that? I pushed her too far. *What if I caused an injury?* The thought turns my stomach.

"Are you OK, angel?" Holding her limp body to my chest, I carry her out to the lagoon.

"Mm-hmm." She nuzzles into me.

"Did I hurt you?" I hold my breath and wait for her answer.

"No. Just sleepy. Feel kinda boneless."

She must be in subspace. The out-of-body euphoria frequently experienced by subs after a scene is a much better reality than the possibility that I'd truly hurt her. With a dizzying sigh of relief, I ease us into the tranquil lagoon's warm saltwater.

I position Elinora so she's facing me in a straddle, her head resting on my shoulder. Her warm breasts mold to my chest as her breathing slows to normal. I softly stroke her hair and rub her back in circles.

She dozes off in my arms, completely and utterly spent from the wringer I put her through.

"I love you, angel." I kiss her shoulders and keep whispering words of praise so she hears my voice and knows I'm here.

"*Jeg elsker dig,*" she murmurs, reverting to her native tongue.

"*A chuisle mo chroí, mo anam cara.*" Reciting the words my Irish grandmother would say to my grandfather, I tighten my arms around her. Because that's what she is—the pulse of my heart, my soulmate.

I can't continue to work here. Not only is it killing me, but it's not just about me anymore. I'm living a lie, and the woman I love deserves better. I'm done with The River. Fuck being Esme's property. Fuck the contract and all its terms. I will find a way out, even if I have to appeal to Maya and beg my family for help.

I can no longer shoulder the costs of Reagan's care alone. As much as I hate it, I need to reach out to my parents and grandparents and confess to how I've been able to afford everything for so long. I'll take the shame and disgust because my family needs to know the truth about their little Catholic school boy with his big job in the city. How I was so desperate to be our hero, I put my body and mind through hell. I'll tell them how I signed my soul over to the devil to keep the status quo.

I can't be the captain and crew of my family's ship. I need some help before everything fucking sinks.

Before I drown in The River and lose Elinora.

# Sixty-Two

## Elinora

The Romance Writer's Conference was an amazing—but exhausting—experience. Attendees ran the gamut from aspiring authors to those consistently on the bestseller lists. It's no mystery why our booth was the convention's hot spot this year. Every woman in the room noticed Lincoln, and I had to beat back my jealousy whenever one approached him. Hopefully, I pulled off the cool, calm, and collected act.

On Monday, we had the published authors' happy hour event, which is a longstanding conference highlight. That theme certainly held true for this year. Seeing so many authors I've signed was like a visual representation of my success—something I seldom get to witness.

My workshop went off without a hitch too. The audience participation was unprecedented—likely due to the gorgeous editor by my side. After my first presentation, Lincoln and I attended the editor roundtable event, during which he was a crowd favorite. God, he's brilliant. The man fielded questions like he's been in the industry for decades.

Lincoln was polite and professional like always, but deep down, I hated the formalities. My veins thrummed with a primal need to mark him. I had to fight back the urge to grab him by the tie and kiss him in the middle of the conference room. Run my fingers through his silken hair. Fuck him right there for everyone to see.

As much as I ached to, I couldn't broadcast to the romance writing world that I'm sleeping with my new—much younger—editor. I can already hear them: *Oh look, the ice queen finally found a boy toy to thaw her frozen heart.* They would probably sit around taking bets on how long Lincoln and I will last before he cheats and makes a fool of me.

Shuddering, I force a deep breath and turn my attention to the dozens of emails I neglected while at the conference. Besides, the negative thoughts don't serve me. Scanning the query inbox, I check to see if anyone from yesterday's pitch sessions sent in their materials. A particular subject line captures my interest.

```
Attn: Lincoln Kennedy - RWC Pitch: requested
materials - Keira Bohannon
```

I remember this author. She stopped by our booth after her pitch. She was adorable when she gushed about how kind Lincoln was and how it thrilled her that he requested her first three chapters. We chatted for a bit, and she told me all about her book, an erotic romance involving an Irish pub owner with a penchant for wild sex with the daughter of a mob boss. I'm not surprised it intrigued Lincoln—he loves anything to do with Ireland.

Deciding to let him do the honors of reading her submission first, I forward him the email without peeking at the attachment. Despite his lack of experience, I believe he has acquiring editor abilities, and I know he'll make sure to keep quality in mind when making his decision.

It's Wednesday afternoon. Lincoln is bartending a special event at The River tonight, so I plan to drop by with a home-cooked meal to surprise him. Last night, I swung over to the grocery store to buy ingredients for beef stew. I threw everything into my crock pot this morning.

I peer through my office window at Lincoln's cubicle. He's at his desk, seemingly deep in thought. He removes his glasses and rubs his temples. It's the third time he's done it in the last half hour. I know he skipped lunch, so his headache is likely due to hunger and eye strain. Good thing it's nearly quitting time.

Unlike most days, I'm leaving the office at five with the rest of my employees. I've been unproductive all day, and I need to whip up a dessert when I get home.

Lincoln looks up at me when I approach his desk. "Hey."

I point to my watch. "Let's call it a day."

He nods, wordlessly gathering his stuff.

I touch his shoulder. "You OK?"

"Yeah. My head's throbbing, but I'm good. I don't feel like working tonight."

"You should play hooky."

He grimaces. "Wish I could, but the place will be packed for the event. I can't screw over my coworkers like that."

"What time does your shift start?"

"Seven."

"Will you come home to me afterward?" I bite my lip and await his reply.

Lincoln rakes a hand through his hair. "I won't be out of there until late, and I don't wanna wake you."

I press my spare house key into his palm. "I want you to keep this. You already know my security code. Let yourself in."

His eyes widen, and he closes his fingers around the key. "Wow. This feels like a big step for us."

"Let's call it a leap of faith."

# Sixty-Three

*Lincoln*

I can't believe she's giving me a key to her place. Maybe if I wasn't so caught up in my head, I could express how much it means to me. Instead, I'm silent.

I spent the entire day strategizing ways to cut ties with The River. Maya and I are going to have a serious discussion about my contract tonight. Hopefully, we can figure out how to get me the fuck out of there. I wish I could come clean to Elinora, but I already know how that would play out. She'd offer me money.

Rising, I sling my messenger bag over my shoulder. "Let's head out."

Elinora's blue gaze searches my face. "Are you sure you're all right?"

"Yeah, I'm just tired. My head hurts. I think I need new glasses." I've been putting off my optometry appointment for months. My vision is exceptionally shitty, and I despise wearing contacts, so the anti-glare lenses cost me a fortune. It's another expense I can't afford right now. I hold the door to the suite open for her. "Eye strain and sleep deprivation."

"You're working too hard."

"Books don't edit themselves."

"True, but I told you we could push out some of the deadlines."

"I *never* miss a deadline, Elinora. Come hell or high water, these edits will be completed on schedule."

"I'm not comfortable with you compromising your health."

"My health is fine," I mumble, pressing the elevator button.

"Bullshit."

"Look, I made a commitment to you. That's not something I take lightly. Please let me do my thing."

"Only if you promise to tell me when your workload gets to be too much."

My workload isn't the issue. It's all the other shit on my plate. Namely, Reagan and The River. Too bad that's not something I can discuss with her.

I grip her shoulders. "I don't make promises I can't keep."

# Sixty-Four

## Elinora

The River is packed. I had to park in one of the employee lots instead of the one reserved for members. According to the security guy I saw on my way in, tonight's event is an auction benefiting sex abuse survivors. I'm not entirely sure what will be auctioned off, but it wouldn't surprise me if it involved sex. Which is, on principle, more than a little ironic.

As I mosey down the corridor to the Aqua Suite bar, carrying a bag with Lincoln's special dinner, I wonder if the poor guy will even get the chance to eat. I hope he likes my version of beef stew. I whipped up a batch of di-rektørsnegls too. Lincoln has given me a new appreciation for my gourmet kitchen. And life.

Up ahead, I spot Madame Esme leading a group of important-look-ing women into Lagoon Eleven. I wave, but she seems too focused on what the one to her left is saying to notice me. That's fine. I didn't come here to see Esme.

As I move deeper into the Aqua Suite, the club music's heavy bass beat vibrates in my chest. Couples gyrate on the dance floor, taking dirty dancing to a whole new level. At the far end of the room, someone erected a small stage equipped with a podium and speaker system. The auction begins at eight. All the bar stools are already taken, and people swarm the area, waving their money at the lone bartender—a handsome, dark-haired man I've never seen before.

*Where's Lincoln?*

I scan the dance floor and scope out the gorgeous group of men setting up chairs in front of the stage. He's not there, either. I glance at my watch. It's seven thirty. *Maybe he's already on break.* Although his shift just started at seven, so why would he take a break thirty minutes after his arrival? *He's probably in the bathroom.* My palms start to sweat, and my heart gallops in my chest.

I could really use a friendly face right now. Where the hell are Ravi and Gideon? I study the shirtless men in the room, and it occurs to me I don't recognize *any* of the concierges on duty. I redirect my focus to the women, hoping to spot Freya's sister.

The bartender appears in front of me, his piercing green eyes meeting mine. The guy is just as stunning as everyone else who works here.

He smiles. "What can I get for you?"

"Is Lincoln working?"

"Yeah, he's with a client."

My heart skids to a stop. "What? I thought he was bartending tonight?"

His gaze widens at my strangled voice. "Nope. He's rarely behind the bar on Wednesdays. Sorry, but you're stuck with yours truly."

"And you are?" I croak, fighting to draw air into my lungs. Tears prick the backs of my eyes.

"I'm Leo. Can I get you a drink?"

"No, thank you." I place the bag on the bar with shaking hands.

He eyes it suspiciously. "What's this?"

"Dinner for Lincoln."

"Tirabassi, get me another whiskey." The voice at my shoulder makes me jump.

"You're already over your limit, Z. I'm not serving you another."

"Fuck limits." Zarek makes his way behind the bar and snatches a whiskey bottle, then fills a tumbler to the brim.

Leo shakes his head. "Esme will have your balls, but whatever. Do what you want—it's not my job to babysit you." He turns back toward me. "Sorry about the interruption. Can I interest you in anything to eat? We have a special menu ton—"

"Where are all your helpers?" Zarek asks.

Leo narrows his eyes. "Can't you see I'm in the middle of a conversation?"

"Hello, Elinora." Zarek looks me up and down. "What are you doing here on a Wednesday?"

"She brought dinner for Linc."

Zarek raises a brow. "Oh? And why's that?"

"C'mon, man." Leo shoves a few shot glasses in his direction. "If you're gonna be back here interrogating her, help me make some fucking drinks. Gideon never showed up for his shift." He reaches around Zarek for a martini glass and pours some vodka inside, then turns his attention to the couple on my right.

"Is Town Car expecting you?" Zarek chugs his whiskey and pours himself some more.

I peer up into his dark eyes and shake my head, swallowing against the bile in my throat. "No, I wanted to surprise him. Where is he?"

"Same place as always. In the lagoon with Maya." He searches my face. "You know about her, right?"

I blink rapidly. "Should I?"

Zarek shrugs. "He's with her anytime you're not here, so I figured you girls had some kind of sharing arrangement."

*Oh God, please, no . . .*

"This is our schedule for the month." He hands over a clipboard. "Town Car's entries are in blue."

Tears blur my vision as I clutch the clipboard and scan the names. Maya Alvarez. Images flash through my mind, and a bone-deep realization turns my stomach.

*No, it can't be her.*

Zarek's lips curve into a smile. "Town Car has a thing for the Chilean beauty. Some might call it an obsession. You'll notice her name listed on every one of his lagoon shifts. Well, not every shift. Just the ones when you're not here, obviously."

My heart shatters into a million pieces when he confirms Maya's identity. Who knew one little family from South America could cause so much heartache? I can't breathe or think as the walls close in around me.

*I need out. Now.*

I make a beeline across the dance floor, hoping to find an exit, but I end up in front of Glacier's entrance. "Let me through."

The guard, a young blond man, takes one look at my face and opens the gate. Blinded by tears, I run down the dark corridors, looking for a way out. The walls look like ice, mirroring my insides.

"Elinora, wait." Zarek jogs down the passageway, catching up to me in no time. "Did you truly believe he'd commit to you?"

"I need to go home," I say on a sob, hyperventilating now.

He grips my elbow, leading me down a different hallway, deeper into The River's bowels. "Let me make it better for you, dollface. I'll kiss those tears away and give you something that'll make Town Car a distant memory."

A chill races down my spine. "No. I'm going home." I yank my arm from his grasp and sidestep him, heading toward an exit at the end of the hall.

"Don't run from me, doll."

Terror squeezes my lungs as I push through the door into a darkened parking garage. My car is nowhere in sight. This isn't the lot I parked in. I take off at a jog, weaving through parked vehicles.

Zarek is right behind me. "Slow down, baby. You're gonna wear yourself out."

"Leave me alone."

"Not a chance, sweetness." He snags me around the waist and spins me to face him, his hardened cock pressing into my belly. The whiskey on his breath is enough to make me drunk. "You don't wanna be alone. Let me keep you company." He slides his grip to my ass and hauls me up against him.

"Get your hands off me." I push against his chest, but he doesn't budge, so I knee him in the balls.

He releases me with a grunt. I turn to run but don't make it more than a few steps before he yanks me back by the hair. "You wanna get nasty?" He slams me up against a utility van and backhands me. "I'll give you nasty."

Pain blooms across my cheek. I claw at him. Try to break free, but he's too strong. He swallows my screams for help with a suffocating kiss. I bite his lip. Hard.

His evil laugh turns my blood to ice. "You've gotta do better than that." With one hand wrapped around my throat, he licks his bloodied lip and hikes up my skirt. "Let me show you what you've been missing."

"You have two seconds to get your fucking hands off her before I rip your throat out."

It takes a moment for the other voice to register, and it's not one I'd expect to hear anywhere near The River. I meet Garrett's furious golden gaze over Zarek's shoulder.

"Fucking try it," Zarek snarls, spinning to face him.

"Time's up." My friend launches himself at my attacker, landing three punches before Zarek even has time to react. Garrett has mentioned his MMA training in the past, but I never knew the man was a lethal weapon.

I scramble out of the way and dig in my purse for my phone. Hopefully, the cops will get here before Garrett kills him.

A dark-haired woman appears out of nowhere and grips my arm, pulling me toward a red BMW idling across the lot. "Come with me."

"What the fuck, Ella?" Garrett flings his arm toward the vehicle. "I told you to stay in the car." The distraction buys Zarek enough time to yank himself from Garrett's grip and take off in a sprint toward the stairwell a few rows over. Garrett regains his focus and starts after him.

"Garrett, stop! Let him go," I plead, tears streaming down my cheeks. "He's not worth getting arrested."

"Beg to differ."

"*Tesoro*, enough. Let's go," she commands.

He reluctantly gives up his pursuit and cups his hands around his mouth. "You better hope I never run into you again, you fucking piece of shit." His warning echoes across the lot as he jogs back to us. "Elinora, you OK?"

"No." Fresh sobs seize my frame as the reality of what nearly happened—for the second time in a month—hits me. "No, I'm not."

Ella fixes the skirt, which was still around my hips, and hugs me tightly. "Take a deep breath. You're safe now."

I cling to her and weep as she gently strokes my hair. Pain, fear, and rage pour out of me in torrents, stealing my ability to breathe.

Garrett wraps his arms around both of us and rubs slow circles on my back. "It's gonna be all right, honey. Tell us what you need, and we'll make it happen, OK?"

"I wanna go home."

# Sixty-Five

## Lincoln

"My innards are digesting themselves," I announce, as my stomach growls for the seventh time this hour.

"So, let's eat." Maya stretches out on the chaise she claimed for herself. "I'm hungry, and I could go for a fruity drink too."

I quickly email myself the manuscript I've been working on. "You hang here, Sea Bass. I'll go get us some food."

"Good call."

We spent an hour brainstorming different ideas to get me the fuck out of here. Then we had a video chat with her boss. Julian agreed to read through my contract in search of loopholes. Meanwhile, Maya researched financing opportunities for me. All in all, I'd call it a productive night.

I head down the hallway toward the Aqua Suite bar. Leo is running back and forth, trying to serve everyone.

"What's up, Tirabassi?" Joining him behind the bar, I snatch a few of the orders he'd scrawled and start pouring drinks. "Why are you alone back here, man?"

"Fucking Gideon never showed up, that's why. I'm losing my mind."

"I'll help you out for the rest of the night."

He shakes his head and points to a red bag. "You have bigger fish to fry."

"What do you mean?"

He pulls out two containers of food. "It's some kind of stew and a dessert. You're lucky I didn't eat it."

"Huh?"

"Jesus, you're dense." Leo rolls his eyes. "Your girl brought you dinner."

"My girl?" I croak, white-knuckling the bar.

"You know, the gorgeous blonde who comes here on weekends to see you. She expected to find *you* behind the bar."

My heart stops, and ice fills my chest. "Fuck."

"No shit, bro. You should've warned me you have someone serious."

"What did you say to her?"

"She asked if you were working, and I told her you were with a client."

My scalp prickles, and the room starts to spin. "What *else* did you say?"

"Nothing." He shakes his head. "I stopped talking when her tears started falling. Z took over from there."

"Zarek?" I grip his shoulders, praying I misheard him.

"Yeah, man. She seemed to know him." He shrugs out of my hold. "Anyway, he told her you were in a private lagoon. He also showed her the schedule and pointed out how Maya's name is listed for all of your shifts."

My stomach lands by my feet. "Where is she?"

"She left over an hour ago. Ran out of here in tears."

"Why the fuck didn't you come get me?"

Leo narrows his eyes and gestures to the bar. "Like I said, I'm alone tonight. Leaving my post is a good way to get canned. Besides, you never told me I'd need to cover for you, asshole."

I grit my teeth. "Where's Z?"

He shifts uneasily and points to the gated entrance across the room. "He followed her."

The glass I was holding shatters on the floor. "To *Glacier?*"

"She ran through that door. He went after her. Dunno their destination."

"Who the fuck let her pass? She doesn't have clearance."

He shrugs. "Probably the new guy."

"Motherfucker." I charge past Leo, bolting for the underground realm. Moments later, I burst through Glacier's lower entrance, charging toward his usual cave. "Zarek!" His name leaves my lips on a battle cry as I pound the door with my fists. "Open the fucking door."

Tobias, a Glacier concierge who's a friend of mine, appears at my side. "He's not in there, man."

"Where the fuck is he?"

His eyes widen at my rabid snarl. "I don't know. He went upstairs a few hours ago. Never came back." He motions to the bartender, a guy I've met but don't know well. "Apollo, did Z say anything before he left?"

Apollo shakes his head. "No, but he was pretty buzzed when I saw him."

Alcohol and Zarek do not mix. I know what he's capable of when drunk. A wave of nausea slams me with the thought.

My phone rings from my back pocket. I yank it out and glance at the screen. *Garrett Casey.* I don't have time for him right now. Stuffing it back into my pocket, I point to Tobias. "Call me if Z comes back. Don't let him bring a blond woman in there. She's mine."

He nods. "Got you covered, L."

"Who else is here tonight?"

"Soren, Raphael, and Kane." The three Glacier concierges seldom visit the Aqua Suite, so I don't know them well, but they're good dudes, according to Darius.

"Are any of the girls working?" I ask, hoping I can get one of them to check the women's restrooms for me.

"Zena was here earlier, but she left."

"Damn. Have you seen Esme?"

He shakes his head. "She left after her meeting. Had some family thing."

"Fuck." Most security footage requests need to go through her, but Darius hates Zarek almost as much as I do, so maybe he'll help me out. "Later, man. Thanks."

Tobias claps my shoulder. "No prob."

I rush up the secret back staircase to Darius's office and pound on the door.

He yanks it open. "What's up, Linc?"

"I need to find someone."

"Now's not a good time. I'm still dealing with the cops."

"The cops?" My phone rings. It's Garrett again, so I decline the call. "What happened?"

"Hit and run." He shakes his head. "Can't discuss it, man."

"Have you seen Z?"

"Nope." Someone inside his office calls his name. "Gotta go." He closes the door in my face.

I hustle outside to the parking lot in search of Elinora's car. It's not here. My next destination is her home. If Zarek is there, I'll drag him out by his throat. I call an Uber and pace the sidewalk while I wait. I'm freezing my ass off because I never even put on a fucking shirt.

When I'd imagined all the worst-case scenarios that could play out with my and Elinora's relationship, I never accounted for the bone-deep terror I'm feeling over the thought of losing her.

My phone rings. Garrett is calling. *Again.*

I answer just so he'll leave me the fuck alone. "Yeah?"

"We need to talk."

"Sorry, but now's a bad time. I'm dealing with some shit."

"How 'bout you deal with *this*? I interrupted your girl's rape."

My legs give out. Sagging against a building, I clench my hand on my phone. "What?"

"You heard me."

"What happened? Is she all right?" The strangled rasp filling my ears can't possibly be my voice. "Oh, God . . ."

"You got time for me now?"

"Yes."

"Good. Now shut the fuck up and listen. My girlfriend was covering to-night's event. She accidentally left some of her camera lenses in her car, so we went out to get them. One thing led to another, and we were fooling around in the back seat when we heard a scream. I went to investigate and found that tattooed, creepy motherfucker who works with you pinning Elinora up against a van. His hands were around her throat, and he'd hiked her skirt to her waist. I threw a few punches, but he took off when Ella distracted me."

"Did he . . . ?" I can't say the words aloud.

"No, but it was *seconds* from happening."

Dizzy with relief, I squeeze my eyes shut. "Where is she?"

"She originally wanted to go home, but changed her mind because she didn't wanna be alone. She asked us to bring her to Freya's. She rode with Ella, and I drove her car over there."

"What's the address?"

"I'm sorry, but I can't tell you that."

I stiffen. "Why the fuck not?"

He sighs heavily. "Elinora found out you were in the lagoon with another chick, and she knows you lied about your supposed bartending shifts. She told me she wants nothing to do with you."

"But—"

"Look, I like you, Linc, but Elinora has been my friend for a long time. I need to respect her wishes. Also, Freya threatened to cut off my balls if I gave you her address."

My heart cracks down the center, my tears flowing freely. "Garrett, *please*."

"We talked about this, remember? I fucking warned you to be careful with her, but you did the worst possible thing by involving yourself with another woman and sneaking around behind her back."

"It's not what it looks like. I swear."

"That's all well and good, but you broke Elinora's trust. There's no coming back from that."

"It wasn't—"

"Then, when she tried to get the hell out of there, that fucking scumbag nearly raped her. Ella said she sobbed the whole ride to Freya's. By the way, Elinora knows her."

"Knows who?"

"Your other girl."

"Wait, how? I'm lost."

"Dunno. Ella said all she kept repeating was, 'it had to be *her*.' I asked Freya about it when I called her after we left, and she told me your side chick ruined Elinora, but she wouldn't elaborate."

"She's not my side chick, and that makes no fucking sense. Maya doesn't have a mean bone in her body—she's not capable of ruining anyone. Besides, I haven't slept with her since I met Elinora. Swear to God," I sputter, tugging on my hair. "And it wasn't *all* lies. I just had to leave some shit out."

"A lie of omission is still a lie."

"My contract was the *only* reason I wasn't totally honest. I didn't have a choice. My fucking sister's life depends on it."

"What contract? What the hell are you talking about?"

I can't answer him through my tears. Seated on a New York City sidewalk, with my world crumbling around me, I'm slammed with the reality that I've failed everyone I love.

An hour later, I knock on the door to Maya's apartment, making sure she can see my face through the peephole. The deadbolt clicks, followed by the metallic scrape of two chain locks.

Light floods the entryway as her mocha gaze meets mine through the crack. "Hey. What happened to you? I waited over an hour, but you never came back. I brought home your laptop and stuff."

"Thanks. I need to talk to you."

She holds the door open for me. "Are you OK?"

"No."

"Talk to me." She closes the door behind us.

I follow her inside, settling on the couch. "Why didn't you tell me you know her?"

"Who?" Shaking her head, she sits beside me. "What's going on, Linc?"

"Does the name Elinora Iverson mean anything to you?"

Maya stiffens, her eyes widening to saucers. "Yeah. Why?"

"She and Elsa are one in the same."

"Oh my God." Her hand flies up to cover her mouth. "Lincoln, why didn't you tell me her real name from the start? I would've warned you." She squeezes her eyes shut. "*Fuck*, this is bad."

Forcing a calm I don't feel, I pull in a slow, deep breath. "Elinora showed up at The River tonight to surprise me. She lost her mind when Leo told her I was in the lagoon with you." I tilt her chin up and pin my gaze to hers. "And right now, *you're* gonna tell me everything I want to know."

# Sixty-Six

## Lincoln

Maya's revelation floored me. Nothing could have prepared me to find out her association with Elinora, and I'm kicking myself for not putting the pieces together sooner.

I called Elinora dozens of times since leaving The River, but she didn't answer. Desperate to explain my side of the story and make things right, I arrive at the office early the following morning. I enter the luxe skyscraper and swipe my badge, but nothing happens. I try again. The card reader doesn't even beep.

Mike from security trudges over, his hands in his pockets. "Your security clearance was revoked, Mr. Kennedy."

My heart sinks. "By whom?"

"Ms. Iverson." He points to the front door. "I'm sorry, but you're not permitted to enter the building."

"But I have work to do."

He grimaces and hands over a piece of paper. "I was instructed to give this to you."

"What's this?" I unfold the letter with shaking hands.

He doesn't answer.

My eyes burn as I scan the page, typed on official Iverson Press letterhead.

Lincoln Kennedy,

Effective immediately, your employment with Iverson Press has been terminated. You must turn in your badge. You are not permitted to enter the premises of Iverson Press headquarters. Furthermore, you are hereby prohibited from <u>all</u> property owned by Elinora Iverson. Please surrender your key to her penthouse. Your belongings will be returned to you via the United States Postal Service.

Your phone number and email accounts have all been blocked. Continued attempts to contact Ms. Iverson (at work, in person, or on her personal phone or computer) will result in the filing of a harassment complaint with the NYPD.

Regards,
Freya Thorne

This can't be happening. Paralyzed by grief, I read the letter three more times. Each pass becomes harder to read through the tears blurring my eyes. Elinora fired and dumped me in one breath. I thought I'd felt pain when Jill told me she was moving to California, but nothing compares to this agony.

"I need your badge, man," Mike murmurs.

I hand it over without looking at him.

"She said you have a house key too."

I reach into my messenger bag and fumble for my keys, nearly dropping them when I pull them out. I'm shaking so badly that my fingers won't work. After a few tries, I finally remove Elinora's house key from my Dublin key ring and place it in Mike's palm. Then I stay rooted to the floor. If I move, it means I'm walking away from my woman. The once-in-a-lifetime love I'd sell my soul to keep.

Mike clears his throat and presses his lips into a grim line, then grips my elbow. "I'm sorry, but I have to escort you out."

Refusing to be humiliated any further, I pull away from him and square my shoulders. "You don't need to walk me out like I'm a fucking criminal. Tell Elinora I'm sorry. If she wants the whole story, she knows where to find me."

# Sixty-Seven

## Elinora

Freya enters her bedroom carrying her phone. "Mike just called. It's done. He turned in his badge and your key and left without causing a scene."

I nod without lifting my head off her pillow. While I'm glad he left willingly, I wouldn't care if Lincoln caused a riot—that man is dead to me.

She settles on the edge of the bed. "He had a message for you. He said—"

I hold up a hand to silence her. "I don't care what he had to say. His time to talk was *before* I found out he was fucking her. Before that monster tried to rape me in a parking garage. I'm all done listening now."

Freya nods and peels back the sheet. "Let me see your neck." Her gaze lands on the bruising and flares with shock. "Jesus Christ."

The handprint encircles my throat. I can still feel Zarek squeezing my neck, his rancid whiskey breath on my skin. His erection against my belly and the cold metal of the van at my back. If Garrett hadn't come to my rescue, I'd feel the evidence of that monster inside me.

"The cops still haven't located Zarek."

I flinch at his name and snatch the sheet, pulling it to my chin. "What about the person he hit?" This morning I'd been horrified to learn that Zarek had plowed into a woman on the sidewalk last night, and then he'd left the scene.

"She's in critical condition."

"Was Garrett able to find out her name, or are the police keeping things under wraps?"

"He got her name from the security guys at The River." She cocks her head to the side. "Why?"

"I want to pay for her hospital bills."

"It wasn't your fault, Elinora. *He* drove drunk."

"Yeah, as a direct result of my actions. Plain and simple, if I didn't go there last night to bring dinner to a fucking liar, a young woman wouldn't be in intensive care. Now, what is her name?"

"Keira Bohannon."

"Oh my God. She's one of the authors I met at the conference. I told her the best way to research kinky sex was to check out some of the sex clubs in the city. I doubt they would've let her in, but she went there because of me."

Freya gapes, opening and closing her mouth a few times. "I'm so sorry, Elle."

Tears roll down my cheeks again, soaking the pillowcase. I will never forgive myself if Keira dies.

Involving myself with Lincoln Kennedy was the biggest mistake of my life.

# Sixty-Eight

## Elinora

Paradise exists on a memory foam mattress with a weighted blanket, black-out shades, and a white noise machine. One day I'll give Freya back her bed. Today is not that day.

As if she can hear my thoughts, Freya taps on her bedroom door. "You awake?"

"Sadly, yes."

"Good. There's someone here to see you."

Panic flares in my chest. "It had better not be—"

"It's not Lincoln. I wouldn't blindside you like that."

Baffled as to who else would visit me, I sit up. The covers pool around my waist, taking the warmth of my cocoon with them. "Who is it?"

"Garrett's girlfriend, Ella."

"Oh. OK." While she was wonderful and sweet when everything happened, I don't know the woman, so I'm more than a little surprised she'd stop by.

"Can I send her in?"

"I look like shit."

Freya rolls her eyes. "She didn't come here to look at you. She came to deliver the food she made."

My stomach growls at her mention of food. "I am a little hungry."

"I'll take that as a yes."

I nod. "As long as she doesn't judge me for being a hot mess, I'm open to the idea of company."

"Be right back."

Moments later, Ella appears in the doorway, carrying an insulated bag. "Hi, Elinora. I hope you don't mind me stopping by, but I wanted to bring you something to eat." She approaches my bedside and sets the bag on the nightstand. Concern fills her Caribbean blue gaze. "And I wanted to make sure you're OK."

Am I OK? No. Absolutely not. Do I want to burden this sweet woman with my trauma? Also, no.

"I'm, uh, hanging in there, I guess."

Freya touches Ella's shoulder. "I'll let you two chat." She leaves the room.

Ella points to Freya's bed. "Mind if I sit?"

"Of course not. Go ahead."

She settles on the edge of the bed and gestures to the bag. "I'm not sure how you feel about Italian food, but I made you some ravioli and tiramisu."

"Oh, wow. Thank you so much. Garrett raves about your cooking."

She smiles. "Does he?"

"All the time."

"That makes me happy. Cooking is my love language. He definitely reaps the benefits." She tucks a lock of mocha-colored hair behind her ear. "I thought maybe you could use a little love too."

"I really appreciate that, Ella."

Her gaze drifts to the bruising on my neck. "I also wanted to see how you're coping with what happened."

"Like this." I point to the bed, which I've yet to leave—aside from bathroom trips, of course—since Wednesday. It's currently Saturday.

She nods sadly. "I get it." Her eyes meet mine once more. "I know we just met, but if you need a friend, I'm here."

"Thank you. I don't have many friends," I murmur. "I have a hard time letting people close to me."

"I can relate."

"Most people think I'm an icy bitch."

"People assume I'm a slut." She rests her hands in her lap. "It's easy to make assumptions about another person when you haven't walked in their shoes. Sometimes, the version of ourselves we show to the world doesn't match what's inside."

"Sounds like you and I are more alike than I realized."

"We are. And that's why I'm here." She touches her neck. "I've been in your shoes. I know the kind of shit running through your head."

"Someone assaulted you?"

She nods. "Many, many times. No one came to my rescue though."

The meaning behind her words is a punch to my gut. Garrett once mentioned his girlfriend endured a lot of trauma. I never imagined he meant she was a rape survivor. "I'm so sorry."

"Thanks. I was in a dark place for a while. I still am sometimes. Thankfully, I found a man who understands and respects me. My healing started when I met Garrett." She touches my arm. "I want you to know I'm here for you. I understand how easy it is to blame yourself, but you can't do that. What happened to you is not your fault."

My eyes well with tears. "I feel so violated."

Ella pulls me into a tight hug. "I get it."

"I also feel like an asshole for complaining to you when I was one of the lucky ones."

"Nope. None of that. My experience doesn't negate yours. I'm happy to be in a place where I can lend my support to another woman." She gently strokes my hair. "It took a long time for me to talk about it. I kept everything locked inside and let it fester for years. I don't want that for you."

Emotion pours out of me, dampening her shirt. "I don't want that, either."

"Elinora, if you let me, I'll be here for you. I will be the friend I so desperately needed back then."

"I'd really like that."

# Sixty-Nine

## Lincoln

(5 days later)

Whoever is pounding on my door can go fuck themselves. My cell rings on my nightstand, but I silence it. The pounding continues. Several texts light up my phone.

It's Myles. They're all Myles.

"Go fuck yourself, Callahan," I mumble into my pillow.

More calls. More texts. More pounding. I finally snatch my phone.

> Myles: Linc, I swear to God, if you don't open this motherfucking door, I'll climb up the fire escape and break a window.

Since the last thing I want is for the guy to fall and break his neck, I lever myself out of bed and trudge to the door, yanking it open. "What?"

His widened gaze sweeps over me. "Jesus. You look like shit."

"I don't need this right now." I move to close the door, but Myles blocks me and bulldozes his way inside.

He gestures to my tattered white T-shirt and boxers. "When's the last time you showered?"

I shrug and rub my furry face. "Dunno."

I don't know what day it is, either. And I don't care.

He points to my fridge. "How about food?"

"Not hungry."

"When did you eat last?"

"Yesterday maybe. Like I said, I'm not hungry."

"You have circles under your eyes."

"That's funny, because all I've done is sleep."

And cry.

Ravi stopped by the day after the fallout to tell me Zarek hit someone with his car while fleeing the premises. He left the woman lying on the sidewalk and drove off like a cowardly piece of shit. When I discovered she was an author who'd pitched me at the conference, I fucking lost it. The impact broke her leg and several ribs, puncturing a lung. Keira is stable now, thank God, but she has a long road to recovery.

The cops found Zarek's abandoned car upstate, but no one has seen or heard from him. My guess is he's hiding out in the Catskills somewhere. After what he did to Elinora, I'd give one of my lungs to smear his entrails across the New York State Thruway.

In the span of a single night, I was the catalyst for Elinora's sexual assault *and* landing a young woman in the hospital. Then I simultaneously lost my job and got dumped. To call me a mess would be the understatement of the century. All the liquor stores in New York City couldn't supply enough whiskey to drown my sorrow.

Elinora blocked all contact, cutting me off like a diseased limb. Maybe that's what I am to her, necrotic tissue festering in a pile somewhere. With flies and maggots too. I can't blame her though—I betrayed her trust.

Then again, maybe things would be a little better if she would let me explain. Instead, she stole a move from Sister Fitzgibbons's playbook and took what she saw at face value. My word, my truth, doesn't matter. Her pain unleashed a vengeance I never saw coming. She ripped my livelihood out from under me. I still can't come to terms with it. When Mike handed me that letter in the lobby, I could have sworn I was back in the parish office being expelled for a crime I didn't commit.

Only this time, the person who hurt me wasn't the villain—she was someone I love.

To make matters worse, I'm still bound to Esme, so I can't escape the place where my life fell apart.

I haven't been at The River all week. Ravi told me Esme is pissed, but I don't give a fuck. I can't deal with her right now. Besides, it's not like she'll fire me.

She had to appear for jury duty this week, and I was hoping she'd be selected as a juror, but no such luck. Since she's blown half the city, she got out of it based on conflict of interest. She called it "slut perks." Meanwhile, my slut perks caused my life to fall apart.

Regardless, The River is currently my only job, so I have no choice but to return—at least until I find something else in publishing. That is, *if* I can find something else.

"Talk to me, Linc."

"Got nothing to say."

He sighs, settling on my couch. "This is what I was afraid of—Elinora going all ice queen on you. That's one of the reasons I didn't want you to get involved with her in the fucking first place."

"Spare me the lecture."

"I'm not lecturing you. I came here because I want to hear your side of it. You've been ignoring me all week. I get that you're hurting, but I'm your best friend."

"I know."

"Then tell me what happened."

I meet his gaze. "First, tell me how she is."

"I don't know, Linc. She hasn't been at work."

"Why?"

"Because . . ." He rubs the back of his neck. "Freya said it's because she doesn't want anyone to see the bruises on her throat. She's having a hard time coping with the assault—both physically and emotionally. She's been staying at Freya's because she doesn't want to be alone."

Angry tears fill my eyes. "I will hunt down Zarek Petrov and *slaughter* that motherfucker."

Myles grips my shoulders. "No, you'll stay the fuck away from him. You can't help Reagan from a prison cell."

I gesture to my messy apartment. "Looks like I can't help her from out here either. I'll need to work seven days a week at The River to make up for what I made at Iverson. And I *still* won't be able to cover the costs of Reagan's housing. How will I find another publishing job? It's not like I can use Iverson Press as a reference. Elinora has probably blacklisted me."

He grimaces. "I'm sorry, man."

"What the fuck am I gonna do, Myles? Even if Maya's boss can get me out of my contract, it'll work against me. If I leave The River now, I'll have no income whatsoever."

"How much is your rent?"

"The landlord cut me a deal, so it's a little over two grand. Why?"

"That's more than my parents' mortgage. When is your lease up?"

"Three months. Why?"

"I have an idea, and I need you to hear me out."

"I'm listening."

"What if you moved back home for a bit? Get the fuck out of the city and stay with your parents. That's an extra two grand in your pocket right there."

I shake my head. "I'm twenty-five years old. I'm not mooching off my parents."

"You've done more for your family than most people do in a lifetime. Besides, I'm not suggesting you live there for free. Pay them some rent if you need to. Also, you can help around the house and assist with transporting your dad."

He has a point there. My dad had to relearn how to walk after his stroke. He still spends most of his time in a wheelchair because he simply doesn't have the strength to stand. Not only is he out of work, but his physical therapy appointments are taking a toll on my mom.

"And you'll get to see Reag-Bear more often."

"Yeah, but how will I find a publishing job in Ulster County?"

"Start your own business. Freelance editors live in all corners of the world. With talent like yours, all you need is a computer and an internet connection."

"How the hell do I make a name for myself?"

"That's where I come in. I'll do all your marketing. I'll set up social media accounts and manage your profiles. You'll join author groups on various platforms, and we'll build your reputation through word of mouth. Maybe Garrett Casey will cut you a deal on website and logo design?"

"He probably would." *Unless he's lost all respect for me too.*

"Think about it, Linc."

I rub my jaw while processing his proposal. Could I really be an entrepreneur? I always imagined myself working for someone else. Do I have what it takes to start a company and go at it alone? The thing is, with friends like

Myles—and Maya—I wouldn't be alone. Maybe I'll ask Gideon his take on it. He's a businessman at heart, maybe he'd help me come up with a plan.

What if I do this? Climb from the ashes of a failed career and start my own venture. Rise like a phoenix and reinvent myself.

Myles leans in. "What are you thinking?"

"I'm thinking you might be on to something."

"Oh, thank God. I didn't think you'd go for it."

"Won't *your* boss have an issue with you moonlighting for me?" I raise a brow.

He waves me off. "I really don't give a fuck. There's nothing in my contract which prohibits me from doing so. And even if there was, I'd do it anyway."

"I love you, man." Tears blur my eyes as I hug my best friend tightly.

Myles hugs me back. "I love you too, Linc. But you need to get your ass in the fucking shower."

About two hours later, after a long overdue shower and full disclosure about everything River-related, Myles and I lounge on the couch eating pizza. Turns out it's Thursday. He called out sick from work to spend time with me.

"This pizza's amazing," he says, gnawing on his third slice.

"Chicken-bacon-ranch is where it's at, bro."

"I'd be five hundred pounds if I lived here."

"Not if you paid this kind of rent."

"True. I guess it pays to have a sugar daddy." Myles lives rent-free in his partner's luxe Fifth Avenue apartment. The place is straight out of a magazine.

"Pizza's expensive. I limit myself to once a month."

"Lucky you. We never have pizza because Richard doesn't like it."

"Who the fuck doesn't like pizza?" I shake my head. "I knew I hated Dick on a fundamental level."

Myles cackles. "And I don't trust pussy."

"Speaking of pussy, do you think I should get a cat?"

"Thought you hated cats?"

"I don't hate all cats. I hated Seamus. He turned me off to the species." My mom's overweight Siamese was an asshole who used to attack my feet when I was little. "But I'm so damn lonely, I'm considering getting a kitten."

"All the more reason for you to move back home. Nothing cures loneliness like a healthy dose of the Kennedy family." Myles shrugs. "That being said, if the idea of a little rebound pussy makes you feel better, I say go for it."

The following morning, I wake with my alarm, then quickly shower, shave, and eat breakfast. I even put on real clothes instead of pajama pants.

I'm feeling much better after my come to Jesus with Myles yesterday. "Wallowing Lincoln" can go fuck himself. I've replayed the events of the past few months over and over in my mind. I can't change the past. The fact remains, I lied to Elinora from the beginning. Regardless of intent, I broke her trust and her heart. *That* is on me.

But I'm done crying over a woman who cut me off like what we shared meant nothing. One who threatened to press harassment charges if I checked in on her after the assault.

I'm responsible for what happened to her. I keep torturing myself with what-ifs, and it kills me that I can't be there to comfort her. Especially after hearing she's missed work. Zarek better hope we never cross paths, because I'll make damn sure he gets what's coming to him. I'd hunt the motherfucker down myself, but like Myles said, I'm no good to my family behind bars. Bottom line, they're my priority now.

My best friend gave me something I haven't felt in a long time. *Hope.*

The more I think about it, the more I love the idea of starting a freelance editing company. I spoke to Gideon last night. He thinks it's a solid plan, and he made a valid point: I'm dominant in the bedroom, so why not take control of my career? Why not make an honorable living and do something I'm proud of? The new and improved "Hopeful Lincoln" is ready for a fresh fucking start.

But I'd give anything for a fresh start with Elinora.

First things first, I need to get out of my contract. I have a meeting with Julian Brooks this afternoon to discuss my options. Afterward, I plan to swing by my bank and inquire about business loans.

I power up my laptop. Since I'm not a bridge-burner by nature, I refuse to let my termination from Iverson Press tarnish my character. I gave Elinora my word that I'd have those manuscripts completed on time. I glance at my calendar. I've got a week to finish them.

One thing's for damn sure, Lincoln Kennedy never misses a deadline. Perhaps this is Hopeful Lincoln reasoning, but maybe Elinora will reach out to me after I send her the manuscripts.

*What happens when she doesn't?*

I stiffen my spine at the thought. There's a strong possibility she won't come around, and that's something I'll have to deal with.

*Whatever happens, happens.*

I shake my head to clear it. No, I'm not going to sit around and hope. I'm going to take some fucking action. I don't know what the appropriate action is yet, but I need to *do* something.

Even though she hates me, I love Elinora enough to fight for her. The devil may have me by the balls, but I'll be damned if I let him win this round.

# Seventy

## Elinora

(Six days later)

Freya marches into my office with a Cheshire cat smirk plastered on her face. She plops a manila envelope onto my desk. "Special delivery."

"What's this?" I ask, setting aside my cup of tea.

"Open it."

I lift the metal fastener and reach inside, then withdraw a thumb drive. "Should this mean something to me?"

"I'd say so, yes."

I glare at her. "I don't have time for riddles."

She settles on the edge of my desk. "Lincoln stopped me on the sidewalk when I was leaving for lunch."

I drop the thumb drive like it might detonate. "Don't say his name around me."

Freya snatches the drive and holds it up. "This contains all five completed manuscripts you've been stressing about."

"What? How do you know?"

"For one, he told me when I saw him. Also, I checked for myself before giving it to you. The time stamp on the edits for the last one is from three o'clock this morning. He finished them, Elle. On time. Just like he said he would. And he didn't sacrifice quality." She smiles. "In fact, these are some of the most detailed edits he's done. Looks like you can call those agents and tell them our deadlines are still intact."

"Why would he do this after I fired him?"

"Uh, maybe because he gave you his word? Or perhaps he truly loves you?"

I squeeze my eyes shut. "No. If he loved me, he would've been honest with me."

"Did you ever consider the possibility that there's more to the story?"

"What are you talking about?"

"Something Garrett said the other day is bothering me."

I raise a brow. "Oh?"

"He called to see how you were doing, but you were in the shower. Anyway, we were discussing the situation, and he said Lincoln's hands are tied. He can't leave The River. When I called him back this morning to ask for clarification, he said Esme *owns* Lincoln."

I roll my eyes. "Yeah, OK. Now he's her fucking sex slave? I don't buy it."

"No, really. He muttered something about legal and financial ramifications. Then he said, 'Linc has no choice. People's lives are at stake.' I begged him to tell me more, but he insisted it would make things harder for Lincoln. He straight-up told me we don't know the whole story. He also said that Lincoln is heartbroken—"

"Enough." I clench my jaw and speak through gritted teeth, "He lied to me. I'm the one who's heartbroken." I stuff some belongings into my purse. "And I had to subject myself to STD testing last week to make sure he didn't give me something he contracted from that woman."

"What time is your appointment?" she asks, glancing at the clock.

"In a half hour. I asked the nurse to fax me my results, but she insisted I need an office visit in case the gynecologist needs to prescribe something." I rise, slinging my purse over my shoulder. "While I'm grateful the manuscripts are complete, that doesn't excuse his behavior."

I stare across my doctor's desk, watching as she peruses my bloodwork and test results. I swear to God, if Lincoln gave me anything, I'm going to show up on his doorstep and slap him. Then I'm going to knee him in the balls.

"Great news. All your STD tests came back negative."

My breath rushes out of me in relief. "Oh, thank God. I was so nervous when your nurse said you wanted to see me in the office."

"That's standard procedure. But in your case, I wanted to discuss the results of one of the other tests we performed. I know you were mostly concerned with STD testing, but since you were almost due for your annual appointment, I checked your hormone levels too. No sense in poking you twice."

"I appreciate that."

"I figured you would." Dr. Terranova points to the value the lab flagged. "Anyway, your FSH levels are elevated."

"And that means?" If I remember correctly from my fertility treatments, it has something to do with ovarian function.

"It can mean a number of things. In your case, it's most likely an indicator of perimenopause."

Her words hit me like a ton of bricks, making my shoulders slump. "Lovely."

Some small, pathetic part of me hoped she called me here to tell me I was pregnant. Even though the situation wouldn't be ideal—given my fallout with Lincoln—a baby would have filled the aching void that has tormented me for years. A chasm that has only deepened since Lincoln and I broke up. A positive pregnancy test would have been a hell of a lot better than hearing that I'm starting menopause.

My struggle with infertility was bad enough. Now Mother Nature is ready to prematurely slam the door on my reproductive system. The finality of my childless state weaves through my ribs and settles in my bones.

"Since you're still very young, I wanted to discuss your options."

"Options?" I repeat, my cloak of sadness getting heavier by the minute.

"Have you ever considered freezing your eggs?"

"It crossed my mind a few times when I was married, but it didn't seem practical back then." Probably because I thought I had plenty of time. Looks like the joke was on me.

"The quality of your remaining eggs will continue to deteriorate as your hormone levels change, so the sooner the better." She taps her pen on the desk. "You don't have to make a decision right away, but it's something to consider. In the meantime, I'd like to run a few more tests to rule out other conditions."

I release a depressed sigh. "Be my guest."

# Seventy-One

## Lincoln

I roll onto my side, pull Maggie's body close, and gently stroke her back. She stretches, peering up at me with those soulful eyes. I kiss the top of her head. "I love you."

She rewards me with a purr and nuzzles into me, her whiskers tickling my chest. I never saw myself with a cat, but now that I have the portly calico, I'm smitten. Maggie is the prettiest cat I've ever seen. I'm so fucking lonely I brought home a pet as comfort. What does that say about my coping skills?

Three days ago, while I wandered the aisles of the pet store, I spotted her in one of the cages in the back. I'd gone there with intentions of getting a kitten, but she was so sweet when they let me pet her, I signed the adoption papers right then and there. They think she's two or three, but it doesn't matter. I love her no matter how old she is.

Her previous owners left her behind when they moved. Sorta like how Elinora kicked me to the curb. Perhaps that solidarity is what moved me. Regardless, my mood is much better with Maggie around.

My phone buzzes on my nightstand with a text. I snatch it and unlock the screen.

Freya: I gave Elinora the manuscripts. Thank you for finishing them. She's been really stressed.

Me: No problem. Like I said earlier, I gave her my word.

Freya: I'm surprised you kept working on them after she fired you.

Me: Yeah, well, when you love someone, you tend to do nice things for them. (Even when they rip your fucking heart out and steamroll it.)

Freya: Do you still love her?

Me: YES.

My eyes start to burn again. I clench my jaw. I don't know when I became such a crier.

Freya: Tell me about Maya. What possessed you to sleep with her?

Me: First of all, I haven't slept with her since I met Elinora. Secondly, I've known Maya a long time. She's my FRIEND.

Freya: You know she's Charles's new sister-in-law, right?

How could I forget that juicy morsel? I still can't wrap my head around it. I literally dry heaved when Maya told me her relationship to Elinora.

Me: I'm well aware of the association.

Freya: Are you aware that SHE introduced Charles to her sister, aka Alyssa Alvarez-Roth? As in, the pregnant slut bride who is partly responsible for Elinora's miscarriage two years ago?

Me: Yes, Maya told me.

Freya: THEN WHY THE FUCK WOULD YOU GO BEHIND ELINORA'S BACK WITH HER?!?!?!?!?!

Me: Again, I have NOT slept with Maya in months. Also, neither one of us made the connection until that night. I always used a nickname when referring to Elinora because I wanted to respect her privacy and reputation—especially since she was my goddamn boss!

Freya: Why can't you leave The River?

Me: If Elinora wants an explanation, tell her to come see me. But I can't talk about it with you.

Freya: WHY?!

I run both hands over my face. I'd give anything to spill my guts to Freya, but Julian Brooks warned me to keep my mouth shut while he figures out how to break my contract. However, I'd gladly ignore his advice if Elinora were the one asking questions.

Me: IT'S COMPLICATED. There's a lot at stake. It's much bigger than just Elinora and me. Please tell her I'm sorry my lies hurt her, but I didn't have a choice.

Freya doesn't reply.

I pull Maggie close and scratch her chin. "Looks like it's just you and me, girlie." Staring at her little face, I realize the truth in that statement. It *will* be just me and my cat if I don't get my shit together and come up with a plan.

Before I realize what I'm doing, I press the call icon next to Freya's name. I hold the phone to my ear and force myself to breathe. I doubt she'll answer when she sees it's me, but a man can pray. Suddenly, I'm in Catholic school again, fiddling with my Rosary beads, saying Hail Mary after Hail Mary, in hopes my parents believe my story over the rotten nun who hated me. Except this time, I'm the one who made my life a living hell—not Sister Fitzgibbons.

"I shouldn't be answering your call, Clark Kent. She'd have my head for this."

"Freya, please just hear me out."

"I'm listening."

"I need your help."

"Why should I help the man who broke my best friend's heart?"

"Listen, I know how it looked, but I swear to God I wasn't cheating on her. I love her. I don't want anyone else—ever. Elinora is it for me."

"Do you really mean that?"

"Yeah, I do. If I thought she'd agree to it, I would've already proposed. I know I fucked up, but I'll do whatever it takes to fix this. I'm begging you to help me. You're my only hope."

"First, tell me what the fuck is going on. Then I'll decide whether you deserve my help."

"It's a long story." I rub my temples. "I don't even know where to start."

"Try the beginning."

"I'm not a free man, Freya."

# Seventy-Two

## Elinora

(Three days later)

As I blow my nose into the box's last tissue, it occurs to me that Hallmark movies probably aren't the wisest choice of viewing material in my current state. I'm curled up on my couch beneath a blanket my mother crocheted for me, inhaling Ben and Jerry's Chunky Monkey ice cream while I watch sappy rom-coms and wallow in perimenopausal misery.

I'm still waiting on the results of my repeat blood draw, and I'm on the fence about freezing my eggs. Mainly because I don't know if I have the strength to endure another failed pregnancy. I wipe my tears and tug the blanket up to my chin. I'd give anything for one of my mother's hugs right now.

Ella is coming over for dinner, so at least I have something to look forward to. She's been a godsend. I'm so grateful to have someone who truly understands the demons I'm battling.

There's a knock at my door.

"Who is it?"

"It's me." Freya's muffled voice reaches my ears. "We need to talk."

"You have a key, don't you?"

She opens the door but stays rooted in the doorway. "Yeah, but I wanted to make sure you didn't come running with your claws out."

"Why would I do that?" I press myself up to a seated position and tilt my head to the side. "Why are you standing in the doorway? Come in for God's sake."

"First, I need you to promise you'll listen and keep an open mind."

I bristle. "The last time you told me to keep an open mind, I wound up in a sex club. What's going on?"

Freya enters my apartment, followed by *her*.

I jump to my feet, toppling the carton of ice cream. "Get out."

"You need to listen to what she has to say."

"No, she needs to get the fuck out of my apartment," I shriek, rushing toward Maya.

Freya blocks me. "Sit down, Elle. It's not what you think. Everything will make sense. Please, just fucking listen."

I point to Maya. "You have five minutes. Then I'm calling the cops." I settle on my couch, arms crossed over my chest, while I glare at the devastatingly beautiful woman in my living room. If looks could kill, she'd be a pile of ash.

"For what it's worth, I'm sorry you're hurting."

"Spare me the pleasantries."

Maya narrows her mocha-colored gaze on me. "Lincoln is my friend."

"You mean fuck buddy?"

"At one point, yeah. But not since he met you."

"You expect me to believe that?"

"I really don't care what you believe, Elinora. I'm telling you the truth." She waves a finger at me. "That man loves you. He's fucking heartbroken."

"Serves him right for lying to me."

"That's easy for you to say without knowing the whole story. Since you won't let him contact you, Lincoln called Freya. She came to me for answers."

"What answers?"

She holds up a sheet of paper. "This is Lincoln's contract with Esme. He gave me a copy two years ago in case something happened to him. Or if she decided to fuck him over."

"What do you mean?"

"Esme really does own him, Elle." Freya moves to stand beside Maya. "I've read the whole thing. We had it all wrong."

"May I see that?"

Maya steps forward and hands it to me. "In case you think I'm making this up, his best friend, Myles, also has a copy. Lincoln didn't want to drag him into this, but if you don't believe me, Myles will confirm."

"Garrett knows too," Freya says. "Lincoln told him about his contract after everything happened."

I scan the document, growing more unsettled by the second. From what I gather, Esme gave Lincoln a lump sum of money in exchange for seven years of his time. He's also required to repay the money within that timeframe.

"OK, so what I'm seeing is an interest-free loan. What's the big deal?"

Maya points to a line on the page. "Did you miss the time obligation part? He's a glorified indentured servant."

"I don't understand. I've offered him money before. Why didn't he just break the contract?"

She shakes her head. "Because other people's lives are at stake."

"Like whom?"

Maya hands me a slip of paper. "This is his address. If you really want the answer, you'll find it there. But you need to go before Sunday."

"What happens on Sunday?"

"That's a question for Lincoln."

I break out into a cold sweat. "Why'd he lie to me?"

"He had no choice. After you two got together, he approached Esme about converting his time to strictly bartending shifts. She refused, telling him if he didn't offer services in the lagoon, he was in violation of their contract. To be clear, that means a twenty percent interest penalty *and* legal ramifications."

"Legal ramifications, my ass. No judge would allow someone to hold another person prisoner like that. News flash—it's called human trafficking."

Maya meets my gaze. "Have you ever heard of emotional blackmail?"

"Of course. What does that have to do with Lincoln?"

"Again, that's a question for him. Anyway, as I was saying, I hadn't seen him in a few weeks. I went to The River that night. When we got to the lagoon, he told me about you."

"You didn't think to explain how your slut of a sister stole my husband?" I clench my jaw. "Or how *you* brought them together? Charles told me you introduced them."

"First of all, I didn't know you two were involved, so my sister wasn't on my radar. When he gushed about the woman he was falling for, Lincoln called you Elsa—not Elinora."

"Elsa?"

"You happen to resemble a certain ice queen. He used the nickname to protect your identity. Especially since you were his boss and all." She crosses her arms over her chest. "For what it's worth, I met your husband when he was fixing the computers in my office, and he was not wearing a wedding ring. He chatted me up, but I had a boyfriend at the time. He saw Alyssa's picture on my desk and asked about her. Charles told me he was single." Maya holds a hand over her heart. "I would've never hooked up my sister with a married man. When I found out about you, I begged Alyssa to stay away from him. I'm sorry they hurt you. I hate what they did, and I'd give anything to go back in time and fix it. I haven't spoken to my sister since I heard what happened with your baby. You can hate me all you want, but I am not Alyssa. And Lincoln is *not* Charles."

I stare at her in shock. I never considered that she'd be on my side of the equation. All these years, I've hated her for something that wasn't her fault.

"Anyway, Lincoln explained his situation, and we came up with a mutually beneficial solution."

"And that was?"

"I went to Esme demanding exclusivity for his lagoon shifts. She owes me for some shit that went down on her property a few years ago, so she agreed. Since that night, any time he wasn't behind the Aqua Suite bar—or with you—he was with me."

"Doing what?"

"Working on manuscripts for you."

"Excuse me?" My jaw drops open.

Maya props her hands on her hips. "How the hell do you think he got everything done? His workload doubled when you fired the mystery and suspense guy. He didn't want to let you down. His top priority was to prove himself and do everything in his power to make your life easier. Even after you fired him and threatened to press charges if he contacted you."

"Oh my God."

"Right. So, yeah, I'd sit on my chaise reading legal shit, while Lincoln edited manuscripts across the lagoon. We both did our work on Esme's dime, and no one was the wiser."

"Why would you agree to do that for him?"

"Lincoln is my friend. There's little I wouldn't do for him."

"But why? If you guys weren't involved, it doesn't make sense—"

"This is why." Maya unzips her plum-colored velour hoodie and shrugs out of it, tossing it onto the couch next to me. She shoves her yoga pants down and kicks them aside, then slowly turns in a circle, wearing nothing but a black lace bra and panties. My hand flies up to cover my mouth at the sight of the scarring on her body. She ties her long, mahogany waves up into a bun so I can see her upper back and shoulders. "Lincoln put a stop to this."

"How did that happen to you?"

My eyes widen as she unhooks her bra and removes her panties. A deep scar crisscrosses her breasts, disfiguring one of her nipples. Another jagged mark runs down the center of the Chilean flag tattoo on her ass. She cups her breasts. "These are just the visible ones." She points to her pussy. "There are plenty more. Not to mention the emotional trauma. This happened because I involved myself with a monster."

"Zarek Petrov?" I whisper.

Maya nods. "I was once his sub. One night, when Z was drunk off his ass, he lost control with me. When he realized he'd gone too far, he left me there all alone, unconscious and bleeding. Lincoln and Zarek were once friends. He went downstairs to Z's room in Glacier and found me bound and gagged. He untied me and drove me to the hospital." Tears roll down her cheeks. "He saved my life and brought me back to life. He taught me that I'm stronger than I give myself credit for. He made me feel beautiful, even through all my ugliness. He cared enough to stick by me when I turned to alcohol and drugs to cope. Lincoln got me away from all that. There is *nothing* I wouldn't do for him."

"Maya, I didn't know," I whisper, feeling like the world's biggest bitch for jumping to conclusions. "I had it all wrong."

Nodding, she puts her panties and bra back on. "Lincoln blames himself for what Zarek did to you. It kills him that he wasn't able to protect you. What wrecks him even more is that he couldn't be there for you afterward." She steps into her yoga pants and pulls them up, then grabs her hoodie and slides it back on. "I'm tired of seeing him cry, Elinora. He's not eating. I stopped by his place with food, and he hadn't touched what I brought two days prior. He's gutted, and I'm tired of not being able to fix it for him." She zips her hoodie and meets my gaze. "He told me you're his once-in-a-lifetime. He's lost without you."

Tears streaming down my cheeks, I slowly climb to my feet and wrap my arms around her. "Thank you for telling me. I'm so sorry."

Maya hugs me tightly. "I'm sorry for all the pain my family has caused you. But please don't hold it against Lincoln. When you came to The River that night, we were brainstorming ways to get him out of his contract. We were so close to figuring it out. He can't give you all of himself until Esme retracts her claws. I introduced him to my boss at the law firm where I work. Julian found a loophole in Lincoln's contract that may help with his time obligation. As far as the financial stuff, I withdrew money from my 401k to help pay her off."

"You'd do that for him?"

"Like I said, he's my friend. I love him, and I'll do everything in my power to repay his kindness and ease his pain. He's a wonderful man, Elinora."

"Had I known about his situation; I would've given him money in a heartbeat. In fact, when he mentioned debts, I did offer him money. He refused it though."

"In case you haven't noticed this, Lincoln has an obscene amount of pride. Unlike Charles, he doesn't want your money; he wants your heart." Maya grips my shoulders. "He was trying to be true to you but went about it the wrong way. Do you think you can forgive him for his methods?"

"Yes," I sob, hugging her once more.

The better question is whether I can forgive myself for the way I treated him.

# Seventy-Three

## Elinora

Seated across the desk from Esme in her office at The River, I fight off the urge to strangle her. I've been here five minutes, and I'm ready to punch the smug look off her face and stuff Lincoln's contract down her throat.

Maya's revelations rocked me to my core yesterday. I played her words in my mind over and over again, trying to fit the missing pieces together. When Ella came over last night, I filled her in on everything to get a neutral party's opinion. She brought up a valid point—desperation makes people do crazy things. While I hate that Lincoln lied to me, I understand why he did it, even if I'm not sure of his motives for accepting Esme's terms.

"Like I said, his contract is nonnegotiable. In fact, he violated its terms by talking about it with you."

"For the record, he's not the one who told me about it. He and I haven't discussed it at all."

"No one else is supposed to know it exists, so that tells me he's in violation of the nondisclosure clause."

"Fuck the contract and its clauses." I snatch my purse, yank out my checkbook, then snag a pen from her desk. "Name your price."

She smiles and toys with the end of an electric blue braid. "It's not the money, baby. It's his *time* that I want."

"Well, guess what? I want his time too." I quickly fill out the check and scrawl my name, shoving it toward her. "Here's your hundred grand back. You'll notice I included interest. Is a hundred and fifty thousand enough, or would you like to name a higher price point for his happiness? What's it gonna be? A million? You tell me. I'll make it happen."

"I don't want your money." She purses her lips, pushing the check away from her. "But it's sweet of you to offer."

"You don't want to tangle with me. My only concern is Lincoln. Understand that I'll do whatever's necessary to get him out of that contract. That includes getting my team of lawyers involved. Tell me, *baby*, are you prepared to go to court?"

She taps her silver nails on the desk. "His case won't hold up in court."

"Oh, I beg to differ, seeing as what you've done to him is essentially human trafficking. But that's another story. Right now, I'm referring to *my* case."

"Excuse me?"

"Don't pretend to be in the dark about what happened to me a few weeks ago. The public will have a field day when they discover you kept a known violent felon on payroll when he sexually assaulted not one, but *two* women on your property. The police can't find him, but something tells me you know his hiding place."

She shakes her head. "I haven't seen or heard from him since."

"But you kept him on staff after he disfigured Maya Alvarez? I've seen what he did to her body, and I'll never forget what he nearly did to mine. You gave that monster a home here. What does that say about you?" I lean in close. "Especially given the nature of your establishment and your supposed mission statement about creating a *safe* place for women to explore pleasure. 'CEO of Iverson Press opens up about her near rape at The River.' Tell me, Esmeralda, what will people think when they read those headlines? Better yet, what does Zarek Petrov have over *your* head? I'm sure my attorneys can dig something up, don'tcha think?"

Her eyes widen, terror flashing across her face. She forces a swallow. "You're a smart businesswoman. You wouldn't bring that kind of media attention onto your company." Her voice comes out on a strangled whisper, confirming my suspicions about her association with Zarek.

"Oh, but I *will*—in a fucking heartbeat—and I'll do it with a smile on my face too. So don't test me." I point to my check. "Here's a bit of friendly advice. I suggest you cash this, take your money, and set Lincoln free." I rise and steel my shoulders. "If the check doesn't clear my account by Monday afternoon, you'll find yourself well acquainted with my legal team. When that happens, I think it's fair to say you can kiss your secrets—and The River—goodbye."

She clutches the edge of her desk. "You drive a hard bargain, Elinora Iverson."

"You have no idea what I'm capable of. Unless you're ready for my army, don't fuck with my man."

# Seventy-Four

## Lincoln

This kitchen has never seen so much love. Now if only I had Elinora in my life to share it with. The bacon and sausage are sizzling. I've got cinnamon buns in the oven. And the omelets are in full swing. Maggie weaves between my legs, rubbing her face on my ankle. "Sorry, girlie, but you've had plenty."

My mom wraps her arm around my shoulders. "I still can't believe you got a bloody cat. Dad's allergic, you know?" God, I've missed her Irish brogue. And her warmth and comfort. My apartment is full, but I still feel empty.

I shake my head. "Sorry, but he's gonna have to deal. Besides, he survived with Seamus around."

"That was different. I had him before I met your dad."

"Maggie is coming with me. Period. End of story." I glance to where my sister is stretched out on my couch. "Reagan, do you want cheese in your omelet?"

She perks up. "Yes, please."

"How about you, Mom? I have cheddar, Swiss, or brie."

"Cheddar." She points to the feast I'm preparing. "You didn't have to do all this for us, love. We would've helped you pack whether you fed us or not."

Today's Saturday. I'm moving back home tomorrow. My landlord let me out of my lease a couple of months early. It works in his favor since he can jack up the rent once I leave. We had an agreement when I moved in a few years ago—I'd do stuff like shovel the sidewalk and fix shit. In return, he never raised my rent. Mom and Reagan came for a visit so I could show them the sights before I leave the city for good.

My eyes burn at the thought. I don't want to leave the city—I want to grovel at Elinora's feet and beg her to take me back. I hope she'll listen to Maya instead of slamming the door in her face. Freya assured me she'd *make* her listen, but Elinora isn't a woman who can be forced into something she has her heart set against. No matter what happens, I won't stop fighting for her. Even if I need to send letters from upstate. I'll find a way to regain her trust and win back my place in her heart.

Hopefully.

A soft knock turns my attention to the door.

"Who could that be?" Mom asks.

Grinning, I point to Reagan. "A surprise for her." I chuckle at my mother's raised eyebrows and whisper, "Please go let Myles in. He's joining us for breakfast."

Nodding, Mom makes her way to the door while I sprinkle some cheese in the omelets. Extra cheddar for Reagan since she's a cheese addict. I drop a chunk on the floor for Maggie because she's too cute to resist.

"Oh, hello," Mom says. "Can I help you?"

"Yes, I'm looking for Lincoln. I'm a friend of his."

"Holy fuck." I drop my spatula and spin toward Elinora's voice. My heart stops beating, and my lungs refuse to fill. She's here. In my tiny apartment.

And she's not pointing a weapon at me.

I blink a few times, but she's not a mirage.

"Hi, Lincoln."

"Hey." I quickly turn off the stove and wipe my hands on a dish towel. "You're here."

Reagan launches herself off my couch, charging for the door. "Oh my God, Lincoln!" Her squeal could shatter glass. "First you get me Jake Bennett's autograph, and now you're friends with *Elsa*?"

*Jesus Christ.*

Mom snags her before she tackles Elinora. "Settle down, Reagan. Remember what we said about boundaries?"

"But Mom, *Elsa* is—"

"Elsa is not a real person." Mom shakes her head.

"She looks real to me."

Elinora chuckles, giving Reagan a warm smile. "My name is Elinora, but oddly enough, you're not the first person to call me Elsa. Unfortunately, I've also been known to behave like an ice queen from time to time." She meets my gaze across the room. "I hurt some people and feel *terrible* about it." Her gaze flicks back to my sister. "And you are?"

"I'm Reagan. Linky is my big brother. He's making me an omelet. With cheese!"

"Hello, Reagan. It's so nice to meet you." Elinora shakes her hand and turns to Mom. "You're Mrs. Kennedy, I presume?"

"Yes, but you're welcome to call me Orla." She shakes Elinora's hand. "Please join us for breakfast, dear."

Before I realize I'm moving, my legs take over, propelling me toward Elinora. "Actually, I need to talk—" I trip over Maggie. "Fuck!" She scampers away while I faceplant in the middle of my kitchen.

# Seventy-Five

## Elinora

All three of us rush toward Lincoln. Despite being the shortest and roundest, Reagan reaches him first, patting the top of his head. "You need to watch where you walk."

"Thanks for the tip, Reag." He presses himself up to his knees and addresses the chunky little cat cowering in the corner. "Daddy gives you bacon and cheese, then you turn around and trip him? Not cool, Mags." He sighs and calls her over, scratching under her chin when she comes.

My insides flutter, hearing him call himself Daddy. One of my hands reflexively finds its way to my belly. What if the egg retrieval I'm considering is not completely in vain?

I shake my head to clear it. First, I need to see if he'll forgive me before I even think about broaching *that* topic. "Are you all right?"

"Yeah, I'm fine. Thanks." He stares up at me like I'm on a pedestal. "I need to talk to you. I need to explain—"

"That's why I'm here." I stoop to pet Maggie. "I didn't know you have a cat."

"He just got her a few days ago," Reagan says, twirling her fiery red hair. "She keeps him company."

Her eyes are the same color blue as Lincoln's, but they're almond-shaped with extra skin at the corners. Taking in her short stature and flattened facial features, I find it more than a little strange he never told me his sister has Down syndrome. Then again, he left out a lot of details courtesy of his contract with Esme. Maya told me someone's life is at stake—I'd be willing to bet my life, she was referring to his sister. What's wrong with Reagan? Does she have underlying health issues? Or did Esme threaten to go after her? If that's the case, I'm really going to give her a war. The thought of anyone harming this spirited young girl turns my stomach.

"That's another reason your father won't be happy havin' a cat in his house," Lincoln's mother says as she watches him climb to his feet. "What happens when Maggie gets in the way of his walker? You know I can't lift him if he falls. He's liable to run over the poor thing's tail with his wheelchair."

"I'll keep her away from him, Mom." He rubs the back of his neck. "But like I said, he needs to get over it. We're a package deal."

I gesture to all the boxes in his tiny studio apartment. "You're *moving*?"

He nods. "Yeah. My goal's to be out of here by tomorrow afternoon, Monday the latest."

"But why?" My heart plummets to my feet. "Where are you going?"

Lincoln stares at my face. A thousand emotions swirl in his gaze, but he doesn't answer me. I hope that doesn't mean I'm too late. An invisible band tightens around my chest.

Reagan loops her arm through the crook of his elbow. "Linky is moving home with our mom and dad because he's really sad."

He squeezes his eyes shut. "Thanks, Reag. How about you tell *all* my secrets?"

She perks up, meeting my gaze. "A mean girl dumped him and hurt his feelings. And she took his job away. He cried a lot."

"*Jesus.* I didn't mean that literally."

"Knock, knock." Myles appears in the doorway, his eyes widening at the sight of me.

"Myles!" Reagan screams. "Mom! Myles is here!" She charges across the room, plowing into him.

"Oof." He grunts and wraps his arms around her. "Hello, kiddo. How have you been?" He kisses her forehead.

Swooning, Reagan hugs him tighter. "I love you."

Myles grins. "Love you too, Reag-Bear."

"OK, let him go now, love." Orla rushes to his rescue. "Boundaries, remember?"

"Hi, Orla." Myles kisses Lincoln's mother on the cheek.

"Hello, Myles, what a pleasant surprise. Let me tend to the cinnamon buns before they burn." She heads for the oven.

"I couldn't miss a chance to see my Reag-Bear." He glances at me. "Hiya, boss lady. What's new? Fancy seeing you on a weekend."

Orla stops in her tracks and slowly turns to face me. Her eyes narrow on mine. "Wait a minute, *you're* the woman who broke my son's heart?" She crosses her arms over her chest and takes a step toward me. "You've got some nerve showin' up here. You plan to rip him apart again?"

*Oh, shit.*

"Mom!" Lincoln knots his hands in his hair. "This is why I don't tell you things. You can't just—"

I clear my throat. "No, Mrs. Kennedy, I'm not here to hurt Lincoln. I came to ask for his forgiveness."

"Well, that's bloody big of you."

"I can't tell you how sorry I am. I made a terrible mistake when I hurt your son."

"You're damn right you did."

"I didn't have all the information and made some false assumptions." I meet Lincoln's widened gaze. "I know I hurt you. I was wrong. It took some persuasion, but I finally understand. I'm so sorry."

Orla gestures to Lincoln. "Are you referring to his contract with that evil sex-peddlin' witch?"

Lincoln's jaw drops. "Wait a minute, how the hell do *you* know about that, Mom?"

Myles crosses the room. "Uh, don't kill me, but I might have told her."

"Are you fucking kidding me? You told my *mother?*" He opens and closes his mouth a few times as redness creeps across his face. "Do you have any idea how embarrassing this is?"

Orla rolls her eyes. "Oh, for the love of God, Lincoln. It's not like I thought you were a virgin. I was the one who caught ya havin' sex with Jill, remember?"

"How could I fucking forget?" He runs both hands over his face, then glares at Myles. "Really, dude?"

"You needed an intervention. I intervened." Myles points to me. "But I definitely wasn't the one who spilled the beans to *her.*"

Lincoln fixes his glasses and searches my face. "Freya talked to Maya?"

"Yes. Maya came to see me. She told me everything. She *showed* me . . ." Tears fill my eyes. "It all makes sense now. I'm sorry I doubted you."

"While I understand your reaction, you did *a lot* more than doubt me, Elinora." He crosses his arms over his chest.

"I'm sorry." My lip quivers. A tear rolls down my cheek. In the past, Lincoln would've brushed it away. Today, he clenches his jaw instead.

*I'm too late.*

"Why's she crying?" Reagan asks.

Myles wraps an arm around her. "How about we go for a stroll so these two can talk?" He raises a brow at Orla. "You coming, mama bear?" She glares at me before following them out.

"Your mom hates me," I say once we're finally alone.

"That's a strong possibility." He shrugs. "But she'll get over it."

I hold up the copy of his contract. "Maya gave this to me."

He nods. "If harassment charges weren't on the table, I would've told you myself." Pointing to the door his family just left through, he adds, "But I'm no good to my family in jail."

"I'm sorry I threatened you with that. It was low of me."

"Yeah. It was." He crosses his arms over his chest again. "I planned to mail you a copy of the contract after I moved. You know, for closure and such."

"What if I don't want closure?"

He narrows his eyes. "You expect me to believe that?"

"Look, I didn't come here to fight with you."

"Then why are you here?"

"I just want to talk. I'm ready to hear your side of things now. But I'm a little confused about your plans to move upstate."

"My lawyer is working on getting me out of the financial part of the contract. He also doesn't think Esme would actually sue me because her case holds no merit. Turns out the contract's terms are borderline illegal. He said I bought into the psychological blackmail game out of fear for Reagan's health."

Bingo.

"Did Esme threaten her?"

"No. It's nothing that sinister." Lincoln sighs heavily and points to his couch. "Sit with me." He waits until I'm seated before speaking. "Reagan has epilepsy and a serious heart condition. She lives in an assisted-living group home. Her care costs my family a fortune. I borrowed money from Esme to cover her housing, but the cost keeps going up."

"Isn't she eligible for financial assistance?"

"She is, but Medicaid won't pay for the facility we want her in."

"Why not use the one they cover?"

A shadow darkens his eyes. "We did, and those neglectful fuckers nearly killed her. After that nightmare, we yanked her out of there and put her in private housing."

"Does her insurance cover any of it?"

"Twenty percent. The rest is self-pay. As in, whatever I can come up with. My parents are strapped for money after my father's stroke." The desperation in his voice matches the haunted look in his eyes. "When I signed that contract, I had no idea what I was doing. All I saw were the dollar signs. I stupidly thought landing a permanent gig at a kink club translated into me hitting the sexual jackpot or something. I never expected to feel so dirty."

"You're not dirty."

"Thanks, but my sexual history proves otherwise. And I lied to you, which makes me a filthy piece of shit."

"While I hate that you weren't truthful, I understand your reasons now."

"For years, I didn't pursue any real relationships because I knew I was bound to Esme. What woman would want anything to do with a man like me? Besides, I never expected to want something real." His gaze burns into me, thawing the parts of me that had iced over. "Everything changed after you showed up in my lagoon." He takes both of my hands in his. "Elinora, I swear to you, there hasn't been anyone else. Maya was trying to help—"

"I know. Like I said, she told me everything. I'm sorry I misjudged her, but can you understand why I reacted the way I did?"

"Yes. Again, I was wrong for not being honest with you. I was scared for Reagan."

"You know I would've given you money in a heartbeat?"

"While I appreciate that, I don't want your money."

That is why I went directly to Esme. But he doesn't need to know that just yet. I'm keeping those details under wraps until she makes her move.

"So, what's your plan? You're just going to move back home and stop showing up at The River?"

"Pretty much. If Esme tries to sue me, I'll fight. In the meantime, I'll funnel the two grand I've been spending on rent into Reagan's housing. Myles said he'll cover the difference while I get on my feet. Now that my *mother* knows,

I'm sure she'll have a plan." He shakes his head. "I can't believe he told her. I didn't want to add to my family's list of problems, I wanted to *solve* them."

"And you've done a damn good job." I squeeze his hand. "But now it's time to let others help. Don't be angry with Myles. He loves you. And so does Maya."

He nods. "I'm blessed to have friends like them. Ravi and Gideon too. And I'm so grateful to Freya for having an open mind. I didn't think she'd listen."

"Thank you for telling her. She and Maya forced me to listen to the truth." I cup his cheek. "Lincoln, I'm so sorry I hurt you."

"It's fine."

"No, it's really not. Please let me make it up to you. Come back to work for me. If you want to stay at your parents' house, that's fine. You can work remotely. I need you on my team."

He squeezes his eyes shut. "I'm sorry, but I can't do that."

"Why not?" Tears fill my eyes once more. "Don't you still have feelings for me?"

Lincoln grips my chin. "I love you, Elinora. But I won't work for you again. You ripped my livelihood out from under me. You wouldn't even let me explain or contact you to make sure you were OK." He slowly shakes his head. "By the way, if I *ever* see that motherfucker again, I'll slit his throat."

"I'm fine, Lincoln."

"Well, I'm not fine. I don't think you realize what that did to me." He holds a hand over his heart. "The thought of you—" He blinks rapidly and forces a swallow.

"You can't hold yourself responsible for his actions."

"I think you know me well enough to know that I do. And what about Keira Bohannon?"

I shake my head. "No. That's on me. She only came there because I told her she needed to research what she planned to write. I visited her at the hospital. She's doing much better. I told her to forward her manuscript to my office when she's ready. I'll publish it even if the damn thing's written in code."

He chuckles. "Let's hope it isn't."

"So, you won't consider being my editor?"

"I'm sorry, but no. My family means everything to me. I can't put myself in the position to hit rock bottom or risk Reagan's life again. Besides, I need to prove to myself—and to the rest of the world—that I'm man enough to do my own thing."

"What do you mean?"

He withdraws a business card and hands it to me. "I'm starting my own company."

*Lincoln Kennedy, editor.* I stare at the colorful design and the words emblazoned beneath a phoenix seated atop a Celtic knot. "Irish Phoenix Revisions?"

"Yeah. Garrett designed my logo. It's awesome, right?"

"It's stunning, just like his artwork always is."

"You know how sometimes you need to crash and burn before rising from the ashes?"

"You mean like your ability to resurrect a shitty manuscript?"

"Exactly. OK, so get this . . ."

I listen intently as he describes his business venture. His plan to tap into the self-publishing realm, in addition to freelancing with traditional publishing houses, impresses me. But what moves me most is the fire in his eyes when he talks about doing what he loves. He reminds me of myself when I started my own little publishing house many years ago.

"Lincoln, this is brilliant."

"You think?"

"As much as I'll hate not having you on my team, I'm truly proud of you."

"You have no idea how much that means to me."

"Will you stay in touch?"

"You say it like this is goodbye."

I blink rapidly. "Isn't it?"

"Just because I can't work for you, doesn't mean I don't want to be together." He brushes the hair back from my face. "Also, I wouldn't be opposed to freelancing some manuscripts while you find my replacement. Speaking of that, since you put Cooper Press out of business, my friend Tess McPherson lost her job. You should consider hiring her. She's an amazing romance editor. Coincidentally, she's also gonna star alongside Garrett in *Prodigy.*"

"Really?"

"Yeah. Broadway is kinda her dream. Anyway, I'm really not sure about her availability, but she'd be a great fit."

"Tell her to give me a call. But for the record, no one can replace you, Lincoln."

Now isn't a good time to ask him about his plans for the future—namely, whether he'd be open to starting a family—because we're both too raw from seeing each other again. Sometimes, I forget how much younger he is. Fatherhood probably isn't even on his radar. Besides, I need to see how much of a fight Esme plans to put up before I even consider subjecting my body to fertility drugs again.

"OK, well, I guess I'll see you later." I rise and rush out of his apartment before I lose the resolve not to throw myself in his arms and make love to him on his couch.

"Elinora, wait." Lincoln jogs after me. "Why are you leaving?"

"I want you to enjoy your visit with your family without me in your hair. Let's take a few days to absorb everything, and then we'll talk about what's next for us. Call me on Tuesday." I hurry down the hall.

"What happens Tuesday?"

I turn to face him. *I'll know what size army to mobilize.* "We'll discuss it after midnight on Monday."

He scratches his head. "I'm confused. Are you turning into a pumpkin?"

No, but I'm going to squash Esme like a bug. Now that I've met Reagan, and witnessed Lincoln's love for her, I'm even more furious that Esme played with his emotions to keep him under her thumb. "Yeah. Something like that."

# Seventy-Six

## Lincoln

It's Sunday afternoon, and for the first time, I'm feeling kind of blue about leaving my little apartment behind. Mom and Reagan headed back upstate this morning with a carload full of my shit. I borrowed a friend's van to load up the rest of it.

Maggie weaves through my legs. Her presence warms me in ways I can't explain. I scoop her into my arms and kiss her furry head. The purring is instantaneous. I carry her around my apartment while I gather the last of my things.

I can't believe Elinora showed up on my doorstep yesterday morning. I thought Mom was going to slap her when she realized she was the woman who hurt me. And I really can't believe fucking Myles told my mother I've spent the past two years as a fuck toy for rich women.

As much as Elinora's apology soothed me, seeing the look on her face when I turned down her job offer ripped my heart to shreds. I love her, but I can't go back to the way things were. We need to figure out our new normal. If we need to do the long-distance thing for a bit, then so be it. I'm still trying to figure out what she meant by all the Cinderella talk.

God, she's beautiful. Even more radiant than I remembered. I can't wait until Tuesday—I need to see her before I head upstate tonight.

A soft knock reaches my ears. My heart leaps into my throat. I rush to the door and fling it open.

*Fuck.*

"Hello, Lincoln." Esme steps into my empty apartment. Her eyes widen and snap to my face. "What the hell is going on?"

Maggie hisses, her hair standing on end.

"What are you doing here?"

"Were you planning to skip town without telling me?" She raises a brow. "That's pretty low, don't you think?"

I force a swallow. "Listen, I—"

She waves a hand at me, her perfectly manicured nails flashing in the light. "I get it."

"Huh?"

She pivots and peers up at my face. "How come you never told me you were unhappy?"

"Seriously? I'm pretty sure I made it known."

"But you had to resort to threats?"

I blink. "What the hell are you talking about?"

"Threats to my establishment, my reputation. Either of those."

"Esme, I'm sorry, but you lost me."

She pulls a folded-up piece of paper out of her pocket and hands it to me.

"What's this?" I unfold it. My jaw drops. "Holy fuck."

"You mean you didn't know your girlfriend planned to storm into my office like a wild woman and threaten to unleash a team of lawyers?"

I gape at Elinora's check for a hundred and fifty thousand dollars. "No."

"Well, she did. She told me if I don't cash it by tomorrow afternoon, she'll drag my name through the mud. Elinora plans to go to the media about Zarek's attack if I don't release you from your contract." She pulls a paper out of her purse and holds it up. "Remember this?"

I glance at my contract and nod.

Esme tears it down the center. "Consider it null and void." She shakes her head sadly. "Give your girlfriend back her check. I don't want her money."

"I will repay the rest of what I owe you, Esme. You have my word."

"I don't want *your* money either. I did some reflecting and didn't like what I realized about myself."

"And that was?"

"Doesn't matter." Shaking her head, she meets my gaze with watery eyes. "I only wanted your time."

"My time?" I repeat, more than a little confused by her sudden about-face.

"Yes, but I don't deserve it. I put a price on your happiness. It was a selfish, fucked-up thing to do. Not to mention it goes against everything I believe in."

"I don't know what to say."

"I never meant to hurt you. I'm so sorry."

"Are you saying—"

"I'm saying you're free to cut ties with me. Consider the remaining debt paid in full. I'm happy to have been able to help with your sister, and I'm sorry I exploited your fear to keep you around."

"Why would you want me around?" The words are out of my mouth before I can stop them.

"There's just something about you, Lincoln. A magnetism I can't explain. Your character and heart are even more appealing than your body, and I couldn't help my desire to keep you. I have always cared about you, but unfortunately my actions didn't translate the way they should have. Again, my behavior was fucking selfish, and I'm truly sorry." She gently touches my arm. "Go to your woman. *She's* the one who needs you around." With that, she tosses her shiny black hair over her shoulder and turns to leave.

"Esme, wait." I grab her wrist and pull her into a hug. "Thank you."

"You know you're always welcome to stop by The River for a visit, baby." She squeezes me tightly. "For the record, your queen was willing to drop millions of dollars *and* wage war with me for you. She's a damn good woman."

"I know."

She cups my cheek. "Now go prove that you're worth it."

# Seventy-Seven

## Elinora

I squint through the peephole at the man standing in the foyer. *Lincoln.* I quickly smooth my hair and yank open the door. "Hey."

"May I please come in?"

"Of course." I step aside so he can enter. "Is everything all right?"

"Yes."

I motion for him to follow me into the kitchen. "Would you like something to drink? Are you hungry?"

"No." He leans against the counter. "Elinora, look at me."

I stop opening cabinets and turn to face him. It's then that I notice his reddened eyes and tearstained cheeks. "What's wrong?"

"Give me your hand."

I tentatively hold out my palm. He places a slip of paper in it—the check I wrote out to Esme. My gaze snaps to his face. "She was supposed to cash it."

"She released me from the contract and told me to give that back to you. She actually apologized for fucking with my head. And my life."

My breath leaves me in a rush. "That's wonderful. You're free now."

He nods, his eyes locking with mine. "She told me what you were willing to do for me." He swallows tightly. "Thank you."

"Lincoln, I love you. I fucked up, but I'll do whatever it takes to win you back."

"Elinora, I—"

"I've been doing some thinking. If you won't come back to Iverson Melt, at least let me help you launch your business. I'm proud of you, and I loved seeing the fire in your eyes when you talked about it. I want to see you succeed, and I'm happy to cheer you on from the sidelines." I trail my fingers down his chest. "Besides . . . being in charge suits you."

His breath rushes out of him as he drops his gaze to the bulge in his jeans. "Jesus, Elinora. It's fucking instantaneous." He gestures over his shoulder to the door. "Would it be all right if I grabbed Maggie from the van and we crashed here until morning? My night vision is shitty, and there are always deer on the Thruway."

"Or you can stay with me *permanently?*"

He widens his eyes. "You mean, like, move in with you?"

"Yes. Maggie is welcome too."

"I'd love to, but I can't let you solve my problems. I need to focus on making money for a few months so I can help Reagan and my parents. Plus, my mom needs some help around the house."

"About that . . ." I pick at my nails and smirk. "So, this might piss you off a little."

He tips my chin up. "What did you do? And why might it piss me off?"

I take a deep breath and peer into his eyes. "After I bulldozed Esme, I had a meeting with Angela from Catskill Manor. Let's put it this way. Reagan's housing is covered for the next ten years."

"Oh, God." Lincoln sinks to his knees and clutches his chest.

I kneel in front of him. "We negotiated the terms so they can't keep increasing their rates. Also, a home health aide will stop by your parents' place for a few hours each day to assist with your father. The agency will contact them this week to set things up. This way, your mom will get a much-needed break."

"Angel, I can't let you do that."

Smiling, I touch his cheek. "It's already been done, darling. The funds cleared my account this morning. We can revisit this discussion in a decade."

"Elinora . . ." His voice breaks, and he pulls me into a bone-crushing hug. "I love you."

# Seventy-Eight

### Lincoln

All I can do is cling to Elinora as tears stream down my cheeks. She solved my every dilemma. I won't have to worry about Reagan's health, Mom will get help with Dad, and I'm finally free from my contract.

She's crying now too. "I love you, Lincoln. Please move in with me. I need to fall asleep in your arms at night."

I pull back to study her face. "Are you sure?"

"I've never been more certain of anything in my life. I want forever with you."

"I want forever with you too, angel. Yes, I'll move in with you." I seize her lips in a soul-melting kiss. She gives it back just as deep, weaving her hands into my hair. One kiss turns into two. Then three. Then twenty. Time stands still, and the world stops turning. Elinora's lips and tongue dance with mine. The kiss erases our pain and the obstacles to our love. Now it's finally just us.

*I'm home.*

"I've missed kissing you," she whispers against my lips. "But I need more. Make love to me."

*Don't forget about Maggie.*

The wayward thought nudges the responsible side of my brain. I have a perpetually hungry kitty—who meowed the whole way over here—waiting outside. Knowing our bedroom activities can go on for hours, I force myself to stop kissing Elinora. "Hold that thought. Let me grab Maggie from the van so she doesn't freak out and gnaw off her own limbs."

"Good call."

After a quick trip outside, we set Maggie up with water, a full bowl of food, a litter box, and some toys. Hopefully, the catnip mice will keep her occupied for a bit.

When everything is said and done, I meet Elinora in her living room and flash a wolfish grin. "Now, where were we?"

"I believe you were about to make me orgasm."

"Damn right I am." I scoop her into my arms and carry her to the bedroom. We shed our clothes in record time, kissing all the while. I nudge her thighs apart and settle on top of her. I take a moment to admire her kiss-swollen mouth before reaching for the drawer where she keeps the condoms.

"Wait." She lifts her hips, coaxing me into the honey between her thighs. "This is definitely the wrong time for this discussion, but what are your feelings about fatherhood?"

I blink a few times and stare down at her face. "Are you pregnant?"

"I wish." She wraps her legs around me. "My doctor kinda talked me into freezing my eggs and trying for IVF. Is that something you'd consider being part of?"

I groan as her body's moisture coats the head of my cock, beckoning me deeper. "Fuck yeah, I would."

The smile that curves her lips is one of pure bliss. "That makes me really, really happy."

"Me too." I stare into her eyes, seeing her truth in the love that shines in them. The profound joy that reaches her soul. I touch her belly, splaying my fingertips out. "When are you going to start the process?"

"I have a consultation next week."

I kiss my way down to her belly, stroking the soft skin in worship. "I'll go with you."

"That means a lot to me. You're still so young—I was worried you wouldn't want to take that step yet."

"Nothing to worry about, angel."

She wants me to be the father of her child. Someone's daddy. The one a kid looks up to for his love and protection. Their shelter and confidante.

Giver of advice and fixer of problems. The man who'd lay down his life for their mother and them.

Me. *A father.*

I trail my lips from hip bone to hip bone, cradling her close. "I love you already, my potential future little one. And I promise to take damn good care of you and your mama. I'm gonna be the best damn father this world has ever seen." I whisper the vow between kisses.

Elinora tousles my hair. "When you're finished chatting with my ovary, I need you to make love to me."

I nuzzle her belly. "But be forewarned, your mother can be pretty bossy."

She laughs. "Minor details. I haven't even ovulated yet and you're already trying to be the favorite parent."

I crawl up the bed and kiss her lips with a reverence that pours from my soul. "I'm sorry, what was that?"

"You heard me. You can't steal everyone's heart." She gives my lip a playful bite.

"You can't stop me from trying." Easing my cock inside her warm body, I fill her to the hilt. Elinora gasps and clutches my shoulders. We both moan as I start to move. She feels like home. I can't believe she welcomed me back into her life, her heart, and her body. No matter what life decides to throw at us, I'm not going anywhere. I roll my hips, stroking her deep inside, loving how her silken body grips my cock.

I bury my face in her neck and make slow, decadent love to her. She tightens her legs around me, flexing her hips to meet my thrusts. She's pulling me closer, chasing the release we both need. Elinora climaxes with a moan of my name, and I follow a moment later.

For the first time in my life, the details align with the big picture. And as I lose myself deep inside her, I find my home in the woman I love.

# *Epilogue*

## *Elinora*
### (Six months later)

Lying on a table, I clutch Lincoln's arm as we wait for the ultrasound technician to return. She'd stopped mid-ultrasound, telling us she needed to speak with Dr. Terranova before proceeding. A million scenarios race through my mind, all of them ending with grief. I don't think I can handle another loss.

Our first IVF cycle was a bust, but Lincoln convinced me to try again. We were cautiously optimistic when implantation was successful this time, but now I'm in a panic. I can't believe I allowed myself to be so hopeful.

A tear rolls down my cheek. Lincoln brushes it away.

"What if I'm miscarrying again? What if something is wrong with the baby? What if—"

"Take a deep breath, angel. Everything is going to be all right."

"But what if it isn't?"

He cups my face. "I love you. No matter what happens, we'll get through it together."

"If it's another loss, I can't handle hosting Thanksgiving tomorrow." The last thing I need is a bunch of people watching me cry into the stuffing.

"We'll cross that bridge if we come to it."

The door opens. The technician steps into the room along with Dr. Terranova, who clasps my hand. "How are you feeling, Elinora?"

"Scared," I whisper.

"Don't be scared. Kim just wanted me to take a look at her findings."

I nod and squeeze Lincoln tighter.

Dr. Terranova studies the screen. "Wow. Look at them in there. How cute."

Lincoln straightens, his eyes widening. "I'm sorry, but what do you mean, *them?*"

She turns to us with a broad smile. "I mean, congratulations on your rapidly expanding family."

"Are you telling us we're having twins?" I squeal, pushing myself upright. Tears of joy spring to my eyes.

"Oh my God." Lincoln's mouth drops open. Then, he grins and kisses me fiercely. "Go big, or go home, right?"

"I'd say you two are going *big*." Dr. Terranova places her hand on Lincoln's shoulder. "Elinora is pregnant with triplets."

"Three babies?" Lincoln repeats, some of the color draining from his face. "Holy shit."

She squeezes his shoulder. "I did tell you multiples were a possibility."

"How are we gonna handle three babies?"

I touch his cheek and repeat his earlier reassurance. "We'll cross that bridge when we come to it. I'm sure we'll have people willing to help us." Not to mention my financial situation could easily allow for a nanny. Or three.

"Given your history, we'll be keeping a close eye on you. I'm going to prescribe vaginal progesterone suppositories as an added precaution. Your job is to take care of your body and mind." She glances at Lincoln. "I don't want her doing any lifting. Not even laundry or grocery bags."

"Got it. I'll take care of that stuff."

I snort a laugh. "Are you kidding? I'll be lucky if he lets me walk."

"You're absolutely right." He eyes me. "I know how stubborn you are. You heard the doctor. Don't give me any shit when I try to do things for you."

Dr. Terranova chuckles. "I know you mentioned a cat. Lincoln, you're on litter box duty until after the babies come."

*Babies. I'm having three babies.*

He nods. "Don't worry. I'll make sure everything gets done and take damn good care of her."

She smiles. "I know you will."

The turkey's nearly done, and all the pies are cooling on the racks. Lincoln is in his glory, cooking a Thanksgiving feast in our gourmet kitchen. My appetite has been weird since I got pregnant, but the gravy he's stirring smells incredible.

It's my first time hosting a holiday, and I'm excited to have a house full of company. Lincoln's family, Freya, Myles, and Maya will be in attendance. We invited Garrett and Ella, but they'd already planned to go to their friend's house.

It feels like Lincoln has lived here forever when it's only been half a year. His business is flourishing, and he actively freelances for Iverson Press. He spends two days a week upstate, helping his parents and visiting his sister, which has done wonders for his mood.

I hired his editor friend, Tess McPherson, as his replacement. Tess is fantastic. Not only does she work for me part-time, but she also stars opposite Garrett in *Prodigy*, which opened two weeks ago. Lincoln and I were fortunate enough to see the production on opening night, and our minds were officially blown.

Ella and I have cultivated a beautiful friendship, and I'm grateful to have another meaningful bond with a female. I've even become close with Maya, who is still a big part of Lincoln's life. I've always been a bit of a loner, with a reputation for being standoffish, so I'm proud of my newfound friend-making abilities.

All in all, I like the new and improved version of myself.

I'm still on cloud nine from our ultrasound appointment. I never imagined I'd be carrying *three* little ones.

"So, do you think we should share our news tonight?" I add a cinnamon stick to the hot apple cider I'm drinking and swirl it around.

He looks over his shoulder at me. "That's up to you."

Everyone knew we were attempting another round of IVF, so it's not like the news will come out of left field. It was so hard to keep it a secret when we first got a positive pregnancy test. I wanted to shout it from the rooftops, but given my history, we thought it would be safest to keep things quiet until after the first ultrasound.

We already told my mom on a video chat this morning. She's ecstatic. Now, if only I can convince her to move back to New York.

Is it too soon to share with the rest of our inner circle? Maybe. But even if the worst happens, I now have the support system I lacked in the past.

"Let's do it. I feel like celebrating."

A sly smile curves his lips. "Oh, we're gonna celebrate later tonight, sugar." He pulls me close and whispers, "In bed, that is."

My insides flutter, but the doorbell interrupts my sexy train of thought. "Be right back."

Freya is the first guest to arrive. She hustles inside, carrying a huge bottle of wine, and kisses my cheek. "Hey. Happy Thanksgiving. Is there anything I can help with?"

"I think we've got everything covered," Lincoln says. "I hope you brought your appetite."

"Always do. Smells amazing in here, Clark Kent."

"Thanks." He turns the burner to its lowest setting. "Everything is done. Just waiting on the turkey."

The doorbell rings again.

"I'll get it." Freya heads for the foyer.

I walk over to Lincoln and wrap my arms around him. "Thanks for doing all the work."

"It's not work, angel. You know I love cooking." He kisses my forehead. "How are you feeling?"

"Fine. Just a little tired."

"Please go sit. I've got this."

"Nope. You can't get rid of me that easily."

He rolls his eyes at my stubbornness. "Why does that not surprise me?"

"Get used to it. I don't have it in me to let someone else handle everything."

Lincoln smirks. "Funny, you have no trouble surrendering control in the bedroom."

The mere thought of his dominance tightens my nipples. "That's different."

"Is it, though?"

Freya returns with Lincoln's family before I can respond. Everyone hugs, and the volume level increases exponentially with Reagan's excitement at learning Myles is on his way. Lincoln wasn't kidding when he told me she's in love with his best friend. The chaos is a bit too much for the cat, who scurries into the spare bedroom to hide.

Maya and Myles arrive a few minutes later. Lincoln makes the necessary introductions, and we all gather around the kitchen island for some light appetizers.

"Who wants wine?" Freya asks, removing the cork from my favorite Riesling.

Myles nudges her. "Is that even a question?"

"Good point. How could I forget you're a lush, Callahan?" She pours him a glass, then motions to Lincoln's parents. "Mr. and Mrs. Kennedy?"

"Please call us Orla and James," his mother chides. "And yes, we'd love some."

"You got it." She fills two glasses and hands them over. "Maya, are you having any?"

"No thanks, I'm driving." She pours herself some hot cider and clinks her mug to mine.

Freya grabs another wine glass. "Elle, I already know you want some of this."

"Um, actually, I think I'll pass tonight."

"Seriously? You never turn down Boss Bitch Riesling."

She's right. I'm obsessed with everything that comes out of Boss Bitch Vineyard, especially their Riesling. I bought an entire case when she and I had our girls' weekend upstate for my birthday this summer. We stayed at Queen Bee Bed and Breakfast, the Airbnb affiliated with the vineyard, and got more than a little drunk while sampling everything.

"Well . . ." Heat crawls up my neck and spreads to my cheeks. "I don't really have a choice."

Freya's eyes widen. "Wait. Are you saying . . ."

Lincoln moves to stand beside me, draping his arm over my shoulders. "Elinora and I have some exciting news."

A hush falls over the room as everyone rivets their gazes to us. Lincoln's father rolls his wheelchair closer.

I clear my throat. "As you know, we've been working with a fertility specialist for several months, and we recently did another round of IVF after our first attempt failed." I smile up at Lincoln, seeing the happiness I'm feeling reflected in his deep blue eyes. "We're thrilled to announce that it was successful this time."

A chorus of "Oh my God" and "Congratulations" fills the room.

"But wait, there's more," Lincoln says in his best impersonation of an infomercial salesman. He grins at our guests. "It's three for the price of one."

Myles tilts his head to the side. "Huh?"

Unable to contain my excitement for another second, I speak up, "He means we're having triplets."

"Holy fucking shit," Freya says, immediately clapping her hand over her mouth when she realizes she swore.

Orla lets out a squeal that could rival one of Reagan's and jumps up and down while clapping her hands. "Triplets! They're having triplets! Jimmy, we're gonna be grandparents three times over!"

"Easy, love. You'll wake the dead. Lincoln, my boy. Well done." He shakes Lincoln's hand before turning to face me. Warmth shines in his eyes. "You're going to be a wonderful mum, dear."

I lean down to kiss his cheek. "Thank you so much, James."

Myles hugs Lincoln and me. "Congrats, you guys. This is incredible."

Freya is still stunned silent, but happy tears sparkle in her eyes as she takes in the scene.

When it's Maya's turn to hug us, she pinches Lincoln's cheek first. "Congratulations, daddy."

"Thanks, Sea Bass. You gonna babysit?"

Maya laughs. "Do I look like someone who can handle three kids?"

Lincoln gestures to himself. "Do I?"

"You'll be fine." Maya smiles at me with genuine warmth. "Look at you. You're already glowing, mama." She squeezes me tightly. "I'm so happy for you."

"Thank you."

"How are you feeling?" Orla asks, making her way over to me.

She stopped hating me about a month after Lincoln and I reconciled. I think she likes me now. Maybe. Once the babies come, I'm hoping her feelings move closer to love.

"So far, so good. Just a little tired. Lincoln has been taking very good care of me."

She gives him an approving smile. "He damn well better."

Reagan, who's been uncharacteristically quiet, stares up at her big brother. "You're not joking, right? Elinora is really pregnant?"

"Yes." He chuckles at the suspicion in her tone. "I know I like to prank you now and then, but I'd never joke about something like this."

Her gaze darts to me and widens. "Oh my God!" Now that all the pieces have fit themselves together in her mind—and she knows we aren't toying with her—she jumps up and down like her mother did moments earlier. "Does this mean I get to be an aunt?"

Grinning, Lincoln pulls her into a hug. "It sure does. How do you feel about that?"

"Excited! I'm gonna be the *best* aunt in the world."

I wrap my arms around both her and Lincoln. "We know you will."

~The End~

**Subscribe to my newsletter for Lincoln and Elinora's bonus epilogue!**

**For Garrett and Ella's story, check out MASQUERADE!**

**Remember nurse Lena, Garrett's bestie? Check out her story in
TRUE NORTH!**
**(What happens when a snarky NY nurse is stranded in the
Alaskan wilderness with a cocky Australian actor? You'll have to
read it to find out.)**

# *Playlist*

**Take Me to the River** by Annie Lennox

**Horns** by Bryce Fox

**I Am Not a Woman, I'm a God** by Halsey

**Play With Fire** by Sam Tinnesz (feat. Yacht Money)

**You Should See Me In a Crown** by Billie Eilish

**Sweet and Sour** by Amelia Moore

**Paradise** by MEDUZA and Dermot Kennedy

**River** by Bishop Briggs

**Feel It** by Michele Morrone

**Streets – Silhouette Remix** by Doja Cat

**Shut Up and Listen** by Nicholas Bonnin (feat. Angelicca)

**Castle** by Halsey

**Movement** by Hozier

**Control** by Zoe Wees

**Dangerous Woman** by Ariana Grande

**Dirty Mind** by Boy Epic

**Wicked Game** by Grace Carter

**Homeward** by Dermot Kennedy

**Comfortable** by H.E.R.

**Trampoline** by SHAED (feat. ZAYN)

**Water** by Bishop Briggs

**Kiss Me – Guitar version** by Dermot Kennedy

**Versions of Violence** by Alanis Morissette

**Heartless** by Dermot Kennedy

**Thing Called Love** by NF

**Colder** by Azee

**Cold** by Chris Stapleton

**Haunting** by Halsey

**Wicked** by Miki Ratsula

**Power** by Isak Danielson

**Won't Back Down** by YoungBoy Never Broke Again, Dermot Kennedy, and Bailey Zimmerman

**Glory** by Dermot Kennedy

**Redemption** by Dermot Kennedy

**Fired Up** by Grace Carter

**Heaven** by FINNEAS

**Waterfall** by P!nk, Stargate, and Sia

**Trouble** by Ray LaMontagne

**Meaning of Life** by Kelly Clarkson

**Power Over Me – Acoustic version** by Dermot Kennedy

**Sweetest Devotion** by Adele

*Books by*

# ARIA WYATT

**Compass Series**
*True North*
*North Star*
*Horizon*

**Prodigy Series**
*Masquerade*

**Standalones**
*Afterglow*
*Devil in the Details*

Thanks so much for reading! It means the world to me. If you enjoyed *Devil in the Details*, please leave me a review.

**For Garrett's story, check out *Masquerade*.**

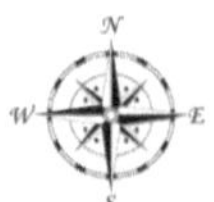

Please visit my website and subscribe to my newsletter for updates and new releases.

# About the Author

Aria Wyatt is a pharmacist mom who spends the inhumane predawn hours with a cup of coffee and her laptop, gleefully indulging in her passion for romance. Her novels range in heat from steamy to scorching, and she doesn't shy away from writing flawed characters with real life issues.

She resides with her husband and two children in New York's picturesque Hudson Valley, near the Catskills and iconic Woodstock. The avid reader balances marriage, motherhood, her pharmacist career, and her romance author dream. When not writing, she dabbles in photography, using the natural beauty of the region to her advantage. She's a self-proclaimed cat lady who cannot live without coffee, chocolate, music, and books.

Author of True North and the Compass Series, Aria has a soft spot for those who are searching, yearning, and ultimately, finding. Whether on a mission to find themselves, find love, find forgiveness or solace, she believes the answer is out there somewhere.

"Journey to Love."

# Author's Note

I covered most of what I wanted to say here in the disclaimer at the beginning of the book.

As I mentioned, I didn't think this story would see the light of day because self-doubt is a bitch. (And I'm a bit of a coward.) That said, The River is one of the most vivid settings I've ever imagined, and I needed to bring it to life on paper. Not going to lie, I wish it was a real place.

I hope you enjoyed Lincoln and Elinora's book. While I absolutely have ideas for more stories set at The River, I haven't made any concrete plans. It all depends on how well *Devil in the Details* is received.

Thank you so much for reading!

# Acknowledgements

**Dana Fisher**, thank you for your valuable insight. Also, I adore you. Thank you for being my best friend since first grade.

**Jen Liese**, I'm blessed to have you in my life with your megaphone and pom-poms. I truly appreciate your friendship, support, and endless encouragement. I love YOU more.

Thank you to my beta reader author friends who always give me constructive feedback and encouragement. You're all amazing and I appreciate the hell out of you. **Liz Schille, Becca L'Amour**, and **Cassandra Cripps**, as always, thank you for your helpful suggestions.

Thank you to my friend **Krystal Dixon**, who wasn't afraid to give the difficult feedback necessary to improve my story. I appreciate your enthusiastic support.

**Claudia Fosca Stahl**, thank you for taking the time to read this one and for boosting my confidence. You're my barometer, lady. It thrilled me to hear that you loved this story.

To my editor, **Karen Cimms**, thank you for fitting me in. Your comments and questions made me dig deeper, and I look forward to working with you in the future!

To my proofreader, **Marla Esposito** of **Proofingstyle, Inc.,** thank you for catching the small stuff.

To **Stacey Blake** of **Champagne Book Design**, as always, thank you for the beautiful book innards and your <u>endless</u> patience.

To my cover designer, **Lori Jackson**, you knocked it out of the park with this one. You deserve a medal for putting up with all of my tweaks. Thank you for bringing my vision to life. To **Kate Farlow** of **Y'all. That Graphic.,** thank you for designing The River's logo. It's perfect.

To **Wander Aguiar**, thank you for taking such drool-worthy pictures! **Andrew Biernat**, thank you for being so sweet and amazing. And for having great muscles.

To my publicist, **Linda Russell** of **Foreword PR & Marketing**. Thank you for always believing in me.

To the bloggers and bookish peeps of Romancelandia, thank you for going out of your way to spread the word. Self-promotion makes my skin crawl, so I truly appreciate every one of you. I see you, **Kelly B., Mikayla S., Katie P., Stacy C., Krystal D., Daria K.**, and the countless others who have taken a chance on me.

To all of **my amazing author friends**, you inspire me. Keep writing.

To my author bestie, **Kristie Wolf**, thank you for loving this story and for encouraging me to move forward with it. I love you, and I'm so happy to have you in my life!

**Dana and Keith Swingle**, thank you for your feedback. I love you guys.

**Kevin Nordstrom**, thank you for providing the "dude perspective" on this one. I appreciate you!

Thank you to **my husband and children** for being supportive and patient with me. I love you so much.

Lastly, thank you to **my readers** for connecting with my words and characters. I couldn't do this without you!

Much love,